'I only did what I thought was best,' Annie said.

'An' yer won't break yer word once yer've given it, will yer?' Tom said.

'Would you have an ounce of respect left for me if I did?' Annie asked him.

Tom didn't answer. Instead, he grasped his hair in his hands and pulled it as hard as he could. Annie reached forward to touch him but he brushed her arm aside.

'Yer've ruined me, Annie Clarke,' he said. 'Yer've ruined the both of us.'

He walked rapidly away down the street. Annie watched him go through eyes blurred with tears, and then he turned a corner and was lost to her.

Sally Spencer was born and brought up in Marston, Cheshire, but now lives in Spain.

Visit Sally's website at
www.arrakis.es/~sspencer

By the same author

Salt of the Earth
Up Our Street
A Picnic in Eden
South of the River
Those Golden Days

OLD FATHER THAMES

Sally Spencer

ORION

An Orion paperback
First published in Great Britain by Orion in 1995
This paperback edition published in 1996 by Orion Books Ltd,
Orion House, 5 Upper St Martin's Lane, London, WC2H 9EA

Reissued 1999

A CIP catalogue record for this book
is available from the British Library

Printed and bound in Great Britain by
Clays Ltd, St Ives plc

For Donald and Sheila

AUTHOR'S NOTE

Anyone who crosses Southwark Bridge Road near the fire station today will look in vain for Lant Place. The street has gone, and even the pub which marked its boundary – the Goldsmiths' Arms – has been rebuilt since the Blitz. But once, Lant Place did exist, and was no doubt populated by the same mixture of busy, worried, happy, sharp, dull and sometimes slightly eccentric people as I describe. I say 'no doubt', but I can never really be sure because the characters in this book *are* simply characters and, as such, no more than products of my own imagination.

Sally Spencer

PROLOGUE

Whenever Lil Clarke thought back to the day Annie, her eldest daughter, was born, it was not the pain of labour she remembered but the fog – a thick, yellow fog of the sort that slinks round street corners and cunningly slides its way in through every opened pub door.

'It's a real peasouper out there,' Mrs Gort, the midwife, had said, brushing down the sleeves of her jacket as if she feared the poisoned air were still clinging to it. 'The trams are crawlin' along, an' even so, I'll swear if it wasn't for the clip-cloppin' of the 'orses' 'ooves, one of 'em could go right past without you even noticin'. I'll tell yer, it's nothin' short of a miracle that I managed to get 'ere at all.'

And Lil, lying in the bed on which she still owed the tally-man seven and sixpence, had merely nodded weakly and thanked her lucky stars that Mrs Gort had had the determination to fight her way through the murk.

It was an easy birth, as first births go, and after it was over the neighbours had all come round to Number Thirty-four to admire Lant Place's newest resident.

'Ain't she pretty,' said Mrs Forest from three doors up. 'Ain't she got a lot of hair.'

'An' just look at them lovely big eyes,' said Mrs Todd, whose husband, the local milkman, was known to be the most bad-tempered man in the whole of Southwark.

'Pity she 'ad to be born on such a bleedin' miserable day,'

3

said Effie Bentley, who never moderated her language, even in front of the vicar. 'A bleedin' miserable day,' she repeated, in case anybody had missed the point the first time through.

Lil looked down at her tiny daughter – at the big laughing eyes and the abundance of reddish-brown hair.

'It don't matter what the weather's like outside,' she said confidently. 'This little gal'll take a ray of sunshine with 'er wherever she goes.'

PART ONE: A NEW LIFE

Spring 1901

CHAPTER ONE

As the cart containing all his wordly possessions trundled slowly down Lant Street, George Taylor caught himself assessing his surroundings as if he were still leading a patrol through hostile territory.

It was a habit he'd have to learn to break, he thought, because he wasn't a sergeant in the 21st Lancers any more – and the ability to smell out a Burmese bandit a mile away was not a quality much valued in timber yard managers.

He looked around him once more, this time trying to see things from a civilian's point of view. On the right-hand side of the street were two small factories. The sign on the first announced that it was a cork manufactory, while the other was a patent leather works. Further up, on the opposite side, was a tall, forbidding building which made him shudder just to look at it – and so could only have been the local board school.

George's wife Colleen, sitting between him and the carman they had hired at London Bridge Station, glanced nervously up at her husband. She seemed to find some reassurance in his face, and that was not surprising, because it was a strong face with its solid jaw, almost square nose and large, alert brown eyes.

'How are you bearin' up, luv?' George asked, sensing his wife's concern and turning to look at her.

'I'm still reelin' from the shock a bit,' Colleen confessed. 'It's not a bit like Marston, is it?'

'No,' George admitted. 'It isn't.'

The small salt-mining village they'd both been brought up in bore no resemblance at all to this street, which was only one of the thousands of roads which made up the capital city of the largest empire the world had ever known. A quiet canal ran through Marston, while not more than a few hundred yards away from Lant Street flowed the mighty River Thames – the throbbing, teeming heart of London – where day and night vessels from the four corners of the earth arrived, weighed down with exotic Eastern spices and humble Dutch eggs, casks of sherry from Spain and chests of tea from India.

'An' I'll soon have me own part to play in the life of the river,' George reflected.

Because, from the following morning, it would be his job to see that the cargoes of Baltic pine and African hardwood which arrived at Hibernia Wharf were properly invoiced, stored and dispatched.

'I mean, it's different for you,' Colleen continued worriedly. 'When you were servin' in the army, you travelled all over the world, didn't you? But look at me! The farthest *I've* ever been in me whole life is Manchester.'

'You'll be fine,' George promised, patting her hand and smiling encouragingly.

Colleen smiled back at him. No one but George would have thought to call her a pretty woman – her nose was far too large and awkward for such praise. Yet she had kind, green eyes and soft brown hair – and when she smiled, she was – for one brief instant – truly beautiful.

They passed St. Michael's Church and soon were crossing Southwark Bridge Road. A few families, dressed in their Sunday best, were out walking, and a small crowd had gathered at the street corner around the Italian organ-grinder and his monkey. Other than that, the road was deserted.

'What's that?' George asked the carman, indicating a building just beyond the corner which was even more imposing than the school on Lant Street.

'It's the Fire Brigade 'eadquarters,' the carman said. 'It'll be really 'andy for yer if yer 'ouse ever goes up in flames, won't it?'

George felt his wife stiffen and wished the carman would keep his thoughts to himself. Colleen was already worried enough about living in London without having the spectre of being burned out of their home presented to her.

The cart turned into Lant Place, which wasn't a square, as Colleen had expected, but a long narrow street lined with terraced houses. Some of the houses had bright curtains at the windows, freshly painted doors and little gardens in the three feet or so of land which separated them from the pavement. Others showed signs of neglect – curtains were faded and dirty, the paint cracked and peeling, the gardens nothing more than a patch of hard-packed earth.

'There's the place I've rented for us,' George said.

Colleen's eyes followed his pointing finger. The first thing she noticed was that there was a neat garden in front of the house, with a rockery made of bright stones and shiny sea-shells. Next she turned her attention to the downstairs window, which positively gleamed in the pale afternoon sun. Yes, she decided, she liked the house – it already had a nice feel about it.

And then she saw the curtain move!

'It looks to me like there's somebody still livin' in it, George,' she said.

'Somebody still livin' in it?' her husband repeated. 'What makes you think that?'

'Because front room curtains don't move on their own,' Colleen told him. 'There's somebody in that parlour right now – an' they're watchin' us.'

George, once more the sergeant on patrol, subjected the window to one of his quick, searching glances.

'You're imaginin' things,' he told his wife.

'I am not imaginin' things,' Colleen replied firmly. 'Look – it's 'appenin' again.'

'Oh, I see what you're on about,' George said as the penny dropped. 'You're lookin' at Number Thirty-four, aren't you? It's Number Thirty-six I've rented for us.'

Colleen looked at the houses on each side of the twitching curtains. The one on the left was not too bad, but the one on the right had the worst paintwork in the street and a garden in which the only things which appeared to be growing were broken bottles and an old, rusting pram.

'Would Number Thirty-six be one up or one down from Number Thirty-four?' Colleen asked apprehensively.

'One up,' George replied, confirming her worst fears.

'Oh Lord – you might've warned me!' Colleen gasped before she could help herself.

'Warned you? Warned you about what?'

'That it was such a dump.'

'It only *looks* a dump,' George assured her. 'The buildin' itself is sound enough. All it needs is a bit of decoratin', and it'll be just as smart as Number Thirty-four.'

'You men!' Colleen said with mild disgust. 'You all think nice homes just happen, don't you?'

Before George had time to answer, they had reached Number Thirty-six and the carman was reining his horse to a halt.

''Ere we are then,' he said cheerfully.

There they were indeed, Colleen thought. And close to, the house looked even worse than it had from a distance.

George twisted round to get off the cart.

'Need an 'and, guv?' the carman asked, glancing down involuntarily at his passenger's wooden leg.

'No thanks, I can manage,' George replied.

There'd been a time, just after he'd lost the leg, when he'd resented any offer of assistance, but he'd long since got over that, and now it merely amused him to show people just *how* well he could cope without help.

Letting his powerful arms take most of the strain, George lowered himself to the ground, reached for his crutch, and then held out his hand to his wife. Once both Colleen's feet were safely on the pavement, he led her through the rickety gate to the front door of Number Thirty-six.

'I suppose I should carry you over the threshold,' he said with a grin, 'but I can't quite manage that.'

'I don't think I'd want to be carried over the threshold of

10

this place,' Colleen said. 'I'm not at all sure the floorboards would stand all that weight on one spot.'

George's grin melted away, and Colleen felt awful. 'I'm sorry, love,' she said.

'It's not like you to set yourself against somethin' right from the start,' George told her. 'You're usually the one who's determined to make the best of things.'

Colleen shrugged helplessly. 'I know,' she admitted. 'But it's not just the house.'

'Then what . . .?'

Colleen glanced over her shoulder to see if the carman was still in earshot. 'It's the people, an' all,' she confessed.

'How do you mean?'

'Well, they all seem so . . . I don't know . . . noisy an' pushy. Look at the way they were all rushin' round that railway station. I'm not used to it, George. I mean, nobody rushes in Marston, do they? There'd be no point.'

She was right, of course, George thought. Life was much less frantic back in the village. And it was going to be hard for her – being uprooted from the place she'd known all her life and transplanted in the middle of this strange tribe of people who went by the name of cockneys.

'If you're havin' second thoughts . . .' he began.

Colleen shook her head firmly.

'No,' she said. 'We talked it over, an' we both decided this job was too good for you to turn down. So now I'm willin' to stick it out – whatever it takes.'

'It won't be half as bad as you seem to think,' George told her. 'I served with any number of cockneys in the army, an' they weren't a bad lot taken all in all. I'm sure you'll like 'em once you've got used to 'em.'

Colleen looked dubiously at the house with the twitching curtain and thought of her mam and her best friend Becky – George's sister – whom she'd left behind her in Cheshire.

'I'll be all right as long as we've got good neighbours,' she said decisively. 'Good neighbours can get you through anythin'.'

In the front parlour of Number Thirty-four, Lil Clarke peeped from behind the curtain out onto the street.

'They're 'ere,' she said.

'Who's 'ere?' asked her husband Sam, though he knew full well who she meant, and was only teasing her.

'The new neighbours,' Lil said. 'The ones that are takin' over the Bentleys' 'ouse.'

'Oh, 'ave the Bentleys moved?' Sam said.

Lil shrugged her shoulders irritatedly. 'Have they moved!' she repeated. 'Well, if they 'aven't, why did you spend 'alf of last Sunday 'elpin' Ned Bentley to load his stuff on that wagon?'

Sam grinned. 'You're right, I did do that,' he admitted. 'It must 'ave slipped me memory some'ow.'

Under normal circumstances, Lil would have turned round and given her husband a piece of her mind for poking fun at her like that, but at the moment she was far too interested in watching what was going on in the street.

'What are they like, Mum?' asked Annie, who was seventeen and worked in Stevenson's match factory.

'Well, they look very respectable,' said Lil, paying the new arrivals her highest compliment. 'Only . . . he's got a wooden leg.'

The Clarkes' son Eddie who, at fourteen, was old enough to have left school but not yet big enough to work on the docks like his dad, got up and rushed to join his mother at the window.

'It only goes up to just below 'is knee,' he said disappointedly as he peered out at George. 'It's 'ardly worth callin' a wooden bacon an' egg at all.'

'You try walkin' round on one of them, an' you'd soon wish you had yer real leg back,' Sam told him.

'An' look at 'er,' Eddie said. 'Cor, she ain't 'alf got a conk on 'er, ain't she?'

Lil clipped her son lightly on the ear. 'We don't make comments like that in this 'ouse,' she said. 'It's not the looks of anybody that matter – it's what people are like inside that counts.'

'But I'll 'ave to admit, she's got a nice shape on 'er,' Eddie continued.

His mother clipped him again – a little harder this time.

'An' we don't make comments like that, either,' she said. 'At least, you don't – not at your age.'

Peggy, the Clarkes' younger daughter, drifted in dreamily from the back yard. 'I think me rabbit's goin' to 'ave babies,' she announced to the world in general.

'How can she be?' asked Lil, still gazing out of the window. 'You can't 'ave babies until . . . well, until you're properly married.'

'Maggie Ross did,' Eddie chirped up, ducking to avoid a third assault on his ear.

'Anyway, my rabbit is married,' Peggy said shyly. 'Or she's got a bloke of 'er own, anyway.'

'An' what do you mean by that?' her mother wanted to know.

'Ossie Wallis 'as got a rabbit,' Peggy said. 'An' it's a boy because . . . well, you can tell it is. Anyway, a couple of weeks back, Ossie brought 'is rabbit round an' we put 'im in the same cage as Beauty for an hour. So I think 'e must have done 'is stuff.'

'Done 'is stuff,' her mother repeated disgustedly. 'I don't know where you kids get it from, honest I don't. The old Queen's 'ardly cold in 'er grave, and 'ere you are talkin' about rabbits doin' their stuff. It'd never 'ave happened when me an' yer dad were children. Would it, Sam?'

'Not if you say it wouldn't 'ave, me old darlin',' her husband replied good-naturedly.

'They don't 'ave much furniture,' Lil said, leaving the subject of rabbits behind her and returning to the drama outside. 'Just a chest of drawers an' a Welsh dresser. Still, I don't s'ppose they need a lot, what with their 'ouse bein' already furnished.'

It was a considerable source of pride to Lil that the furniture in Number Thirty-four was all their own. 'Or, at any rate, it *will* be our own when we've finished makin' the payments,' she'd say to her husband after each and every one of the tallyman's weekly visits.

'When we've finished makin' the payments!' Sam would think to himself. 'Me grandkids won't live long enough to see the end of the payments on this lot.' But though he thought it, he was wise enough never to say it out loud.

'Ain't you goin' to ask the new people in for a cup of rosie, Mum?' Annie asked.

'Course I am,' Lil replied. 'It's only right an' proper that they should get a good first impression of the street. But before I do that, yer dad'll probably want to go round there and give 'em an 'and shiftin' their belongin's in.'

Sam sighed theatrically and rose to his feet.

'I was wonderin' 'ow long it would take you to get round to that idea,' he said.

The house wasn't too bad after all, Colleen decided as she stood in the back yard and looked around her. The front door opened onto a passageway, with doors leading off to the front parlour and the room which must have been the kitchen until someone had built an extension in the yard. Now the kitchen was in the extension, and so was the washhouse. Add to that the two bedrooms upstairs, and they should have plenty of space.

'A lot of the families in the street have lodgers livin' in their upstairs rooms,' George had told her when he'd returned to Cheshire after renting the house.

'And will we need to do that?' Colleen had asked.

'No. I'll be earnin' thirty-five bob a week at the wood yard, and we should be able to manage very comfortably on that without havin' to put up with strangers in our home,' George had said, with just a hint of pride in his voice.

No strangers in their home. No grown-up strangers – and perhaps no tiny ones, either.

A frown crossed Colleen's face as she remembered the final thing her father-in-law had said to her just before she'd left Marston.

'I've got some beautiful grandchildren,' Ted Taylor told her as they stood by the cart which was to take her and George to the railway station.

'You certainly have, Dad,' Colleen agreed.

'Beautiful grandchildren,' Ted repeated. 'An' I love 'em all dearly – but they're all me daughters' kids, you see.'

'I'm not sure I'm followin' you.'

Ted shifted awkwardly from one foot to the other.

'I know it sounds daft,' he said, 'but I've always had this yearnin' to have grandkids with me own name. Well, there's not much chance of our Jack ever settlin' down. And as for our Phillip – I'm not sure I'd like to see him have any children by that flighty piece he's married to.' He looked her straight in the eye. 'So that leaves you an' George. Do you see what I'm gettin' at?'

How could she *not* see what he was getting at?

'Have some babies,' he was telling her. *'And have 'em soon – while I'm still young enough to enjoy 'em.'*

As if she didn't want to! As if it wasn't her deepest desire to be a mother and to make George a proud father.

But it wasn't as easy as that, was it? She and George had been married for over a year, and so far nothing had happened. Every time she was late with her monthly cycle she felt hope spring up – even though she had been irregular all her life – but then the discomfort would arrive and she would have to accept the fact that once again she'd failed.

'Perhaps we're not doin' it right,' she thought, gazing around the yard of her new home.

Yet that couldn't be the case. True, she'd been a virgin on her wedding night, but from the gentle yet masterful way George had guided her through what was expected, it was obvious that she was far from being the first woman he'd ever slept with.

And if they weren't doing it right, surely she wouldn't enjoy it so much!

Maybe her real problem – the reason she was so edgy these days – had nothing to do with moving to this strange new place. Maybe her real problem was a deep-seated fear that she and George would *never* have kids – and that somehow it would all be her fault.

'A penny for yer thoughts,' said a voice which was so close that it made her jump.

Colleen whirled round, her heart beating furiously, to find herself looking straight at a stocky man who was standing just by the kitchen door.

15

'Mrs Taylor?' the man said, and when Colleen nodded he added, 'Well, yer'd 'ave to be, wouldn't yer? My name's Sam Clarke. I'm yer next-door neighbour. Yer 'usband said it'd be all right for me to come through an' make meself known. I never meant to scare you.'

'You didn't, really,' Colleen lied. She held out her hand to him. 'It's a pleasure to meet you, Mr Clarke,' she said.

Sam took her hand in his and gave it a gentle shake. He was about forty-two or forty-three, she guessed, with thick black hair, just turning grey, and the sort of sparkling dark eyes which suggested a wry sense of humour. Though first appearances could sometimes be deceptive, Colleen thought that she was really going to get on with Sam Clarke.

'Anyway,' Sam continued, 'I'm just about to give yer 'usband an' the carman a hand with shiftin' yer stuff, an' my missis was wonderin' if you'd like to nip next door for a cup o' rosie?'

'A cup of rosie?' Colleen asked, totally mystified.

Sam grinned. 'Rosie Lea,' he said. 'Tea.'

'I'm afraid you're not making much . . .' Colleen began.

'Cockney rhymin' slang,' Sam explained. 'If yer goin' to live round 'ere, you'll 'ave to learn to speak like the natives do, won't yer?'

'I'll do my best,' Colleen told him. 'Is it easy?'

'I should cocoa,' Sam replied. 'A woman like you, with a good crust on her shoulders, should soon be rabbiting to my old Dutch like you was born under Bow Bells.'

A worried look crossed Colleen's face, but it was soon replaced by a smile. 'You're makin' fun of me, aren't you, Mr Clarke? she asked.

'Course I am, me old china,' Sam agreed. 'Now if you'd like to pick up yer plates, yer'd be very welcome next door.'

'For a nice of cup of rosie,' Colleen said.

'That's right,' Sam agreed.

The Goldsmiths' Arms stood at the corner of Lant Place and Southwark Bridge Road, right in the shadow of the fire station. It was a good boozer, George decided as he and

Sam stepped through the door of the public bar – simple but not scruffy. It reminded him a bit of the pub his father-in-law, Paddy O'Leary, ran.

The two men walked up to the bar.

'Two pints 'o best, darlin',' Sam called out to the dumpy little barmaid. Then he turned to George and said, 'If there's one thing I've learned in life, it's never trust a woman – specially if you 'appen to be married to 'er.'

George saw the twinkle in the other man's eyes, and grinned.

'How d'you mean?' he asked.

'Take what my old Dutch said just before we come out,' Sam answered. 'What was 'er exact words?' He screwed up his face in concentration. ' "Yer've worked 'ard unloadin' that furniture",' he continued in a fair imitation of Lil. ' "Why don't yer take yerselves off for a drink?" That was it, wasn't it?'

'More or less,' George agreed.

'Now a bloke like you, who hasn't been married that long, might just take it at face value.' Sam said. 'But us old 'ands know better. We can see what's lyin' be'ind all this sudden kindness and concern.'

'An' what *is* lyin' behind it?' George asked, the grin on his face broadening.

'What she really meant was, "I want to 'ave a decent chin wag with Missis Taylor, an' I can't do that with you two blokes clutterin' up me parlour",' Sam explained. He shook his head in frank admiration. 'I tell yer, when it comes to bein' crafty, women are 'alf way round the track before we've even come out of the startin' gate.'

The dumpy barmaid brought the drinks over to them. 'That'll be fourpence, gents,' she said.

George was just reaching into his pocket when the other man put a restraining hand on his arm.

'Leave yer money where it is,' Sam said. 'It's yer first time 'ere, so it's my treat.' He slid some coins across the counter to the barmaid, then glanced down at George's wooden leg. 'Did yer lose that in the army?' he asked.

'Yes, I did,' George said.

17

'A big battle, was it?'

'Omdurman. I was in the Lancers.'

Sam whistled softly. 'So you was in that cavalry charge, was you? That must have been bleedin' awful.'

'It was no picnic,' George admitted.

'I was in the army meself,' Sam said. 'I was with Wolseley when 'e marched to Khartoum to try an' save Gordon.'

'It was that campaign that made me join up in the first place,' George said, remembering how avidly he had followed the details of it in the newspapers.

'Was it now,' Sam said. 'Well, there's a coincidence. What rank was you?'

'Sergeant,' George told him.

'The backbone of the army, yer sergeants,' Sam said.

'An' you?' George asked.

'Corporal,' Sam replied.

'Us sergeants'd never have been able to do our job properly without you,' George said.

'D'you want me to fill 'em up, gents?' the barmaid asked.

George looked down at his pot and was surprised to find it was already empty. 'Yes, fill 'em up,' he said. 'Only this time, I'm payin'.'

'Fair enough,' Sam agreed.

As George sorted through his change, he thought how lucky he'd been to find a mate so soon. He could only hope that Colleen was getting on as well with *Mrs* Clarke.

A three-piece suite in imitation velvet dominated the Clarkes' front room, but there were several other pieces of furniture which had also staked a claim to their own territory. There was a sideboard in walnut veneer against one wall, and a heavy circular table in ebony, on which sat a vase of china tulips, against another. To the left of the fireplace stood a large and elaborately carved display case, while to the right was a nest of mahogany coffee tables. A grandfather clock gazed sternly from the corner and chimed on the hour in furious competition with the cuckoo clock which hung over the mantelpiece.

'If she tries to cram anythin' more in here, there'll be no room for the people,' Colleen thought to herself.

She looked around, from Lil and Annie – who were sitting in the armchairs – to Eddie, slouching at the other end of the couch, and Peggy, who was sitting cross-legged in front of the fireplace. Yes, a couple more people in there and it would be a real squeeze.

Yet for all that it was so overdone, the parlour was a cheerful, friendly room, perhaps because it had obviously been furnished with love and care.

'More tea, Mrs Taylor?' Lil Clarke asked solicitously, pointing to one of her best china cups which Colleen was balancing delicately on her lap.

'You've only just poured me this one,' Colleen replied.

' 'Ow about another fancy, then?' Lil said, reaching towards the cake-stand which was resting on yet another occasional table. 'They're made with real cream, yer know.'

Colleen held up her free hand in protest. 'I couldn't eat another thing. I'm full to burstin',' she said, and then added silently to herself, 'a bit like this room.'

Still, she couldn't help liking Lil Clarke. She was about the same age as her husband, Colleen guessed, and though she had started to fade a bit now, she must have been a very pretty woman when she was younger.

Annie, her eldest daughter, seemed to have inherited Lil's looks. Her hair was a deep, rich brown with a natural springiness which most women would envy. Her green eyes were intelligent and lively. And there'd been a time – before George had convinced her that he loved her as she was – when Colleen would have signed away her soul for a slim, delicate nose like this girl had.

'So yer 'usband's goin' to be managin' 'Ibbert's wood yard, is he?' Lil asked.

'However did you know that?' Colleen asked, so surprised that she almost dropped Lil's precious cup.

Annie laughed.

'Mum ain't nosey, yer understand,' she said with an impish look in her eye. 'It's just that she 'ears things – even when she don't really want to.'

'Yer cheeky young devil,' Lil said – though she didn't clip Annie's ear as she would have clipped Eddie's if he'd been the one who'd made the comment.

'But how did you find out?' asked Colleen, intrigued to hear the full story.

Lil looked embarrassed.

'Well, I'm a great friend of Mrs Todd's, yer see,' she said, as if that were all the explanation that was necessary.

'Yes?' Colleen said, still mystified.

'Well, 'er 'usband's the milkman,' Lil continued, 'an' he used to deliver a pint of milk every day to Mr Baker, the boss of 'Ibbert's. Very particular, Mr Baker was, wouldn't use condensed milk in 'is tea like some of the other blokes – it 'ad to be fresh.'

'I see,' Colleen said.

'Well, I don't, said Eddie, whose wild hair and restless energy made him remind Colleen a bit of George's brother Jack.

'Mrs Todd 'appened to mention to me that 'er husband 'ad told 'er that Mr Baker 'ad cancelled 'is pint,' Lil explained. 'So, o' course, I knew he must be movin'.'

'O' course,' Annie said, winking at Colleen. 'But yer still 'aven't explained 'ow yer got from that to knowin' that Mrs Taylor's 'usband was takin' over from 'im.'

'Well, I knew for a fact that the landlord would put up the rent on next door when the Bentleys' left,' Lil continued.

'And . . .?' Annie pressed her.

'An' the rent collector just 'appened to mention to me that 'e'd had a number of inquiries about whether the new people would be takin' lodgers, and 'e'd 'ad to tell 'em no,' Lil said triumphantly.

'So?' Annie said.

'So, ain't it obvious?' Lil demanded. 'I knew that the new people movin' into Number Thirty-six 'ad enough money to pay a big rent on their own, which 'ad to mean the 'usband 'ad a good job, didn't it? An' the only good job goin' spare round 'ere is boss of 'Ibbert's timber yard.'

Colleen's mouth fell open in astonishment. She'd known a few gossips in her time – Not-Stopping Bracegirdle back in Marston, to name but one – but Lil Clarke was above the run of ordinary gossips; she was the Sherlock Holmes of Lant Place and the surrounding district.

Seeing the expression on Colleen's face, Annie Clarke laughed out loud.

'Mum's always addin' two an' two together,' she said, 'an' the really amazin' thing is that most of the time she manages to come up with four.'

Peggy, who had not said a word all the time the guest had been in the parlour – hadn't, in fact, even seemed to notice what was going on – now turned to Colleen and said, 'Have you ever 'ad a pet goat of yer own?'

'A goat?' Colleen replied. 'Whatever made you ask me a thing like that?'

'Just wonderin',' Peggy said vaguely.

She was a strange little girl, Colleen thought. She was much fairer and paler than her sister Annie. And whereas Annie had the look of a young woman prepared to take on life with determined good humour, Peggy's expression was wistful and other-worldly. It was almost as if she didn't belong in the East End at all, but would have been happier being a character in a children's story book. The good fairy, perhaps. Or maybe Little Bo Peep.

'*Did* yer 'ave a goat?' Peggy asked.

'No,' Colleen admitted. 'But I did have a big tabby cat once. Is that any good?'

Peggy smiled at her, to show she'd appreciated the fact that Colleen had been trying to be helpful, then slowly shook her head.

'Don't go worryin' yerself over Peggy,' Lil said, noticing the look of mild concern creeping onto Colleen's face. 'She's all right in the 'ead, really she is. She's a good scholar when she wants to be – when they're learnin' about animals an' things like that at school – but 'alf the time, even *I* don't know what she's talkin' about. Ain't it true what I'm sayin', Peggy?'

But Peggy's mind had already drifted off somewhere else entirely.

'Are yer ready for another cup of rosie now, Mrs Taylor?' Annie asked.

'Yes please,' Colleen said. 'But you mustn't keep sayin' "Mrs Taylor". My name's Colleen. That's what everybody calls me back home. Won't you do the same?'

'Right-ho, Colleen,' said the wild-haired Eddie, with a great deal of enthusiasm.

Lil shot him a look which would have frozen the blood of most people, but seemed to have little effect on her son.

'When Mrs Taylor says "everybody" calls her Colleen, she means everybody 'oo's grown-up,' Lil told her son tartly. 'An' grown-up definitely don't include lads 'oo 'ave only just left school. Ain't that right, Colleen?'

'Well, yes, I suppose so,' admitted Colleen, although it was a fact that even the smallest kids in Marston had used her first name.

'So you watch yer manners,' Lil warned her son, then, turning to her guest, she said, 'My old man works down on the water, you know.'

'Does he?' Colleen replied. 'At the Hibernia Wharf?'

'No,' Lil said.' 'E's not a wharfman. 'E's a docker, my Sam.'

Colleen wondered what the difference was, but since it seemed so obvious to Lil, she would have felt foolish asking, so she contented herself with saying, 'That's nice.'

' 'E's not a Royal,' Lil confessed, 'though o' course one day 'e's 'opin' 'e will be. But at least he's not a casual, like some of the people who live round 'ere. He's a ticket man!'

'Is he?' said Colleen politely, though she had no idea what a ticket man was.

'A ticket man Class B!' Lil told her triumphantly. ' 'E works on the other side of the river, down at St Katherine's Dock. Yer probably noticed it when you were comin' 'ere. It's right by the Tower.'

'No, I can't say I did notice it,' Colleen admitted. 'I've seen so many new things today, they're all startin' to blur together.'

'O' course they are, gal,' Lil said sympathetically. 'But don't worry. Yer'll soon get used to it.'

Colleen took a thoughtful sip of her tea – of her *Rosie Lea*. Soon get used to it? What with Royals and ticket men, crusts, dutches and plates, not to mention amateur detectives and elf-like children as next-door neighbours, there seemed to be a lot more to moving into Southwark than just putting up new curtains.

CHAPTER TWO

Lil Clarke woke up, as she always did, at exactly a quarter past four. It was still dark outside, but already there was activity in the street. She listened to the clip-clop of horse's hooves under her window, and guessed that the cart passing below was a fruit wagon heading for the Borough Market.

No sooner had the first hoof-beats died away than Lil heard fresh ones, this time accompanied by the sound of a man's voice.

'Ger on, yer idle bleeder,' the man shouted. 'I 'aven't got all day, yer know.'

Lil smiled to herself. Dick Todd, the worst-tempered man in the whole of Southwark, was on his way to meet one of the milk trains at Paddington Station, and even at this early hour managed to summon up enough energy to curse his horse. Not that the animal seemed to mind – he knew where he was going, so most of the time he simply ignored his driver and went there at his own pace.

Lil climbed out of bed and groped around for her clothes, which were hanging over the chair. She could have turned on the gas light, but she didn't, because that would have disturbed Sam – and though she might nag him in the daytime, she did appreciate how hard he worked and how much he needed his sleep.

'Yer a good man, Sam Clarke,' she said softly, then

worried for a moment that he might be just awake enough to hear her.

She opened the bedroom door and tiptoed quietly downstairs. Once in the kitchen, the first thing she did was strike a match and light the fire Sam had laid the previous evening. She watched as the paper blazed up and the sticks started to burn.

'It's lovely always havin' enough coal to light a fire with,' she thought.

There were families in the street who had to keep an ear peeled for the coalman every single day, and when they heard his cart, they'd rush out and buy a few pounds, or even just a shovelful. The Clarkes didn't do things like that. When Sam had a slack week, they might all have to tighten their belts a bit – but they still always managed to buy their coal by the bag.

It was the same with their other purchases, too. Lil never had to go to Mr Southern's shop in Lant Street and ask for just a twist of tea or sugar. It was always packets for her.

'Not that people can always 'elp bein' poor,' she told herself.

There were any number of decent, willing men in the district who'd just been unlucky, and she'd always drummed it into her kids that it wouldn't be right for them to look down their noses at families that were not as comfortably off as they were. Still, she was grateful that *she* didn't have to traipse across Southwark Bridge Road to Lant Street every time she felt like a nice, warmin' cup of rosie.

By the time Sam Clarke came downstairs, the fire was burning brightly and Lil had his dinner already bundled up in a big, red-check handkerchief.

'Do yer think there'll be work today?' she asked her husband as he ate his bread and marge.

'Should be,' Sam replied. 'We're expectin' a couple o' Spanish steamers in.'

'Pigs o' lead and casks o' sherry?' asked Lil, who, with the constant need to find money for the tallyman and the gasman, knew almost as much about the workings of the docks as her husband did.

'That's right,' Sam agreed. 'Probably them little round Spanish potaters, as well.'

He spoke seriously – because the one thing he never joked about to his wife was his job. Getting regular work mattered, and though, being a Class B Ticket man, he could usually rely on being taken on most days, there were times when only the Royals – who got paid whether there was work or not – came away with any money.

There was the sound of reluctant footsteps on the stairs, and then Eddie entered the room, rubbing his eyes.

'Fancy gettin' up at this time o' day,' he complained. 'An' all for six bob a week.'

'There's lots o' kids your age'd be glad of the chance to be earnin' six bob a week,' his mother told him sternly.

She worried about Eddie. He'd had several jobs since he'd left Lant Street Board School, and lost them all – either through laziness or lack of interest. He'd been very lucky to get his latest at the stables in Union Street. Stablin' work was steady work, she'd told him, because tradesmen would always need to hire horses to pull their carts. An' the gentry weren't about to start walkin' everywhere, now were they? So *they'd* always need 'orses, too. Yes, she'd *told* him, but had he taken any of it in? Had he hell!

'It'll all be motors soon, Mum,' he'd said cockily. ' 'Orses are on the way out.'

On the way out? When you could hardly cross the street in London without puttin' yer foot in a pile of 'orse manure! Honestly, Eddie talked like he was soft in the head sometimes.

Yes, Eddie was a problem, all right. But maybe when he was a bit older, he'd settle down to steady work like his sister, Annie. His mother certainly hoped so, anyway.

Annie came downstairs at five, just as The Goldsmiths' Arms was opening its doors to the first customers of the day.

' 'Ave Dad an' our Eddie already gone off to work?' she asked sleepily.

'Yer dad 'as,' Lil said. 'An' I 'ope yer brother 'as, too – though there's no tellin' with 'im.'

As Annie ate her breakfast, her mother looked at her and thought – not for the first time – what a beautiful young woman she'd grown into. And that, in its own way, was almost as worrying as Eddie's idleness, because beautiful young women got a lot more attention than was good for 'em – and sometimes it all ended in tears.

Annie was a sensible girl, Lil told herself, but even sensible girls could make mistakes now and again – and she should know, because she'd once nearly made one herself.

Peggy was the last to arrive at the breakfast table, her fluffy blonde hair all over the place and a dreamy, thoughtful expression filling her face.

'We should get ourselves a nice goat, Mum,' she said, without any preamble.

'Oh, we're back to that, are we?' Lil asked.

'It'd pay for itself in no time,' Peggy said earnestly.

'An' 'ow do you figure that out?' Lil wondered.

'Well, there's the milk for a start,' Peggy told her. 'Goat's milk's very 'ealthy. We could sell it to all the neighbours.'

'Could we now?' her mother replied, with a slight smile coming to her lips. 'Well, yer must be plannin' on gettin' a very big goat if yer think yer can feed the whole street. An' how's Mr Todd goin' to feel about losin' all his customers to us?'

'Then if I got a little cart, I could fasten the goat between the shafts an' charge all the kids in the street a farthin' a ride,' Peggy said, attacking on a new front.

'An 'ow many kids round 'ere d'yer think 'ave money to spend on ridin' in goat carts?' Lil asked sceptically.

'I could run errands, too,' Peggy persisted. 'It's easy runnin' errands when yer've got a goat.'

Experience told Lil that Peggy could go on like this all day, and she knew that if she was to have any chance of getting her daughter to school before the last bell, it was time to finish with the subject of goats.

'We've no spare money for buyin' animals,' Lil said, 'even if they would pay themselves in no time.'

A cunning look came to Peggy's eyes. 'But what if I got one free or bought it meself?' she said. 'Could I keep it then?'

Lil examined her younger daughter suspiciously.

'Do you 'appen to know where you can get a goat for nuffink?' she demanded.

'No,' Peggy admitted. 'But you never know what might 'appen, do you, Mum? So *could* I 'ave one, I mean if it really didn't cost you an' Dad anyfink?'

Time was ticking by, and the whole thing seemed so unlikely anyway that Lil simply nodded her head. 'Provided you kept it in the yard an' it didn't cause no damage,' she said.

'Oh, my goat wouldn't cause no damage,' Peggy assured her. 'My goat would be'ave like a perfec' Christian, my goat would.'

Messers. J.L. Stevenson's match factory was located on the other side of Waterloo Road, between Stone Wharf and the Lion Brewery. It was a fair distance from Lant Place to the factory, but Annie didn't mind the walk.

'It's the best part of me day, really,' she thought to herself as she cut down Pocock Street – because nothing exciting, or even pleasant, would happen to her once she'd passed through the imposing doorway and entered her daytime prison.

Annie reached the factory gate just as the hooter was blowing, and joined the stream of women who, like her, were all wearing long dark dresses and had their hair up in sensible buns.

'Nine 'undred an' thirty-one,' Annie said, almost to herself, as the women made their way towards the door.

'What was that?' the girl next to her asked.

'Nine 'undred an' thirty-one,' Annie repeated. 'That's 'ow many days I've been packin' matches. I worked it out.'

She could still picture the first of those days vividly. She remembered her shock at seeing the boxing room, with its row upon row of benches that seemed to go on for ever. And if that had not been bad enough, there was her first encounter with Miss Hunt, the boxing room supervisor.

Miss Hunt was a tall woman with a hooked nose and eyebrows as thick as a man's. It would have been cruel to call her ugly, Annie thought, but it was difficult to come up with any other word which might describe her as accurately.

'So you're the new girl they've sent me, are you?' the supervisor had demanded.

And Annie, fresh out of Lant Street Board School, had curtsied and said, 'Yes, ma'am.'

'Your name's Clarke, isn't it?'

'That's right, ma'am. Annie Clarke.'

'I shall not be requiring your Christian name,' Miss Hunt said witheringly. 'Follow me, Clarke.'

The supervisor led Annie to a row of pegs from which dozens of white aprons were hanging. She selected one of them and held it up before Annie with such reverence that it could have been a sacred object.

'This will be *your* apron, Clarke,' she'd said in hushed tones. 'The company kindly provides it absolutely free, but in return they expect, quite rightly, that you will look after it. You are to take it home every Saturday and wash it thoroughly. And when I say "thoroughly", Clarke,' she continued, her voice louder and harsher now, 'that is exactly what I mean. A soaking simply will not do. You must scrub it. Do you understand?'

'Yes, ma'am.'

'Then kindly repeat my instructions.'

'I 'ave to take it 'ome on a Saturday an' give it a good old scrubbin'.'

'It will also be your duty to repair it, should that be required,' the supervisor said. 'And I will expect your repairs to be so neat and tidy that they will be almost invisible. Is that clear?'

'Yes, ma'am,' Annie said again.

Finally satisfied that the new girl knew how to look after the valuable gift the company was bestowing on her, Miss Hunt handed over the apron. 'One more thing, Clarke,' she said. 'Do you see those windows over there?'

Annie looked towards where the supervisor was

pointing, saw a row of windows running along the far wall and nodded.

'There is a wonderful view over the Thames through them,' Miss Hunt told her.

Annie wondered for a moment how to respond, and eventually settled on, 'Smashin'.'

'It is not "smashin'," Clarke,' Miss Hunt said viciously. 'Those windows exist to let in the light by which you can see to do your work – and for no other purpose! If I catch you so much as glancing through them, you will be in serious trouble. Now follow me, and I'll show you where your workbench is.'

That first day on the line had been awful. The other girls seemed to pack matches so much more quickly than Annie could ever hope to. But even working at what was comparatively a snail's pace, Annie's fingers began to ache after a couple of hours, and then, because she was not used to standing for so long, her legs started to hurt her, too.

At the end of the day, Miss Hunt had come over to her bench and said, 'You're going to have to learn to work much faster than that, Clarke.'

'I'll try, ma'am,' Annie promised.

Miss Hunt frowned, so that her bushy eyebrows almost met. 'You're a pretty girl, Clarke,' she said.

'Thank you, ma'am,' replied Annie with a lack of caution she would soon learn to abandon.

'And I've noticed that pretty girls think they can get away with murder,' Miss Hunt hissed through almost clenched teeth. 'Well, they can't – not when they're working under me. So you'd better do more than just *try* to pack quicker, because there are plenty of others who would be glad of this job.'

That had been over three years ago, and now Annie was the fastest packer on her line. Her fingers and legs no longer ached at the end of the day, either. She had got used to the match factory – but that didn't mean she had to like it.

The two men in the rowing boat were dressed identically in long-sleeved vests and broad-cut trousers. They'd been

30

wearing reefer jackets, too, when they walked down Wapping Police Stairs to their boat, but these had been quickly discarded. Rowing was hot work, and the Thames Police – or 'Wet Bobs' as they were commonly known – wore their jackets only in the coldest weather.

The senior constable in the boat had sandy hair, intelligent brown eyes and a strong chin. His name was Harry Roberts, and he was twenty-six years old, with five years of solid service already behind him. Jack Davies – the junior constable – had been with the Thames Police for only eight months. It was no coincidence that he had been assigned to the same boat as Harry. The powers-that-be back in Wapping Station thought a great deal of Constable Roberts, and considered him just the right person to break in a new bobby.

'Yer've got to keep yer eyes open all the time, because you never know what's goin' to 'appen next on the river,' Harry said as his powerful arms pulled on his oar.

They glided past a 'dummy' – a barge without its mast – which was moored under Southwark Bridge. 'What do you make o' that?' Harry asked.

'It's just a barge, ain't it?' Jack replied. 'Looks 'armless enough to me.'

'It might be 'armless,' Harry agreed. 'Then again, it just might not be.'

' 'Ow d'yer mean?' Jack said.

'There was a barge just like it moored up near Blackfriars Bridge last year,' Harry explained. 'We thought it was just laid up because trade was slack.'

'But it wasn't?'

'I 'appened to notice some shifty lookin' characters 'angin' around the barge, so I checked up with Customs 'n' Excise and found it was s'pposed to 'ave a cargo of oil-cakes on it. Then I started to ask meself why a bunch of villains should be so interested in it. I mean, it's not as if they'd be likely to want to steal oil-cakes, is it?'

'An' did yer come up with an answer?' Jack asked.

'Yes, I did,' Harry replied. 'If they wasn't watchin' it with a view to nickin' things, then what they 'ad to be doin' was *guardin'* it. Which meant that there 'ad to be somefink much more valuable than oil-cakes on board.'

'So what did yer do?'

'Went to the Super with it. An' 'e got us permission to raid the barge.'

'An' what did yer find?'

'There was cakes all right – cakes o' snuff that 'ad never seen the insides of a customs 'ouse. That's what I mean, yer see – keep lookin' 'cos you never know what you'll find.'

Following his own advice, Harry looked up-river himself. On the starboard side of the police boat, a steamer was discharging broken chunks of granite into the lighter anchored alongside it. Harry watched as the granite came tumbling down the chute and the trimmers on the lighter spread it evenly over the deck. It was marvellous, the speed at which these trimmers worked, he thought – and nothing short of a miracle they could manage both to do their jobs and keep out of the way of the falling stone.

'But they don't always manage to keep out o' the way,' he reminded himself sombrely. Sometimes the trimmers would trip, or else the granite would come down the chute faster than they'd anticipated. If they were lucky, they'd get away with a broken leg when such a thing happened. If they weren't, the heavy stone would crush the life out of them.

And then, the friends of the dead man would start handing black-edged cards round. The name of a pub – usually one the dead man used himself – would be at the top of the card, and beneath it an invitation to attend a 'harmonic meeting' – or 'friendly lead' as most people preferred to call it.

The friendly lead would duly take place – and whenever his duty permitted it, Harry would go to it himself. Everybody there would have a good time, joining in the singing and laughing at the amateur comedian's jokes. But no one would forget the real reason they were there, and at the end of the evening, when the collection plate went round, everyone would contribute generously – including the dead man's worst enemy, who would make it a point of pride to see that he gave more than anybody else.

The funerals which followed the friendly leads were often magnificent affairs. A man who'd never had two ha'pennies to rub together in life would be buried in style, with a string of doleful undertaker's mutes leading a procession of carriages pulled by black horses and decked in flowers.

Harry shook his head. They were a breed apart, the river folk. They could be hard as nails one minute and as soft as putty the next. They'd fight each other with a fury on Saturday night and then pay off their opponents' fines in the magistrate's court on Monday morning. There was no understandin' 'em – you just 'ad to take 'em as they were, because they'd never change. And Harry rather liked them the way they were.

The police duty boat had almost drawn level with Battle Bridge Stairs. 'Let's head towards the bank an' see what's going' on,' Harry said to Jack.

The two policemen turned their boat towards the shore. Three or four watermen had moored their skiffs at the foot of the stone steps and were just standing around, waiting for customers. One of them, a handsome young man with jet-black hair and an infectious smile, seemed to be telling a joke, and when he finished it, the others roared with laughter.

Jack noticed Harry stiffen, and then the senior constable raised his cupped hands to his mouth.

'You always was a bit of a comedian, wasn't yer now, Tom?' he called out.

The young man turned round, and when he saw who had hailed him, the smile quickly vanished from his face.

'I said, yer always was a bit of a comedian,' Harry repeated.

'Course I was,' Tom replied. 'I got a lot to laugh about, ain't I – like that time I made a monkey out of you, fer instance.'

The two men's eyes locked. Ten seconds passed, then another ten. Neither man moved a muscle. It seemed to Jack that both of them would rather have cut off their own right arms than be the first to turn away.

A wharfinger, dressed in a frock coat and with a cargo invoice tucked under his arm, bustled down the steps.

'I need ferrying out to The Balmoral,' he said self-importantly. 'Which of you men will take me?'

The young waterman regretfully broke off his silent battle with the policeman and turned to face his potential customer. 'It's my turn,' he said.

'Then let's get started,' the wharfinger replied. 'I'm in something of a hurry.'

As the waterman led his customer down to his skiff, Harry and Jack began to pull away from the shore.

'What the bleedin' 'ell was that all about?' Jack asked.

'That was me just lettin' Tom Bates know I won't be 'appy until I've driven 'im off the river,' Harry replied.

'An' why's that?' Jack asked.

'Because 'e's a nasty piece o' work,' Harry told him. ' 'E lives up in Southwark – Lant Place – an' until a couple o' years ago, 'e was the leader of the Borough 'Ooligans. A real menace, they was, 'specially while they was at war with the 'ooligans from Newington. I tell you, some nights the streets was runnin' with blood.'

'So how did you get to know about 'im?' Jack asked. 'I mean, trouble on land ain't our business, is it?'

'Some of the fightin' spilled over onto the Embankment, an' as far as I was concerned, that made it my business.'

'Did yer ever manage to nick 'im?' Jack said.

Harry shook his head.

'I nearly 'ad 'im once, but the bleeder managed to slip out of it. But there's still time.'

'I thought yer said he wasn't with the 'ooligans no more,' Jack said. ' 'Ow are yer goin' ter nick 'im if 'e's gone straight?'

' 'E only sez he's gone straight,' Harry replied. ' 'E claims that when 'is dad died, 'e got hi'self an honest job so he could support 'is brother an' sisters.'

'But you don't believe 'im?'

'I've always 'ad me doubts about blokes like 'im ever goin' completely straight,' Harry said. 'An' that's what I

34

was doin' just now – remindin' Tom Bates that I've always 'ad me doubts.'

Miss Hunt – her hands clasped behind her back and her whistle hanging from a dark-blue ribbon round her neck – stopped briefly to glance at a couple of the packers' trays and then began to walk towards the other end of the boxing room. Annie silently counted to twenty, then risked looking up from her work. The supervisor was a long way away now – certainly out of earshot. If there was ever going to be an opportunity to chat to Maisie – the girl on the next bench – this was it.

' 'Ow was yer day off, Maisie?' Annie asked, speaking out of the corner of her mouth in a whisper.

'Awright,' Maisie replied. 'Ernie took me up West, an' we went rowin' on the Serpentine. What did you do?'

'Just stayed at 'ome,' Annie said.

'Poor old you,' Maisie commiserated.

'Oh, it wasn't too bad,' Annie told her friend. 'It give me a chance to meet the new neighbours, an' they seemed quite nice.'

'You want to get yerself a chap,' Maisie advised her.

'There's things I want before I go about getting meself a chap,' Annie said.

'Like what?' Maisie wondered.

'Like a new job. I'm just about sick to me guts of this one.'

'A new job? You mean, yer want to go an' work at the jam factory or the tannery?'

'No, not the jam factory or the stinkin' tannery,' Annie said firmly. 'I'm after somefink a bit more excitin' than that.'

'Huh!' Maisie replied.

'You're talking, Clarke!' said a loud voice just behind Annie's left shoulder.

Somehow, without her noticing it, Miss Hunt had managed to circle round and sneak up on her blind side.

'Sorry, ma'am,' Annie said.

'Sorry doesn't get matches packed!' Miss Hunt told her,

although looking at the pile that Annie had already boxed, talking didn't seem to have slowed her up at all.

'I was only asking Maisie if . . .' Annie began.

'You aren't paid to ask Stowe *anything*,' Miss Hunt interrupted. 'Keep packing while I check the work you've done so far.'

The boxes which had already been filled with matches were stacked at the end of the bench. Miss Hunt stared at them for a few seconds – as if she could tell, just by looking at their outsides, how many matches they contained – then she selected three boxes from three different rows and tipped the contents of one of them out onto the bench. With practised fingers, she began to divide them up into small piles.

'Five . . . ten . . . fifteen . . . twenty – twenty-five . . .' she counted out loudly.

It promised on the boxes that each would contain an average of forty-three matches. As far as J.L. Stevenson and Co. were concerned, a few less than that was acceptable, because, after all, the customers were unlikely to count them out themselves. A few more than forty-three was – grudgingly – permissible, too, since, up to a point, speed of packing was more important than accuracy. But *only* up to a point! So woe betide any girl who consistently packed less than thirty-eight and thus damaged the company's reputation, or packed more than forty-six and so cut into the profits.

Miss Hunt had finished counting. There were eight piles of five matches and three left over.

'Forty-three,' she said disappointedly.

She picked up a second box and began the process all over again.

'Five . . . ten . . . fifteen . . .'

There were exactly forty-three in this box, too. And in the third. From the corner of her eye, Annie could see the frown on the supervisor's face, and it was all she could do to stop herself from laughing.

One of the workmen from the dipping room appeared, carrying several trays of recently-dipped matches. 'Where d'yer want 'em, Miss Hunt?' he asked the grim-faced supervisor.

'Empty them into Clarke's trough.' Miss Hunt said.

'All of 'em!' the man asked, surprised.

'All of them,' Miss Hunt said.

The man tipped the matches and Annie's trough was full to overflowing.

'That's not fair, ma'am!' Annie protested.

'Not fair, isn't it?' Miss Hunt demanded. 'Would you rather I reported you to the manager?'

'No, ma'am,' Annie replied.

'Then you'd better work a bit faster, hadn't you?' Miss Hunt said. 'You've got a lot of catching up to do.'

The police duty boat had moved further down the river, keeping in close to the bank, and it was about five hundred yards beyond Battle Bridge Stairs when Harry noticed the fish box bobbing up and down on the water.

'What do yer make of that?' he asked Jack.

'It's just an old fish box, ain't it?' Jack answered. 'The river's full of 'em.'

'It may be,' Harry replied, 'But most of 'em are movin' with the current.'

Jack looked at the fish box again. 'You're right,' he said. 'This one ain't movin' at all. Why's that, 'Arry?'

'You'll find out in a minute,' Harry said, rowing the boat towards the bobbing box.

The moment the duty boat was close enough, Jack reached out for the box.

'Don't do that!' Harry said. 'You might break the thread!'

'The thread?' Jack repeated. 'What the devil are yer talkin' about, 'Arry?'

'Instead of tuggin' at the box, just feel underneath it,' Harry advised him.

Jack reached over the side of the boat and slid his hand into the murky water. 'There *is* a piece of rope 'angin' from under it,' he said with surprise in his voice.

'Pull it in gently,' Harry urged him. 'Tease it out o' the water, like yer'd do if you was fishin'.'

Jack did as he'd been told and soon was pulling a parcel, which was wrapped in waterproof material, into the boat. He carefully undid it and his eyes grew wide when he saw what was inside.

'Watches!' he said. 'Dozens of 'em!'

'It's a trick some of the old fences still use,' Harry explained. 'The fence is worried that the bobbies might raid him, yer see, but he don't trust nobody else with 'is booty. So what he does is, he hides 'em in the river, leavin' a fish box or a bit of old mattin' as a marker buoy.' He chuckled. 'Well, this partic'lar fence ain't goin' to be very pleased when 'e comes back for 'is stash, now is 'e?'

Jack shook his head in wonder. At Wapping Station, they'd told him there wasn't much you could teach Harry Roberts about police work. He had the sharpest eyes on the river, the other coppers said. And they'd not been exaggerating! Left to himself, Jack would never have noticed the fish box, but Harry had gone straight for it.

Feeling well pleased with their work, they rowed further down the river towards Tower Bridge. To their right, they saw a score of lighters and a dozen or so small cargo steamers with gaudily painted funnels which were unloading goods onto the cranes of the great Tooley Street warehouses. On their left they noted the Dutch sloops which brought eels for the Billingsgate Fish Market – sloops which looked very little different from the ones which these sailors' great-grandfathers had sailed into London two centuries before. In the distance a clock was sounding the hour, which meant that five hours of their six-hour shift were already over.

'Got used to workin' water police hours yet, 'ave yer, Jack?' Harry asked.

'Just about,' Jack said, 'though I did find it a bit confusin' at first, workin' for six hours, then taking twelve off and comin' back for another six. I mean, it ain't natural goin' to bed at a different time every day, is it?'

'Maybe it ain't natural,' Harry agreed, 'but it does make sure that over any three days, you get to see the river at every hour o' the day an' night.'

'An' is that important?' Jack asked.

'It's vital,' Harry told him. 'The river's like a woman. You see her out on the street, dressed up to the nines, an' yer think yer know 'er. But yer don't. Before yer can get a proper picture, yer 'ave to see 'er last thing at night, when she's fallin' asleep, an' first thing in the mornin' when she's just wakin' up.'

Jack grinned. 'Yer seem to know as much about women as yer know about the river,' he said. 'Got a gal of yer own, 'ave yer, 'Arry?'

In his mind's eye, Harry could picture Stevenson's match factory, back up the river. And with that picture came another one - of a lovely girl with shining brown hair who worked in the factory and lived up the same street as Tom Bates, the ex-Hooligan.

'I said, 'ave you got a gal?' Jack repeated.

'Not yet,' Harry told him. 'But I'm livin' in 'ope!'

CHAPTER THREE

The hooter which crowned the roof of Stevenson's match factory sounded right on time, but the women in the boxing room knew better than to stop work immediately. For another minute and a half, their agile fingers continued to pack matches – never more than forty-six never less than thirty-eight – until, finally, Miss Hunt chose to blow her whistle.

Annie let out a sigh of relief and made her way across the room to the coat hooks. Miss Hunt was standing with her back to the wall, and the supervisor's gaze, Annie noticed, was following her every step.

'Well, yer can watch me as much as yer like, you nasty old cow,' the girl thought to herself. 'You ain't got no power over me between now and tomorrer mornin'.'

But already, tomorrow was only a few hours away – already a few precious moments of freedom were lost and gone forever.

As she hung her apron on her hook, Annie suddenly realised just how hungry she was. Still, what did she expect, she asked herself. You were bound to feel hungry when you'd had no dinner. And there hadn't really been any choice *but* to miss dinner – because there'd been so many extra matches heaped into her bench-well on Miss Hunt's instructions that when the other girls had trooped off for their twopenny or threepenny meals, she'd had to stay at her bench in order to box them.

Maisie Stowe appeared and hung her apron up on the peg next to Annie's.

'I'll die if I don't 'ave somefink to eat in the next few minutes,' Annie said to her friend. 'How d'yer fancy comin' to Lock'art's Cocoa Rooms with me?'

Maisie looked doubtful. 'I'm not sure I can afford it after the Sunday that me an' my Ernie 'ad,' she said. 'Goin' up West don't exac'ly come cheap, yer know. Not even if you're careful.'

'I'll treat you,' Annie said.

'Are yer sure yer can afford it?' Maisie asked.

Annie jingled the coins in the pocket of her dress. 'Course I can afford it,' she said. 'I wouldn't 'ave asked yer if I couldn't.'

She had plenty of money left over after the weekend. *She* didn't have any young man to go up West with.

Annie liked Lockhart's Cocoa Rooms. They were bright and clean and the manager didn't mind if you brought your own breakfast or dinner in with you, as long as you bought at least one drink per head. Tonight, however, her hunger made her go the whole hog and she'd ordered a sausage sandwich.

While she munched her way through the spicy banger and crusty bread, she glanced through the situations vacant columns of the evening paper.

'Just what kind of job are yer expectin' to find in there?' Maisie asked.

'Somefink that's better than what I've got now,' Annie told her. 'Somefink a lot more interestin' than packin' boxes of matches day in an' day out.'

Maisie scoffed. 'Fat chance!' she said. 'I mean, think about it. You ain't got no trainin', 'ave yer?'

'I could learn,' Annie protested. 'I was a good scholar when I was at Lant Street, yer know.'

Maisie shook her head pityingly.

'Gals like you an' me don't get good jobs,' she said. 'We work at places like the match factory or the jam factory. Then, if we're lucky, we meet a decent bloke with a trade, marry 'im, an' start havin' 'is kids. An' when yer think about it, what's wrong with that, anyway? Don't yer want kids?'

'Course I do,' Annie answered. 'But before I settle down, I'd like to prove to meself that I can do somefink else.'

'Prove to yerself that yer can't do *nuffink* else, more like,' Maisie said gloomily.

But Annie was no longer listening to her friend. Her eyes were firmly fixed on an advertisement which almost seemed to leap out from the page at her.

' 'Ere, 'ow about this?' she asked. 'The National Telephone Company is currently recruitin' operators for its London Switchboards. Applicants should be of good moral character . . .'

'Well, that lets you out for a start, don't it?' Maisie said mischievously.

' . . . good moral character an' education,' Annie continued, determined to ignore her friend's interruption. 'Hours – nine daily, includin' time allowed for luncheon an' afternoon tea.'

'Luncheon!' Maisie said in disgust. 'What's wrong with callin' it dinner?'

'Perquisites . . . whatever them are . . . include pension scheme, membership of the Company's various social clubs . . . Oh, I see, they're talkin' about *perks* . . .'

'Can't call anyfink by its proper name, can they?' Maisie sniffed.

' . . . launch trips on the Thames an' lectures an' lantern displays in the Association Rooms, St George's Hall.'

'An' what's it pay?' Maisie asked.

'Eleven bob a week, risin' to a pound after nine years,' Annie told her.

'Huh! You're earnin' more that nine bob a week now,' Maisie reminded her.

'I know I am,' Annie agreed, 'but bein' an operator sounds so excitin'. Don't *you* think it's excitin'?'

Maisie stirred her cocoa moodily. 'I don't want to see you gettin' yerself 'urt,' she said.

'What d'yer mean by that?' Annie asked.

'We're not the sort of gals for luncheons, launch trips on the river an' pension schemes,' Maisie said. 'You'd be wastin' your time goin' after a posh job like that.'

'Well, I'd like to 'ave a crack at applyin', anyway,' Annie said decisively.

'Do what yer want,' Maisie told her, 'but don't come cryin' to me when they turn yer down flat.'

It was almost dark by the time Annie reached Lant Place, but the street still teemed with life. A fly-paper vendor, his wares stuck to his tall top-hat, was going from door to door, trying to persuade the residents that they'd better buy now, because the first flies of summer were due any day. An elderly chair-mender, bowed down by the years, was making his way up the other side of the Place, hoping to find at least one broken chair which he could fix for the price of a decent supper.

But it was the kids who really owned the street for those hours between tea and bedtime, and there was a score of them out now. Some were playing football with an old rag ball. Others were rolling rusty metal hoops from old cart wheels or butter churns. And there was third group – exclusively girls – who were playing Horsey with home-made multi-coloured woollen reins.

On any other day, Annie would have taken a minute or two to stop and watch the kids. She enjoyed seeing the eager looks on their faces as they played Ugly Bear or 'Charley Knacker . . . one, two, three.' She laughed indulgently at the girls' lip-licking concentration as they launched themselves perilously from one chalked hop-scotch square to another. But on this particular Monday evening, the advertisement in the paper weighed too heavily on her mind for her to take any pleasure in the children's antics.

'*Gals like you an' me don't get good jobs like that,*' Maisie had told her, less than an hour earlier.

'But if yer don't try, yer'll *never* get what yer want, will yer?' Annie said aloud, as if Maisie were by her side and she was still arguing her case.

43

'*We're not the sort of gals for luncheons, launch trips on the river an' pension schemes,*' the phantom Maisie quickly responded inside her head.

Annie was so wrapped up in her own thoughts that she didn't notice the beer dray trundling, unusually quickly, up the street ahead of her. Nor did she notice that in his haste to make up for time lost earlier, the drayman had not made a proper job of tightening the restraining rope at the back of the wagon – and now one of the barrels was rocking dangerously against it.

Maybe Maisie *did* have a point, Annie conceded grudgingly. Why go to the bother of gettin' all worked up over a job which you knew, deep in your heart, they'd never give to someone like you? Wasn't it better, in the long run, just to forget the whole idea and save yourself the disappointment?

The first real warning that anything was wrong on the beer dray came with a loud crash which echoed up and down the whole length of the narrow street. Startled, Annie looked in the direction of the noise. She saw the trailing rope first – and then she saw the barrel!

The barrel had fallen into the road and was bouncing along the cobblestones at a frightening speed – straight towards her.

'Get out o' the way, Annie!' screamed half a dozen frightened children further up the street.

'Get out o' the way!' Annie told herself.

But she couldn't. The sight of that massive cask – getting closer and closer with every second – simply made her freeze. The rumbling noise got louder and louder, and soon the sound filled her ears. The barrel grew larger and larger, until it blocked out the rest of the world.

She could read the name of the brewery stencilled on the side of it! She could smell the mixture of hops and malt! And still she couldn't bring herself to move.

'Get out o' the way,' she repeated desperately.

But her legs seemed rooted to the ground, and any second now the great heavy thing would hit her – bowling her over as if she were no more than a wooden skittle.

At the very last moment, just when escape seemed impossible, she felt a strong pair of hands grab her, lift her effortlessly off her feet, and swing her out of the way. And even as she swung, she could still see the barrel and feel a whoosh of air as it rolled past, only inches away.

Her rescuer put her on the ground again, though he continued to hold onto her waist in case she still needed support.

Annie looked up into his face, and saw he was a handsome young man with jet-black hair and an infectious grin.

'You should watch where yer goin', Annie Clarke,' he said. 'If I let go of yer now, yer won't fall over, will yer?'

'I d . . . don't think so,' Annie said shakily.

The young man removed his hands, and Annie discovered that though her legs felt a little wobbly, she could stand without help.

'Are yer sure yer all right?' the young man asked.

Who was he – this knight in shining armour? He knew her name, and it seemed rude not to use his in return when she thanked him for saving her.

'Well done, Tom!' called one of the kids up the street.

Tom? Yes, of course – that was who he was! Tom Bates, whose family lived right at the other end of Lant Place.

'I said, are yer sure yer all right?' her rescuer repeated.

'I'm fine . . . Tom,' Annie said. 'An' thanks for pullin' me out o' the way.'

'Think nuffink of it,' Tom said generously.

The drayman, a huge man with arms like tree trunks and a chest almost the size of one of his barrels, had got out of his wagon and came running down the street.

'What 'appened?' he asked.

'What 'appened?' Tom said. 'Yer very nearly killed 'er – that's what 'appened!'

'Yer not blamin' me for a simple accident, I 'ope!' the drayman said aggressively.

'If my boat springs a leak, I blame meself,' Tom told him, 'an' if a rope comes loose on your dray, I blame you. So I think you owe the young lady an apology.'

He'd said it nicely, but he left no doubt that it was an order rather than a request.

The drayman seemed about to argue, but, despite his size, one look at Tom's determined eyes was enough to persuade him that it was not a good idea.

'I'm sorry, gal,' he said. 'Maybe I should 'ave been a bit more careful with me ropes.'

'Maybe you should 'ave been,' Tom agreed. 'Well, there's yer barrel. If I was you, I'd go an' see if it's all right.'

Annie turned her head in the direction Tom was pointing and saw that the barrel had come to rest against a gas lamp down the street. The cask itself looked fine, but there was a noticeable dent in the lamp-post. She shuddered at the thought of the harm it would have done if it had hit *her*.

The drayman set off to rescue his barrel, leaving Annie and Tom alone.

'You look like yer could use a drink,' Tom said. 'D'yer fancy nippin' into The Goldsmiths' with me?'

Annie wanted to say yes – yet she hesitated. The fact that he lived at the other end of the street was only one of the reasons she didn't know Tom Bates better. The other, more important one, was that she'd been warned off by her mum.

'You keep well away from that Tom Bates,' Lil had said in that voice she kept in reserve for when she was *really* serious. ' 'E's an 'ooligan, make no mistake about that, an' no respectable gal wants to get 'erself involved with an 'ooligan.'

Annie looked Tom up and down. He certainly wasn't dressed like a hooligan. He had on a collar rather than one of the neckcloths that hooligans favoured. And he was wearing braces, whereas most of the lads in the gangs preferred a belt, because it came in useful as an extra weapon.

'Well?' Tom asked, grinning. ' 'Ave yer made up yer mind whether or not yer ashamed to be seen with me?'

After he'd just gone an' saved her life, how *could* she tell him she was ashamed to be seen with him?

'I'd be 'onoured to go an' 'ave a drink with yer,' she told him.

And when Tom held out his arm to her – like a proper gent – she really didn't see she had any choice but to take it.

The saloon bar of The Goldsmiths' Arms opened onto the billiard room, and from where they were sitting, Annie could hear the constant click of the ivory balls. It felt strange at first, to be with a man she hardly knew – especially when most of the other customers were courting couples – but Tom was easy to talk to, and Annie soon found herself starting to relax.

She told him about the match factory and her argument with Miss Hunt.

'I wouldn't go takin' any apples off that Miss 'Unt if I was you,' Tom advised.

'Apples?' Annie said. 'What ever makes yer think she'd want ter give apples to me?'

'Don't the wicked witch always try to give the beautiful princess poison apples?' Tom asked.

Annie felt herself reddening, and laughed to cover her embarrassment.

'Miss 'Unt might be a witch, all right,' she said, 'but I've a long way to go before I'm a princess.'

'You ain't got far to go before yer beautiful, though,' Tom said quietly. 'No distance at all.'

'Tell me what life's like on the river,' Annie said hastily, to save herself more blushes.

Tom shrugged. 'Not much to tell. It can be freezin' in the winter an' boilin' hot in the summer. When yer rowin' against the current, it's 'ard work, but when you're goin' with it, yer don't 'ave to do much more than sit there.'

'Is it a good livin'?'

'It can be. Sometimes, when there's a lot of ships in, you can make reasonable bees an' honey ferryin' people across to 'em, but there's times when business is slack as well. An' you still have to pay out rent for yer skiff, 'owever little yer've taken in yerself.' His eyes twinkled. 'That's why the watermen in the old days used to 'ave a sideline to make 'em a bit extra.'

'What sort of sideline?' asked Annie, who couldn't

47

imagine what it was they could have done that Tom would think was amusing.

'Findin' bodies in the river,' Tom said. 'They used to get a 'andsome fee for fishin' corpses out o' the old Thames. An' of course, they always knew exactly where to look.'

'Always knew exactly where to look? But 'ow could they?'

'Because it was them who put the bodies in the water in the first place,' Tom explained.

'You mean, they'd kill people just so they could get the fee!' Annie said, horrified.

'That's right,' Tom agreed cheerfully. 'But the council's put a stop to all that, now.'

'I should 'ope they 'ad.'

'Yes, these days, you only get two bob a corpse, an' that includes havin' to take it to the mortuary yourself an' giving evidence at the inquest.' Tom grinned. 'So with all that bother, it's not really worth our while doin' it any more, is it?'

'Yer jokin', ain't yer?' Annie said.

'About the old watermen?' Tom asked. 'No, that's true enough. But the only stiffs I'm ever likely to fish out of the Thames'll be me own kind.'

'Other watermen?'

'That's right. There's a waterman drowned nearly every week somewhere along the river. Most of the blokes who work it ain't never learned to swim, yer see.'

'But you can, can't you?' Annie asked, wondering, even as she spoke, why she should find the idea that he might not be able to swim himself so alarming.

'I can swim like a fish,' Tom assured her. 'I was a real mudlark when I was a kid – yer couldn't keep me out of the river.'

Though Annie had decided that she would tell no one but Maisie about the advertisement for the telephonist's job, she found she was so relaxed in Tom's company that she was repeating the details to him almost before she realised it.

'Maisie thinks I've got ideas above me station,' she said,

when she'd finished outlining what the advertisement had said. 'Do yer think she's right?'

'Right?' Tom said. 'I think she's off her bloomin' 'ead. I can see just by lookin' at you that yer a good little worker an' as smart as paint. If I was the guv'nor of that telephone company, I'd give yer a job like a shot.'

'Yer not just soft-soapin' me, are yer?' Annie asked.

Tom looked shocked. 'I'd never do that,' he said earnestly. 'Cross me 'eart an' 'ope to die.'

'Then I *will* 'ave a try for it.' Annie said. She glanced up at the big wall-clock, then swallowed the last of her port wine. 'An' now, if yer'll excuse me, I'll 'ave ter go 'ome.'

' 'Aven't yer got time to stop for just one more?' Tom asked disappointedly.

'I'd like to,' Annie confessed, 'but I'm late already, an' if I don't turn up soon, me mum'll start worryin'.'

Tom sighed lightly, then stood up and offered her his arm.

'*You* don't 'ave to leave as well,' Annie said. She reached into her pocket. 'Stay an' 'ave another one. An' this time, I'll pay.'

Tom shook his head. 'I should be gettin' 'ome meself,' he told her. 'Anyway, I'll 'ave to see yer as far as yer front door. If yer go on yer own, yer might get run down by another beer barrel.'

Annie could just picture the look on her mother's face if she arrived home in the company of Tom Bates. Lil would go absolutely spare – you could bet money on it. Yet how the dickens could she explain that to him?

'I'll go on me own,' she said. 'There's no point in takin' you out of yer way.'

'It won't kill me to walk an extra few 'undred yards, now will it?' Tom asked.

It was Annie's turn to sigh. 'If yer don't mind, I'd really much rather go on me own,' she told him.

For a moment, Tom look hurt, and then he nodded his head as if to say that he knew he had a bad name in the street, and however unfair it was, he was stuck with it.

' 'Ow about a compromise?' he suggested. 'I'll walk *part* o' the way with yer.'

Annie smiled. 'All right,' she said, standing up and taking his arm. 'Walk me part o' the way.'

They reached the door and found their way blocked by a sandy-haired man in a Thames Police uniform.

'Ain't 'e an 'andsome bloke,' Annie thought before she could stop herself. What was wrong with her? she wondered. She didn't usually pay any attention to what men looked like, but today, in the space of an hour, she'd caught herself admirin' two different ones. Maybe she was comin' down with the 'flu or somefink.

The policeman had made no move to get of their way, nor did Tom make any attempt to walk round him. For several seconds, the two men just stood there.

Then the policeman spoke. 'We always seem to be runnin' into one another, don't we Tom?' he said coldly.

'The last time I saw yer was at Battle Bridge Stairs,' Tom replied, his own tone matching the policeman's, 'which – in case yer didn't know – is where I 'appen to work. An' this pub is my local boozer. So if anybody's runnin' into anybody, Constable Roberts, I'd say it was you runnin' into me.'

Harry Robert's powerful shoulder muscles tensed, and for a moment Annie was afraid that he was going to take a swing at Tom. Then the policeman relaxed again and he turned towards her.

'I'm sorry, I'm forgettin' me manners,' he said.

'Yer what?' Annie replied, knocked off her balance by the fact that whereas his voice had had a hard edge when he was talking to Tom, it was now much softer and . . . well, friendly.

'I'm forgettin' me manners an' 'olding you up, Miss . . . Miss . . . ?' Harry said.

'Clarke,' Annie told him. Yes, the voice was definitely friendly. 'Annie Clarke.'

'Well, I'll detain yer no longer,' Harry said, stepping to one side. 'Good night, Miss Clarke.'

'Good night,' Annie replied, wondering whether she was being disloyal to Tom in speaking so politely to this policeman who was obviously his enemy.

And then she suddenly felt ridiculous. Disloyal to Tom? Crikey, she 'ardly knew the bloke!

Harry stayed in the doorway and watched the couple make their way up Lant Place. So the girl who'd first caught his attention so forcibly outside the match factory was called Annie Clarke, was she? he thought to himself. The name suited her. And she was even prettier close up than she was from a distance.

Annie still had her arm linked with Tom's, Harry noted, but surely that was no more than common courtesy on her part. Yes, he decided, you could tell just by looking at her that she was the kind of girl who would treat everybody decently – even a bleedin' hooligan like Tom Bates.

Still, the policeman didn't like the situation one bit. For all that Tom was a villain, Harry had to admit that he was a good-looking lad, and it was just possible that someone as young and innocent as Annie Clarke might fall victim to his charms.

'I won't let it 'appen,' Harry promised himself. 'Not to a nice girl like that.'

He had pledged to drive Tom off the river – and he would drive him away from Annie Clarke, too.

It had been dark for quite a while by the time Tom Bates approached his own home, and a gas light was burning brightly in the parlour. Tom unlocked the front door, and then, instead of going straight to the kitchen, he stuck his head round the parlour door.

There was hardly any furniture in the room any more – much of it had been sold to pay his dad's doctor's bill, and most of the rest had gone to cover the costs of the funeral. But even if they hadn't so desperately needed the money, the furniture would have had to go anyway, because ever since her husband's death, the parlour had been May Bates' workshop.

She was there now, sitting on a stool in the centre of the room. In front of her was a hollow cardboard cylinder which she had just glued together, and while she held it firmly with one hand, she sewed a lid onto it with the other. To her left was a stack of cardboard from which she would make more of the cylinders, and to her right were several teetering towers of completed hat boxes.

'Hello, Old Gal,' Tom said, smiling at his mother. 'You're still at it, I see.'

May returned his smile, though there were definite signs of tiredness in hers.

'Only another couple of dozen o' these to do, an' I'll 'ave finished me gross,' she said. 'An' that'll be another two an' a tanner towards the rent.'

She could turn her hand to anything, Tom thought admiringly. When there was no demand for hat boxes, she made paper flowers, and when the trade in them was a bit slack, she turned her hand to scrubbing brushes and shoe brushes. Once in a while, she even boiled beetroots in her washhouse boiler and sold them from a basket down at the Saturday night market.

'You want to be careful you don't overdo it, Old Gal,' Tom warned her.

'Look who's talkin',' May replied. ''Ow many hours do yer reckon you spend on that river?'

Tom shrugged uncomfortably. 'I'm only down there as long as any of the other watermen are,' he said.

'You start tellin' fibs to me an' yer'll get a clip round yer ear,' May told him. 'I know for a certain fact that yer always the first one down at Battle Bridge Stairs, an' as often as not yer the last to leave as well.'

Tom grinned like a little boy whose mother had caught him out. And in a way, he supposed, that was what he was. Blokes were always little boys to their mums, even when the mum in question barely reached their shoulders.

'If I do work more than the others – an' I'm not admittin' I do, mind – it's only 'cos we need the bees an' 'oney,' he said. 'Left to meself, I'd be a real idle devil.'

His mother smiled again.

'You're a good lad, Tom,' she said. 'Yer dad – God rest 'is soul – used to worry about yer when you was runnin' around with them 'ooligans, but I always said to 'im, our

Tom'll sort 'imself out before 'e's very much older. And yer did, didn't yer?'

'I did, Old Gal,' Tom agreed.

Not that he'd had much choice, he thought to himself. It had been a fine thing to be one of the Borough Hooligans as long as he was a single chap, but the second his father had been taken ill, he'd realised that with all his extra responsibilities, he didn't dare risk getting into trouble with the police.

And there was something else – something he wasn't sure he fully understood himself. He watched his dear old dad slowly dying, yet fighting his illness every inch of the way, and Tom had become convinced that life was far too precious to chance carelessly in a street battle.

Even so, there were times when he was rowing some sailor or wharfinger out to a ship when he'd catch himself missing the old days – the thrill of planning an attack, the excitement of leading his gang into the fray.

'Fancy a cup o' rosie, Old Gal?' he asked his mother.

'If yer goin' to make one anyway, then I wouldn't say no,' May admitted.

Tom was just about to step into the hallway when he stopped himself and said, casually, 'What d'yer think of the Clarkes?'

'Yer mean the Clarkes 'oo live down the street at Number Thirty-four?' May asked.

'That's right,' Tom agreed.

Now why should he want to know about the Clarkes from Number Thirty-four all of a sudden? May wondered. Could it have anythin' to do with the fact that over the last year or so, young Annie Clarke had really started to blossom?

'*Lil* Clarke's all right,' she said, her hands continuing to stitch away at the hat box. 'Some o' the people in this street think she gets a bit above 'erself at times. An' maybe she does sometimes – but for all that, she's got a good 'eart. Just look at the way she looks after Nettie Walnut whenever the poor old soul turns up.'

'Looks after who?' Tom asked.

'Nettie Walnut,' May repeated. 'Don't yer know 'er?'

'No. 'Oo is she?'

'She's an old tramp. Wanders all over the country, she does, but always 'eads for the Smoke when winter sets in. Anyway, most of the neighbours'll 'ave nothin' at all to do with 'er – but she can always be sure of a nice, warm cup of rosie an' a slice of bread in Lil Clarke's kitchen.'

'An' the rest of the family?' Tom asked.

Only a slight twitch of his left eye betrayed his impatience, but his mother did not miss it.

'Sam's a really nice bloke,' May said. 'A bit of a comedian on the quiet, though most of the time, people don't even realise he's bein' funny. An' then there's the kids . . .'

She paused and turned her head so that Tom couldn't see she was smiling.

'What about the kids?' her son asked when several seconds had passed in silence.

'They've a daughter called Peggy,' May said. 'Mad about animals, the gal is. She'd turn their 'ouse into a zoo if Lil'd let 'er. And then there's Eddie. I've lost count o' the number of jobs 'e's 'ad since 'e left school, an' if you ask me, e's turnin' into a right little loafer.'

The hatbox was finished. May stacked it carefully on top of the wobbly towers and reached for another sheet of cardboard. With hands made expert by long practice, she applied glue to one edge, then bent the cardboard round until it formed the shape she needed.

Behind her, she heard her son sigh, and then he said, 'I thought they 'ad three kids.'

'Oh, d'yer mean Annie?' his mother replied.

'Yes. I think that's 'er name.'

'She works at Stevenson's match factory. She's a really nice girl. Very pretty, as well!'

'Is she?' Tom asked. 'I can't say I've ever noticed that meself.'

CHAPTER FOUR

'Well, now yer've 'ad a bit o' time to settle in, what do yer think o' the place?' Lily Clarke said to her new next-door neighbour on Saturday morning.

'It's different to what I'm used to,' Colleen said cautiously. 'Very different.'

It was, in fact, worlds apart from Marston. The village had been such a sleepy place, populated in the daytime only by gossiping wives and children too young for school, but London – or at least, Lant Place – seemed to teem with life from dawn to dusk.

Colleen thought back to the previous Monday. She'd seen George off to his new job and then, with nothing to distract her, had set about getting the house straight.

With nothing to distract her! What a piece of wishful thinking that had been!

The milkman had come round at nine, his churn rattling noisily against the guard rail of his three-wheeled trolley as he'd made his way down the street.

'Me name's Todd,' he said. 'I don't normally come knockin' on people's doors – if they want any milk, I'm out in the street an' they can come to me – but since it's yer first day 'ere, I've gone out of me way for yer.'

'That was very kind of you, Mr Todd,' Colleen said.

'But, mind you, it'll be the last time I'll call on yer,' Todd told her. 'I've got better things to do with me time than go chasin' after people who need milk.'

The fishmonger had appeared next, pushing a long barrow packed with ice.

'I don't usually make 'ouse calls,' he said as if he were a doctor, 'but as yer a newcomer, I thought I'd better set yer straight. See them fish?' He pointed to his barrow. 'They're so fresh they've 'ardly 'ad time to stop breathin'. But not everybody's got my 'igh standards. There's blokes who'd sell yer cod that 'adn't seen the sea since Adam was a lad.'

'Have you got anybody in particular in mind?' Colleen asked, doing her best to hide her amusement.

'It's not for me to say,' the fishmonger replied warily. 'But I'll tell you this – even stray cats stay well clear o' ole Tubby Townsend's barrer.'

The coalman had turned up shortly after the fishmonger had taken his leave.

'I don't usually . . .' he began.

'Come to people's doors,' Colleen said.

'That's right,' the coalman agreed. 'Leastways, not unless they're wantin' a full bag.'

'I'll be needin' *two* bags,' Colleen said, thinking of all the cleaning she would have to do, and how many gallons of water that would mean heating up in the washhouse copper.

The coalman raised his eyebrows in surprise. 'Two bags, eh?' he said. 'The neighbour'ood's goin' up in the world – my word it is.'

The coalman had barely left when another man turned up to take his place – this time, a salt seller.

'Do you happen to know where that salt comes from?' Colleen asked nostalgically as she watched him chip several large splinters off the big block he had on his barrow.

'No idea, missus,' he replied. 'I mean, when all's said an' done, salt's just salt, ain't it?'

Not if you came from Cheshire, it wasn't. If you came from Cheshire there was all the difference in the world between rock salt and brine salt, between salt which had been produced by Ashton's and that panned by Worrell's.

'Oh, I can't help wishin' I was back home again,' Colleen thought to herself.

A woman in a flowery hat, her hands full of feather dusters, came in the salt seller's wake.

'Yer'll be needin' one or two o' these, havin' only just moved in,' she said.

'Oh really!' Colleen said exasperatedly. 'Is there anybody in the whole of Southwark who *doesn't* know that we've only just moved into Lant Place?'

'Beg yer pardon, gal?' the woman said.

'Doesn't matter,' Colleen told her. 'How much were you askin' for your dusters?'

'I'd be doin' meself to let 'em go at less than one an' six a piece,' the woman replied.

Colleen laughed. 'Me mum an' dad might be Irish, but that doesn't mean I'm green all the way through,' she said. 'I'll tell you what – I'll give you a tanner for a pair of 'em.'

Several minutes' hard bargaining followed, at the end of which Colleen managed to buy one duster for only a little more than twice the price she'd have paid if she'd known the ropes.

The interruptions had continued all day. An old man who repaired chairs had asked if she needed his services. A street hawker had tried to sell her a gent's hat.

'Only five bob,' he'd said. 'The reason they're so cheap is that I make 'em meself. Look a treat on yer old man's loaf, this 'ere titfer would.'

'I think my "old man" would rather buy his own "titfers",' Colleen said, and wondered how the women of Lant Place ever managed to get any work done with such constant interruptions.

Yet somehow she had been able to squeeze in a little time for housework, and now, less than a week after she'd first seen it from her vantage point on the cart, Number Thirty-six had been so thoroughly cleaned and scrubbed out that she could even have invited her mam round to tea.

Lil Clarke approved too. 'Yer've done wonders,' she said, looking round the spotless kitchen. 'An' now it's time for a bit o' fun. Are yer goin' to let yer old man off 'is leash, tonight?'

'How do you mean?' Colleen asked.

'Are yer goin' to let 'im slip 'is rope an' nip down the road to the boozer?'

'I suppose so – if he wants to,' Colleen said.

' 'E'll want to,' Lil said confidently. 'An' with the men out of our 'air, we can 'ave a bit of fun of our own – doin' the shopping.'

'All right,' Colleen said, although she wasn't sure that the shopping would be quite as much fun for her as Lil Clarke seemed to think it would be.

'An' since the gas man's been, I might treat yer to a few jellied ells,' Lil said.

Even in the brief time they had known each other, Colleen had come to understand that there were leaps in Lil's conversation that were impossible to follow in any logical manner – and that the quickest way to fill in gaps was simply to ask what she meant. Which was what she did now.

'What's the gas man comin' got to do with you treatin' me to jellied eels?' she said.

'Well, 'e emptied me meter for me, didn't he?' Lil replied.

'Yes?' Colleen said, still mystified. 'That's what gas men usually do, isn't it?'

'An' when 'e'd emptied it, 'e gave me the two bobs.'

'What two bobs?'

'The two bobs that were in me meter,' Lil explained.

'But the meter takes pennies, doesn't it?' Colleen asked.

'O' course it does,' Lil said. 'It's be a fine thing, wouldn't it, if we 'ad to put an 'ole two bob in the meter every time we wanted a bit o' light?'

'So if the meter doesn't work off two shillin' pieces, how did they get in there?' Colleen asked.

'I put 'em in meself,' Lil replied, looking at her as if she were demented. 'Who else d'yer think's going to put money in my meter – the coalman?'

'But why?' Colleen said, almost – but not quite – ready to strangle her neighbour at this point.

A look of realisation came to Lil's face.

'Oh, I see what yer mean,' she said. 'Whenever I've got a spare couple of bob, I put 'em in the meter, 'cos once they're in there, I can't spend 'em. Everybody in the street does that. It's like bein' in the Post Office Savin's Bank, but without the walk.'

'Yes,' Collen said. 'I suppose it must be.'

'I'll come round for yer at about eight o'clock, then, shall I?' Lil asked.

'Eight o'clock!' Colleen exclaimed. 'But it'll be nearly dark by then, won't it?'

'Best time to do the shoppin' – after dark,' Lil said. 'That's when yer get the best bargains.'

'But aren't all the shops closed by then?' Colleen asked her neighbour.

Lil laughed, as if she found Colleen's remark the funniest thing she'd ever heard.

'Closed at eight?' she said. 'This is London, gal. It'll be nearer to midnight before most of 'em start thinkin' about puttin' their shutters up.'

It was, in fact, a little after eight when the two women set out from Lant Place.

'Still, there's no 'urry,' Lil said. 'Things won't even have started warmin' up yet.'

Their journey took them along Southwark Bridge Road and then up Great Guildford Street. Lil provided a commentary as they walked along, describing each place as if it were as historic as the Tower of London, as exotic as an Eastern harem.

'That's the Congregational Chapel,' she said at the corner of Orange Street. 'An' over there, you can just see the top o' All 'allows Church. It's got seats for a thousand, it 'as, not that that'll be of interest to you, bein' a Catholic.'

'How on earth did you know that I was a Catholic?' Colleen asked sharply.

'I couldn't 'elp noticin' yer washing 'anging out on the line,' Lil confessed.

Colleen tried to guess what about her washing had given her away, but not having the skills of Lant Place's Sherlock Holmes, she soon gave up. 'What did my washin' tell you?' she asked.

'Well, I just 'appened to see this one dress,' Lil explained, 'a brown one, it was, with lace on the sleeves.'

'Yes, I know the one you mean,' Colleen said. 'I used to wear it quite a lot, but now I only keep for when I'm doin' really dirty work around the house.'

'An' I couldn't fail but see that it was worn round the neck,' Lil continued.

She must have eyes like an eagle, Colleen thought, but aloud she said, 'It *is* worn. I told you it was an old dress.'

'Yes, but it ain't worn evenly,' Lil said. 'The middle of the neck is all right. It's a bit to each side where it's frayed.'

'An' what did that tell you?' Colleen asked, starting to enjoy Lil's games.

'It told me that most o' the time yer'd 'ad that dress on, yer'd been wearin' somefink on a chain,' Lil said. 'Somefink quite 'eavy. An' what could that be but a crucifix?'

Colleen laughed. What was it Annie had said? *'Mum's always addin' two an' two together, an' the amazin' thing is that most of the time she comes up with four.'*

Well, she'd certainly come up with four about George taking over as manager of the wood yard – and she'd got her sums right on Colleen's religion, too.

Within sight of the railway viaduct, they turned left onto Union Street.

'Yer don't wear yer crucifix much now though, do yer, Colleen?' Lil asked.

'I don't wear it at all,' Colleen said. 'I 'aven't really worn it since I got married.'

'Is that because yer old man ain't really one of your lot, then?' Lil wondered.

'Now howdid you know that he wasn't brought up a Cath . . . ?' Colleen began, then she chuckled and continued. 'Well, however you worked it out, you're right – again! George went through the motions of bein' received into the Church, but I know he doesn't really believe in it, and I thought it'd just be pushin' me religion down his throat to keep on wearin' me cross.'

'You did right,' Lil said. 'It's easy enough to aggravate yer old man by accident, without goin' out of yer way to do it deliberate. But what's goin' to 'appen when you 'ave children? I mean, won't your George care when you want to bring them up as . . .'

'What's that buildin' over there?' Colleen said hastily.

'Oh, that the seamen's mission house,' said Lil, who could sometimes be easily sidetracked. 'An' a right odd crowd there is in there sometimes. Foreigners, most of 'em, and yer wouldn't believe the things they get up to. Why, only last week . . .'

In the public bar of The Goldsmiths' Arms, Sam and George were already half-way down their pints.

'So 'ows the first week at the wood yard gone down with yer?' Sam asked.

'Not too badly,' George replied. 'The yard could do with some reorganisin' and the men need a bit of lickin' into shape, but I think I can manage that easily enough.'

Sam looked George up and down. A lot of crippled ex-servicemen had a hangdog look about them, but there was no evidence of that in George's strong features. He acted and talked like a man who didn't realise he'd lost his leg at all. And that was probably just was well, because there were some tough characters working on the Southwark wharfs. But then, there'd probably been tough characters in George's regiment too, and if George hadn't been able to deal with them, he wouldn't have stayed a sergeant for long.

'Course, yer main problem's the blokes who do the unloadin' from the boats for yer,' Sam said. 'I mean, I'm not sayin' they don't know their jobs, but if they was any good, they'd be working down at the real docks instead o' wastin' their time in a piddlin' little wharf like the 'Ibernia.'

George grinned. It hadn't taken him long to learn about the rivalry that existed between the stevedores of the London docklands and the men who worked on the wharfs of Southwark and Bermondsey. Listen to any member of either group for five minutes and you'd be convinced that while he and his mates kept the business of the river running smoothly, their rivals were nothing but a bunch of completely useless berks who couldn't unload a crate of bananas without taking a long tea break first.

'It's St. Katherine's Dock you work at it, isn't it, Sam?' George asked.

'That's right,' Sam replied. 'An' believe me, it's the finest dock in the 'ole o' London.'

'But it's a long way to have to go to work every day,' George reflected.

'You're dead right, there,' Sam agreed. 'Specially in winter, when it's blowing a gale across the river.'

'So haven't you ever thought of moving somewhere closer to the docks?' George asked. 'I mean, there must be 'ouses up for rent around there.'

'Oh, there are,' Sam conceded. 'Probably better an' cheaper 'ouses than the one we're livin' in now. But my Lil'd never stand for it, yer know. She'd put 'er foot down good an' proper if I even 'inted at movin'.'

'But why?' George said. 'We wouldn't be in Lant Place if it wasn't handy for my work.'

'It's like this,' Sam explained. 'Me an' my old dutch got married when I was in the army. She was expectin' our Annie at the time.' He stopped suddenly, and looked around him to see if anybody had overheard. 'For Gawd's sake, don't repeat that,' he continued, when he'd made sure that nobody but George *had* heard. 'Lil ain't one for violence, but she'd kill me if she ever found out I'd told yer.'

'Your secret's safe with me,' George assured him.

'Anyway, she moved into Lant Place as soon as we was married – an' I got sent to fight for Queen an' Country,' Sam said. 'Well, by the time I came back, I'd got a two-year-old daughter an' an 'ouse I didn't recognise. I'd left 'er in a dump with nuffink but a few old orange boxes to sit on an' eat off. When I got 'ome she'd decorated the whole 'ouse an' managed to scrounge up enough furniture – an' Gawd alone knows from where – to make it quite comfortable.'

'I see,' George said.

'No, yer don't,' Sam replied. 'She was worried about me gettin' killed yer understand – almost frantic at times – an'

62

what kept 'er goin' while I was away was makin' that 'ouse nice for me. Because as long as she was doin' that, it meant I *'ad to* be comin' home. Sort of superstition, like. That's why Lil'll never move, 'cos while she keeps that 'ouse nice, she thinks I'll always come 'ome safe.' He grinned. 'She doesn't know I know that.'

George shook his head in amazement. 'You're a remarkable man, Sam,' he said.

'We're all remarkable,' Sam said, signalling to the barmaid for another round of drinks. ' 'Ow's your old gal settlin' in?'

'Fine,' George said – perhaps a little too quickly.

'But . . .?' Sam pressed him.

'There somethin' been botherin' her for the last couple of months,' George told him. 'I can see it in her face. Not all the time, mind, but at odd moments when she thinks I'm not watchin' her. It got a bit buried in all the excitement of the packin', but now we're gettin' settled, it's come back to the surface again. An' I can't think what it could be.'

'Can't yer, now?' asked Sam, taking a long, thoughtful slug of his pint.

'I'm not tirin' you out, am I, gal?' Lil asked as the two women approached the end of Union Street.

'No,' Colleen assured her. 'I used to go for long walks when I lived in Marston.'

But for a country girl like her, it did feel strange to have walked so far yet still be surrounded by houses. And why did Lil want to go such a distance to do her shopping when there were perfectly good shops only a couple of minutes away from home?

It was when they crossed Blackfriars Road that Colleen felt the atmosphere around her change. The street was suddenly full of all kinds of people. The air buzzed with excitement and anticipation. And ahead of them, Colleen could see lights – hundreds of them – floating in the sea of darkness. She could hear the sounds of musical intruments, too – fiddles and trumpets and big bass drums – wafting towards her on the breeze.

'Bloomin' heck!' she gasped.

'Did yer say somefink, gal?' Lil asked, with a knowing smile on her lips.

'What's goin' on down there?' said Colleen.

'That,' Lil replied, waving her hand in front of her like a magician who has just completed a particularly successful trick, 'is the New Cut Market.'

Lil and Colleen made their way between the rows of barrows – brightly lit up with naphtha lamps – which were packed tightly together on both sides of the street.

'It's more like a fairground than a market,' Colleen thought to herself.

To her left, a cornet player and two men with tubas were playing a strident military march. To her right, another musician was squeezing his accordian for all he was worth. And just up the road, a flautist was fingering his instrument feverishly, though whatever sound he might be making was drowned out by his noisier brethren.

Nor were the musicians the only entertainment on offer.

'Step right up an' get the shock of yer life!' called out one costermonger, pointing to the large electric battery which was resting on his barrow. 'Only an 'a'penny, an' I'll give yer a tingle yer'll never forget!'

'Come 'an test yer lungs,' roared a second costermonger, on whose barrow rested a strange-looking machine with a clock face attacked to it. 'Blow down the rubber tube an' find out just 'ow much puff yer've got in yer!'

Lil and Colleen stopped in front of a stall piled high with women's jackets, blouses, dresses and shawls, where a female huckster was about to deliver her patter.

'Lovely blouse, ain't it?' the huckster said, pointing to a garment her assistant was holding up. 'Second, and I'm not denyin' it, but I 'appen to know that its last owner was a haristocrat, who only wore it the once – when she went to Bucking'am Palace.'

'Crystal Palace, more like,' someone in the growing crowd shouted out.

'An' what am I askin' for it?' the huckster continued, not

the least put off. 'Did I 'ear somebody over there say five pound?' She pointed dramatically into the middle of her audience. 'No, me old china, I ain't askin' nuffink like that. So what do I want for this magnificent garment, which is almost 'istoric as yer might say.' She banged her hand down on the counter. 'Ten bob, ladies and gents! An' I swear to yer, I'm robbin' meself blind at that price.'

But her audience, kind souls that they were, seemed unwilling to see her rob herself, and there were no takers.

'All right,' the huckster said. 'I can see yer tempted an' just need a bit more encouragement. Five bob, an' I'm givin' it away.'

'That tatty old thing wouldn't even make a rubbin' rag,' some wit in the audience called out.

'It's a finer piece o' cloth than yer'll ever 'ope to see on your back,' the huckster retorted. 'Tell yer what I'll do. I'll drop me price to two an' a tanner, an' I'll throw in a lovely pair o' silk stockin's that yer can 'ardly see the ladder in.'

Lil nudged Colleen. 'Let's get out of 'ere quick before she talks me into buyin' it,' she said.

'Good idea,' replied Colleen, who had been starting to think that the blouse was just what *she* needed.

They walked further up the New Cut until they came to a large shop packed to the doorway with women. Colleen, standing on tiptoe, looked inside to try and see what it was that had attracted so many eager customers.

A heavy mahogany counter ran the entire length of the far wall, and behind it stood a number of harassed-looking assistants. One of the assistants was passing a battered tin bowl along, and as it reached them, the women closest to the counter threw square pasteboard cards into it.

'No need to push, ladies,' the man with the tin bowl said, as one of the waiting women was elbowed out of the way. 'I swear I won't go 'ome till yer've all been seen to.'

Several of the women laughed good-naturedly, but Colleen noticed that the man's words didn't seem to have stopped them jockeying for position.

The assistant took his bowl of cards and emptied them into a cloth bag which was hanging from the ceiling by a rope.

'Haul away, Fred!' he called out, looking up.

'An' move yerself, Fred!' shouted one of the women in front of the counter. 'My old man'll play 'ell if I ain't warmin' 'is bed for 'im by closing time.'

Several of the other women giggled, and the bag disappeared through a trap door in the ceiling.

'We won't keep yer a minute, ladies,' the assistant promised the waiting women.

He was as good as his word. Barely sixty seconds passed before parcels started to rain through the trap door and hit the floor below with a dull thud.

'What is this place?' Colleen asked.

'Yer mean yer don't know?' Lil said, surprised. 'It's a pawnbroker's. Don't yer have pawnbrokers up North?'

'Well, yes,' Colleen admitted. 'But I've never been inside one. An' they're little shops – not like this place at all.'

'As I keep tellin' yer, this is London,' Lil replied. 'We do everyfink big in London.'

Colleen saw a huge woman with bare, washerwoman's arms push a bundle over the counter, just at the same time as her painfully thin neighbour was being handed a package by another of the clerks.

'Are they takin' their pledges out or puttin' 'em in?' she asked, confused.

'Some are doin' one, some are doin' the other,' Lil told her. 'Depends on their circumstances. Yer see that one,' she pointed to the thin woman, who was now trying to make her way to the door with her parcel under her arm. ' 'Er old man's just 'anded 'er 'is wage packet, an' she's got 'er bundle out of 'ock 'cos the family need some decent togs to wear for their Sunday outin'. Course, she'll be bringin' 'em back again on Tuesday or Wednesday, when she starts to feel the pinch.'

'That's terrible,' Colleen said.

'That's life,' Lil told her philosophically. 'Now take the other one,' she continued, indicating the big washerwoman, 'well, she's a different story altogether. 'Er old man probably ain't come 'ome at all, an' she knows that by the time 'e does, most of 'is wages will 'ave gone in drink.

So what's she to do – there's still the Sunday dinner to buy and she's boracic.'

'She's what?'

'Boracic lint – skint,' Lil answered. 'Crikey, gal, don't yer know nuffink? Anyway, as I was saying, 'ow's she goin' to put food on the table when 'er 'usband's let 'er down like that? Why, she can come down 'ere to 'er uncle's an' raise a bit 'o money on the drunken devil's best suit.'

'And serves him right,' Colleen said with feeling.

'You've never said a truer word,' Lil agreed. 'A man who don't look after 'is family wants 'anging from the nearest lamppost. We're lucky, you an' me – me with my Sam and you with your George.'

Yes, but was George lucky to have *her*, Colleen wondered. She'd make a nice home for him, but was that enough? A man was entitled to children, especially when he wanted them as badly as George did, and however she looked at it, she ended up feeling that by not getting pregnant she was letting him down.

The two women walked on. The deeper they got into the market, the greater the variety of stalls. One sold second-hand books, while another specialised in cheap crockery. A third stall contained a mountain of spectacles, and several old men and women were rummaging through them, searching for a pair which would transform the swimming black lines on the cards they held in front of them into letters of the alphabet.

There were costermongers selling rolls of lino, and others peddling old boots. There was a tall, grey-haired man who was holding up a bottle of pink liquid and proclaiming loudly that it would cure all known diseases and knit a broken leg so quickly that, 'Yer'll be back on yer bacons an' doin' a knees-up before yer know it.'

Lil bought them both a bag of jellied eels, as she'd promised she would, and while they were eating their treat, they stood outside one of the New Cut pubs and listened as a band of blacked-up musicians performed their act.

'I always did like nigger minstrels better'n anyfink,' Lil said, as she popped her last piece of eel into her mouth.

'Still, it must be nearly ten o'clock by now. I think it's about time we got on with doin' our shoppin', don't you?'

'Whatever you say,' replied Colleen, who had decided, hours ago, that the only thing to do in this outdoor madhouse was to put herself completely in her neighbour's hands.

Lil led Colleen to a huge, open-sided wagon which served as a butcher's stall. There were countless joints of meat hanging from hooks all over the stall, but the butcher, a jolly, red-faced man, did not seem to mind in the least that he still had so much of his stock left on his hands.

'It's Sat'day night an' 'ere we all are again,' he said to the small crowd which had gathered round. He picked up the joint which was closest to him and held it out for the spectators to see. 'Prime beef, this is,' he promised. ' 'Alf an hour ago, I'd 'ave been sellin' at two and fourpence a pound, but since it's gettin' late, an' I want to get 'ome to me wife an' kids . . .'

'You ain't never been married, Ned,' someone called out from the crowd.

'. . . since I want to get 'ome to me wife and kids,' the butcher continued unashamedly, 'I'm willin' to let yer 'ave it at a bargain price. Who'll give me two bob a pound?'

'Yer must be jokin',' another heckler called out. 'Two bob – for that scrag-end!'

'What will yer give me, then?' the butcher asked.

'A tanner a pound,' the heckler responded.

'I'd rather feed it to me dog than sell it at that price,' the butcher said stoutly.

'Yer don't 'ave no dog, neither,' the first heckler chipped in. 'An' if yer did, I bet 'e'd turn 'is nose up at a piece of 'orse-flesh like that.'

But not everyone seemed to share the heckler's opinion. A woman at the front of the crowd bid a shilling a pound, one to the left of the butcher upped it to one and tuppence, and the piece of 'orse-flesh which even the butcher's nonexistent dog would turn its nose up at was eventually sold at one and five a pound.

Even before his assistant had started to weigh it, the

butcher had a fresh piece of meat on his block. Now that the crowd had had their fun, they were ready to get down to business, and the bidding became brisker, so that by the time Colleen and Lil had bought pieces of meat, round about a quarter past ten, the butcher had managed to shift nearly half his stock.

'Fruit an' veg next,' Lil said decisively.

They were auctioning at the fruit and veg stalls, too. Colleen was surprised, when she'd bought all she needed, to see how little she'd spent. And what surprised her even more was how much she'd enjoyed herself.

'Do you come here every Saturday, Lil?' she asked.

'Every Sat'day,' Lil said. 'Wouldn't miss it for the world. Are yer ready for 'ome now?'

'Yes,' Colleen agreed. 'I'm ready for home.'

They made their way back towards Blackfriars Road. At the very edge of the market, just beyond the glow of the naphtha lamps, Colleen noticed a woman and child standing huddled together. The woman was wearing an old, darned shawl, and the little girl, who couldn't have been more than three, had big hollow eyes, the sight of which almost broke Colleen's heart.

As Colleen and Lil drew closer, the woman took a couple of timid steps forward. 'Could yer spare a copper so I can get a bit o' grub for me little one?' she asked.

'O' course I can, gal,' Lil said, stopping immediately and opening her purse.

Colleen looked down at the little girl. How long was it since the poor mite had had a decent meal? she wondered. Lil had already given the woman a penny. On impulse, Colleen reached into her shopping basket, took out the leg of pork she'd bought, and handed it over to the beggar.

'Get some of that in the little lass's belly,' she said.

The other woman looked at her in amazement.

'Gawd bless yer, missus,' she said, taking the meat. 'If there's such a thing as 'eaven, I'd bet me life yer 'eadin' for it.'

She took her daughter's hand and led her off towards the market, where, with the penny Lil had given her, she would buy some vegetable scraps.

'What did yer go an' do that for?' Lil asked, sounding almost as surprised as the beggar had done.

'You gave her money,' Colleen said defensively.

'I didn't give 'er me 'usband's Sunday dinner, though,' Lil pointed out.

'I've got some sausages in the pantry,' Colleen said. 'George won't mind havin' them.'

Lil put her hand on Colleen's shoulder. 'Yer can't go feedin' everybody in Southwark who's 'ungry,' she said. 'You do know that, don't yer?'

'Of course I know that,' Colleen replied. It was just that looking at that little girl, with her hollow cheeks and big, empty eyes, she'd not been able to help herself. How terrible it was that the poor child's mother couldn't afford to feed her properly. And how wrong it seemed that she and George, who could have given such a child a good home, seemed destined to be denied any children of their own.

The sound of the bells of All Hallows Chruch drifted across George's mind and slowly eased him out of his sleep.

'Sunday morning,' he thought with satisfaction. If there was one Cockney habit that George didn't need teaching, it was that Sunday morning was specially created so that working men could have a decent lie-in.

He rolled over and, eyes still closed, reached for his sleeping wife. Sunday morning was one of her favourite moments, too. They would lie there for an hour or more, not speaking but simply holding each other. Sometimes they'd fall asleep again, but whether they did or not, they usually ended up making love.

George's hand felt around the bed, but instead of finding his wife's soft body, it touched only a cold sheet.

He opened his eyes. Colleen was not there. And now, as he grew more aware of what was going on, he realised that he could hear someone moving downstairs.

'Collie?' he called out.

There was the sound of footsteps in the hallway, and then a scraping as the front-door latch was lifted.

'Is that you, Colleen?' George shouted.

'Yes, it's me,' his wife replied from the foot of the stairs.

'What are you doin'?'

'Goin' out.'

'Goin' out? But where . . .?'

'I won't be long,' Colleen said, and then George heard the front door shut behind her and the noise of her heels as she walked rapidly down the street.

'Now why should she want to go out at this time of day?' George asked himself. 'An' where exactly is she goin'?'

Though he had no recollection of doing so, George must have fallen asleep again, because the next time he opened his eyes, Colleen was standing over him with a smile on her face and a breakfast tray in her hands.

Using his strong arms - more powerful than ever now they had to do some of the work of his missing left leg – George moved himself into a sitting position. Colleen placed the tray on his lap and pecked him lightly on the cheek.

'You went out,' George said gruffly, still only half-awake but already feeling a little peeved that his Sunday morning had not gone as anticipated.

'Yes, I did go out,' Colleen admitted, turning away as if she did not want to look him in the face.

'An' where did you go?' George asked.

'Only down to The Goldsmiths' Arms,' Colleen replied.

'The Goldsmiths' Arms? But whatever made you go there?' George reached onto the bedside table and checked his pocket watch. 'It won't be open for a couple of hours yet.'

'I didn't go for a drink,' Colleen told him. 'I went down there to see Mr Wilkins.'

'The gaffer?' George said. 'I didn't think you even knew him.'

'I don't,' Colleen replied, still looking at the wall. 'But I saw a notice in the pub window sayin' that he was lookin' for barmaids.'

Suddenly, George was wide awake. 'Barmaids!' he exploded. 'I'm not havin' my wife workin' as a barmaid.'

'That's what I was when you met me,' Colleen reminded him. 'That's what I was when we fell in love.'

'That was different,' George said. 'It was your dad's pub you were workin' in. Besides, we weren't married then, but now we are – an' it's my job to earn the money.'

Colleen whirled round, and George saw that she was almost as angry as he was.

'An' what's my job?' she demanded.

'To stay at home,' George said. 'To stay at home and cook an' clean an' have me ch . . .'

'Have your what?' Colleen screamed.

'Have me . . . have me meals waitin' for me when I get home from work,' George said uncomfortably.

'To have your children – that's what you were goin' to say, isn't it?'

'Yes,' George admitted. 'I was.'

'But I don't think that's goin' to happen,' Colleen said, her anger evaporating and a sudden deep sadness replacing it. 'I don't think I'm capable. I'm no good to you, George – no good at all.'

Tears began to run down her cheeks.

'Come here,' George said.

'I don't . . . I can't . . .'

'Come here,' George said, more firmly this time.

Colleen moved hesitantly towards the bed, then suddenly flung herself at her husband and buried her head in his massive chest.

'Maybe God's punishin' me for somethin',' she sobbed. 'Maybe I did somethin' very wicked. I can't remember doin' it but . . . but maybe that's it.'

George stroked his wife's hair. 'It's too early to say yet whether we can have children,' he said. 'If we can't, it could be my fault just as easy as it could be yours . . .'

'But George . . .'

'. . . an' whatever happens, you've got to believe one thing – I'd rather have you without kids than another woman who could give me a houseful of 'em.'

Colleen lifted her head and looked into his eyes. 'Is that true?' she sniffed. 'Do you *really* mean it?'

'You know I mean it,' George said.

'Don't try an' stop me goin' out to work,' Colleen begged. 'Please, George.'

'Why is it so important to you?' George said.

'Because I want to feel useful,' Colleen said. 'An' because if I stay in this house on me own all day, I'll go mad. I know I will.'

George gave the prospect of her working the same thoughtful consideration he would have given to planning a patrol through enemy territory in the old days.

'I can't say I like the idea much,' he said firmly, 'but if it'll make you happy, I won't stand in your way.'

Colleen slithered up the bed and kissed him softly on the lips.

'You're the best husband a woman ever had,' she said.

'Get away with you,' George replied awkwardly.

Colleen ran the nail of her little finger up and down George's thick neck and gazed at the counterpane. 'Even if it turns out later we can't have kids, there's no harm in us trying, is there?' she asked shyly.

'You mean, now?' George asked.

'Yes,' Colleen said, almost in a whisper.

George smiled. 'No harm at all,' he said.

CHAPTER FIVE

As she waited for the tram at a stop on Blackfriars Road, Annie did her best not to panic.

'After all, what's the worst thing they could possibly say to me down at the National Telephone Company?' she asked herself. 'No thank you, Clarke – yer just not what we was lookin' for? Well, that ain't *too* bad, is it?'

But if it wasn't too bad, then why was she worrying about it so much?

To distract herself, she turned round and examined her reflection in a shop wondow. She was wearing a panelled skirt which was a delicate shade of pink, a white blouse and a shaped bolero with a patch pocket. Her hat was trimmed with stiff bows and lacquered feathers. She'd bought the whole outfit at the New Cut Market. The man behind the stall had insisted it was almost new, and from its appearance, she had no reason to doubt his word. Studying herself now, she thought she looked very smart indeed.

She only wished she felt as good as she looked. Tom Bates had told her that if he was the guv'nor of the telephone company, he'd give her a job like a shot.

'But he *ain't* the guv'nor of the company, is 'e, though?' she thought.

And not everybody she knew had been as quite as encouraging as Tom.

'Yes, you may take the time off to go to the interview if

you wish, Clarke,' Miss Hunt had said when Annie had shown her the letter, 'but if you want my opinion, you'll be doing no more than losing a day's wages unnecessarily.'

' 'Ere, take this an' wear it at yer interview,' Maisie Stowe had said, handing her an enamel brooch with gilt edging. 'It'll bring yer luck.' Yet even though Maisie had *wished* her good luck, she could tell that her friend still didn't really think she stood any chance at all of getting the job.

Annie glanced up nervously at the clock hanging over Feinman's Jewellers and Watchmakers. 'What's 'appened to all the trams this mornin'?' she wondered frantically.

She'd been told to report to the National Telephone Company's school on London Wall at precisely eleven o'clock, and because she'd known she'd have to change from tram to omnibus once she crossed the river, she'd set out in plenty of time. At least, she'd *thought* she had – but if the bloody tram didn't come soon, she was going to be late. And that, as Miss Hunt might say, would be starting out on a very bad footing indeed.

She looked down the street again and saw a tram approaching in the distance.

'Thank 'eavens for that!' she said aloud.

The tram was close enough for her to be able to pick out details now – the two strong brown horses which were pulling it, the moustached driver holding their reins, the advertisement for Bryant and May's matches which ran along the open top-deck – and yet, although it was still moving towards her, it didn't seem to Annie to be getting any closer.

' 'Urry up!' she urged horses and driver alike. 'For goodness sake, 'urry up.'

The tram finally drew level with the stop and Annie was faced with the choice of taking the stairs which twisted round in front of the driver, or of travelling on the lower deck.

'I s'ppose it'd be a lot more ladylike if I was to go downstairs,' she thought. And there was certainly less danger of messing up her hat and her hair-do if she went inside.

75

'On the other 'and, it's a luverly day,' she told herself, 'an' yer get a smashin' view of the river from up top.'

Annie stepped smartly onto the platform and began to climb up the stairs.

'Well, I must say, yer look a real picture,' the conductor called after her. 'Proper brightened up me mornin', yer 'ave.'

'Thanks a lot,' Annie said, looking back over her shoulder and smiling at him.

She was starting to feel better again.

Eddie Clarke ran one hand through his wild hair and looked briefly around the stable he had been sent to muck out. Then, with a shrug, he took a copy of *The Automobilist* from his back pocket and made himself comfortable on a pile of straw in the corner. Within seconds, he was lost in another world – a world made up of crankshafts and double-cylinder V-type engines.

He was half-way through a fascinating article on the newest car to come from the Daimler works when he heard a horse neighing in the stable yard.

' 'Orses!' he said contemptuously. 'Who needs 'em?'

Nasty, smelly creatures, 'orses were. An' not just smelly, but practically useless as well. People saw 'orses pullin' an omnibus and thought they were doin' a grand job – but what the ignorant buggers didn't realise was that after a couple of trips the 'orses got tired an' had to be changed over.

'It takes *ten* 'orses to keep to keep *one* omnibus going,' he reminded himself. 'Ten!'

Still, their days was numbered. The engineers workin' on motor buses 'adn't got the design quite right yet, but it could only be a matter of time. An' then they'd show the 'orses a thing or two!

'Yer'll be for the 'igh jump if Mr 'Orrocks catches yer slackin' on the job,' said a sneering voice from the stable doorway.

Eddie sprang to his feet and reached for his shovel. Then he saw that the newcomer was only Len Spriggs, another of the apprentice grooms, and he relaxed again.

'Yer shouldn't sneak up on me like that,' Eddie told Len, though he tried to keep any trace of anger out of his voice, because Len was not only two years older and three inches taller than him, but was also a bully who would use any excuse to make him suffer.

'What's that yer readin?' Spriggs demanded.

'Nuffink,' Eddie said, trying, belatedly, to hide the magazine behind his back.

Spriggs held out his hand. 'Give it 'ere,' he said in a voice which made it clear that he was willing to accept no argument.

'But . . .' Eddie protested.

'Now!' Spriggs ordered him.

Eddie sighed and handed the magazine over.

'Be careful with it, won't yer?' he pleaded.

Spriggs flicked through the pages. Once or twice his lips moved as he tried to read one of the articles, but after a few words he got lost and gave up. 'What a waste o' time!' he said aggressively. 'Ortemobeels are bleedin' rubbish. Yer want to stick to 'orses an' donkeys. There's a future in 'orses an' donkeys.'

'D'yer think so?' Eddie asked, unable to tear his eyes away from the precious magazine which was still in the bigger boy's large, rough hands.

'Course I think so,' Spriggs replied. 'What is it yer see all over London! 'Orses! 'Orses pullin' trams an' buses. 'Orses between the shafts of bakers' vans, butchers' vans, grocers' vans. 'Orses takin' doctors on their rounds and toffs to the theatre. An' do yer know where most of them 'orses come from?'

'They're rented,' said Eddie in a bored voice. 'Even the ones what pull the fire engines.'

'They're rented,' Spriggs said, full of enthusiasm. 'Even the ones what pull the fire engines. So when I say there's a real future in 'orses, I know what I'm talkin' about. The blokes what own the big stables 'ave got London by the throat. An' some day, I'm goin' to be one of 'em!'

'Course you are, Len!' Eddie said. 'A bright bloke like you is bound to end up ownin' 'undreds of 'orses.'

He realised he had gone too far the moment the words were out of his mouth. For a second, Spriggs' face was filled with sadness, and then his lips twisted into an angry snarl.

'Yer makin' fun of me now, ain't yer, yer young bleeder?' he said aggressively.

'No . . . yes . . . I'm sorry, Len,' Eddie said.

He meant it. He might not like Spriggs very much but that was no excuse, he told himself, for pointing out to Len just how thick he really was.

Spriggs glanced down at the precious magazine he was still holding in his hands.

'Bleedin' waste o' time – like you,' he said, and began, slowly and deliberately, to tear it in two.

Eddie flung himself across the stable at the other boy, but it was a very unequal contest and almost before he knew what was happening he was lying on his stomach with his arm twisted up painfully behind his back.

'Yer believe me about 'avin a stable of me own one day, don't yer?' Spriggs demanded, twisting the arm even harder. 'Tell me yer believe me.'

'I believe yer! I believe yer!' Eddie gasped.

He hoped that Spriggs would get his wish, and end up owning every horse in London. Then he, Edward Clarke of the Clarke Motor Omnibus Company, could ride past in style – and laugh.

Spriggs pressed his head deeper into the dirt of the stable floor, and the stink of horses filled Eddie's nostrils.

Oh, for the luverly smell of a petrol engine, he thought through his pain.

When Annie was shown into the waiting room at the National Telephone Company's training school in London Wall, there were already a number of other girls there. Some of them looked up and nodded at her, but others, absorbed in magazines or conversations, barely seemed to notice that she had arrived.

Annie went over to a chair in the corner, sat down and placed her cupped hands primly on her lap. Once settled, she looked around the room and – without making it obvious – counted the other girls.

Eleven!

The advertisement in the paper hadn't said how many jobs the company was offering, but Annie thought it was unlikely there would be an even dozen.

Time passed, with the only distractions being the hiss of whispered conversation and the turning of pages. Annie began to wish she'd brought something to read, too. She sneaked a few quick glances at the titles of some of the other applicants' magazines.

The Lady's Home Companion, she read. *Sussex Life, Town and Country*. She'd never seen any of these on sale in the newsagent's shop in Lant Street, and now she thought it was perhaps just as well that she hadn't brought a magazine of her own – because she'd have looked pretty stupid sitting there reading *Comic Cuts*.

A severe, efficient-looking lady of indeterminate age appeared in the waiting room doorway and consulted the piece of paper she was holding in her hand.

'The Board will see Miss Pringle first,' she said.

A fair-haired girl in a dress with a fine lace trim stood and walked confidently towards the door. She looked very smart indeed, Annie thought. In fact, *all* the girls looked smart, and their dresses – unlike hers – didn't seem *almost* new, but gave the impression of having been taken off the dress-maker's dummy that very morning.

A few more minutes ticked slowly by, and Annie found herself straining her ears to listen to what some of the other candidates were talking about.

'We have quite a party staying at the house during the shooting season.'

'The chief clerk is such a sweet man. I don't know how Father would ever manage without him.'

'And when he heard the Bishop was coming to luncheon, Papa went into such a tizz . . .'

'I told the carriage to wait, because, you see, I had no idea how long we'd be here.'

'Oh crikey,' Annie thought. 'Whatever 'ave I got meself into this time?'

The woman with the list came back, though there was no sign of the blonde girl in the lace dress.

'The Board will see Miss Clarke next,' the list-carrier announced ominously.

Annie rose shakily to her feet and followed the woman to the room where 'The Board' – whatever that was – was waiting to devour her.

'The Board' turned out to be three men in frock coats sitting along one side of a heavy mahogany table. Two of them were old men with long white whiskers and serious expressions, but the third was younger and had kind eyes.

'Would you sit down, please, Miss Clarke?' said one of the white-whiskered men, and he pointed to a chair which had been placed in front of the table.

Annie sat, clenched her hands nervously, unclenched them again, and then, feeling that they looked odd apart, quickly put them back together.

'My name is Haynes,' said the second white-whiskers. 'This,' indicating the younger man, 'is Mr Archer, and the gentleman on my right is Mr Spring.'

' 'Ow do yer do?' Annie said. 'Pleased to meet yer.'

The man who called himself Haynes frowned and then glanced down at a piece of paper which she recognised as the application form she had so painstakingly filled in.

'I see you hail from Southwark,' he said.

'I beg your pardon?' Annie replied, completely mystified – and not a little panicked.

'He means, Southwark is the place you come from,' Mr Archer explained.

'That's right,' Annie agreed.

The frown was still deeply embedded in Mr Haynes' forehead, but as if to make the best of a bad job, he said, 'Well, I'm sure there are some very pleasant parts of Southwark if only you know where to look. Where exactly is Lant Place?'

'Just off Southwark Bridge Road,' Annie said, and when

that didn't seem to help him, she added. 'Near Stamford's Engineerin' works . . . about five minutes' walk from St. Saviour's Work'ouse.'

The frown grew even deeper and Mr Haynes said, 'I see. And what does your father do for a living?'

' 'E's a docker,' Annie replied.

'A docker!' Mr Haynes exclaimed. 'Your father is a docker?'

' 'E's not casual labour nor nuffink like that,' Annie said in her father's defence. ' 'E's a ticket man, is my dad.'

The information did not seem to impress Mr Haynes, and for several seconds there was an uncomfortable silence.

Then Mr Archer said, 'Why do you want to become a telephonist, Miss Clarke? For the money?'

His gentle, interested voice immediately put her at her ease, and Annie laughed. 'Well, everybody needs money,' she said, 'but it ain't the main reason I applied. I want a job that's more interestin' than workin' in the match factory.'

'A match girl!' Mr Haynes muttered, almost to himself. He turned to Annie and said, 'Thank you, Miss Clarke. I think we've heard quite enough.'

Mr Archer, his kind eyes full of sympathy for her, got up out of his seat. 'Please allow me to escort you to the exit, Miss Clarke,' he said softly.

'I can find me own way out,' Annie said, doing her best to fight back her tears.

'I insist,' Mr Archer said, more firmly this time, and walking round the table he held out his arm to help her to her feet.

There was nothing to do but take the arm, and so Annie did. Mr Archer opened the door and led her into the corridor.

'I won't get the job, will I?' she asked miserably.

'No,' Mr Archer replied. 'I'm afraid that I have to say that you won't.'

'It's 'cos me family's not posh, ain't it?' Annie said as they walked along the corridor. 'It's 'cos we don't 'ave no carriage an' the Bishop don't often drop in for luncheon at our 'ouse.'

Mr Archer laughed. 'What an extraordinary notion,' he said. Then, becoming more serious again, he continued, 'It's true that most of the young ladies we employ come from the professional classes . . .'

'What's that mean?' Annie asked.

'That they have fathers who are doctors, lawyers or clergymen,' Mr Archer explained, 'but the fact that your father is a docker is not the reason I feel unable to recommend you for a position with the company, Not directly, anyway.'

'Is it 'cos I come from the East End, then?' Annie demanded, anger beginning to replace her misery. 'Do you think that just 'cos I come from Lant Place I must be stupid?'

'Certainly not,' Mr Archer assured her. 'One has only to look at you to realise you are an intelligent young woman who would have no difficulty mastering the switchboard and furthermore, would be able to keep her head in a crisis.'

'So what is the matter with me?' Annie asked.

'It's the way that you talk, Miss Clarke,' Mr Archer said sympathetically.

'What's the matter with the way I talk? Yer can understand me, can't yer?'

'Of course I can. But you have to put yourself in the position of our subscribers. They won't be able to see you, as I can. To them, you would just be a voice, and I'm afraid yours is not a voice which would inspire confidence in the telephone company.'

'I see,' Annie said dully.

'I'm so sorry,' Mr Archer continued, opening the door which led onto London Wall, 'but our subscribers – however unfairly – associate a well-ordered mind with a well-ordered speech pattern, and yours, I'm afraid, simply will not pass muster.'

They'd been right – Maisie, Miss Hunt, all the other people who'd said she'd had no chance – they'd been right all along.

She held out her hand to Mr Archer.

'Thanks for showin' me out anyway,' Annie said. 'An' thanks for botherin' to take the time to explain to me why I'm not suitable.'

'I really am sorry, Miss Clarke,' Mr Archer said, shaking her hand gently but warmly.

'I know you are,' Annie replied.

She stepped out into the street and heard the door of opportunity click softly shut behind her.

Annie had gone barely a hundred yards up London Wall when she heard a voice say, 'Miss Clarke!'

She turned and found herself facing a man with sandy hair who was wearing a smart blue double-breasted jacket and a silk tie. He looked very familiar to her, but for the moment she just couldn't seem to place him.

'I'm sorry,' she said. 'I'm not sure . . .'

'Harry Roberts,' the man told her.

'O' course,' Annie replied. 'Yer look a bit diff'rent out o' uniform, Constable Roberts.'

'So most people tell me,' Harry said. 'Anyway, it's a bit of an 'appy coincidence meetin' yer on the street like this. I was just on me way to grab a spot of dinner at the ABC restaurant. Would yer care to join me?'

It was tempting. Annie was feeling ravenously hungry, and a good dinner might be just the thing to cheer her up. But even so, she hardly knew the man. In fact, if truth be told, she didn't *really* know him at all.

'I'm invitin' yer to have a bite to eat with me, Miss Clarke, not proposin' marriage,' Harry said, reading her thoughts. 'An' if yer worried about me behavin' meself, well, all I can tell yer is that if I don't, yer'll 'ave about an 'undred witnesses when yer want to bring yer case against me – 'cos that's 'ow many people there'll be in the ABC at this time o' day.'

The last time she had seen him – standing in the doorway of The Goldsmiths' Arms – his expression had been severe and disapproving, but now he grinned and his whole face lit up.

'All right, I'll come to the ABC with yer,' Annie said. 'But yer talked about invitin' me, an' I'm not havin' that. I've got me own money an' I'll pay me own way.'

'Fair enough,' Harry agreed.

The ABC restaurant had high moulded ceilings and elaborate gas mantles. The walls were decorated with heavy, floral paper, the floor cheerfully tiled.

Harry had promised there would be a hundred customers – and he wasn't far out, Annie thought, as she looked around her. There were men in top hats, bowler hats and – now that summer was almost on them – a few sporting straw boaters. There were women out with their children and women surrounded by mountains of brightly wrapped parcels. Yes, there must have been *at least* a hundred customers there, waiting to be served by a small army of waitresses in dark dresses and spotless white aprons.

'What d'yer think of the ABC?' Harry asked her.

'I like it,' Annie said.

And she really did. It was without any doubt the smartest place she'd ever gone to eat in, and she only hoped that after she'd insisted she pay for herself, she'd have enough money to cover her share of the bill.

A waitress came to the table and handed them both menus – real *printed* menus.

'What do yer fancy?' Harry asked.

'I don't know,' Annie said, beginning to feel out of her depth. 'What're you 'aving?'

'Yer can't go wrong with meat and three veg,' Harry told her. 'And the mutton in 'ere's supposed to be good.'

'I'll 'ave that, then,' Annie said.

Harry gave their orders to the waitress, and she actually wrote it down on a piece of paper, instead of just shouting it across to the kitchen.

Harry leaned back in his chair, as if he was completely at home in these surroundings.

'D'you come 'ere often?' Annie asked him.

Harry grinned again. 'Not very often,' he admitted. 'I couldn't afford it on a Wet Bob's pay. Most of the time, I take me meals in the police canteen at Wappin' Station. But I do like to come to the ABC now an' again – if it's a special occasion.'

'An' what's so special about today?' Annie asked.

Harry looked her straight in the eyes. 'You're with me,' he said.

Annie felt herself start to blush.

'What's . . . what's it like, bein' a river policeman?' she asked hurriedly.

'Yer surely don't want to 'ear anyfink about me job, do yer?' Harry said.

'I do!' Annie insisted. 'Honestly!' Anything to steer the conversation away from the direction it had been going in! 'It must be really interestin' to spend all yer time catchin' criminals.'

Harry laughed. 'There's a lot more to bein' a copper than just catchin' criminals,' he said.

'Like what?'

'Well, sometimes we 'ave to 'elp the fire brigade fight a blaze on one o' the ships moored in the river. An' sometimes, we 'ave to pull people out o' the water before they drown.'

'Yer mean people who've fallen in?' Annie asked.

'Or jumped in,' Harry said darkly. 'Yer'd be surprised 'ow many people throw themselves in the river – Waterloo Bridge's the favourite place for that.'

Despite herself Annie giggled. 'What's so special about Waterloo Bridge?' she asked.

'Beats me,' Harry replied. 'All I know is that there's so many suicide attempts from that partic'lar bridge that we keep a special boat there – one with a roller across the stern.'

'Why's that?'

'So that the bobby who's gone into the water after the poor, tormented soul can get 'im or 'er into the boat easier. Roll 'em in, yer see.'

' 'Ave you ever done that?' Annie asked. ' 'Ave you ever saved anybody's life?'

Harry shrugged uncomfortably. 'Once or twice,' he admitted.

The waitress brought their food. The mutton lived up to its promise, and by the time Annie had finished eating, she was feeling *much* better than she had an hour earlier.

'Now yer've got some grub inside yer, do yer want to talk about what 'appened this mornin'?' Harry asked.

' 'Ow d'yer mean?' Annie said.

'Do yer want ter talk about the interview that you 'ad with the telephone company?' Harry replied.

Annie looked at him through narrowed eyes.

'It wasn't just a coincidence that we ran into each other on the street, was it?' she asked.

'No, it wasn't,' Harry confessed. 'I wanted to see yer again – an' in better circumstances than last time – so after I came off me shift this mornin' I 'ung about outside the factory.'

'Yer never!' Annie said, giggling again.

'As God's my witness, I did,' Harry replied with a grin. 'An' if 'E's not good enough for yer, you can ask yer pal Maisie – 'cos it was 'er that told me about yer interview.'

'Yer can't trust anybody these days, can yer?' Annie asked – though she really didn't mind, because if Maisie had kept her mouth shut, they wouldn't have been having this nice dinner now.

'So I thought to meself, she'll either be in a mood to celebrate or else want somefink to take 'er mind off 'er disappointment,' Harry continued, 'and whichever it is, it can't do any 'arm to see she gets properly fed. An' so 'ere we are.'

'Thanks ever so much, 'Arry,' Annie said. 'It really 'as cheered me up a lot.'

'Yer didn't get the job, then?' Harry said.

'No,' Annie replied. 'Of course I didn't.'

'Why d'yer say "of course"?' Harry asked.

Annie told him about the interview, and what Mr Archer had said to her after it was all over.

'Well, there yer are,' Harry said when she'd finished. 'There's 'ope for yer yet.'

' 'Ope!' Annie repeated. ' 'Ow can yer think that, after I've just told yer what Mr Archer said? I don't speak proper, 'Arry. An' there's nuffink I can do about that, is there?'

'If 'e'd said you was too pretty, there'd be nuffink yer could do about it,' Harry said, 'but yer can do somefink about not talkin' the way they want yer to.'

'Like what?'

'Like takin' a few lessons from somebody 'oo *does* know 'ow ter speak proper.'

Annie turned the idea over in her mind for a few seconds, then shook her head. 'It'd never work,' she said. 'I'm an East End gal, an' that's all I'll ever be. Maisie was right – I'll be stuck in one factory or another until I get married.'

Harry's eyes flashed with anger. 'Don't give up on yerself like that,' he said, reaching across the table and grabbing hold of Annie's arm. 'Don't you ever *dare* give up on yerself.'

'It's easy for you to say that,' Annie said defensively.

'It ain't easy for me,' Harry told her, and now he was squeezing her arm so tightly that he was almost hurting her. 'It ain't easy at all. Do yer know what my old man did for a livin'?'

'No. 'Ow could I?'

'Then take a guess.'

What sort of homes *did* policemen come from, Annie wondered. 'Was 'e a soldier?' she asked.

'No.'

'Or maybe a docker, like my dad?'

'No, not that either.'

'Then I give up.'

' 'E was a villain,' Harry said. 'A cat burglar an' a fence. I grew up in an 'ouse which the bobbies visited more often than the rent man did. I was the 'ead of the family from the time I was ten or eleven – because my old man was always away doin' time.'

'Oh, I'm so sorry, 'Arry,' Annie said. 'It must 'ave been awful for you.'

'People said I'd never make a policeman, comin' from an' 'ome like that,' Harry continued. 'But I did! It was a bloody struggle most of the way – but I got there in the end.'

He suddenly seemed to realise how tightly he was holding her. He released her arm and looked around him, embarrassed.

'I'm sorry,' he said. 'I know I shouldn't get all steamed up about it, but sometimes I can't help meself.'

The hand which had been gripping her was now resting

awkwardly on the table. Annie reached across and put her own hand gently on top of it.

'It's all right,' she said soothingly. 'We all get in a bit of a state about the 'ard times. An' you're quite right, yer know – you should never give up on yerself.'

Annie stood outside Lant Street Board School and watched as the stream of scholars poured out through the big double gates. She'd only left the school a few years earlier herself, she thought, but already it felt like a different world to her – perhaps one that she'd only dreamed.

Miss Crosby had been no dream, though! Miss Crosby had been frighteningly real. She was about a hundred years old – but for all that she was a giant of a woman, whose rages could reduce the toughest boy in the class to tears.

'Crikey, but she scared us!' Annie said aloud. Put her next to Miss Crosby, and even the tyrannical Miss Hunt would seem no more frightening than a kindly, slightly absent-minded, grandmother.

A small middle-aged woman in an old-fashioned grey dress came through the gate and began to walk across the street to where Annie was standing. There seemed to be something vaguely familiar about her, although Annie was not sure.

And then it hit her like a sledgehammer! The woman was Miss Crosby. How much smaller she had become in a few years. And how much younger!

Miss Crosby stopped in her tracks and gave Annie a cold, quizzical look. 'I know you,' she said.

'I'm . . .' Annie began.

'Don't tell me!' Miss Crosby commanded.

And Annie couldn't have, even if she'd wanted to, because the sharpness of her old teacher's words and the glare which accompanied them seemed somehow to have robbed her of the power of speech.

Miss Crosby tilted her head first to one side and then the other, and Annie stood frozen to the spot, not sure she would be able to move even if she'd dared.

'You're Clarke,' the teacher said finally.

'That's right, Miss,' Annie said, though if Miss Crosby had told her her name was Bungawallah, she'd probably have agreed.

'And what are you doing here, Clarke?' Miss Crosby demanded. 'If my memory serves me well – and it usually does – you were a fair scholar, but you had no particular liking for school.'

Annie swallowed hard. Heavens, but this was even more difficult than she'd thought it would be.

'I want to learn to speak proper, Miss,' she said. 'I want yer to give me lessons.'

'Do you, indeed,' Miss Crosby said. 'And what has brought on this sudden desire to speak *properly*?'

'A job,' Annie admitted.

'A job!' Miss Crosby snorted. 'When I first came to this school, twenty-five years ago, I thought of myself as a missionary. Do you remember what a missionary is, Clarke?'

'A . . . good man who goes to work among the ignorant 'eathen,' Annie stuttered, hoping she'd got the answer right.

'Precisely,' Miss Crosby agreed. 'I was going to bring you the light – to open the doors to the wonderful world of knowledge for each and every one of you. What a fool I was! The ignorant heathen of Lant Street care nothing about learning for its own sake – only about whether it will earn them more money once they are free at last of school.'

'I can pay yer for me lessons,' Annie said, looking down at the ground and wishing she was dead.

'Money again,' Miss Crosby said. 'And tell me, Clarke, how much do you think I'm worth?'

'I could give you two an' a tanner – two an' sixpence – a lesson,' Annie mumbled, amazed at herself for having the nerve to attempt to hire her old teacher.

'Two and sixpence a lesson,' Miss Crosby repeated, savouring the words. 'That, I believe, is exactly the amount you would pay for a lesson in bicycling. So I'm worth just about as much as a bicycle instructor, am I, Clarke?'

'Course not,' Annie said. 'Yer worth a lot more than that. But I can't afford to give yer what yer worth.'

'How much do you earn?' Miss Crosby asked.

'Nine bob a week.'

'And how much of that do you give to your mother?'

'Six bob.'

'So if I were to give you one lesson a week, and you were to pay me two and sixpence for it,' Miss Crosby mused, 'you'd have exactly sixpence left over to cover your other expenses. Do you think you could survive on that, Clarke?'

'I'd manage some'ow,' Annie said, her eyes still firmly fixed on the ground.

Miss Crosby was silent for perhaps half a minute, then she said, 'It must be really important to you.'

Annie raised her head and looked straight into her old teacher's eyes. 'Yes, Miss,' she said firmly. 'There ain't nuffink I want more in the whole world.'

'Not *ain't nuffink*, Clarke,' Miss Crosby said. '*Isn't anything* – that's the proper way to say it.'

'Yes, Miss,' Annie said humbly.

'And don't just say, "Yes, Miss",' her old teacher told her. 'Correct your mistake.'

'There *isn't anyfink* I want more in the whole world.'

'Anything!' Miss Crosby corrected.

'Anything,' Annie repeated.

'You know, Clarke, if you're going to be paying out a small fortune for your lessons, you really should take advantage of the time you have with me,' Miss Crosby said.

'Does that . . . does that mean yer willin' to teach me after all?' Annie gasped.

'Yes,' Miss Crosby replied. 'That is exactly what it means.'

And then a miracle occurred. Right there – in front of Lant Street Board School – Miss Crosby's stern expression, which had terrified generations of schoolchildren, began to melt away and was replaced by a broad smile.

PART TWO: BANK HOLIDAY

Summer 1901

CHAPTER SIX

The disturbance started shortly after dawn broke. In Streatley Place and Gayton Well Walk, in Pilgrim's Lane and Willoughby Road, residents were rudely awakened by a cacophony of sound. There was the clip-clop of horses' and donkeys' hooves, the creaking of badly-oiled cartwheels, the cracking of whips. There was shouting and laughter and the occasional curse.

Had any of those sleepy residents climbed out of their beds and gone over to the window, they would have seen a strange procession passing their front doors. Several donkey carts trundled by, laden with the makings of coconut shies. A couple of huge vans, weighed down by boat-swings, moved ponderously along, wobbling dangerously as they went. Italians with huge waxed moustaches pushed barrows of ice cream, and London costermongers followed, their barrows loaded with nuts or fruits or winkles.

The householders would have seen all this, if they'd bothered to stir themselves. But it is unlikely that any of them did. Once the drowsiness had cleared from their minds, they would have remembered that it was August Bank Holiday, and done their best to go back to sleep again. For this one summer day, Hampstead Heath did not belong to them – the genteel people whose houses surrounded it – but to the brash, noisy, fun-loving folk of the East End, who would be arriving later by train and tram, by bicycle, donkey-cart and on foot, to claim it as their own.

It was around half-past twelve when the Clarke family arrived on the Heath, and by that time the festivities were well under way. Lil looked around her at the coconut shies and shooting galleries, the test-your-strength machine and the barrows selling cheap jewellery, pigs' trotters and penny mechanical toys.

'It does yer good to get out once in a while, don't it?' she said to her husband.

'If you say so, gal,' replied Sam, who'd been made to wear a new collar which felt as if it were almost cutting his neck in two.

'Where's our Annie?' Eddie asked.

' 'Ow d'yer expect me to know that?' Lil demanded. 'Wasn't you there yerself when she said that 'er an' 'Arry would be makin' their own way 'ere?'

'Well, I 'ope she comes an' finds us,' Eddie grumbled. 'She promised me a tanner for cleaning her boots for a week, an' now she ain't 'ere to give it to me.'

'I'd be ashamed to take money off me own sister if I was you,' Lil told him. 'I know for a fact that she only let yer clean 'er boots so yer'd stop pesterin' 'er. An' she can't really afford to give yer anythin', yer know, what with 'avin' to pay out for them elic . . . eelic . . . speakin' lessons she's gettin' from Miss Crosby.'

'It ain't my fault she spends all 'er money tryin' to learn to speak proper, is it?' Eddie asked.

'It ain't a crime to want to better yerself, neither,' his mother told him. 'Yer'd do well to foller yer big sister's example yerself, wouldn't 'e, Peggy?'

But Peggy was not listening. Instead, her eyes were firmly fixed on a goat-chaise which was parked near the boat swings.

'I said 'e'd do well to foller 'is big sister's example, wouldn't 'e?' Lil said sharply.

Peggy looked up at her mother. 'Can I go off on me own for a bit, Mum?' she said.

'Yer 'aven't 'eard a word I've been sayin', 'ave yer, Peggy?' Lil asked.

'No, Mum,' her daughter replied, with a sweet, vague smile on her face. 'Can I go off on me own for a bit?'

'If yer do, we'll 'ave to arrange to meet somewhere,' Lil told her. 'I ain't goin' through the 'umiliation of 'aving to pick you up at the lost children's tent. I'm too old for that sort of thing.'

'We could meet in one o' the tea gardens,' Sam said hopefully. 'You an' me could go straight there now, so we'd be sure of bein' there when our Peggy comes back.'

'Go there straight away!' Lil said, as if it was the most scandalous thing she'd ever heard. 'An' us only just arrived on the 'Eath! Certainly not!'

'It was only a suggestion,' Sam said in the meek voice he reserved for calming down his wife.

'An' a very bad suggestion it was,' Lil told him. 'We've come all the way to 'Ampstead to 'ave a good time, an' there'll be no rest nor cups o' tea for you until we've 'ad one.'

'Whatever you say, gal,' said Sam, running his finger round his stiff new collar and deciding that it was definitely getting tighter by the minute.

Annie and Harry made their way between the rows of costermongers' stalls towards the part of the Heath where the fairground had been set up. She had her arm linked through his, and thought to herself that anyone seeing them like that would be bound to assume they were walking out together.

But they weren't – she'd made that plain from the start.

'I like yer – like *you* Harry,' she'd said. 'An' I like bein' with you. But I'm not ready to get serious with anybody.'

'I never said I wanted to get serious, either,' Harry had replied, 'but would yer mind tellin' me – just to satisfy me curiosity, as yer might say – exac'ly what yer've got against it? Don't yer want to get married an' 'ave kids?'

'Of course I do,' Annie replied. 'But not yet.'

Not before she'd achieved her big ambition. Not before

she had something more to look back on in her old age than simply being a wife and a mother. And she was getting closer to reaching her goal all the time.

'Another few months . . .' said Miss Crosby, who sometimes forgot to collect her two and sixpence at the end of a lesson but would always insist, the following week, that she distinctly remembered Annie paying her, '. . . another few months and you'll talk just as correctly as any of the other young ladies who apply for positions as telephonists.'

As any of the other *young ladies!*

Annie had felt the urge to laugh out loud at that, but she hadn't dared – because although she no longer thought of Miss Crosby as a fire-breathing dragon, there were still things it was wiser not to do in the presence of her old teacher.

Yes, Annie thought, she had her life clearly planned out – and in that plan there was no room for walking out with any chap. As Miss Crosby had told her, in a few more months she would be ready to apply again. Then, if she got the job, there would be weeks of training before she finally became a real telephonist. Even after that there could be no romance, because it was a telephone company rule that once a woman was married, she had to give up her job. And though she sometimes caught herself wishing that she could have her cake and eat it too, she knew that if she gave up her ambition now she would never forgive herself.

'A penny for 'em,' Harry said.

'What?' Annie asked, startled out of her vision of the future and brought back to the present – and Hampstead Heath – with a jolt.

'A penny for yer thoughts,' Harry repeated.

'I was just thinking it might be nice to go and listen to one of them barrel organs over there,' Annie replied. 'I mean, if that's all right with you.'

'Course it is,' Harry said easily. 'I like to listen to a good tune now an' again.'

There were three barrel organs, so close together that their music mingled in one crazy melody, and by each of them a group of young men and women were dancing for all they were worth.

As they strolled towards the organs, Harry said, 'Do yer still see Tom Bates?' and though he tried to sound casual, there was a hard edge to his voice.

'I've *never* seen him like you mean,' Annie said. 'I've told you before, he's just a friend.'

'An' what kinds of things do yer get up to with this "friend" of yours?'

'We go for a drink when I can afford it . . .'

'Yer won't let him pay for yer, then?' Harry said.

'Of course I won't,' Annie replied, a little crossly. 'Just like I won't let *you* pay for me.'

'An' where else 'as he taken yer?'

'We went out on the river last Sunday. He rowed me all the way from the Tower to Blackfriars Bridge.'

'If yer wanted takin' out on the river, why didn't yer ask me?' Harry said.

'Harry?' said Annie, with a smile on her face, 'will you take me out on the river some time?'

And Harry, despite himself, was forced to laugh. 'Yer impossible,' he said.

'Does that mean "no"?' Annie asked.

'It means "yes",' Harry told her. 'But yer still impossible.'

They had reached the nearest barrel organ and were forced to step smartly to one side to avoid being crashed into by some of the more enthusiastic dancers.

'Do yer fancy a dance?' Annie asked, and then, remembering her lessons with Miss Crosby, she said, 'I mean, would you care to dance, Harry?'

'I'm game if you are,' Harry said. He took her in his arms and they began to waltz in and out of the other couples.

It felt good to have a man's arms around her, Annie thought. It was a pity, really, that she was so set on getting on in the world – but that was the way she was, and there was nothing she could do about it.

'It was really good of yer to bring us up 'ere to the 'Eath, Tom,' May Bates said to her eldest son.

'My pleasure, Old Gal,' Tom replied. 'Think nuffink of it.'

'I don't know 'ow you ever managed to scrape the money together,' his mother insisted.

By putting in even more hours on the river than he normally did, Tom thought – by working until even *his* strong back felt it was broken. Still, it was worth it, he told himself. It was a real pleasure to see his old mum lookin' relaxed an' happy for once. His sisters seemed to be 'avin' a good time, too. Doris, who had just turned twelve, was contentedly chewin' away on a pig's trotter, and Mary, all of fifteen, was showin' quite a lot of interest in the young chaps who were paradin' past her.

Tom frowned. Over the previous few months, Mary's puppy fat had melted away and now, though he still found it hard to accept, she was no longer a girl, but a young woman. Somebody should have a word with her about the blokes who'd soon be buzzing round her like flies to a honey pot, he decided, and since his dad was dead, he supposed it was up to him.

'I'm fed up,' said a voice just behind him.

Tom turned round to look at his younger brother Joey. The boy's thin shoulders were hunched up and he was scuffing the ground discontentedly.

'Somethin' the matter, Joey?' Tom asked.

'I thought it was goin' to be excitin' on the 'Eath,' Joey complained. 'But it ain't. Not even a little bit.'

'Instead o' gripin', yer should be thankin' yer brother for givin' yer a day out,' May Bates said.

'Thankin' 'im? Huh!' Joey retorted. ' 'E only brought us 'cos that Annie Clarke couldn't come with 'im.'

'That ain't true,' May told him, with a warning note creeping into her voice. 'Tom's been plannin' this trip for weeks. An' I'll tell yer somethin', Joey Bates – I'll not 'ave you talkin' to me like that, an' I'll not 'ave yer spoilin' the day for everybody else. Yer've got about four secs to say yer sorry to our Tom or yer'll have me to answer to when we get 'ome.'

Joey looked a little ashamed of himself. 'Sorry, Tom,' he

said. 'I know yer'd 'ave brought us even if Annie Clarke 'ad been able to come with yer.'

'Let's go for a walk,' Tom said to his brother. 'Yer don't mind us going off for a bit, do yer, Old Gal?'

'No, I don't mind,' May replied. 'I've got the girls to keep me company, ain't I? An' at least *they* appreciate bein' 'ere.'

Tom put his arm around Joey's shoulder and led him away from the rest of the family. 'Now, what's botherin' yer, Joey?' he asked, when he was sure they were out of their mother's range of hearing.

'I'm just a bit out o' sorts, that's all.'

'Any special reason?'

'Not really,' Joe admitted. 'It's not one thing – it's everyfink. I couldn't wait to get out o' school, yer know. An' now I'm a butcher's apprentice, I can't wait to get out o' work either. In a few years, I'll 'ave a wife an' 'ouseful o' kids – an' then I'll die. Ain't much of a life, is it?'

Tom sighed softly. It was hard work filling his dad's shoes, and it wasn't made any easier by the fact that although he had the body of a man whilst his brother's was that of a scrawny child, there weren't really that many years between them. Still, he'd do what he could for the boy.

'There's a lot to be said for findin' a good woman an' settlin' down, yer know,' he told Joey, and when his brother merely snorted he added, 'Why, what else are you lookin' for outta life?'

'When you was a little kid, did yer ever pay yer ha'penny to get an electric shock from one o' them big batteries in the New Cut market?' Joey asked.

'Course I did,' Tom replied. 'We all did.'

'Funny thing to want to do, ain't it – give yerself an electric shock?' Joey said. 'I mean, you're a bit scared when yer waiting for it, an' it ain't exactly pleasant while yer 'avin' it, but when it's over, yer glad yer've done it.'

'I suppose yer right,' Tom admitted, wondering when his little brother had begun to get so deep.

'That's what I want me life to be like,' Joey said. 'Like one electric shock after another.'

'Well, well, well,' said a harsh voice behind him. 'If it ain't Tom Bates.'

Tom and Joey whirled round to find themselves facing three young men who were wearing loose-fitting jackets, and neck-cloths instead of collars.

' 'Ow are yer, Tom?' asked one of them, a thickset man with a badly stitched-up scar on his left cheek.

'I'm doin' fine, Rollo,' Tom replied, in a flat, emotionless tone. 'Thanks for askin'.'

'Yer remember me pals Chas an' Blackie, don't yer, Tom?' Rollo said, gesturing with his hand.

Tom turned to look at the other two men. Blackie was a little shorter than Rollo and had small, cunning eyes, while Chas was a big, solid bloke with a vacant look on his face.

'Yes, I remember 'em,' Tom agreed. 'Rollo's lootenant, are yer now, Blackie? You 'ave come up in the world.'

Blackie scowled, but said nothing.

'We ain't seen much of yer down Newington way lately, Tom,' Rollo continued, smiling unpleasantly and revealing several broken teeth.

'I ain't *been* down Newington way lately,' Tom told him. ' 'Aven't you 'eard? I stopped runnin' the Borough Gang when me old man died. I ain't an 'ooligan no more.'

'Maybe you ain't now,' Rollo said. 'But I reckon I still owe yer somethin' for that thrashin' yer give me when yer were.'

'I don't want to fight yer, Rollo,' Tom said evenly. 'This ain't the time or place for it. Besides, as I told yer, I've put all that be'ind me now.'

'I bet yer don't want to fight,' Rollo replied. 'Not when there's three of us an' one o' you.'

'Two of us,' Joey chipped in.

'Stay out o' this, Joey,' Tom said, not taking his eyes off the Newington Hooligan even for a second. 'It ain't your fight.'

'I'm yer brother!' Joey protested.

'Oh, yer brother, is 'e?' Rollo said, running his eyes over Joey's thin arms and puny chest. 'Must be the runt of the litter. Still, if 'e's family, 'e's due for a pasting as well.'

The hooligans had started to fan out, so that now Tom could only see Rollo's lieutenants from the corners of his eyes. 'If anyfink starts, you make a run for it,' he told Joey.

Rollo put his hand in his pocket and when he pulled it out again he was holding a cosh. 'This is goin' to 'urt you a lot more than it 'urts me,' he said, with another ugly grin.

'The last time you an' me 'ad a fight, I 'eld meself back,' Tom said, almost conversationally.

'Yer what?' Rollo asked.

'I 'eld meself back,' Tom repeated. 'I could 'ave put yer in 'ospital if I'd wanted to.'

'Maybe yer could,' Rollo admitted.

'If yer start anyfink now, I won't 'old back,' Tom said. 'Yer pals might give me a good workin' over, but before they do, I'll make sure I fix it so yer'll never be the same again.'

Rollo thudded his cosh thoughtfully against his palm two or three times.

'Pe'raps yer right,' he said. 'Maybe this ain't the time or place for settlin' our differences.'

'We can 'ave 'im on the ground before 'e even touches yer,' Blackie told his leader.

'I said we'd leave it for now,' Rollo replied coldly.

'Yer not the only one what wants to get their own back, yer know,' Blackie persisted. 'I reckon I owe the bugger a few kicks to the 'ead meself.'

Rollo raised a warning finger and pointed it straight at Blackie's face. 'This is *my* gang,' he said, 'an' you'll do as yer bleedin' well told.' He pocketed his cosh and turned back to Tom. 'The time *will* come for settlin' up between us, and when it does, yer'd better be ready.'

'I'll be ready,' Tom promised.

Rollo turned on his heel and marched off. The other two hooligans hesitated for a second and then followed him.

Only when he was sure they'd really gone did Tom turn to look at his brother. He'd expected Joey to be pale with fear, but instead his cheeks were flushed and his eyes positively glowed.

'It was the biggest mistake I ever made in me life,

becomin' an 'ooligan,' Tom said. 'An' as yer've just seen for yerself, I'm still payin' for it.'

But Joey did not seem to hear him. Instead, he was gazing into the distance, as if he could see his own future.

'I said it was the biggest mistake I ever made in me life,' Tom repeated.

'Bloody 'ell!' Joey gasped, almost to himself. 'That was better'n an electric shock any day o' the week.'

The goat was fastened between the shafts of the chaise. It smelled a bit, but Peggy didn't mind that. Nor did she really mind that it seemed more interested in chewing at the grass than paying attention to its visitor. She was happy to stand by it, stroke it and pretend that it was hers – which was precisely what she'd been doing for the last half hour.

' 'Ere, take yer hands off my goat!' shouted a thin, reedy voice behind her.

Peggy turned round. A boy about her own age, with a very dark complexion and black, curly hair, was glaring at her from beside the coconut shy.

'I wasn't doin' any 'arm,' she said. 'Only pettin' it. Is it really *your* goat?'

'Said it was, didn't I?' the boy asked aggressively.

'I mean, does it belong to yer dad, or is it yer very own?' Peggy asked.

'Mine,' the boy told her.

Imagine havin' yer own goat. Heaven.

'Where do yer live?' Peggy asked.

'That depends,' the boy replied evasively.

' 'Ow can it depend?' Peggy said scornfully.

Her tone stung the boy. 'We foller the races,' he said. 'So sometimes I'm in 'Aydock, sometimes I'm in Doncaster an' now an' again yer'll find me in Ascot.'

'An' yer 'ave an 'ouse in them places, I suppose,' Peggy said sceptically.

The boy grinned, and Peggy noticed what a nice face he had when he wasn't scowling.

'Course I ain't got an 'ouse in all them places,' he said. 'D'yer think I look like Lord Muck or somefink?'

No, Peggy had to admit, he didn't look like Lord Muck. In fact, he looked quite poor. But he still had a goat of his own.

'Yer must 'ave one real 'ome, somewhere yer come back to,' Peggy persisted, still trying to pin down the goat's address.

The boy grinned again. 'I take me 'ome with me when I go travellin',' he said.

' 'Ow can yer do that?' Peggy asked.

' 'Cos I live in a van,' the boy said. 'We're camped in Newin'ton for now.'

'That's near where I live,' Peggy told him. 'Well, not too far away, anyway.'

The boy looked at her strangely, as if it were only now that he was seeing her as anything more than someone who had been bothering his goat. 'Yer quite pretty, ain't yer?' he said. 'What are yer called?'

'Peggy.'

The boy thought about it. 'That's a nice name,' he decided.

'An' what's yours?' Peggy said.

'Pedro,' the boy replied.

'That sounds foreign,' Peggy said. 'Yer don't speak like no foreigner.'

'That's 'cos I ain't,' Pedro said. 'But me grandad was. 'E was a genwin Spanish gypsy.'

How lucky he was, Peggy thought. Not only did he have a goat of his very own, but he'd also had a grandad who'd been a genwin foreign Spanish gypsy.

A man as dark-faced as the boy appeared round the corner of the coconut shy. 'Are yer goin' to stand there yatterin' all day or are yer goin' to do some work for a change?' he demanded.

'Sorry, Dad, I'm comin' now,' Pedro said.

He turned to walk away, then changed his mind and swung round again.

'Why don't yer come an' see us?' he said. 'Just ask anybody in Newin'ton where the camp is. Everybody knows about us.'

'Pedro!' the boy's father shouted loudly from the other side of the sacking.

'Right, Dad,' Pedro called back. He gave Peggy one last, imploring look. 'You will come an' see me, won't yer?'

'Course, I'll come,' Peggy said. 'Cross me 'eart an' 'ope to die if I don't.'

She watched the boy disappear behind the sacking. She liked his smile and his curly hair, she thought. She'd probably have promised to go and see him even if he hadn't had a goat.

'D'yer think that tea'll be ready yet?' Sam asked, glancing down hopefully at the teapot which sat on the scrubbed table in front of him.

'No, but give it another minute or so an' it will be,' Lil replied. 'An' I'll tell yer somefink for nuffink, Sam Clarke. Yer'll enjoy it a lot more now than yer would 'ave done if we'd come straight 'ere – because yer've earned it.'

He'd enjoy it all the more because paradin' over half the Heath had given him a raging thirst. Still, if the walk had put Lil in a good mood – and it must have done, or she'd never have allowed him to take off his jacket and roll up his shirt sleeves in public – then it had been worth it.

Lil poured the tea. 'Nice to be on our own for a change, ain't it?' she said.

'It is, gal,' Sam agreed.

And it was. Lil might be a bit bossy now and again, and he might take the mickey in return, but the words of the old Cockney song might have been written for Sam Clarke – there wasn't a lady livin' in the land as 'e'd swop for 'is dear old dutch.

'Yes, it's nice to get away from the kids,' Lil said, 'but you can't 'elp missin' 'em, can yer?'

'Missin' 'em!' Sam responded. 'They can't 'ave been gone for more than an hour.'

'Can't they?' Lil said. 'It seems like longer to me.'

' 'Ow're yer goin' to manage when they've grown up an' got married?' Sam asked.

'I don't know,' Lil confessed. 'D'yer think our Annie will marry that policeman of 'ers?'

Sam laughed. 'Yer a funny devil, you are,' he said. 'One minute yer sayin' that yer miss yer kids, an' the next yer talkin' as if yer can't wait to get 'em out of the 'ouse. Our Annie's not even eighteen yet, you know.'

'O' course I know,' Lil replied. 'I'm 'er mother, ain't I? If I don't know 'ow old she is, who does? But I'm worried about what'll 'appen if she don't marry 'Arry.'

' 'Ow d'yer mean?' Sam asked.

Lil hesitated for a second, then said, 'She's not told me about it 'erself, but she's been seein' Tom Bates as well as 'Arry.'

'Tom Bates from up our street? May Bates' son? Are yer sure? I mean, 'ave you seen 'em together yerself, or are yer just takin' some nasty-minded busybody's word for it?'

'Neither,' Lil said.

'Then 'ow can yer be so sure?'

' 'Cos when our Annie come 'ome last Sunday, she 'ad a lot of colour in 'er cheeks, as if she'd been out on the river. An' Tom Bates 'as got a boat.'

'She could've just been to the park,' Sam said. 'An' even if she 'ad been on the river, there's thousands of people apart from young Tom 'oo 'ave boats.'

'An' then there was the button,' Lil said, sweeping her husband's objection aside.

'What button?' Sam asked.

'I 'appened to see Tom on the street,' Lil explained, 'an' I couldn't 'elp noticin' that one of the buttons on 'is jacket didn't match the others. 'E must have lost one, yer see, an' somebody stitched 'im on an odd one they 'ad.'

'Imagine anybody doin' that,' Sam said. 'Amazin', ain't it?'

'Annie's got a card o' buttons in 'er sewin' basket just like that odd one,' Lil told him.

'So 'ave 'alf the 'aberdashers in London, prob'ly,' Sam pointed out.

'D'yer want me to tell yer the rest?'

'Yer mean there's more?'

'A lot more. For a start, I couldn't 'elp seein' that last Thursday our Annie . . .' Lil stopped, and glared at her

husband, who seemed to be having an attack of the giggles.
' 'Ave I said somethin' to amuse yer?' she demanded.

'No, gal,' Sam said, wiping his eyes with his handkerchief. 'It's just that after all these years, I still can't get used to the way yer can piece a story together.'

'I can't see what's so funny about that,' Lil said, sounding a little annoyed. 'Anyway, I was tellin' yer . . .'

Sam, who looked as if he was about to burst out laughing again, held up his hand to stop her. 'That's enough, gal. If you say our Annie's been seein' Tom Bates, then I'll believe yer.'

'Yer takin it very calm,' Lil said.

' 'Ow else should I take it?' Sam asked.

'Well, I would 'ave thought yer'd 'ave been a bit more concerned,' Lil admitted. 'I mean, Tom is an 'ooligan.'

'*Was* an 'ooligan,' Sam corrected her. 'From all accounts, 'e's settled down since 'is old man died. An' it don't really matter what 'e's like 'cos I trust our Annie not to do anythin' stupid.'

'It's all right for you,' Lil said, aggrieved. 'Yer only 'er father. It's always mothers who 'ave to bear the brunt o' these things.'

'I'll tell yer what,' Sam said, 'the next time I run into Tom in the pub, I'll have a quiet word with 'im – drop the 'int that if our Annie's got any complaints, it's me 'e'll have to deal with.'

'Would yer, Sam?' Lil said. 'That'd make me a lot easier in me mind.' She looked around the tea garden. 'I wonder what our Eddie's up to. I 'ope 'e's not gettin' into trouble.'

The afternoon was not going well for Eddie. He wasn't getting into any trouble but, on the other hand, he wasn't having much fun either. Going to the boxing match had been a mistake, for a start. A whole penny it had cost him and it had been a pretty poor show. Besides, the sight of the swaggering winner holding his gloved hands above his head had only served to remind Eddie that tomorrow he would be back at the stables – and once more in the power of that bully Len Spriggs.

After the match, he wandered aimlessly around the other sideshows. There was a dancing bear and a fire eater, but they didn't hold his attention, nor did the acrobat who picked up a chair, with a small child in it, and balanced it on his chin.

'Ain't 'e marvellous!' one of the other spectators said to Eddie as the acrobat slowly revolved, the whole weight of child and chair pressing down on his jaw.

'I s'ppose he is,' the boy agreed. But he was being no more than polite. Human beings and their tricks didn't interest him. Anything a man could do, he thought to himself, a machine could repeat with greater precision and far less effort.

He was just about to write the day off as a complete loss when he heard the sound that would change his life. It was something between a roar and a loud cough – perhaps the sort of noise a sick lion would make – but to Eddie it had a magical quality, and without even thinking about it, he rushed towards the source.

Motor cars had become quite common in the City, but to people who came from south of the river they were still a novelty, and by the time Eddie arrived on the scene, this particular vehicle was surrounded by a group of excited Cockneys bombarding the driver with questions.

' 'Ow fast will it go, mister?'

'If yer 'ad a race with an 'orse, which of yer would win?'

' 'Ow much did it cost yer?'

The driver, a plump, prosperous-looking man in a heavy motoring cloak and goggles, didn't seem to mind the questions. In fact, he answered them all with the intensity of an evangelist out to make converts.

The automobile could travel at a speed of seventeen miles an hour, he told them. A horse could more than match it over a short distance, but the motor car would go on long after the animal had collapsed. And as for the cost – well, if you wanted one of these, you wouldn't see much change out of two hundred pounds.

Each new fact brought a fresh gasp from the crowd, but

this was all stale stuff to Eddie, and instead of listening he merely gaped at the car. It was a magnificent machine, he thought – one of the new Lanchesters. The spokes in its wheels were gleaming, the leather upholstery shone in the sunlight. And underneath the bonnet was an engine which, as the automobilist had said, would go on long after the strongest horse had dropped to the ground.

'Are there any more questions?' the driver asked indulgently.

Eddie put his hand up, as if he were still in school.

'Yes?' the man said.

' 'Ow is this better'n the old model?' Eddie asked. And once he'd put one question, he couldn't stop himself asking a desperate, eager, flood of others. ' 'Ow many cylinders 'as it got? 'Ow 'igh's the torque? 'As it got one of them new water-cooled engines in it?'

The people around him looked at Eddie strangely, as if he had suddenly started talking a foreign language, but the automobilist began to regard him with new respect.

'You seem to know a lot about motor cars, young man,' he said.

Eddie felt himself start to blush. 'N . . . not enough,' he stuttered. 'Not as much as I want to.'

The automobilist considered him for a second longer, then said, 'I keep my vehicle garaged in Queen Street. Do you happen to know where that is?'

'It's just the other side of the river from where I live,' Eddie replied.

The man nodded his head, as if he found the answer satisfactory.

'I've been looking around for a likely lad to take care of Besty here,' he said, stroking the vehicle lovingly. 'Nothing mechanical, mind,' he added, raising a warning finger. 'I just want someone to give the upholstery and coachwork a thorough polishing once a week. But whoever I hire will have to really care about automobiles. Would you like the job?'

'Would I like it?' Eddie gasped. 'You bet, mister!'

'Then you can start next Saturday,' the man said.

'Right, mister,' Eddie said, hardly able to believe that this wonderful, incredible thing had actually happened to *him*.

Annie was watching Harry test his skill in the shooting gallery when she noticed Tom Bates walking in their direction.

'Oh Crikey!' she thought. 'Whatever's going to happen now?'

Then she told herself she was being silly. After all, she'd made it quite clear to both the men that she was seeing the other. And she'd made it equally clear that neither was anything more than a friend. So why should there be any trouble, just because she'd happened to run into Tom when she was out with Harry? Maybe he wouldn't even see them.

Tom saw them at the same moment as Harry – finishing his last shot and putting down his rifle – saw Tom.

'Did yer plan to meet 'im 'ere?' Harry asked in a hiss that showed just how angry he was.

'Course I didn't,' Annie said.

If she'd been hoping that Tom would simply walk away, she was in for a disappointment. Walking away was not Tom Bates' style, and he made a beeline for them.

'I don't wany any trouble,' Annie said, sensing her companion begin to tense up as Tom got closer.

'There won't be no trouble,' Harry said. 'None that I'm responsible for startin', anyway.'

Tom drew level with them. ' 'Ello, Annie,' he said, completely ignoring Harry.

'Hello,' Annie replied, wishing she was somewhere else entirely.

'I thought yer told me yer couldn't come out today,' Tom said accusingly.

Harry took a step forward, his hands bunched into fists. 'You mind 'ow yer speak to my gal, you toe-rag,' he warned Tom.

'An' you mind 'ow yer talk to me,' Tom countered. 'Just 'cos yer a copper don't mean I can't give yer a bloody good 'idin'.'

Any moment now, they would come to blows. Annie

stepped between them, her arms outstretched to keep them apart.

'Stop it, the pair of you!' she said exasperatedly. 'I'm *not* your gal, Harry Roberts. I'm not anybody's gal.' She turned to Tom. 'And as for you, Tom Bates, don't try to make me out to be a liar. I never said I couldn't come out. I said I couldn't come out *with you*. And I couldn't – 'cos Harry asked me first.'

Her words had an instant effect. Both Harry and Tom looked like naughty boys who'd been caught out by their mothers, and if she hadn't been worried that they still might have a go at each other, Annie would have found the whole situation comic.

'Sorry, Annie,' Tom said.

'I didn't mean to offend yer when I called yer my gal,' Harry told her.

Annie looked from Tom to Harry and saw that beneath their shamefaced expressions there burned a mutual animosity which bordered on hatred.

'I don't like bein' in this position,' she said, 'an' as far as I can see, there's only one way out of it.'

'Yer'll 'ave to choose between us,' Tom said.

'That's right,' Harry agreed.

'All right,' Annie said. 'I've chosen.'

'Which one of us is it to be?' Tom asked.

'Neither of you,' Annie told him.

'Yer what?' Harry gasped.

'I know you two'd never have got on, even if it hadn't been for me,' Annie said, 'but the way things are now, it's bloody ridiculous – an' that's swearing. I won't have you at each other's throats, an' if the only way I can stop that is not to see either of you, then that's what I'm going to have to do.'

The two men had both been looking at Annie, but now they exchanged a glance which spoke volumes.

'Yer don't 'ave to go that far,' Harry said.

'I do,' Annie insisted. 'A couple of minutes ago you were about ready to kill each other.'

'It won't 'appen again,' Tom promised.

'At least, not as long as you're there to come between us,' Harry said.

'I see,' Annie said. 'So what you're tellin' me is that the only way to stop you having a fight is to keep on seeing both of you.'

Tom, who was always the first to see the funny side of any situation, saw it now – and grinned. 'Somefink like that,' he admitted.

'Well then, I suppose I don't have much choice after all, do I?' Annie said. 'But just as a sign that you really mean what you're sayin', I'd like to see you shake on it.'

Neither of the men made a move.

'Go on!' Annie ordered them. 'Do it!'

Slowly, as if there were great weights tied to them, the men lifted their arms and stiffly shook hands.

'And now, since I'm out with Harry, I think you'd better go, Tom,' Annie said. 'I'll see you sometime in the week.'

'I'll 'old yer to that,' Tom told her. He turned towards Harry. 'Goodbye, Constable Roberts,' he said flatly.

'Goodbye, *Mr* Bates,' Harry replied.

Annie watched Tom walk away into the crowd. He had rescued her from a runaway beer barrel, she thought. And Harry, for his part, had cheered her up after she'd failed her interview and encouraged her to apply again. She owed them both something. But I don't owe either of them the right to call me his gal, she thought.

She didn't want to be *anybody's* gal – she wanted to be a telephonist. And she was certain in her own mind that she'd made that perfectly plain to both of them. So why was it that not five minutes earlier the two men had been prepared to knock each other senseless over her?

'Ain't life complicated?' she sighed, forgetting, for a moment, everything Miss Crosby had taught her.

CHAPTER SEVEN

The worst thing about bank holidays, Sam Clarke told himself as he made his way down Burr Street the following morning, was that after the extra day off it was hard to get back into the swing of work again. Not that he really minded going to work – it was just that if he could afford not to, he didn't think he'd bother.

The approach to the dock gates led him past The Albion, and as he drew level with the pub, he noticed a group of scruffily dressed men hanging about outside its front door.

'It must be a terrible thing to be desperate for a drink at this time o' day,' Sam thought.

And even worse not to have the money in your pocket to buy one. But desperation was a feeling that this group of stevedores – the casuals – were all too familiar with. They were the last dockers to be taken on, and long after the Royals, the B ticket men and the C ticket men had started work, the casuals could be seen hanging about the dock gates in the pathetic hope that another ship would un-expectedly arrive.

They were an odd lot altogether, the casuals, Sam reflected. Many of them were just the sort you'd expect to find living a hand-to-mouth existence – ex-convicts, tramps, long-time dossers – but then there were also a fair number of blokes who'd simply come down in the world. There were skilled men who'd lost their jobs and couldn't find others like them; policemen who'd been dismissed for some irregularity; shopkeepers who'd gone bankrupt; barristers who'd been disbarred and doctors who'd been struck off. In other words, they were a proper mixed bunch, and the only thing they had in common was a constant struggle for survival.

'Sam!' called a croaking voice from the edge of the circle of casuals. 'Sam Clarke! Is it really you?'

Sam turned in the direction of the voice and saw a man in a ragged frock coat waving frantically at him.

'Yes, I'm Sam Clarke, all right,' he admitted, 'But I don't think I know *you*.'

The man advanced hesitantly towards him, and Sam studied his face. He was somewhere in middle age, with pale, thin hair and a protruding Adam's apple. Deep lines were etched on his cheeks, and there was a compulsive twitch in his bloodshot left eye. Gawd, but he looked a mess, though, didn't he just?'

The man stopped a few feet away from him, but even at that distance the smell of stale whisky which lay heavy on his breath was enough to make Sam wince.

'I'm . . . I'm not surprised you don't recognise me,' the casual said. 'I'm much changed since we last met.'

There was something about his voice which rang a bell, Sam realised. And now he came to think about it, there was something familiar about that Adam's apple – which was so big it looked he'd got a real apple stuck in his throat.

Was he . . .? Sam wondered. No, he couldn't possibly be! And yet there was something . . .

'Padre?' he asked uncertainly.

The other man threw up his hands in horror. 'Don't call me that!' he implored. 'I don't have the right to be called that any more.'

'Then what *shall* I . . .' Sam asked awkwardly.

'Bertram,' the priest replied. 'You can just call me Bert if you want to.'

A lot of the casuals had come down in the world, Sam reminded himself. But still, he had never expected to find his old regimental chaplain among them. How could this man – who had been a tower of strength to many of the soldiers serving under Wolseley in the Egyptian Campaign – have sunk so low?

'What 'appened to yer, Bert?' Sam asked.

'Drink,' the other man said simply. 'When you've seen as much suffering and uncertainty as I have, you soon find out that you need the odd drink just to carry on going. And then you have another, and another – until, in the end, you lose the ability to help others – because you can't even help yourself.'

'Well, if there's anyfink that I can do for yer . . .' Sam said awkwardly.

In the distance, a clock chimed seven and Bert licked his lips nervously. 'There is *something* you could do,' he said.

'Just tell me what it is.'

'I've come here looking for work . . .'

'An' yer just might be in luck. There was a wool ship due in from Australia last night.'

'. . . but before I start work, it would help me . . . it would set me up for the day, as you might say . . . if I could have just one little drink.'

'An' yer skint, are yer?' Sam asked.

'I am temporarily out of funds,' Bertram admitted.

Sam struck his hand into his trouser pocket and pulled out some coins. ' 'Ere y'are,' he said, placing them in Bert's outstretched, trembling palm.

'God bless you, Sam,' Bert said. But even before he'd finished speaking, he'd turned and was heading for the pub door.

The docks were slowly coming to life as Royals, warehousemen and bowler-hatted customs officers made their way to the main entrances. Sam was not a man given to envy, but he couldn't avoid a small twinge of it now, as he watched the Royals pass through the gates.

'No linin' up for you, is there?' he said to their disappearing backs. 'Even when there's no shippin' to speak of, you'll still be gettin' paid, won't yer?'

There was a sound of clanking metal as the Dock Police

dragged heavy chains across the cobbles in front of the gates. It would take the coppers at least ten minutes to set everything up, Sam estimated. Just time for a smoke.

A clock struck the half hour. The street was jam-packed now, with ticket men at the centre of the crowd and casuals on the fringe. At a signal from one of the dock gangers on duty, the B ticket men started to move into a square bounded by the heavy chains which the policemen had dragged out earlier.

'Get yer papers out,' the ganger shouted, and Sam reached into his pocket for the red ticket without which life would have been as desperate for him as it was for the poor bloody casuals.

Some days, when work was slack, the ganger would let his eyes rove over the waiting dockers and select only a few of the biggest and strongest, but today there was work for all the B men, and they were soon passing through the narrow gap in the chain fence and heading towards the docks.

If the wool ship was in, there'd be work for all the C men, too, Sam thought, and maybe even for some of the casuals. He hoped that Bert would get taken on, even if the poor bugger did blow all his wages on drink the moment he left the docks.

Sam and the rest of the B men followed the ganger along the quayside. Work was already well under way on some of the ships. A gang of Royals was unloading pigs of lead from a Spanish steamer, while the two clerks – one representing the ship's owners and the other employed by the docks – were scrupulously noting down each piece of cargo as it reached dry land.

Further along the quay, a second group of Royals stood on the deck of another ship, each one with a pick-axe in his hands.

'What's goin' on up there?' Sam called out as he and his gang passed the ship.

'Cargo o' sugar,' one of the Royals answered. 'Got wet some'ow, didn't it? An' now all the bags are stuck together an' the bleedin' sugar's as 'ard as treacle toffee.'

Sam grinned. Hard as treacle toffee, was it? And because the Royals had been admitted to the docks first, they had been landed with the unpleasant job of hacking it out. Maybe there were some advantages to only being a ticket man after all.

There were only four customers in the saloon bar of The Goldsmiths' Arms – a couple of young off-duty firemen called Fred Simpson and Stan Watts, a bookie's runner, and an old man with heavy whiskers who could spin out a gill of ale for hours.

'Not that the peace an' quiet's likely to last for long,' Colleen thought.

Come noon, the place would be heaving with men from the leather factory and the engineering works, all of them slamming their coppers on the counter and wanting a drink double quick, because they'd had a hard morning and there was nothing like beer for taking away the taste of their labours.

Colleen would welcome the rush, because as long as she was busy serving up pints, it was easier to keep her mind off . . . off the other matters that had been troubling her.

'What's the matter with you, Colleen?' called Fred Simpson. 'Yer look like yer've lost a tanner an' only found thruppence.'

'I was just thinkin',' Colleen said, forcing a smile to her lips because the customers were entitled to a bit of cheerfulness in return for handing over their hard-earned money.

'Thinkin'?' Fred said. 'Yer should never do that. Look at Stan, 'ere.' He pointed to the other fireman. 'He ain't never thought in 'is blinkin' life, an' it ain't done 'im any 'arm. 'As it, Stan?'

'No 'arm at all,' Stan agreed cheerfully.

The smile on Colleen's face was genuine now. She liked most of the firemen who came into the pub, but Fred was her favourite. He had a boyish face, all round and smooth, and it was almost impossible to believe that he was old enough to be in the fire service – despite the fact that he topped six foot.

The bell rang in the Jug and Bottle Department, which was situated on the other side of the partition from the saloon. When Colleen went to see who the new customer was, she found a small boy with an impish grin on his face and a jug in his hands which seemed almost as big as he was.

'Two pints o' best, please,' he said, standing on tiptoe to place the jug on the bar counter.

'Where do you live?' Colleen asked as she pumped the beer.

'The other end o' Sturge Street.'

'And are you sure you can carry this big, heavy jug all that way by yourself?'

'Course I can!' said the child, clearly offended but still grinning. 'I'm strong, I am, missis.'

Colleen smiled. You could never be sure what kids were going to say – that was one of the great joys of them. She thought of the other children who regularly brought jugs in: Lennie, who always said, 'Fill it right up wiv beer, please, missis. Me dad don't want no frof.' Eileen, who had once explained artlessly, 'This is for me Uncle Jack. 'E always comes to see me mum when me dad's away. Ain't that kind of 'im?' And little Sid, pint-sized himself, who always bragged that, 'I'll 'ave this 'alf drunk by the time I get 'ome. I'm a devil for the beer, I am.'

She loved them all, and sometimes it was all she could do to stop herself picking them up and hugging them.

The boy handed over his coppers, and Colleen, leaning over the bar, lowered the jug into his hands.

' 'Ave yer got any sweets, missis?' he asked hopefully.

'No – but even if I had I wouldn't be allowed to give 'em to you,' Colleen said.

'Why not?'

'Because it's the law.'

'Are yer sure about that?' the child asked. 'It seems a daft sort o' law to me.'

'It's not daft at all,' Colleen told him. 'The government doesn't want us barmaids bribin' all you kids to come to our pub rather than one of the other ones, so none of us are allowed to give out sweets to you.'

'Is that right?' the boy asked. But a flicker in his eyes gave him away.

'You knew it already, didn't you?' Colleen demanded.

The boy looked a little shame-faced. 'Maybe I did know it,' he admitted reluctantly, 'but I wasn't to know that *you* did, now was I?'

Colleen put her hands on her hips. 'You ought to be ashamed of yourself, tryin' to trick me like that,' she said sternly.

'Yes, missis,' the boy agreed, and then, whether he willed it or not, the grin was back on his face and he said, 'I'm a rum little bugger, ain't I just?'

Colleen felt her heart melt. 'You are that,' she agreed. 'Now, listen. I might not be able to give you any sweets in the pub, but if you ever happen to see me on the street, you can asked me then. I always carry a few in me pocket in case I meet one of me friends.'

'I'll remember that, missis,' the boy said, turning and heading for the door.

'Are you sure you can manage that jug?' Colleen asked anxiously after him.

'I can manage,' the boy grunted.

For a few seconds after he had gone, Colleen stood staring at the doorway. He was right, she thought – he was a rum little bugger. But she hoped he'd come and see her again.

A vague feeling of depression swept over her, but it soon went away again when she returned to the saloon and saw that Annie Clarke had just walked in.

'What're you doin' 'ere at this time, Annie?' she asked. 'Got a day off work?'

'*Taken* a day off work,' Annie said. 'I had to. Both me mum and our Peggy have come down with a stomach bug. Must have been something they picked up on Hampstead Heath.'

'What a shame!' Colleen clucked sympathetically. 'What can I get you to drink?'

'Well, I really came in for some soda water for me mum,' Annie said, 'but while I'm here I don't suppose there'd be any harm in having a port and lemon.'

Colleen poured the drink and slid it across the counter. 'How's Tom?' she asked mischievously.

'He was fine the last time I saw him,' Annie replied, looking at her drink rather than at the barmaid.

'And Harry?' Colleen said.

'He was fine as well.'

'The last time that you saw *him*.'

'That's right.'

'You're goin' to 'ave to make your mind up between 'em sooner or later, you know,' Colleen said.

'Not as long as I can keep them both as just friends,' Annie replied firmly.

'But you must prefer one of them to the other,' Colleen persisted. 'I mean, that's only natural.'

'They're both lovely men,' Annie said, 'and I . . . I try not to think about which I like the best – because I can't afford to go falling in love. Not yet.'

'So what you really mean is, as long as you're seeing 'em both, you think you'll be able to stop yourself gettin' serious about either of 'em,' Colleen said.

'Yes,' Annie agreed reluctantly. 'I suppose that *is* what I mean.'

'Well, I wish you luck,' Colleen said, 'but if you ask me to bet on your chances . . .'

The door swung open with a loud crash, and a group of rough-looking young men with iron bars burst into the saloon. There were three of them, Colleen counted – a very big one who looked a bit weak in the brain department, a smaller one with cunning eyes, and a thickset one with a badly-stitched scar on his left cheek.

The hooligans fanned out, and the one with a scar was starting to make his way towards the bar when Fred Simpson stood up and blocked his way.

'You lookin' for trouble, Baby-Face?' the hooligan asked.

'Not *lookin'* for it, no,' Fred said calmly.

' 'Cos if yer are, I can give yer plenty of it,' the hooligan told him. 'There's three of us against two of you, an' I've got another 'alf a dozen of me boys waiting outside.'

'Why don't yer plant one on 'im, Rollo?' shouted the hooligan with the sly eyes.

Rollo turned to look at his lieutenant. 'I will – when I'm ready,' he told him.

When you'd been brought up in a pub as Colleen had, you learned how to assess all kinds of trouble, and this, she thought, was the worst kind. Unless she did something quickly, she was sure that things would turn very nasty indeed.

'Sit down, Fred,' she said quietly.

'Yer can't just let blokes like these push yer around,' the fireman replied.

'Sit down,' Colleen repeated. 'Please, Fred! If I need you, I'll call on you.'

With a great show of reluctance, the young fireman stepped aside and sat down.

'That's better,' Rollo said. He swaggered up to the bar counter. 'I'm lookin' for somebody,' he told Colleen.

'L . . . lookin' for somebody?' stuttered Colleen, who was starting to lose her composure now that the hooligan was so close to her.

'That's right,' Rollo said. 'I'm lookin' for a bloke name o' Tom Bates. 'E comes in 'ere a lot, don't 'e?'

To her left, Colleen heard Annie gasp, but she didn't dare to turn and look at her. 'He's not one of my customers,' she said shakily. 'I've never even heard of anyone called Tom Bates.'

Rollo lifted his iron bar to shoulder height, then slammed it down hard on the counter. The wood splintered and glasses at the other end of the bar rattled.

' 'Ow about now?' he demanded. 'Are yer still sure yer've never 'eard of 'im?'

'Yes,' Colleen replied, more firmly this time.

Rollo smiled, and revealed a row of broken teeth. 'Yer lyin',' he said, 'but it don't matter. 'E ain't 'ere now, an' that's all I care about.'

He turned and walked towards the door. Chas and Blackie, their iron bars still held in front of them and their eyes fixed on the firemen, backed up to join him. Once he'd reached the exit, Rollo turned round again.

'If yer do 'appen to see Tom, give 'im a message from me, will yer?' he said. 'Tell 'im I've got better things to do with me time than to wait for 'im today, but I'll be back. It might be a week or it might be a month – but I'll be comin' for 'im.'

The three hooligans left as abruptly as they'd entered.

'Oh Gawd!' Annie said. She rushed towards the door, and would have been through it and out into the street if Fred Simpson hadn't stood up and grabbed hold of her first.

'You'd better give 'em a couple o' minutes to get clear of the area,' the young fireman said soothingly.

'I daren't!' Annie told him as she struggled to break free of his firm fireman's grip. 'You 'eard what they said. They're after Tom. I 'ave to go an' warn 'im.'

'An' I also 'eard 'em say they got other things to do today,' Fred said. 'So it won't do no 'arm to wait a few minutes before yer go an' find Tom.'

'You don't know that!' Annie said, crying now. 'You can't be completely sure.'

'I'm sure I don't want you out on the street until that lot 'ave buggered off,' Fred said. 'Look, Tom's a pal o' mine an' all, but I honestly don't think 'e's in any danger right now. So why don't yer just take a seat till yer've calmed down a bit.'

With his hands still on her shoulders, Fred steered Annie to his table and forced her into a chair.

'I've got to tell 'im!' Annie sobbed. 'You must understand – I've *got* to.'

'We'll give it ten minutes, an' then I'll go with yer meself,' Fred promised her.

Watching the scene from behind the bar, Colleen forgot her own fears and found herself wondering if Annie would have been *quite* so hysterical and foolhardy if it had been Harry – not Tom – that the hooligans were after.

There were waiters swarming all over the docks – pushing tea trolleys, dragging beer barrels on wheels, holding up

121

doorstep corned beef sandwiches to tempt the hungry stevedores.

'Babies' 'eads'!' one of the waiters called enthusiastically. 'Get yer luverly babies' 'eads 'ere – I promise yer, they're just like mother used to make.'

'I wonder *why* they call beef-steak puddin's "babies 'eads"?' Sam Clarke said, as he made himself comfortable on an empty packing case.

'No reason at all, prob'ly,' replied the man next to him, ' 'cept that they always 'ave been called that.'

'We 'ad a clever bloke come down from the university once to take a look at us,' Sam said. ' 'E told me that the docks was a bleedin' marvellous place for Cockney culture – whatever that's supp'sed to mean.'

'P'raps it means we 'ave our own way of doin' things down 'ere,' the other man suggested.

'Yer could 'ave a point there,' Sam agreed. 'I mean, take 'andkerchiefs fer instance.'

' 'Andkerchiefs?'

'That's right. Every docker 'oo brings 'is own dinner to work carries it in a big red-check 'andkerchief, don't 'e?'

'Well, o' course 'e does!'

'But why? There ain't no law says the 'andkerchief *'as* to be red-check, is there?'

'Maybe not,' the other man said. 'But I wouldn't feel comfortable carryin' an 'andkerchief that was any other colour.'

'No, neither would I,' Sam admitted.

He opened his own red-checked handkerchief and examined his food – potted meat sandwiches, a hard-boiled egg and an apple.

'You've done all right for yerself,' the other docker said.

'Oh yes,' Sam said proudly. 'My Lil always does me well.'

He pictured her standing in their cosy kitchen, handing him his bundle and saying, 'I'm not 'avin yer buyin' yer dinner at the docks, even if I am rushed off me feet. I just wouldn't trust any o' them dockside cafés to live up to my 'igh standards.'

Sam grinned and took a sip of the hot, sweet tea he'd bought from one of the passing trolleys. Work wasn't so bad, he decided – not once yer'd got back into it.

'Clear a way!' somebody shouted. 'For Gawd's sake, clear a bleedin' way, can't yer?'

Sam looked up. Four of the casuals, led by a ganger, were trotting along with something held between them. As they got closer, Sam could see arms and legs, and realised that what they were carrying was a man – a man in a ragged frock coat.

'Bert!' he said. 'Bloody 'ell, it's Bert!'

The casuals veered to the left and headed for the main gate. Forgetting his food, Sam jumped to his feet and ran after them.

The chaplain looked in a bad way. His jaw was slack, and though his eyes were open, his pupils were not to be seen.

'What's the matter with 'im?' Sam asked the ganger. 'Was 'e in some kind o' accident?'

'In an accident?' the ganger snorted. 'Was he 'ell in an accident. The silly bleeder's been suckin' the monkey, an' now we've got to miss our dinner hour to take 'im to 'ospital.'

'Will 'e pull through?' Sam asked worriedly.

'Who knows?' the ganger replied, puffing from his exertions. 'Some of 'em do, an' some of 'em don't. Yer can never tell till after yer've 'ad the stomach pump on 'em.'

Sam dropped back. There was really no point in going any further with the unconscious man, he realised. All he would be doing was getting in the way – and only the doctors could help his old chaplain now.

Sucking the monkey was a very dangerous game, he thought, as he made his way back to the packing case where he'd left his dinner. And the real problem was that it was so simple to play – all you needed was a brown-paper tube, and then you were free to suck up as much port or brandy through the bung-hole of a cask as you wanted to. Some of the men who played the game knew when to stop, but there were always a few – like poor Bert – who'd keep on sucking and sucking until they passed out.

'Was that a mate o' yours?' asked the docker he'd been talking to earlier.

'No, not a mate,' Sam said. 'Just somebody I used to know.'

He looked down at this dinner. Five minutes earlier he'd been looking forward to it, but now he had no appetite at all.

'What a waste,' he said softly to himself, though he was thinking more of his old chaplain than of the food Lil had packed him. 'What a bloody tragic waste.'

It had just turned three o'clock when Eddie Clarke was summoned to the store room that Mr Horrocks, the head groom, used as his office. Horrocks, a tall man with thin, pointed features, was sitting behind his rickety desk. He did not look pleased.

'I never seem to 'ear nuffink but complaints about you, Clarke,' he said.

Eddie looked down at his boots. 'Sorry, Mr 'Orrocks,' he mumbled.

'Sorry yer've done things that get complained about, or sorry I've got to 'ear about 'em?' the head groom said.

'Sorry I've done things wrong,' Eddie said.

'Yer've been late for work more times that I can count, an' even when yer do turn up, yer generally slapdash,' Mr Horrocks told him. The head groom leaned forward, his bony elbows resting on the desk. 'Do yer see any future for yerself in this line o' work, Clarke?' he asked. 'Do yer really want to learn to be a top-notch groom?'

Now there's an interestin' question, Eddie thought. A future in grooming was the closest thing he could think of to purgatory. But – and it was a very big 'but' – he'd had so many jobs since he left school that his mum's patience had about run dry. Which meant that however much he might hate working in the stables, he'd have to stick it out for a little while longer.

'Well, Clarke?' Mr Horrocks asked impatiently.

'Yes, Mr 'Orrocks,' Eddie said. 'I want to learn to be a top-notch groom.'

Mr Horrocks shook his head in wonder. 'Well, yer've a funny way o' goin' about it,' he said. 'I'll tell yer the truth, Clarke – if I 'adn't served with yer dad in the army, I'd've sacked yer weeks ago. An' even allowin' for the fact that me an' Sam are old comrades, I'm on the point o' sackin' yer now. And d'yer 'ave any idea why?'

Eddie quickly ran through the number of things he might have done which could have caused Horrocks to call him in. It was a depressingly long list.

'Any idea at all?' the head groom prompted.

'I can't think of anyfink off 'and,' Eddie lied.

'Can't yer? Well, why don't yer just cast yer mince pies over that mess in the corner.'

Eddie did. Horrocks was pointing at a snarled-up mess of bridles, harnesses, reins and horse brasses.

'Recognise that?' the head groom asked.

'Yes, I do, Mr 'Orrocks,' Eddie said, feeling his stomach lurch as he spoke.

'It's quality stuff,' the head groom told him. 'Only, we ain't used it for months. Well, I got word yesterday that Lord Kensal was in town an' wanted to 'ire a team of our best 'orses. Now, when we got a posh customer like 'im, we can't send in 'orses tied up with bits o' string, can we?'

'O' course we can't,' Eddie agreed in a desperate, belated attempt to win himself a place in his boss's good books.

'So I went down to the tack room an' pulled this gear out,' Mr Horrocks continued. 'An' just look at the state of it! The brass is turnin' green, an' it's only a miracle the leather ain't rotted. An' who's job was it to see that didn't 'appen?'

Eddie's stomach turned over again.

'Mine, Mr 'Orrocks,' he admitted.

'Yours,' the head groom agreed. 'An' tomorrow mornin', when Lord Kensal's coachman comes round to pick up the 'orses, d'yer think 'e'll be 'appy with tack in that condition?'

'I don't know,' Eddie said.

The moment the words were out of his mouth he knew it was the worst possible answer he could have given.

'Don't know!' Horrocks repeated, suddenly angry. 'Don't know! Would *you* be 'appy with it?'

'No, Mr 'Orrocks,' Eddie admitted.

'An' neither will the coachman o' one the richest lords in the land,' Mr Horrocks said. He shook his head sadly. 'It's no good, Clarke . . . Eddie . . . I'm goin' to 'ave to let yer go.'

Eddie thought about how his mother would receive the news – and was surprised to discover that he was more concerned about her being hurt and worried than he was about her being angry.

'Please give me another chance, Mr 'Orrocks,' he said. 'I'll try 'arder this time. Honest I will.'

Horrocks shook his head again. 'Yer've 'ad chance after chance after chance,' he said, 'an' it's done no good . . .'

The office door flew open and one of the senior grooms burst into the room.

'We've just 'ad word from Lord Kensal's 'ouse'old,' he said in a rush. ' 'Is lordship's decided 'e wants the 'orses earlier than 'e thought 'e did. 'E's sendin' 'is coachman round to pick 'em up today, instead of tomorrer.'

Horrocks frowned. 'They think nuffink about buggerin' us about, the toffs, do they? Can yer get the 'orses ready on time?'

'It'll be a push, but if yer'll let me take a couple o' blokes off of the other jobs, I should be able to just about do it,' said the groom after a couple of seconds' thought.

' 'E's a good customer, Lord Kensal,' Horrocks said. 'Take whoever yer need.' His eyes fell on the tack in the corner. 'An' yer'd better put a couple o' the blokes on cleanin' that up, as well.'

'Let me do it, Mr 'Orrocks,' Eddie said.

The head groom hesitated for a second and then said, 'All right. You an' . . .'

'Just me,' Eddie interrupted. 'On me own.'

'Yer'll never finish it in time on yer own,' Horrocks told him.

'I will,' Eddie promised. 'Give me the chance to show what I'm worth, Mr 'Orrocks.'

Horrocks looked dubiously at the heap of tack. 'As I told yer, Lord Kensal's one of our best customers an' I ain't doin' anyfink that'll . . .'

'Please,' Eddie begged. 'I know I can do it.'

Horrocks shook his head again, though this time it was in amazement at his own thoughts.

'I prob'ly want me 'ead testin' for sayin' this,' he told Eddie, 'but I'm goin' to let yer try.'

'Yer won't regret it, Mr 'Orrocks,' Eddie said, going over to the corner and picking up the tangle of harnesses and brasses. 'I swear yer won't regret it.'

Eddie was sitting on a box in the corner Number Three Stable, vigorously rubbing saddle soap into the last of the harnesses. It hadn't been an easy task he'd set himself, he thought as he rubbed. Mr Horrocks had been right when he'd said it was only by a miracle that the leather hadn't been ruined. But Eddie had worked solidly – and harder than he'd ever done in his life – and now his task was almost completed.

'I've been runnin' an errand for Mr 'Orrocks,' said a slurred voice from across the stable.

Eddie glanced up to see Len Spriggs standing in the doorway. And from the way the older boy was swaying, it was obvious that Len had done more than just run an errand – he'd called in at least one boozer on the way back. Eddie went back to his work, rubbing hard at the leather, bringing it up to a perfect shine.

'I'm talkin' to you, Clarkie!' Len Spriggs shouted. 'You got cloth ears or somefink?'

Eddie sighed. It was difficult to know how to deal with Spriggs when he had one of his moods on him. Sometimes it was best just to ignore him, but on other occasions, like now, that was the course of action to infuriate him.

'Did yer 'ear me?' Spriggs demanded.

'I 'eard yer,' Eddie admitted. 'What d'yer want me to say?'

' 'E trusts me, yer see,' Spriggs said, leaning heavily against the door jamb. ' 'E knows I love 'orses. An' he know I got faith in 'em. Not like you.'

Eddie went back to his polishing, hoping that Spriggs would get bored and go away. But instead of leaving, the older boy walked across the stable with the careful steps of someone who is drunk enough to pretend that he isn't. Eddie did not look up, but from the corner of his eye he could see Spriggs kneeling down in front of him.

'I'd do somefink about me breath if I was you,' Eddie said, as the stink of cheap whisky hit him in the face. 'Yer don't want Mr 'Orrocks to know yer've been boozin, now do yer?'

But Len Spriggs, once he had got his teeth into a subject, was not to be distracted by talk of drinking.

'You ain't got no faith in 'orses, 'ave yer, Clarke?' he demanded. 'You think it'll all be motors in a few years, don't yer?'

'No,' Eddie mumbled.

'Yes, yer do!' Spriggs bellowed. 'An' look at me when I'm talkin' to yer.'

Eddie sighed, and raised his head so that his own clear eyes were meeting Spriggs' bloodshot ones. 'I never said it would *all* be motors,' he told the other boy, wishing to himself that Len would get fed up and go away so he could finish his job in peace.

'Yer never said it, but it's what yer think,' Sprigg said. The drink was beginning to make him maudlin now, and tears appeared in the corners of his eyes. 'It's all right for you,' he continued. 'Yer a clever bugger. You can do anyfink yer put yer mind to. But I can't. 'Orses is the only thing I know.'

Having lived in fear of Spriggs for months, it was a strange thing now to start feeling sorry for him, but that was exactly what Eddie *did* begin to feel.

'The motors won't take over from the 'orses right away,' he said kindly. 'Whatever 'appens, there'll always be plenty o' work for a good groom like you.'

For the first time, Spriggs seemed to notice the harness in Eddie's hands. 'What yer doin'?' he asked.

Eddie was tempted to tell him that he was polishing a harness, but he was afraid that Spriggs would take that as cheek, so instead he said, 'Lord Somebody-or-Other wants the best 'orses this afternoon, so I'm gettin' all the tack ready.'

Spriggs eyes narrowed, as if he was turning something over in his mind. 'Wants 'em this afternoon, does 'e?' he said. 'An' I bet 'e wouldn't be pleased if they wasn't ready on time.'

'No, 'e wouldn't be,' Eddie agreed.

'If yer worked at it, yer could 'ave 'Orrocks's job before yer was much older,' Spriggs said.

'But I don't want 'Orrocks's job,' Eddie protested.

'An' then yer'd be my boss, wouldn't yer?' Spriggs said, with an icy edge to his voice.

'It'll never 'appen,' Eddie told him.

'No,' Spriggs said. 'It won't. I'll make sure it don't.' And, moving very smoothly for a drunk, he pushed Eddie backwards over the box, grabbed the harness, and began to rub it in the dirt.

Eddie stood in front of Mr Horrocks' desk with his head bent low – and wished he was dead.

'I trusted yer,' Horrocks said. 'I trusted yer an' yer let me down.' He held up the harness and waved it in front of Eddie's eyes. 'Do yer call this clean? Do yer call this good enough to put on the 'orses I'm sendin' to Lord Kensal?'

'It was clean!' Eddie protested. 'It 'ad come up a real treat. Honest, it 'ad!'

'Then what 'appened to it?'

Eddie was tempted to tell him – but what would have been the point? If Horrocks took Len's word over his, it would all have been a wasted effort. And if Horrocks didn't, then Len would lose his job – and whatever he'd done, Eddie couldn't see that happen to someone who loved horses as much as he did.

'Well, what did 'appen to it?' Horrocks demanded.

'I don't know,' Eddie said.

'Yer don't know!' Mr Horrocks repeated in disgust. 'Go an' see Mr Cunnin'am an' tell 'im I've said 'e's to pay yer what we owe yer. An' once yer've got yer money, get out. I don't ever want to see yer face round these stables again.'

CHAPTER EIGHT

Sam Clarke turned right at the end of East Mount Street, looked up at the imposing facade of the London Hospital – and shuddered. He didn't like hospitals one bit. Full of sick people, hospitals were, and Sam, who'd not had a day's serious illness in his life, would never have come near this particular building if it hadn't been for his sense of duty.

He looked at the queue of people waiting in front of the out-patients' entrance, and then at the bottle seller who had set up her stall near them. 'Funny thing about 'ospitals,' he thought. 'They'll give yer the medicine for free, yet they won't provide yer with anyfink to carry it away in.'

Not that this fact seemed to be of much advantage to the bottle seller doing business outside the London that day, because most of the people standing in line had had the foresight to bring their own containers. And what a wonderful collection they had – sauce bottles, whisky bottles and even marmalade jars.

Putting the hospital out of his mind for the moment, Sam turned his thoughts to Eddie. The boy had been very quiet the night before – unnaturally quiet for him. Even when Lil had presented her son with some wonderful opportunities to be cheeky, Eddie hadn't taken them. And that wasn't like him at all! Something wasn't right. Sam wondered if it had anything to do with his work at the stables.

'Stop worryin',' he told himself. 'I swear, yer gettin' as bad as yer old gal.'

The great double doors of the hospital swung open. The crowd began to surge forward and Sam joined them. They did not move very far. Just inside the doorway, a nurse and a uniformed porter stood inspecting the letters from the patients' own doctors and then splitting them up into groups.

'Bad chest? Over there.'

'Aches an' pains in yer legs? Join that lot in the corner.'

'Eyes? See if yer can find yer way to that bunch standin' next to the door.'

The porter held his hand for Sam's letter.

'I'm not 'ere for meself,' Sam said, slightly offended that the porter should think he was sick.

'Then why *are* yer 'ere?' the porter asked grumpily.

'I've come to see one of yer patients,' Sam explained. ' 'E got took sick yesterday.'

'Well 'e's nuffink to do with me,' the porter said. 'Yer'll 'ave to go down to the main desk.'

'An' where's that?'

'Straight through that door an' to yer right,' the porter said, pointing.

'Thanks,' Sam replied, glad of any excuse to get away from all these pale, coughing people.

A bright young nurse sat at the reception desk, and when Sam smiled at her, she smiled back.

'How can I help you?' she asked.

'I'd like to see one of yer patients,' Sam told her.

'I'm afraid that won't be possible,' the nurse said. 'Visiting hours aren't until this evening.'

'I thought that might be the case,' Sam said. 'Only I'm a docker, yer see, an' we're expectin' a cargo of Spanish potaters in later this afternoon.'

'A cargo of potatoes? I'm not sure I quite take your meaning.'

'We'll be workin' 'alf the night to get the potaters unloaded,' Sam explained. 'So I won't be able to come at yer regular visitin' time. To tell yer the truth, it was as much as I could do to get me ganger to give me an hour off now.'

'Even so, it would be highly irregular to let you in outside normal hours,' the nurse said, frowning slightly. 'Is the patient perhaps a relative of yours?'

'Would it 'elp if 'e was?'

'Well, it certainly wouldn't count against you.'

' 'E's me brother,' Sam lied.

'I see,' said the nurse, opening the thick ledger which lay on the desk in front of her. 'And what's his name?'

Now there was a puzzler, and no mistake.

'I don't know what 'is last name is, but 'is first name's Bertram,' Sam said.

The nurse's frown deepened. 'You don't know your brother's last name,' she said. 'Isn't it the same as yours?'

Dead clever, ain't you, Sam? the docker thought to himself. Now 'ow do you get out o' that one?

'Don't you know your own last name?' the nurse asked.

'It's Clarke,' Sam said. 'But . . . er . . . me brother might not be usin' it at the moment. 'E uses a lot o' different names. 'E's a bit of a black sheep, if the truth be told.'

'Then if you don't know what name he's using, how do you know he's even been admitted to this hospital?' the nurse asked.

Another good question. Sam felt his mouth flap open helplessly, then forced himself to say, 'A . . . a bloke I met in a pub told me that 'e was in 'ere.'

The nurse studied him intently for a second, then her face broke out into a grin. 'You're not a very good liar, are you, Mr Clarke?' she said.

Sam grinned back. 'I don't think I'd win any cups for it,' he admitted. 'But really, Miss, I do want to see this bloke. 'E was me chaplain in the army, only now 'e's fallen to pieces, yer see. 'E got alcoholic poisonin' an' I'm worried about 'im.'

The nurse was still smiling, though now her smile showed sympathy as well as amusement. 'You're a nice man, aren't you, Mr Clarke?' she asked softly.

It normally took quite a lot to embarrass Sam, but he felt himself reddening now. 'I'm not doin' anythin' nobody else wouldn't 'ave done in my place,' he mumbled.

'You'd be surprised, Mr Clarke,' the nurse told him as she ran her finger down the long list of names in the ledger. 'There *was* a man admitted yersterday with acute alcoholic poisoning. He didn't give us a name – it's hard to when you're unconscious – but he was brought in from the St. Katherine's Dock. That would be the man you're looking for, would it?'

'Yes,' Sam said. 'That'd be 'im.'

'Well he hasn't left – one way or the other – so he must still be here,' the nurse said. 'I'll tell you what, Mr Clarke. I can't let you go up and see him, but if I were to turn in the opposite direction, you could just slip past and make your way up to Ward Seven. Then, if you can sweet-talk the ward sister like you've just sweet-talked me, you might get to see this chaplain of yours.'

Sam felt himself growing hotter and hotter with embarrassment. Sweet-talking? Nobody had ever accused him of that before! But when the nice young nurse turned her head, he took advantage of the fact and made his way quickly along the corridor.

'Maybe I really do know 'ow to sweet-talk,' Sam reflected as he walked down the ward.

It had certainly been much easier than he'd thought it would be to get past the sister on duty.

'Yes,' she'd said, looking him up and down when he'd told her why he'd come. 'Yes, a visit would do the patient the world of good.'

The ward wasn't as bad a place as he'd expected it to be, either, Sam decided. True, it was so long and thin that it was almost like a corridor, but there were plenty of windows to let the light in, and in between the windows hung cheerful pictures and framed texts.

He found Bert in a bed half-way down the room. The former chaplain, dressed in a red flannel bed-jacket, was sitting up and seemed to be absorbed in the newspaper he was reading. Sam stepped to one side to take a closer look at him.

The patient's hair had been neatly combed. The lines on his face didn't appear to be quite so deep as they'd been the day before, either – though maybe they simply looked shallower now the dirt had been cleaned out of them. And the twitch in his eye, which had been so prominent down at the docks, was entirely absent.

Sam coughed to attract Bert's attention, but the other man simply went on with his reading.

'Er . . . 'ello, Padre – I mean, Bert,' Sam said awkwardly.

The chaplain lowered his newspaper. 'Sam,' he said, delightedly. 'Whatever are you doing here?' A look of concern came to his face. 'I hope that neither yourself nor any of your family has been taken . . .'

'No, it's nuffink like that,' Sam interrupted hastily. 'We're all as fit as fleas.'

Bert's concerned expression was replaced by one of astonishment. 'But you can't mean . . . you haven't . . . you've not come here to see *me*, have you?'

'Well, since I don't know nobody else 'ere, I reckon I must 'ave done,' Sam said awkwardly.

'But how kind of you,' Bert said, overcome. 'I didn't think anyone would care enough to visit me.'

'Get on with yer,' Sam said, wondering how many times it was possible to be embarrassed in one morning. 'Fact is, I was just passin' and I thought I might as well pop in.'

'God bless you,' Bert said.

' 'E 'as so far,' Sam replied. 'So 'ow are yer feelin', Bert?'

'My abdomen's still a little sore,' he admitted. He smiled, remembering an old joke. 'I'm allowed to have an abdomen, you know, having been an officer.'

Sam smiled, too. 'That's right,' he agreed. 'Officers 'ave abdomens, sergeants 'ave stomachs, an' all other ranks just 'ave bellies.'

'But apart from being sore and feeling a little weak, I'm absolutely fine,' Bert said. 'Do you realise, Sam, that is the first time in years I've slept between clean sheets?'

'I supp'se it must be,' Sam replied.

'It's reminded me of what my drinking's made me lose,' Bert said. 'And I've made myself a promise that once I get out of here, I won't slip back into my old ways.'

'Good for you,' Sam said encouragingly.

'I was never actually defrocked,' Bert continued. 'I could still get myself a new living – a nice little parish in the country. Somewhere not too demanding.'

'Course yer could,' Sam assured him.

'And I'll tell you something else,' Bert said. 'I'll not forget your kindness to me. If it's the last thing I do, I'll find a way to pay you back somehow.'

'I didn't do nuffink,' Sam said.

'You stood by me in my hour of need,' Bert insisted.

Sam was beginning to feel uncomfortable again. 'Is there anyfink I can get yer while I'm 'ere?' he asked.

Bert's huge Adam's apple began to bob up and down and the twitch was back in his eye. He licked his lips and glanced nervously up and down the long ward.

'You wouldn't happen to have a bottle in your pocket, would you?' he said.

'A bottle?'

'Whisky. Brandy. Methylated spirits, if that's all you have,' Bert said desperately, and then, seeing the look on Sam's face, he added, 'I am going to give it up. I swear I am. But you have to do these things slowly, you know – cut down in stages. So have you got anything, Sam? Please!'

'No,' Sam said sadly. 'No, I'm afraid I 'aven't.'

For the first three or four hours after he'd supposedly set out for the stables, Eddie wandered the streets of Southwark wrapped up in a cloak of his own misery. He couldn't keep up this pretence for ever, he told himself. Someone was bound to see him and have a word with his mum.

Your Eddie was 'angin' about all day. 'Asn't lost hi'self another job, as 'e?

Or Mr Horrocks might run into his dad in the pub. *'I'm sorry, Sam. I kept 'im on as long as I could, but we can't afford to carry no dead weight in the stables.'*

Even if neither of those things happened, Saturday would soon roll around and his mum would be holding out her hand, expecting most of his wages.

'*One and twopence ha'penny! Where's the rest of it, Eddie?*'

'*There ain't no more, Mum. It's all that Mr Cunnin'am give me when 'e paid me off.*'

'*Paid yer off? What d'yer mean – paid yer off?*'

'*After Mr 'Orrocks sacked me. I'm sorry, Mum. Honest I am.*'

But sorry wasn't good enough. He saw that now. He was going to hurt his mum deeply – and there was nothing he could do about it.

It was despair, more than anything else, which drove him to cross Southwark Bridge. The automobilist he'd met on Hampstead Heath – Mr Peterson – had told him not to turn up at the Queen Street garage until Saturday afternoon, and yet here he was already – on Wednesday morning – heading straight for the place. For all he knew, Mr Peterson's Lanchester might not even be parked there.

An' even if it is, there's no sayin' the garage manager'll let me get anywhere near it, he thought. But then, what else did he have to do with his time?

The garage had big double doors, painted green. The sight of them was almost enough to make Eddie lose his nerve, but then he told himself that he was in so much trouble already that a little more wasn't going to make much difference.

He turned the handle and found that the doors were locked, but then he noticed that inset into one of them was a smaller door, and when he pushed it tentatively, it swung open. Taking his courage in both hands, Eddie stepped through the gap – and froze.

'Bloody 'ell!' he said.

The garage was huge, and was full of automobiles of all kinds. Eddie let his eyes wander around the room. At one end, a couple of mechanics had the bonnet of a vehicle open and were bent over its petrol engine. Further on, another team was tinkering with the boiler of a steam-powered car. And at the far end were a row of electric automobiles, plugged into brass wall sockets and slowly charging up.

Never in his wildest dreams had Eddie imagined that a place like this could exist. It was heaven on earth – a heady mixture of smells, noises and confusion which made him feel almost giddy.

'What the 'ell d'yer think you're doin' 'ere?' demanded a voice from his left.

Eddie turned and saw a big, red-faced man who had his shirt sleeves rolled up and whose arms were covered right to the elbow with grease.

'I've . . . I've come to clean Mr P . . . Peterson's Lanchester,' Eddie stuttered.

'Is yer name Clarke?' the big man asked.

'Yes,' Eddie replied.

The man looked him up and down.

'Can't say I like 'im gettin' outside elp,' he told Eddie. 'We've got blokes 'ere who could clean 'is car for 'im as nice as 'e could wish. Still, it's 'is Lanchester, and I suppose 'e'll do what he wants with it.' The man's eyes narrowed. 'But didn't 'e say somethin' about yer comin' on Sat'day?'

'Yes,' Eddie agreed, 'but I've some time on me 'ands – and wasn't that the truth! – so I thought I'd come an' do it now. If it's 'ere, I mean.'

'It's 'ere,' the big man said.

He wiped his hands on a piece of rag which was sticking out of his trouser pocket, put his fingers to his mouth and whistled so loudly that even with all the racket going on around him, the noise must have carried from one end of the garage to the other.

An apprentice appeared almost before the sound had died away. 'Yes, Mr Rockcliffe?' he said.

'What kept yer?' the big man asked.

'Sorry,' the boy said.

'This bloke's 'ere to clean the Lanchester, since Mr Peterson don't seem to think we can do a decent job of it ourselves,' Rockcliffe said.

He paused, as if to invite comment from his employee.

'Is that right?' the apprentice asked, giving Eddie a brief but hostile look.

'No, it ain't right, but it's what we're stuck with,'

Rockcliff replied. 'So I s'ppose yer'd better take 'im to the Lanchester so 'e can get workin'.'

'Foller me,' the apprentice said, turning on his heel and striding rapidly away towards the other end of the garage. By the time Eddie had caught up to him, the boy was standing in front of a pair of large metal doors.

'Is it in there?' Eddie asked.

'Course it ain't,' the apprentice said scornfully. 'But we gotta use this to get to where we *do* keep it.'

Eddie was still trying to work out exactly what the apprentice meant when the double doors suddenly slid open to reveal a metal-lined room. Only then did he see the button on the wall and realise that what he was looking at was a lift.

'It's enormous!' he gasped, before he could stop himself.

'I s'ppose it *must* seem like that to a bloke what's never been inside a proper garage before,' the apprentice said maliciously. 'But if it was any smaller, we'd never get the motors in it, would we?'

'There's another floor to the garage!' Eddie said, amazed.

The apprentice chuckled. 'Yer don't know nuffink, do yer?' he asked.

It was all right for him, Eddie thought. He was one of the chosen ones. He got to come to this wonderful place every day, and it held no mysteries for him – the lucky devil!

'Well, are we goin' to stand 'ere all day?' the apprentice asked. 'Or shall we go upstairs?'

'We'll go upstairs,' Eddie said, stepping into the lift.

The apprentice pressed the button, the door slid closed, and the lift shuddered. Eddie did his best to assume a casual expression, as if what he was doing were the most natural thing in the world to him. Yet try as he might, he couldn't hide the thrill he felt surge through him as the lift began to go up. And how could he ever have hoped to hide his excitement? He'd never travelled in *any* sort of lift before – let alone a huge one like this.

The Lanchester was a work of art, and Eddie paid it the reverence it was due. First he polished the bodywork, and then the upholstery. That finished, he cleaned the wheel spokes, the tyres and the headlamps. And finally, when there was nothing else left to do, he lifted the bonnet.

He'd intended only to admire the engine at first, but when he saw it right in front of him, he couldn't help touching it. Once he'd done that – and given the fact that he'd already noticed a set of tools in the corner – what could have been more natural than that he should start dismantling it – just a little bit?

His enthusiasm ran away with him, and before he realised what was happening, he had all the easily detachable pieces of the engine lying on the ground around him.

'Crikey, what am I goin' to do now?' he asked himself in a sudden panic.

There was only one thing he *could* do, and, praying that he'd remember everything correctly, he began to put the engine back together again.

He'd just about finished his task when he heard heavy footsteps behind him, and turned round to see Mr Rockcliffe approaching. The garage foreman had a smile on his face. It was not a pleasant smile – rather it was the smirk of a man who's known right from the start that a mistake was being made, and has been perfectly content to sit back and let events prove him right.

'Could 'ave stopped yer earlier,' he told Eddie, 'but then I said to meself, "No, Mr Peterson's got confidence in this bloke – more confidence than 'e 'as in us 'ere at the garage, it seems. So why don't I let 'im go ahead an' do whatever he wants to the Lanchester".'

'I . . . I . . .' Eddie spluttered.

Mr Rockcliffe closed the car's bonnet. Oh, why had he fiddled with the engine? Eddie wondered silently. Why couldn't he have just cleaned the car and left it at that?

'Do yer know where the startin' 'andle to this thing is?' Mr Rockcliffe asked.

'Yes,' Eddie replied in a voice that was almost a moan.

'Right,' Rockcliffe climbed into the driver's seat. 'Let's see yer start 'er up then.'

'What for?'

'So we can see exactly 'ow much damage yer've done.'

Eddie bent down in front of the Lanchester, inserted the starting handle and cranked it round. The engine caught first time.

Mr Rockcliffe listened to it turn over for perhaps half a minute, the frown on his broad forehead deepening with every second that passed. Then he switched it off.

'Is it all right?' Eddie said – praying that, by some miracle, it was.

'Just 'ow many engines 'ave you taken to pieces by yerself?' Rockcliffe asked.

'This is me first one,' Eddie admitted.

'Then 'ow many 'ave yer dismantled with somebody supervisin' yer?'

'None.'

'Yer've got to be jokin',' Rockcliffe said contemptuously.

'This is the *first* engine I've ever touched,' Eddie insisted. 'Honest it is.'

Rockcliffe scratched his head. 'Well, I'll tell yer somefink for nuffink,' he said. 'I've never 'eard this beauty run smoother.'

When Peggy got home from school, the first thing she did was announce that she'd been invited to a birthday party.

'What! Now?' Lil asked.

'Now,' Peggy confirmed.

'But I've not got yer best dress ready or anyfink,' Lil said.

'We're not s'pposed to dress up special.'

'An' then there's the present. Yer can't go to a party without takin' a present.'

'Gertie's mum said we wasn't to take no presents. She says Gertie's got everyfink she needs.'

'Well, it seems an odd sort o' party to me when there's no presents an' no dressin' up,' Lil said, and for a moment Peggy was afraid that her mother wouldn't let her go. Then Lil smiled. 'Still, I s'ppose I should be grateful yer've started makin' friends of yer own age,' she continued. 'P'raps now yer'll be spendin' less of yer time with all them daft animals.'

'P'raps,' Peggy agreed.

It was a lie about the party, of course, but it had been in a good cause. Pedro's goat wanted to see her – Pedro's goat would be very upset if she didn't come as she'd promised.

When Fred Simpson saw the girl with fair hair, blue eyes and a slightly turned-up nose walking towards him on Lant Street, he felt as if he'd been struck by a bolt of lightning. She brought to mind all the poems they'd made him learn at school about visions of loveliness and beauty beyond compare. The poems hadn't meant anything to him then, but they did now.

The vision of loveliness was getting closer to him with every second that passed, and though he tried to tear his eyes away from her face he found it impossible. And then, as they drew level with each other, she stopped and smiled at him.

' 'Ello, Fred,' she said. ' 'Ow are things at the fire station?'

'Do I . . . do I know yer?' Fred gasped.

The girl laughed. 'Well, o' course yer do,' she said. 'I'm Tom Bates's sister.'

'Mary?' Fred said. 'But you're a . . .'

'But I'm a what?'

He'd been about to say that, as far as he remembered, she was a chubby little girl – but that plainly would not do now. 'You're . . . you're lookin' very pretty today, Mary.'

Mary reddened slightly. 'Thanks,' she said. 'I . . . I better be goin'.'

'Yes,' Fred agreed. 'I better be goin', too. It's been nice talkin' to yer.'

'Likewise,' Mary said, and hurried away.

' 'Oo would 'ave believed it?' Fred thought as he watched her cross Southwark Bridge Road. ' 'Oo ever would 'ave believed that little Mary Bates would 'ave turned out like that?'

Pedro had told Peggy that it would be easy to find his encampment – everyone in Walworth would know where it was – but what he hadn't told her was she was as likely as not to get a warning thrown in with the directions.

'Watch yerself with that lot, my little love,' said the kindly old gent whom she stopped to ask the way.

Peggy set off in the right direction, but her thoughts were so firmly fixed on seeing the goat that within five minutes she'd forgotten everything the old gent had told her and was forced to ask again.

'Keep yer eyes open or they'll 'ave the dress off yer back,' warned the washerwoman as she put her on the right track.

Peggy paid no heed. She'd have gone through fire and water for a chance of seeing Pedro's goat again.

Finally – with perhaps more luck than judgement – she reached the patch of waste ground near the Walworth Road coal depot where the van dwellers had set up camp. Peggy walked between the rows of wagons, looking out for Pedro but not failing to notice, as she did so, how different it all was from Lant Place.

Brown-skinned men sat on the steps of their vans smoking clay pipes. Women with shiny black hair stood over braziers, frying sausages or cooking stews – and filling the air with a mixture of delicious smells which made Peggy's mouth water.

' 'Ello, gal!' called a cheery voice from the gap between two of the vans.

' 'Ello, Pedro,' Peggy said. 'Where's yer goat?'

The gypsy boy made a long face. 'An' I thought yer'd come to see me,' he told her.

'I have,' Peggy said hurriedly. 'Only I thought that while I was 'ere, I might 'ave a look at the goat as well.'

'Me mum's took 'im off to Union Street recreation ground,' Pedro said.

And now it was Peggy's turn to make a long face. 'Why's yer mum gone an' done that?' she asked.

Pedro laughed. ' 'Cos 'e fancied a game of football, o' course!'

' 'E what?'

'Ain't got much of a sense of humour, 'ave yer, gal?'

Pedro asked. 'She took 'im to the rec. 'cos there's better grazin' there than there is 'ere.'

'Oh, I see,' Peggy said, disappointed.

'If yer like goats so much, why don't yer get one yerself?' Pedro asked.

'I would,' Peggy said, 'but me mum won't buy me one, an' I ain't got no bees an' 'oney of me own.'

Pedro shook his head in amazement. 'Gawd love us,' he said, 'if dosh is yer only problem then yer don't 'ave no problem at all. There's lots o' ways yer can make money if yer really want to.'

'Tell me some of 'em,' Peggy said eagerly.

'I'll do better than that,' Pedro promised her. 'I'll show yer some of 'em.'

'There yer are, gal,' said Tom, placing a port and lemon in front of Annie and sitting down opposite her.

They were in The Crown on Lant Street, because after Rollo's visit to The Goldsmiths' Arms the day before, Annie had no intention of running the risk of meeting Tom in their local.

Annie took a sip of her drink. 'Well, are you going to bring the subject up, or do I have to do it?' she asked.

'What are yer on about?' Tom replied.

He could be so infuriating sometimes, Annie thought, but she wasn't going to lose her temper – not when they had important matters to discuss.

'You know very well what I'm on about,' she told him.

'Yes, I s'ppose I do,' Tom admitted. And then he smiled that infectious smile of his – which Annie decided really wasn't playing fair.

'We can't just pretend it didn't happen,' she said, determined not to be sidetracked.

Tom sighed. 'Once yer've got yer teeth into somefink, yer don't let go, do yer?' he asked. 'All right, then. It was very good of yer to come all the way down to Battle Bridge Stairs yesterday to tell me about Rollo – but yer could 'ave saved yerself the effort.'

'You didn't see them hooligans like I did,' Annie told

him. 'If you had, you wouldn't be acting so casual about it now.'

'I might not 'ave seen 'em yesterday, but I do know 'em pretty well, an' I'm sure Rollo wasn't really lookin' for me.'

'Then just what *was* he doing up at The Goldsmiths' with an iron bar in his hand?'

'Puttin' on a show.'

'Putting on a show!' Annie echoed. 'How can you say that when he brought two other members of his gang with him and had another six waiting outside?'

'If 'e'd really wanted to fix me, 'e'd just 'ave taken Chas and Blackie with 'im.'

'You're not making a lot of sense, you know,' Annie told him.

'If 'e 'ad found me when 'e 'ad 'alf his gang with 'im, 'e'd 'ave 'ad to play it by the rules – an' 'e wouldn't fancy that,' Tom explained.

'Rules? What rules?'

'If yer workin' over somebody from outside the gangs, it don't matter 'ow many of yer pile into 'im. But if 'e's one of yer own kind – even if 'e's from a gang you 'ate – then it 'as to be a fair fight, man to man. An' Rollo won't fight me, 'cos 'e knows 'e'd lose.'

'So if he didn't want to fight you, why did he turn up at The Goldsmiths' with his gang in tow?' Annie asked.

'I think 'e was forced into it,' Tom replied.

'Who by?'

'Prob'ly by Blackie.'

'You've lost me again.'

'Blackie was 'opin' I would be there, an' Rollo'd 'ave to fight me.'

'Why should he hope that?'

''Cos Blackie's fed up with bein' the lootenant – I could see that when I met 'em on 'Ampstead 'Eath. Blackie fancies 'imself as leader of Newin'ton 'Ooligans, an' if 'e could 'ave got me to 'umiliate Rollo in front of all the others, 'e'd 'ave been 'alf way there.'

'Then he'll try again, won't he?'

' 'E might, but Rollo won't be caught out by the same trick twice.'

'So what you're saying is, you're in no real danger.'

'That's right.'

But there was something in his voice which stopped his words from ringing true.

'Be honest with me, Tom,' Annie pleaded.

'Rollo didn't get where 'e is by bein' brave – 'e got there by bein' cunnin'. So 'e won't face me 'ead on again, but 'e might try somethink else to get 'is revenge.'

'Like what?'

Tom shrugged. 'If I knew, I'd be as devious as what 'e is.'

'You have to go the police,' Annie told him.

'No police. I don't trust 'em. Anyhow, they know I've been a 'ooligan so they'd never listen to me.'

'Harry would listen to you – if I asked him to,' Annie said.

'I don't want no 'elp from 'Arry Roberts, thank you very much,' Tom said firmly.

Despite what she'd promised herself about keeping calm, a sudden anger swept through Annie, and she banged her fist down on the table.

'You've no right to be so proud and so stubborn when you could be in danger,' she said. 'What if something happened to you? How could I ever . . .'

' 'Ow could yer ever what?'

'How could I ever face your family again?'

'Face my family again? Was that really what yer were goin' to say?' Tom asked.

'Of course it was,' Annie replied, not looking at him. 'What else would I have said?'

When Eddie got back to Lant Place, there was only his mother at home – which was a pity, as he'd have appreciated a bigger audience.

'Where's the rest o' the family?' he asked as he sat down at the tea table opposite Lil.

'There's a lot o' ships in the docks, so yer dad's workin' a ghost,' Lil said. 'Our Peggy's gone to some sort o' birthday

145

party, and tonight's the night yer sister Annie 'as 'er lesson in talkin' proper. So it looks like there's just you an' me for . . .' She stopped suddenly, her keen eyes having picked out a speck of something black on Eddie's left hand. 'Stretch out yer arms,' she ordered her son.

Eddie did so, and two stained shirt cuffs appeared from inside the sleeves of his jacket.

'It'll wash off,' he said hopefully.

'Wash off!' his mother repeated. 'I'll give yer "wash off"! That shirt was clean on this morning, and 'ow yer managed to get in such a filthy state workin' a stable, I'll never know.'

'I don't work at the stables no more,' Eddie told her.

'Yer don't what!'

'I got fed up with it, so I 'anded in me notice.'

Lil clamped her hands on her hips, which was a clear sign to anyone who knew her that it was time to apologise, or make her laugh, or do something – anything – to avoid the oncoming storm.

'Now just you listen to me, Eddie,' she said. 'First thing in the mornin' yer to go down to the stables, cap in 'and, and tell Mr 'Orrocks yer nothin' but an 'alf-wit – which ain't really stretching the truth much. An' then yer'll ask him for yer job back, 'cos in times like these new jobs is 'ard to find.'

'But I've already found meself one,' Eddie told her gleefully. 'When yer look at me, yer not lookin' at a stable lad any more – yer seein' an apprentice mechanical engineer.'

For once in her life, Lil didn't know how to react. Part of her was furious with Eddie for throwing up his job, while another part was relieved that he'd got a new one. And so, unsure of whether to slap him or hug him, she decided on a middle course – at least until she knew more about it.

'So what exactly does bein' an apprentice mecknanical whatsit . . .'

'Mechanical engineer,' Eddie supplied.

'. . . mechanical engineer,' Lil corrected herself. 'What exactly does it mean?'

'It means I'll be learnin' how to fix cars,' Eddie said with enthusiasm, 'an' maybe even build 'em in time. An' Mr Rockcliffe – 'e's the boss – says I'm a natural at it, a real natural.'

'An' just what will this fine job be payin'?' Lil asked.

'Five bob a week to start with,' Eddie told her.

'Huh!' Lil said. 'Yer used to complain all the time that the stables weren't payin' yer enough, an' they were given yer *six* bob a week there.'

But Eddie wasn't really listening to her.

'Just think of it, Mum,' he said dreamily. 'Me – a mechanical engineer.'

Pedro and Peggy looked down from the Embankment at the river below. It was low tide, and where earlier the Thames had flowed freely, there was now only a stretch of mud.

'We just come 'ere at the right time,' Pedro said. 'There'll be 'undreds of the little beggars down there now, just waitin' to be caught.'

At the bottom of the stairs, Peggy stopped. ' 'Adn't we better take our boots an' stockin's off before we go walkin' through all that lot?' she asked, looking out towards the mud.

'Yer can do if yer like,' Pedro said. 'I ain't usually so partic'lar meself.'

They sat down on the step and began to unfasten their laces. Pedro finished first – since he had no stockings to remove – and set out alone.

'Wait for me!' Peggy called after him.

'No time for waitin', gal,' Pedro replied. 'Not when there's work to be done.'

Peggy discarded her second stocking and stepped into the mud. It felt unpleasantly cold and squidgy between her toes, and it was only the thought of her goat which forced her on.

By the time she reached the edge of the water, Pedro had already selected a likely spot.

'Now 'ave yer still got the fork what I give yer back at the van?' he asked.

'Course I 'ave,' Peggy said haughtily. 'D'yer think I'm stupid or somefink?'

'Well, there's times when I *do* 'ave doubts about yer,' Pedro admitted.

'I got it right 'ere,' Peggy said, waving the fork in front of his nose as proof of her intelligence.

'Let's get started then,' Pedro said. He knelt down and slid his fork gently into the river. 'Now just copy me an' yer'll be catchin' big fat eels in no time.'

'There's one!' Peggy said excitedly, pointing to a thin black shape which was snaking through the water. 'Catch it, Pedro!'

'It ain't as simple as that,' the gypsy boy told her. 'Yer've got to 'ave patience.'

Pedro let several more eels go by, and then, when one appeared which seemed more sluggish than the rest, he plunged his fork down, forced the creature to the bottom and impaled it on the prongs.

'There y'are,' he said, holding up the wriggling eel in triumph. 'A nice juicy one!'

It seemed so easy, watching Pedro do it, but when Peggy tried to imitate him, she had no luck at all. 'They keep gettin' away,' she complained.

'Well, o' course they do,' Pedro replied. 'They don't want to end up as somebody's dinner any more than you would.'

They crouched in the mud for another hour, at the end of which Pedro had managed to catch two more eels and Peggy hadn't landed any at all.

'These'll sell for two-pence-ha'penny each,' Pedro said, holding the two biggest eels and examining them with an expert eye. 'An' this other one ain't worth much, so I'll give it to me mum to cook for our supper tonight.'

'Are we goin' to stop so soon?' Peggy asked, surprised.

'Course we are. We'll not get no more bitin' with the tide comin' in again.'

'But we've only caught two that we can sell,' Peggy said.

'An' that's what I call a good day's work,' Pedro told her. 'I ain't always as lucky as this.'

A good day's work – and all they had was a fivepence between them, Peggy thought. ' 'Ow much does a goat cost?' she wondered.

'Don't know,' Pedro confessed. 'I didn't exactly buy mine.'

Peggy screwed up her eyes and tried to do the calculations. Say she could get one for thirty bob. That was two hundred and forty pence plus one hundred and twenty pence. Divide that by the fivepence they should get for their eels . . .

'It ain't possible,' she moaned.

'What ain't?' Pedro asked.

'I'm never goin' to 'ave enough for me goat at this rate.'

A crafty look came into Pedro's eyes. 'Well, if yer not too partic'lar, there are easier ways of makin' money,' he said.

'Like what?' Peggy asked.

'Like the broken milk jug dodge, for one thing,' he said. 'Yes – that'd be a good one for us to try, 'cos all that yeller 'air of yours, yer'll have the punters all cryin' into their 'ankies in no time.'

'An' can we make more bees an' 'oney with that?' Peggy asked, though she had no idea what the broken milk jug dodge was.

'Course we can,' Pedro said confidently. 'Only thing is, we'll 'ave to keep our eyes peeled for the coppers.'

CHAPTER NINE

Joey Bates ambled down Southwark Bridge Road, jangling the coins in his pocket. He was feeling good, because it was Saturday night and he was free of the rest of his family at last.

Mum'll be down at the New Cut market, doin' the shoppin', he thought, an' Tom'll be moonin' around Lant Place in the 'ope of runnin' into Annie Clarke.

Then there were his sisters. Mary was probably in her bedroom, staring at herself in the mirror. She'd been doing that a lot since Fred Simpson had just happened to smile at her on the street a couple of days earlier. And as for Doris, the last he'd seen of her, she'd been playing hopscotch with her pals under the gas lamp outside their front door.

Joey chuckled at the thought of what they'd say if they knew where he was heading now. His mum would throw up her hands in horror. Mary would shake her head disapprovingly. Tom would go all serious and try to act like he thought their dad might have done if he'd still been alive. And even Doris, who was younger than him and so by rights should keep her mouth shut, would probably feel she had to chip in *her* two penn'orth.

He crossed Borough Road. The London, Chatham and Dover Railway viaduct loomed up ahead of him, and a locomotive bound for the coast was steaming its way furiously along the track. Joey watched it for a few seconds

– enjoying the way the smoke snaked its way through the air and the tiny glowing cinders floated gently towards the ground before burning themselves out. Then, suddenly angry with himself, he turned away.

'Puffin' Billies ain't nuffink but kids' stuff,' he said contemptuously to the empty street.

And he wasn't a kid any longer, was he? Since his fourteenth birthday, he'd started to think of himself as a man. True, whenever he looked in the mirror he could still see the narrow shoulders and thin arms of a boy, but that wasn't important. He might not be a man in his body yet, but he already was in his head. And if any proof were needed of that, there was the fact that whereas a few months earlier he would have hung around in the hope that more locomotives would go rushing past, he was now making his way resolutely towards a place where something really *manly* was about to happen.

Joey let his mind wander back to the previous Monday on Hampstead Heath. How exciting it had been – that feeling of violence in the air which had run through his entire body like a charge of electricity. And how much he was looking forward to experiencing the feeling all over again!

He had almost reached his destination – a boarded-up railway arch guarded by two large men who looked like boxers gone to seed – and, for the first time, Joey began to have self-doubts. What if they won't let me in? he wondered as he looked at the bruisers. Because if they wouldn't – if they laughed at him and said he'd better run home to his mum – he was sure he'd die of shame.

'Go on!' he urged himself. 'Take the chance!'

Heart pounding furiously, he stepped off the pavement and began to cross the road. The two men watched his approach with interest, and as soon as he had reached the other side, one of them stepped forward to block his way.

'An' just where do yer think yer goin', yer little runt?' he demanded.

'To see the fight,' Joey said, doing his best to make his voice sound deeper than it actually was.

'Been before, 'ave yer?' the man asked.

'Lots o' times,' Joey said unconvincingly.

The two men exchanged a quick, amused glance. 'Well, if 'e's been 'ere before, 'e'll know the drill, won't 'e, Chalkie?' one of them asked.

' 'E certainly will, Dick,' the second replied, as if he were the straight man in a music hall double act.

'So why ain't 'e doin' it?' Dick inquired.

'Why ain't I doin' what?' Joey asked.

'The drill,' Chalkie said.

The only drill Joey could remember was the sort he'd done in the school playground, but that couldn't possibly be what they wanted him to do.

'Arms straight up in the air!' said Dick, who was obviously getting tired of playing the fool.

It *was* like the drill at school, Joey thought as he did as he'd been instructed. But in the drill at school, the teacher didn't come up to you and run the flat of his hands up and down your body, like Dick was doing now.

'What's this all about?' Joey asked.

'Mr Brody don't like nobody takin' weapons inside,' Dick told him, and then, turning to his partner, he added, ' 'E's not got nuffink on 'im.'

'Right, then, give us yer bob an' yer can go straight inside,' Chalkie said.

A bob was all the money Joey had brought with him, and he'd been hoping the admission would be less, so that later he'd have enough left over to go and sink a pint with all the other men who'd come to see the fight. Still, if that was what they wanted from him, he was willing to pay it – just as long as they didn't change their minds and turn him away.

Joey handed over his money and Chalkie opened the door. 'In yer go then, young shaver,' said Dick, sounding much friendlier than he had earlier.

Joey stepped through the door into a cavern illuminated by the eerie glow of a single gas-jet, which hung from the ceiling and shot out flame like a blow-lamp.

The boy looked around him. In the very centre was an

open square, but the rest of the space was filled with tiered benches which were already packed with eager spectators. Joey felt a stab of disappointment. The place was nowhere as big – and not half as impressive – as he'd expected it to be.

Joey found himself a seat at the very back of the room. He could see the boxers, stripped down to fighting tights, sitting on the front row. It would not be long now before the first match started.

A large man wearing a collar and tie – and he must have been the only person in the whole archway who was – stepped into the centre of the ring.

'Gen'lemen – the first bout of the evenin',' he announced, 'between, on my right, Sid Savage . . .'

A youth of about seventeen stood and waved his gloved hands at the audience.

'. . . an' on my left, Wally "The Whacker" Dixon.'

A man with tattoos all over his chest rose to his feet and acknowledged the cheers of his supporters.

Sid Savage, despite his name, was no match for Wally the Whacker, and the fight only lasted a couple of minutes. A second bout followed, then a third, and it came as something of a surprise to Joey to realise that he was not enjoying the spectacle half as much as he'd thought he would. It wasn't that the fighting was in any way faked – the bleeding noses and swelling eyes were real enough – but somehow it didn't give him the same tingle as the idea of a running battle on the street.

It was only when the last fight had finished, and the master of ceremonies was holding up the battered winner's hand, that Joey noticed a man across the other side of the ring who was staring very intently at him.

'An' 'e looks familiar to me,' Joey thought.

Then the man turned to talk to one of his pals and Joey saw the badly-stitched scar on his cheek.

Rollo!

Rollo from the Newington Hooligans, who had promised to fix Tom and had said that since Joey was his brother, they might as well fix him as well!

Joey felt his legs turn to quivering jelly. He was doomed – he knew he was.

The spectators were slowly beginning to file their way out – and suddenly Joey saw a faint glimmer of hope. He was closer to the exit than Rollo – and there were at least fifty people between them. If he acted quickly, he told himself, he might – just might – manage to get away.

He forced himself to his feet, climbed shakily down from the bench, and joined the stream of men heading for the door. All around him there was a buzz of animated conversation.

' 'E's some boxer, that Whacker.'

' 'E'll end up in the ring at the Whitechapel Wonderland, you mark my words.'

' 'E might even make it to the National Sporting Club. An' yer 'ave to wear a dinner jacket to watch a fight there.'

This was the sort of talk Joey had hoped there'd be after the fight – real manly talk – but now, in his panicked state, he didn't even hear it. He glanced over his shoulder and saw Rollo and his two pals pushing their way through the crowd and getting closer to him every second.

Maybe the people around him would protect him if the hooligans caught up with him, he thought desperately. But why should they? Why should they risk getting hurt for a kid they'd never seen before?

It was only when he felt a cool breeze blowing against his cheek that Joey realised he'd passed through the gate and was finally outside the archway.

'Run for it!' his brain screamed – and run for it he did, straight up Borough Road.

As he turned onto Southwark Bridge, Joey heard the sound of pounding footsteps behind him. He looked round – and wished he hadn't! There was no sign of Rollo, but his two pals were on Joey's tail and gaining ground with every step.

Joey's lungs were on fire and he knew that he couldn't keep the pace up for much longer. There was only one thing to do, and that was to try and lose his pursuers.

Collinson Street was just ahead, and a number of alleys

ran off it. Gasping for breath, Joey turned right – and saw Rollo standing just down the street and grinning at him.

Joey stopped running and simply stood there, his head bowed, waiting to take what was coming to him.

He didn't have to wait long. The other two – Chas and Blackie – were so close behind that even before his heart had begun to slow down they were on him, pushing him viciously against the wall. Rollo, for his part, strolled up as if he had all the time in the world.

'Well, if it ain't the little brother of my worst enemy,' he said. 'An' I reckon that makes *you* me enemy as well.'

'No, it don't,' Joey lied desperately. 'I 'ate that brother of mine. I'm on your side. That's why I come to the fight tonight – 'cos I wanted to see yer.'

'Is that right?' Rollo asked. 'Then why did yer run like 'ell the second yer got yer wish?'

'From the way yer was lookin' at me, I could tell yer'd got the wrong idea,' Joey improvised. 'I was goin' to write yer a letter when I got 'ome to explain everyfink.'

Rollo chucked nastily. 'An' where would yer 'ave sent this letter to, once yer'd written it?' he asked.

'I don't know,' Joey admitted. He realised that Rollo was only playing cat and mouse with him, and that all he was doing was putting off the beating – but still he had to *try* to talk his way out of it. 'I was goin' to write,' he persisted. 'Honest!'

Blackie stuck his face right up against Joey's. 'Yer a lyin' little toe-rag,' he said, 'an' yer just about to get the thrashin' of yer life.'

'No, he ain't,' Rollo said. 'Not till I give the word. I'm int'rested in this letter o' yours,' he continued, turning his attention back to Joey. 'If yer 'ad 'ad me address, what would yer 'ave said in it?'

'That I wanted to join yer gang,' Joey told him.

'Yer 'ave to come from Newington to join us,' Blackie said. He poked Joey nastily in the ribs. 'An' even if yer did, we still wouldn't 'ave a pipsqueak like you.'

'So now it's you what decides 'oo joins the gang an' 'oo don't, is it?' Rollo said, with a dangerous edge to his voice.

'Well . . . no . . .' Blackie backtracked.

'Funny,' Rollo mused, 'I always thought that I was in charge – but maybe I was wrong.'

'No, yer wasn't wrong, Rollo,' Blackie assured him. 'It's just that I didn't think . . .'

'That's right!' Rollo said. 'Don't think! Leave the thinkin' up to me. An' *I* think that this shaver should become one o' the Newin'ton 'Ooligans.'

This was too much, even for the slow-thinking Chas. 'But Rollo . . .' he protested.

'There's advantages to 'avin me worst enemy's brother in me gang,' Rollo said.

A look of realisation came into Blackie's eyes. 'I see what yer mean,' he said.

'I thought yer would,' Rollo replied.

'Bleedin' clever,' Blackie said, with reluctant admiration.

'Ain't it,' Rollo agreed. 'Course *you* still don't see what I'm getting' at, do yer, Chas?'

'No,' Chas admitted.

'Well, don't go worryin' yer 'ead about it,' Rollo told him. He looked down at Chas's big hands, which were still tightly clamped around Joey's thin arm. 'Yer can let 'im go now,' he said.

Chas relaxed his grip and Joey shook himself free. Gawd, but it still 'urt though, he thought to himself. He'd be covered in bruises in the mornin' – but not as many as if he'd got the real thrashin' that Blackie had threatened him with.

When Rollo moved towards him, Joey instinctively cowered. But he need not have worried, because all the gang leader did was to put his arm around his shoulder – as if he were an old friend.

'So what's yer name, young shaver?' Rollo asked.

'Joey,' the boy said, and then, because it sounded more manly, he added, 'I mean, Joe.'

'Well, Joe, welcome to the Newin'ton 'Ooligans,' Rollo said.

'Thanks,' Joey replied.

Rollo clicked his fingers. 'There's one thing I forgot to mention,' he said. 'Before yer can be a proper member, yer 'ave to do somefink to prove yerself.'

'Like what?' Joey asked, feeling his heart sink right down into his boots.

'Nuffink much,' Rollo said reassuringly. 'Just some bit o' mischief that shows yer really are one of us.'

'A bit o' mischief?' Joey repeated. 'What kind o' mischief?'

'I 'aven't really given it any thought,' Rollo admitted, 'what with yer joinin' us so sudden, like. I'll tell yer what. We'll see yer back 'ome. Somefink's bound to come to me between 'ere and there.'

As the four of them made their way back towards Lant Place, Rollo's words pounded through Joey's head in time to his footsteps . . . a bit o' mischief . . . a bit o' mischief . . .

What could the gang leader possibly ask him to do, he wondered worriedly. And would he be up to it?

At the corner of Bittern Street, Rollo called a halt. 'See that?' he asked, pointing to a large cobblestone which was lying in the gutter.

'Yes,' Joey replied.

'Pick it up.'

'Pick it up?'

'That's what I said.'

It could be a trick, Joey thought fearfully. The hooligans could still be playing cat and mouse with him, and the moment he bent down he might feel a sharp boot up his backside.

'Go on,' Rollo said impatiently.

Joey bent down. No one tried to kick him. He quickly straightened up again and offered the stone to Rollo.

'It ain't for me,' the gang leader told him. 'Sling it through one o' them winders.'

'What for?'

'Cos that's yer test.'

'Is that all I have to do to join the gang?' Joey asked with considerable relief.

157

'It's all yer 'ave to do to *join*, yes,' Rollo said. 'But if yer want to become more important, like Chas an' Blackie 'ere, yer'll 'ave to take another test.'

But that was in the future, Joey thought happily. For the moment, he only had to break a window. He looked down the street at the row of front parlours, each with their respectably drawn curtains through which he could just see the glowing gas mantles.

'Which one d'yer want me to smash?' he asked.

'Take yer choice,' Rollo told him.

Joey selected a window, lifted back his thin arm, and hurled the stone with all his might. The window shattered, and Joey felt a sense of power he had never known before.

He was about to turn and run for his life when he noticed that Rollo and his gang were making no effort to go, but instead were lounging in the middle of the road as if they had all the time in the world. Not knowing what else to do, Joey went and joined them.

The front door of the house with the broken window was flung violently open, and a furious householder, in his shirt sleeves, stepped out into the street. 'You bleedin' kids . . .' he began.

And then he noticed the hooligans, grinning at him.

Slowly and casually, Rollo began to walk towards him – and the man started to back away.

'I'll set the law on yer,' he blustered.

But as Rollo got closer, he retreated into his house and shut the door behind him.

Joey saw the whole scene through wide, amazed eyes. The man was afraid of Rollo – who wasn't much more than a kid! What a wonderful thing it was to have so much power! What a wonderful thing to be a Newington Hooligan.

And he *was* one, he told himself, hardly able to believe it. He was one of the gang. He had grown up at last.

Rollo, who had now walked a few yards up the street, beckoned Blackie to join him.

'Look at 'im,' he whispered, pointing discreetly to Joey. 'As pleased as punch, ain't 'e? But then 'e don't know what plans I got for 'im. 'E don't know 'ow I'm goin' to use 'im to get back at 'is brother.'

It was well past midnight when Colleen finally left The Goldsmiths' Arms and made her way up Lant Place, but there was still a light burning in the window of Number Thirty-six.

'Bless him. I told him he could go to bed, but he's waited up for me anyway,' she said to herself.

As a matter of fact, George usually waited up for her, though he was often so tired after his work in the wood yard that she would find him sound asleep in his favourite armchair.

That night, however, he hadn't dozed off but was sitting at the table, holding a long letter in his hands.

'Who's that from?' Colleen asked, as she took off her coat and hung it up behind the door.

'Our Becky,' George told her.

Yes, a letter that bulky could only be from her, Colleen thought. Of the whole Taylor family, it was Becky who wrote the longest letters – Becky who made the goings-on in the village they had left behind them come alive for her.

Colleen sat down, full of anticipation, opposite her husband. 'So what does your sister have to say for herself this time?' she asked.

'I don't know yet,' George said. 'The letter must have come by the last post. I've only found it in the hallway just now. D'you want to read it first?'

'No', Colleen said reluctantly. 'She's your sister, an' it's only right you should read it first. Only . . .'

'Only what?'

'Only don't read it like you usually do – slow and carefully, as if it was some kind of military dispatch.'

George grinned. 'Would you like me to read the interestin' bits out loud to you?' he asked.

'Yes, that would be nice,' Colleen said.

George skimmed the first page of the letter.

'My mam an' dad are both in good health,' he said, 'an' your dad's talkin' of finally givin' up the pub.'

Colleen laughed. 'He's been sayin' that for years,' she told her husband, 'but he'll not go. He'd be lost without that bar counter to lean on an' a pump handle to pull.'

'Our Becky's expanded her bakery, her husband's back in Africa an' her kids are gettin' to be more of a handful every day,' George continued. 'She says that sometimes they almost drive her to distraction.'

He did not look up from the letter, but if he had done, he would have seen Colleen's happy expression cloud over. *Becky's kids were getting to be more of a handful every day and sometimes they almost drove her to distraction.*

'Nobody's heard from me brother Philip – well, we never do unless he's in trouble – but Becky thinks he's probably still in London,' George said.

'I'm sorry, I didn't catch that bit,' Colleen told him.

Now George did look up. 'Is anythin' the matter, love?' he asked.

'No,' Colleen said, 'I was just thinkin' about somethin' else, that's all.' She forced a smile back on to her face. 'Go on with your sister's letter, love.'

'Nobody knows where Philip is an' . . .' George stopped reading and chuckled. 'Hey, listen to this. "You will be pleased, an' I think surprised, to hear that our Jack is gettin' married at last. He's chosen a very nice girl, though perhaps *chosen* is the wrong word, because he didn't really have any choice once she told him she was in *a certain condition*".' George laughed again. 'Imagine that! Our Jack's gettin' caught out after all these years.'

People were having babies all over the place – people who hadn't planned them and probably didn't even want them. It just didn't seem fair.

'Have I lost you again?' George asked.

'No', Colleen replied dully. 'You said your Jack's havin' to get married.'

'And don't you think it's funny?'

'Funny!' Colleen was starting to get angry, though if anyone had asked her why, she'd have had no answer. 'No, George, I don't think it's funny. I think it's sad.'

'Oh, come on, love,' George said playfully. 'Our Jack's

sowed more wild oats than a mountain goat. He was bound to slip up sooner or later.'

'Slip up!' Colleen said. 'Slip up! You make it all sound like some sort of game.'

'In a way, I suppose it is,' George admitted.

'An' did you sow your wild oats while you were servin' overseas?' Colleen demanded, feeling an overpowering urge to strike out, to hurt somebody – even if it had to be her dear husband. 'Well? Did you?'

'Well, you know . . .' George said uncomfortably.

'No, I don't know,' Colleen told him. 'It's somethin' we've never talked about before.'

George shifted awkwardly in his armchair. 'When I was in the army,' he said, 'there were certain ladies – well, more like women really – who made their livin' out of enter-tainin' the soldiers.'

'And did they "entertain" you?' Colleen asked.

'I . . . er . . .' George mumbled.

He had never seen his wife like this, and he was completely at a loss as to how to handle it.

'How do you know there isn't some little dark-skinned kiddie in Africa or India who's got your nose an' your eyes?' Colleen went on relentlessly.

'Don't talk daft,' George said.

'You can't be sure there isn't one, can you?' Colleen demanded, almost screaming now.

'No,' George admitted unwillingly. 'I suppose I can't be absolutely sure.'

Colleen felt her anger drain away as quickly as it had appeared, and in its place there was only a feeling of total hopelessness and exhaustion.

'I'm goin' to bed,' she said heavily, getting to her feet.

'I'll come with you, love,' George told her.

'Would you mind sleepin' in the spare bedroom, tonight, George?' Colleen asked.

'In the spare bedroom?' George repeated.

He was frowning. More than that – he looked hurt.

An' well he might, Colleen thought. They'd never spent a night apart since their marriage – but she didn't want him with her that night! She couldn't stand the thought of having him near her, of him embracing her and . . . doing that thing to her which should make babies – but wouldn't.

'*Why* do you want me to sleep in the spare bedroom?' George asked, still trying to take it all in.

'I'm not feelin' very well,' Colleen lied.

'What's the matter with you?'

'I'm . . . I'm just feelin' a bit feverish, that's all.'

'Can I get you somethin' for it?' George asked worriedly. 'A glass of warm milk or . . .'

'No!' Colleen said. Oh, why was he making it so difficult? 'No, I . . . I just want to sleep on me own till the sweatin' goes away.'

'Perhaps we should call a doctor,' George suggested.

'I don't want a doctor, for God's sake!' Colleen screamed. 'All I want is to be left alone!'

She rushed upstairs and locked the bedroom door behind her. And then she listened. There was no noise from below – no sound of George's crutch tapping its way across the parlour floor. He must still be sitting where she'd left him – thoroughly miserable or too shocked to move.

Colleen went across to her underwear drawer and rummaged around under her bloomers until her hand felt the reassuring touch of the gin bottle.

'I'll only have a drop,' she promised herself.

She uncapped the bottle, held it to her lips and took a generous swig.

'Never used to drink,' she thought as the oily liquid burned her throat. 'Not when I lived back in Marston. Not before I got married to George.'

She didn't *really* drink now, she told herself – just the occasional one in the pub and an odd nip when she came home.

She held up the bottle to the light. When had she bought it? Thursday? No, it couldn't have been Thursday, because today was only Saturday, and it was already half empty.

She took another swig, and sank slowly down onto the bed.

★

On Sunday morning, just after breakfast, Peggy announced that she was going out and would not be back till teatime.

'Goin' out?' her mother said suspiciously. 'Not back till teatime? An' where are you thinkin' of goin', may I ask?'

Up to Charlotte Street, which Pedro had decided would be the ideal place to try out the broken milk jug dodge.

'To Bessie Wimbush's 'ouse,' Peggy said. 'She's 'avin' a birthday party, 'an I've got an invite.'

Suspicion lingered on Lil's face. 'Yer never used to 'ave so many friends,' she said. 'Yer never seemed to 'ave time for anyfink but yer precious animals before.'

'Maybe I've grown up, like yer were always tellin' me to,' Peggy told her.

'An' 'ow is that all these new pals of yours keep 'avin' birthday parties?' Lil asked.

Peggy shrugged. 'Maybe 'cos they all keep 'avin' birthdays,' she suggested. 'Can I go, Mum?'

Lil clucked her tongue disapprovingly. 'I don't know,' she said. 'Birthday parties on a Sunday. It don't seem right, some'ow.'

'It's the only day Bessie could 'ave it,' Peggy said. 'An' 'er Gran's comin' down from Shoreditch, special.'

'What time does this party start?' Lil asked.

'Eleven o'clock,' said Peggy, who had arranged to meet Pedro at a quarter past.

'Well, all I can say is, it seems to me like a very funny time to 'old a party,' Lil told her.

Sensing that she was losing the argument, Peggy played her trump card. 'They're a very respectable family, the Wimbushes,' she said. 'Very respectable indeed.'

'Are they?' Lil asked. 'An' what makes yer think that?'

' 'Er dad's got four diff'rent shirts an' they 'ave a pianner in their front parlour – a new one.'

Lil nodded her head as if to say that, yes, it did sound as if they were *quite* respectable.

'An' would yer be goin' in yer school clothes, like last time?' she asked. 'Or would yer 'ave to be dressed up?'

'I'd 'ave to be dressed up,' Peggy said cunningly,

knowing that if anything could tip the balance in her favour, it would be a willingness to put on her best clothes.

'Well, I supp'se there'll be no 'arm in yer goin',' Lil said. 'But if the party's at eleven, we'll 'ave to go straight upstairs an' start gettin' you ready for it now.'

'Thanks, Mum,' Peggy replied, doing her best to hide a triumphant smile.

Pedro, holding something bundled up in a red-checked handkerchief in his hand, was waiting for her on the corner of Charlotte Street and Gravel Lane.

' 'Ello,' Peggy said cheerfully.

'Just stand there while I take a proper look at yer,' Pedro answered, with a crispness in his voice she had never heard before.

She did as she had been told, and Pedro walked round her, now examining her dress, now glancing at her boots.

'Yer look just right,' he pronounced finally.

'Thanks a lot,' Peggy replied, wondering why his words had made her feel a warm glow all over.

'Poor but decent – that's 'ow yer look,' Pedro told her, nodding his head in approval.

Peggy was shattered. 'These are me best clothes,' she said. 'Don't yer like 'em?'

'I told yer, they're perfect fer the job in 'and,' Pedro replied. 'Now let's get started.'

Peggy glanced at the long line of crumbling terraced houses which lined Charlotte Street. 'This place is a dump,' she said. 'Ain't we better goin' somewhere posher?'

Pedro shook his head. 'It ain't the toffs that usually give yer the odd copper,' he told her. 'It's people with 'ardly two ha'pennies to rub together themselves what end up diggin' in their pockets.'

He looked around him to make sure the street was deserted, then bent down and put the bundle he'd been carrying onto the pavement. His deft fingers undid the knot in the red-ckeck handkerchief and he opened it to reveal the fragments of what had once been a large milk jug. While

Peggy watched him, he quickly picked up several pieces of the jug and laid them on the pavement.

'Sunday's a good day for it, yer see,' he said as he worked, ' 'cos even if people ain't churchgoers, they're still goin' to feel more full of 'oliness an' Christian charity today than they do on any other day in the week.'

He stood up, stuffed his handkerchief into his pocket, and surveyed his work critically.

'There y'are,' he said. 'Looks like it might 'ave just fallen out of yer 'and this very second, that does. Now, d'yer remember 'ow to run the dodge?'

'Course I do,' Peggy said.

'Right, then all yer 'ave to do is stand 'ere an' wait for yer first punter,' Pedro told her. 'An' don't forget to rub yer eyes just before yer look up at 'em.'

He started to walk away.

'Won't you be stayin' with me?' Peggy asked, suddenly feeling very nervous.

Pedro turned round, looked at her, and shook her head. 'Yer make a better picture on yer own,' he told her. 'But don't you worry yourself, gal – I won't be far away, an' I'll come an' join yer if I think yer need it.'

And with that, he sauntered off down the street, leaving Peggy by herself.

She wasn't alone for long. Scarcely a minute passed before the door of one of the houses opened, and a middle-aged woman in her Sunday best stepped out onto the street.

Peggy looked down at the jug as Pedro had told her to, and when she heard the woman getting closer, she secretly started rubbing her eyes.

The woman stopped a couple of feet short of where Peggy was standing. 'What 'appened, gal?' she asked.

Peggy looked up again. 'Me mum sent me out to get some milk,' she said, 'I was on me way to the dairy when I tripped over. An' now I don't know what I'm goin' to do.'

'There's not much yer *can* do,' said the woman, surveying the wreckage of the jug. 'The best thing is to go straight 'ome an' tell yer mum all about it.'

'Oh, I couldn't do that,' Peggy moaned. 'Me dad'd kill me. I know 'e would.'

'Yer'll be all right as long as yer explain to 'em that it was an accident,' the woman said soothingly. 'Nobody can 'elp 'avin accidents, can they?'

She patted Peggy on the head and was on the point of moving away when Pedro suddenly appeared from out of nowhere.

'Oh Gawd, look at that,' he said. 'I wouldn't like to be in your shoes when yer get 'ome, Effie Smith. Yer dad'll give yer such a pastin' yer'll not be able to sit down for a week.' He looked up into the woman's eyes. ' 'E's got a terrible temper, 'as Effie's dad. Well known for it down our street, 'e is.'

'Well, there's nuffink I can do about it,' said the woman, in a voice that was a mixture of sympathy and helplessness. 'I mean, it's not as if I could afford to buy her a new milk jug meself, is it?'

'Course it ain't,' Pedro agreed gloomily. Then his face lit up as if he'd suddenly had a good idea. 'But yer could spare 'er a penny, couldn't yer, missis?' he asked.

'I supp'se so,' the woman replied. 'But she won't get a new jug for a penny, will she?'

'No,' Pedro said. 'But if she stays 'ere for a bit, an' some more kind souls like yerself come past, an' *they* give 'er a penny as well, then she'll soon 'ave enough for a new jug, won't she?'

'Yer right,' the woman said, reaching into her pocket and taking out a coin. ' 'Ere y'are, gal. That'll start yer off.'

By the end of the afternoon, when Pedro carefully collected up the fragments of the milk jug and wrapped them in his handkerchief, they had scrounged one and eightpence, her share of which, Peggy calculated, would just about buy her half a back leg of her goat.

'How d'yer fancy pullin' the dodge again, next Sunday?' Pedro asked her.

'All right,' Peggy agreed. 'But I'll 'ave to come up with some new excuse to tell me mum. She's gettin' a bit sick of me goin' to so many birthday parties.'

'You'll think o' somethin',' Pedro said cheerfully. 'Tell yer what. If I can get me hands on 'em, we might try the pawnbroker's ticket dodge instead of o' usin' the old milk jug.'

'What's the pawnbroker's ticket dodge?' Peggy asked.

'It's a real beauty,' Pedro said. 'I'll tell yer all about it next week.'

'An' will it make us more money than the milk jug?' Peggy said, thinking about her goat.

'A lot more,' Pedro told her. 'Course, it's a bit riskier as well. Not frightened of doin' somethin' a bit riskier, are yer?'

'No,' Peggy said.

She was more than willing to do anything that would please Pedro *and* help her to get her goat quicker.

PART THREE: SECOND CHANCES

Winter 1901

CHAPTER TEN

It was bitterly cold that late November morning when Annie Clarke made her way along London Wall to the National Telephone Company's training school, but Annie had so much on her mind that she hardly noticed the weather at all.

This was her second chance, she told herself, and if she failed this time she would not get another one, but instead would be condemned to a life of drudgery in the match factory.

'But I won't fail!' she said aloud.

Why should she? After her last interview, Mr Archer had said she was an intelligent young woman who should have no difficulty mastering a switch board and that the only thing wrong was her accent. Well, she'd done something about that, 'adn't she?

Hadn't she?

And not only did she sound good, but she looked good as well. Her mum had done her hair a real treat. She was wearing Colleen Taylor's very best green velvet dress, which perfectly complemented her eyes. And the hat with the light feather trim – which Miss Crosby had given her – made her look serious without being severe.

'I'll get the job, I'll get the job,' she chanted in time with the sound of her footsteps. 'I'll get the bleedin' job.'

Yet the closer she got to the training school, the more she

felt her confidence ebbing. Talking properly didn't make her a vicar's or lawyer's daughter, she thought. Even if she did manage to avoid dropping her aitches, she would still be little Annie Clarke, a docker's daughter from Lant Place.

She was shown into the same room as before, and just like last time there was a number of other applicants reading magazines or talking quietly to each other.

Annie sat down and opened the copy of the *Tatler* she'd gone all the way up West to buy.

'I say, could you help me?' said a voice to her left.

Annie turned, and found herself looking at a girl with chubby cheeks and sulky eyes.

'I was just wondering if you had any idea how long all this will take?' the girl said.

'No, I'm afraid I don't,' Annie replied, not wishing to admit that she'd been through the process before – and been rejected.

'Because, you see, I'm spending the weekend in the country,' the girl continued, 'and I do so want to supervise the packing personally.'

Why's she talking about weekends in the country? Annie wondered. Is she tryin' to impress me, or what? Common sense told her to nod vaguely and return to her *Tatler*, but suddenly, from out of nowhere, a mischievous imp seemed to leap into her head and take over her voice.

'Actually, I *never* supervise my own packing,' she said. 'But then I suppose I'm lucky, because I have a *very* good maid.'

The other girl's sulky eyes flashed with envy, and she could hardly conceal her gasp.

'You have a maid of your own, do you?' she said.

Annie wished she'd never spoken, but the imp, now in complete control, was really starting to enjoy itself.

'Actually, Peggy – that's her name by the way, Peggy – is not so much my maid, as Mother's,' the imp said. 'But with Mother being away so much, I have her pretty much to myself.'

From the look of malicious glee which came to the other girl's face, Annie knew that she'd made a mistake – but she had no idea what it was.

'I see,' the girl said. 'You have her pretty much to yourself, do you? Your mother must be a rather eccentric person if she doesn't take her personal maid *with* her when she's travelling.'

Annie felt her new-found self-confidence crumble around her. Her mouth was dry, and she was sure that when she spoke again, it would be with a strong Cockney accent.

And worse was yet to come! Looking around the room, she suddenly realised that all other conversation had stopped – and that everyone there was waiting expectantly for her to say something in reply.

'I expect the dear woman simply *refuses* to travel,' said a new voice from the opposite corner. 'Some of these old family retainers can be very stubborn, you know.'

Annie glanced across at her rescuer – a big-boned girl with laughing blue eyes and a wide, generous mouth.

'That's right,' she agreed. 'She simply *refuses* to travel. Mother finds it rather an inconvenience, but Peggy's such a treasure that she can never bring herself to sack – to dismiss – her.'

The girl with the chubby cheeks looked more than a little disappointed. 'Is your family very rich?' she asked, giving Annie more rope to hang herself with.

But the docker's daughter had no intention of making the same mistake twice.

'It's rather vulgar to talk about money, don't you think?' she said. 'Besides, I don't really care about what Father has. I want to make my own way in the world.'

The woman who had shown Annie into the room appeared in the doorway with a piece of paper in her hand.

'The Board will see Miss Clarke now,' she said.

Annie stood up. 'If you'll excuse me . . .' she said.

The girl with the chubby face watched as she walked through the door, then turned to the other applicants. 'There's something not quite *right* about her, you know,' she said.

The rest of the applicants took it as an invitation to start a general discussion.

'I see what you mean.'

'So do I, but perhaps if her family has only *recently* come into money . . .'

'I believe there *are* servants who can be quite difficult about things like travelling.'

The big-boned girl listened with growing amusement. What a bunch of crashing snobs these rural deans' and county solicitors' daughters really were, she thought.

She waited patiently until most of the chatter had died down, then said, 'I thought having an uncle in the House of Lords would stand me in good stead for getting an appointment here, but I'm not so sure after meeting Miss Clarke.'

'What do you mean?' asked the girl with the sulky eyes.

'Well, isn't it obvious? You could tell by that dress she was wearing that she doesn't *really* need to impress the Board at all. In fact, it would surprise me if Miss Clarke's uncle isn't one of the company's directors.'

'Do you really think so?'

'Oh yes,' the big-boned girl said cheerfully. 'If there's only one position going, you can bet your last guinea that Miss Clarke will be the person to get it.'

An air of gloom descended over the whole room, and it was all she could do to stop herself laughing out loud.

As Annie followed the woman with the list along the corridor, she was feeling on top form. With just a little help from the girl in the corner, she had fooled all the others! They might not believe that she had a rich father – probably most of them didn't – but at least they had no idea she came from the East End.

'Thank you, Miss Crosby,' she prayed silently. 'Thank you, thank you, thank you.'

It was the same selection board as on her last visit. Sour Mr Haynes – who had never heard of Lant Place – sat in the middle, with Mr Spring on his left and the younger man, Mr Archer, on her right.

Mr Haynes looked at one of the pieces of paper in front of him and sniffed. 'We appear to have interviewed you on a previous occasion, Miss Clarke,' he said.

'Yes, sir. You have,' Annie replied.

'Then if we've once found you unsuitable, I can't really see the point of going through the same . . .'

'Let me explain, since it's partly my doing that Miss Clarke is here,' Mr Archer interrupted. 'We rejected her last time because of some slight irregularities in her grammar and accent, but since then she has made a considerable effort to correct her faults, and after she wrote and told me that, I thought it was only fair to interview her again.'

Mr Haynes scowled. 'I think I'm starting to remember you, Miss Clarke,' he said. 'You work in a jam factory, do you not?'

'No, sir, I work in a match manufactory,' Annie corrected him, 'but I have my sights set on wider horizons.'

Mr Haynes' eyebrows shot up.

'Wider horizons!' he said. 'Indeed!'

And Annie thought, 'Good old Miss Crosby. She said that'd impress 'em.'

'You do realise that we employ only single ladies as telephonists, don't you, Miss Clarke?' Haynes said.

'Yes, I do,' Annie said. 'It's all very clearly explained in your brochure.'

'What I mean to say, Miss Clarke, is that persons from your side of the river – Southwark if my memory serves me well – do tend to get married rather earlier than those who hail from, for example, Marylebone.'

'Most of the weddings in Southwark take place in the afternoon,' Annie said. 'When do they get married in Marylebone? At night?'

'I don't think you quite understand my . . .' Mr Haynes began, only to be interrupted by a sudden burst of laughter from Mr Archer.

'Very good,' Mr Archer said, slapping his thigh. 'Very good indeed.'

Mr Haynes turned to his fellow board member with a look of irritation of his face. 'Have I said something funny, Archer?' he demanded.

'Not you,' Mr Archer replied between chuckles. 'Miss Clarke. Do they get married at night in Marylebone! Don't you understand, Mr Haynes – she was making a joke.'

'I see,' Haynes said, though he plainly didn't. He turned back to Annie and pushed his glasses forward on his nose. 'Let me express it another way, then, Miss Clarke. Is there any young man that you see regularly – who takes you to brass band concerts or rows you on the Serpentine, perhaps?'

Harry had taken her to concerts, and Tom had rowed her – though on the Thames, not the Serpentine. But Mr Haynes wasn't talking about music or rowing. 'Is there a man you're serious about?' – that was what he meant.

And there wasn't! She might give Harry a good night peck when he saw her to her door, and sometimes when she was out with Tom she felt the urge to . . . to . . .

Mr Haynes was waiting for his answer.

'No, sir. There isn't any young man,' Annie said.

The interview continued for another ten minutes, and when it was over she could tell from Mr Archer's face that – at least as far as he was concerned – it had gone well.

'Thank you ever so much,' she said, when Mr Archer showed her to the street door.

'There's nothing to thank me for,' he replied. 'It's my job to recruit the best people I possibly can. I'm not able to promise you here and now that we *will* be offering you a post,' he winked, 'but I'm sure that if we do, you'll be a great asset to the company.'

They shook hands and Annie began to walk sedately down the street – at least until she heard the door close behind Mr Archer. Then she stopped, took off her hat, and threw it into the air.

'I've got it, ain't I?' she shouted to the amazed passers-by. 'I got me job with the telephone comp'ny!'

Gawd, but it was luverly to be talkin' like normal people again!

She bent over and picked up her hat. She had shared her news with the world in general, but now that she'd calmed down a little, she felt that she wanted to share it with just one person – someone special. And it came almost as a shock to her to realise who that special person was.

George Taylor and Sam Clarke leant against the polished counter of the Crown Inn's public bar with freshly pulled pints of ale in their hands.

George looked around to see if anyone was in earshot, then said, 'I'm worried, Sam.'

'I know yer are,' Sam replied.

'Does it show that much?' George asked.

Sam shook his head. 'It don't show at all,' he said. 'It never does with you ex-sergeants. But I knew when yer suggested that we come 'ere instead o' The Goldsmiths' that yer 'ad somethin' yer wanted to get off yer chest without 'avin' Colleen hoverin' in the background. It is yer old woman yer want to talk about, ain't it?'

George nodded.

'She's growin' more an' more desperate about the fact that she's not gettin' pregnant,' he said. 'I can see it on her face. It's like she's got a knife in her guts, an' every day that passes the knife twists a little bit extra an' sinks in that little bit deeper. In the end, it'll be the death of her, I'll swear it will.'

'Is she drinkin'?' Sam asked.

'Yes, she is,' George admitted. 'It's not too bad most of the time, but now an' again she'll go on a bender, an' then she can hardly stand up. I've even found gin bottles hidden in our bedroom.' He laughed hollowly. '*Our* bedroom!' he repeated bitterly.

'What does that mean?' Sam asked. 'That yer not sleepin' together any more?'

'We do sometimes,' George said. 'But most nights, she wants to be left alone.'

'So let me get this straight,' Sam said. 'She's upset 'cos she ain't got no babies yet.'

'Yes.'

'An' that's makin' her act in a way that pretty much *guarantees* she won't never 'ave none.'

'That's about it,' George confessed. 'I don't know what to do, Sam. You might not have seen her at her best . . .'

Sam raised a hand to cut him off. 'I may not 'ave seen 'er at 'er best,' he said, 'but I've seen enough to know that she's a woman in a million. An' yer love 'er, don't yer?'

'God, yes!' George said. He paused for a second, then asked, 'Have you ever been really scared, Sam?'

'More times than I care to remember,' Sam replied. 'Specially when I was in the army.'

'It was the army I was thinkin' about just now. There was this one time when I was leadin' a patrol up in the North-West Frontier. Army Intelligence had told us we wouldn't have any trouble, but they were talkin' through their backsides . . .'

'They usually do.'

'We must have been thirty miles from base camp when the Pathan Irregulars found us. There were well over a hundred of them an' only ten of us. They had us surrounded, a great ring of some of the finest fightin' men in the world – an' the circle was gettin' smaller an' smaller all the time. I knew they'd kill us, an' that our only chance was to make a headlong charge an' try an' cut out way through. So that's what we did.'

'Go on,' said Sam, content to let George make his point at his own speed.

'I came closer to death that day than I'd ever done before,' George told him. 'Or since, for that matter. Even the Battle of Omdurman was a picnic compared to that Pathan ambush.'

'An' . . .?' Sam said patiently.

'An' I wasn't scared,' George said. 'Believe me, I wasn't scared – not for a second.'

'Oh, I believe yer' alright,' Sam assured him. 'Yer wouldn't be scared. Yer not that kind o' bloke.'

'I'm scared now. I'm scared that me marriage isn't goin' to last. I'm scared I'll lose Collie.'

Sam took a reflective sip of his pint. 'We're out of our depth,' he said.

'We're what?' George asked.

'Out of our depth,' Sam repeated. 'Men are very well when it comes to bringin' 'ome the wage packet, but we've no idea 'ow to handle a situation like this.'

'So what can I do?' George asked.

'People laugh at my old woman, with all 'er talk of respectability, an' her furniture an' her gossipin'. I know, I've done it meself,' Sam said, 'but for all that, my Lil's got an 'eart big enough to sink a battleship an' an 'ead on 'er shoulders that'd be the envy of many a bloke with all the learnin' in the world.'

'I'm not sure I'm followin' you,' George said.

'Talk to 'er,' Sam replied. 'Tell 'er yer troubles, and then let 'er 'ave a word with Colleen. I'm not sayin' she'll come up with an answer – maybe there ain't no answer – but she's got a damn sight better chance o' findin' a way out of this than either you or me 'as.'

George turned the idea over in his mind. It had only been desperation which had made him confide in Sam, and he didn't want news of his problems with Colleen spreading any further. On the other hand, Lil just might be the person to help. After all, she had three kids of her own and was Colleen's best friend in London.

'All right, I'll talk to her,' he said.

'You won't regret it,' Sam promised him.

And George prayed that Sam was right.

Annie rushed recklessly down Battle Bridge Stairs and threw her arms around Tom's neck.

'I think I've got the job!' she said excitedly. 'No! I'm sure I've got the job!'

'O' course you 'ave,' Tom said, hugging her to him. 'I never doubted yer would for a minute.'

The embrace was getting uncomfortable – uncomfortably nice – and Annie broke free. 'Could you take an hour off?' she asked. 'So that we can go and have a drink or something to celebrate.'

'Only if, for just this once, yer don't insist on payin' yer own 'alf,' Tom told her.

'But that's stupid,' Annie protested. 'I'm the one

who's . . .' She stopped, and smiled. 'All right, Tom, if that's what you want,' she agreed.

They walked arm in arm down Battle Bridge Lane. A fog was starting to come up off the river, and it seemed to have driven everyone else off the street.

'I s'ppose yer'll 'ave a very different life now yer goin' to be a telephonist,' Tom said.

An edge of gloom had started to creep into his voice, but Annie, still full of her own success, missed it completely.

'Yes, it will be different,' she bubbled. 'No more matches to pack. No more Miss Hunt breathing down my neck . . .'

'I didn't mean the work,' Tom said.

'Then what *did* you mean?' Annie asked, beginning now to realise that something was wrong.

'I meant what yer'll be doin' after work's finished. Yer bound to meet new people, ain't yer? Posher people? More educated people?'

'I suppose so,' Annie agreed.

'Yer already talk more like them than what yer talk like us.'

'What's that got to do with anyfink?' Annie asked.

'Yer mean, what's it got to with *anything*,' Tom corrected her.

Annie stopped in her tracks, put her hands on Tom's arms and turned him round to face her.

'Just what are you trying to say, Tom Bates?' she demanded. 'That because I'll be meeting people who talk differently from you, I'll think they're somehow better or more interesting?'

'There was this coalman 'oo used to deliver up our street when I was a nipper,' Tom said. 'Nice bloke, 'e was. Used to let me ride on 'is cart. Then one day 'e got a contract to deliver to a bakery, so 'e bought 'imself a second cart. By the end o' two years, 'e 'ad six carts, an' 'e moved to an 'ouse on the other side 'o the river.'

'Where's all this leading?' Annie asked.

' 'E don't come down our street no more,' Tom told her. 'An' when I saw 'im at Battle Bridge Stairs once, 'e looked right through me.'

'Are you saying I'll be like that?' Annie asked angrily. 'Are you saying I'll go and turn my back on everybody I know – everybody I love?'

'It's 'appened to others,' Tom said.

Annie's anger gave way to blind fury, and she lashed out – slapping Tom across the face as hard as she could. He saw the blow coming, but did not try to avoid it. Nor did he flinch when it landed.

'I'm sorry, Tom,' Annie said, as remorse quickly replaced anger.

'I'm sorry, too,' Tom replied. 'I shouldn't 'ave said it. But sometimes I get so scared I'm goin' to lose yer.'

She only meant to reach up and stroke his cheek, but almost before she knew what was happening, her arms were round his neck and she was kissing him.

She felt his powerful body press against hers, felt his hands running down her back and his tongue exploring her mouth – and she knew that nothing as wonderful as this had ever happened to her before.

'Tom, oh Tom!' she gasped.

His hands stroked the backs of her thighs, and he was pressing himself harder – even harder – against her. She wanted him to caress her breasts . . . to lift her skirt and take her right then and there. She wanted it – wanted *him* – with an urgency which was new and exciting . . . and frightening.

The sound of men's voices drifted towards them through the gathering gloom – voices which were growing louder every second. Annie broke away from Tom, stepped back and looked up into his eyes.

'You won't lose me,' she said.

The men they'd heard in the distance were almost level with them now, and more were approaching from the opposite direction.

'Busy all of a sudden, ain't it?' Tom said, knowing that the moment was gone. 'S'ppose I should buy yer that port an' lemon I promised yer.'

'After what just nearly happened, I think yer'd better make it a double brandy,' Annie said, taking his arm.

★

Peggy and Pedro stood at the top of Customs House Stairs. The fog was rising, and they had to hug themselves to keep warm. Peggy wished her friend had let her bring her coat, but Pedro had been very firmly against that.

'No point in pleadin' poverty if yer don't look bleedin' poor, is there?' he'd said.

Pedro's family was supposed to have moved on soon after the Bank Holiday, but then there'd been some sort of trouble and now his dad was, as Pedro had put it, 'a guest of 'Is Majesty for the next six months.'

It seemed unlikely to Peggy that the King would invite a van dweller to stay with him for a week, let alone six months. Yet Pedro swore it was true, and Peggy was glad the monarch had been so generous, because it gave her more time to be with Pedro – and to raise the money for her goat.

A skiff pulled in at the bottom of the stairs and a man stepped out. He was wearing a smart naval uniform, and sported a black, bushy beard.

' 'E's a good mark if I ever saw one,' Pedro whispered. 'Now remember, play 'im for all 'e's worth.'

Peggy didn't need reminding. They'd been pulling the pawn ticket dodge for several weeks now, and she'd become something of an expert at it.

The naval man took the stairs two at a time, but came to a halt when the fair-haired girl in rags stepped in front of him.

'Want to buy some cloves, sir?' Peggy asked.

The sailor looked her up and down. 'Some clothes?' he repeated.

'Yes, sir,' Peggy said. She held out some pawnbroker's tickets for him to see. 'Good cloves, they are. Me dad's suit cost him two an' a tanner on the market, an' me mam's dress would look lovely on any lady – once yer'd sewn up the tear.'

The sailor squatted down so his eyes were on a level with hers. 'Now look here,' he said, 'you can't go round selling your family's clothes.'

'But me mum told me to,' Peggy said plaintively. 'She says what's the use of 'avin' cloves when yer belly's empty.'

'You're hungry, are you?'

'We ain't 'ad nuffink to eat since the day afore yesterday.'

The sailor examined her suspiciously. 'You don't look underfed to me,' he said.

'That's 'cos me dad 'ad a job till last week,' Peggy replied. 'Then 'is war wound started playin' 'im up again, an' he got the sack.'

The sailor shook his head. 'I'm not sure I entirely believe you,' he said.

A few weeks earlier, Peggy would have given up on the man, but since then Pedro had taught her some tricks – and she'd made up a few of her own. So now, instead of turning and running away, she held out the pawnbroker's tickets for a second time.

'There's sheets an' blankets, as well,' she said. 'Good, warm blankets they are.' She let her eyes mist over. 'You could sleep nice under them blankets.'

'And what are you sleeping under now your blankets are in pawn?' the sailor asked.

'We got a couple o' old sacks. If yer all snuggle up close together, yer don't really notice the cold. Well, not much, anyway.'

'You poor little mite,' the sailor said.

'So will yer buy me tickets, sir?' Peggy begged.

The man put his hand into his pocket and pulled out coins. He sorted through them in his palm, then handed her a shilling.

'You make sure your family gets some decent, hot food this evening,' he said.

'Thank you, sir,' Peggy said gratefully. She held out the tickets. 'An' these are for you.'

'Good God, you don't suppose I want to take those, do you?' the sailor asked.

'Me mum said I've got to . . .' Peggy began.

'Keep them,' the sailor said. 'And perhaps when your father's fit to go to work again, you'll be able to get your blankets back.'

He side-stepped her and walked quickly on towards the Customs House.

'They never do want to take the bleedin' tickets,' Peggy thought to herself. Which was just as well, because, although they were genuine, the goods described on them had been long since redeemed.

Peggy looked down at the coin in her hand. Another shillin'! At this rate, she'd have her goat by Christmas.

Joey Bates stood at the corner of Tooley Street and Morgan's Lane, watching the fog curl around the gas lamp and feeling the cold bite into him.

He wished that he could have worn a warm overcoat, but a coat didn't go with the part he was playing. Newington Hooligans ignored the weather, as they ignored so many of life's hardships, and, winter or summer, a thin jacket was all the protection they needed against the elements.

Joey heard the sound of footsteps, and through the thick fog he saw three black shapes approaching. As they got closer, he could see that it was – as he expected – Rollo, Blackie and Chas. He was glad they'd turned up so soon because, though he'd never have admitted it to them, it had been a bit frightening standing on the empty, fog-engulfed street all by himself.

He thought back to the day when Rollo had told him to sling that stone through a window in Bittern Street. *'Is that all I 'ave to do to join the gang?'* he'd asked.

'It's all yer 'ave to do to join, yes,' Rollo had told him. *'But if yer ever want to become more important, like Chas an' Blackie 'ere, yer'll 'ave to take another test.'*

He hadn't really understood what Rollo meant about being important back then – but he did now.

The 'lootenants' had it made. They always got to sit near Rollo in the pub, whereas Joey, as the newest recruit, was always seated furthest away from him. Whenever there was any money to share out – and Joey never did understand where the money had come from – it was Blackie and Chas who took the biggest shares after Rollo. And when the leader wasn't around, the 'lootenants' could boss the lesser gang members about to their hearts' content!

Yes, they'd got it made – and now Joey was going to be given the chance to have it made, too!

It had been Blackie, waiting for him outside the butcher's shop where he worked, who had told him of his good fortune. Rollo wanted him to take the second test, Blackie had said, and if he passed it, well, the gang could always use another lootenant.

Rollo, Chas and Blackie had drawn almost level with the gas lamp now.

' 'Ello, Rollo. 'Ow yer doin',' Joey said, proud to be addressing the leader of the gang in such casual terms.

'Watcha, Joe,' Rollo replied. 'Ready to see a bit o' mischief done, are yer?'

'See it?' Joey said disappointedly. 'I thought I was goin' to be the one that *did* it.'

Rollo chuckled. 'There's some spirit in this young shaver, ain't there, Blackie?' he said.

'Loads o' spirit,' Blackie agreed.

'I'll tell yer 'ow it is,' Rollo said, turning back to Joey. 'Tonight, yer see *'ow* it's done, an' next time, it'll be your turn to do it. Fair enough?'

'Fair enough,' Joey said.

'What time is it?' Rollo asked.

Chas took a big fob watch out of his pocket, and stared down it. Joey noticed the other boy's lips moving as he did some tortuous mental calculations.

'It's 'alf-past . . . 'alf-past eight,' he said finally.

'An' what time does this bloke us'lly leave the ware'ouse?' Rollo asked.

'About now,' Blackie said.

'Right, we'd better all get ready then, 'adn't we?' Rollo said. 'Blackie, you take the front, me an' Chas an' young Joe 'ere'll come at it from behind.'

Blackie walked a little further along the street and disappeared into a doorway, while Rollo led the other two into an alley just beyond the gas lamp. 'An' when this is over, we'll all go an' 'ave a good drink,' Rollo promised.

'When all what's over?' Joey asked.

'You just wait an' see, young Joe,' Rollo told him. 'You just wait an' see.'

There was the sound of footsteps coming along Tooley Street, and then a tall man in a frock coat and top hat crossed the head of the alley.

'Is that 'im?' Rollo whispered to Chas, once the man had gone.

'That's 'im,' Chas said.

'Let's get goin', then,' Rollo said.

As lightly as cats, Rollo and Chas slipped along the alley. Joey knew he should have been following them – but he didn't want to. Being a part of the gang had been a game so far, but this had a nasty feel about it, and he didn't like it all.

At the top of the alley, Rollo turned and gestured impatiently that he should be with them. For a second, Joey almost turned tail and fled in the opposite direction, but then, slowly and reluctantly, he made his way towards where Rollo was waiting.

'After all, what choice 'ave I got but to go along with 'em?' he asked himself.

Rollo was the boss, and he didn't take kindly to anybody disobeying orders. Besides, Joey thought, it probably wouldn't turn out half as badly as his stomach was telling him it would.

The three hooligans stalked their victim up the street, and had almost reached him when Blackie stepped out from his hiding place and blocked the man's way.

' 'Scuse me, guv,' Joey heard Blackie said. 'Can yer tell me the way to Tooley Street?'

The man's body went rigid, as if he were already beginning to suspect that something was wrong. '*This* is Tooley Street,' he said.

'Is it, now?' Blackie said easily. He put his hand in his pocket and pulled out a packet of cigarettes. 'Yer couldn't oblige me with a light, then, could yer, guv?'

'I'm afraid not,' the man replied, a hint of panic creeping into his voice. 'Now, if you would just let me pass . . .'

'Plenty o' time for that,' Blackie told him. 'We should 'ave a talk first.'

The man was about to step out into the road when Rollo and Chas moved in. Chas, coming at him from the left, removed his top hat, while Rollo, on the right, swung a sand-filled cosh down hard on his victim's skull. The man groaned, and then his legs crumpled beneath him and he fell to the ground.

'We always take their 'ats off 'em first,' Rollo said to Joey. 'Makes it easier to 'it 'em. Anyway, there ain't no point in wastin' a good titfer, is there?'

' 'Adn't we better take 'is wallet so that it looks like a robbery?' Blackie asked.

'Good idea,' Rollo agreed.

'*Ain't* it robbery, then?' Joey asked, wondering why he was bothering to whisper on the deserted street.

'No, it ain't,' Rollo said, as Blackie bent over the fallen man and began to go through his pockets. 'It's more what yer might call settlin' a score.'

'How d'yer mean?' Joey said, with fascinated horror.

'This bloke's a wharfinger,' Rollo explained, 'an' one of the other wharfingers don't like the way 'e does business. Yer understand what I'm sayin'?'

'No,' Joey admitted.

'This other bloke, the one 'oo don't like him, comes up to us an' offers us ten bob if we'll put 'im in 'ospital.'

Joey looked down at the fallen wharfinger. He had not moved all the time Blackie had been going through his pockets – and he was not moving now.

'I think you might 'ave done more than just put 'im in 'ospital,' he said in a terrified whisper. 'I think yer might 'ave killed 'im stone dead.'

'An' what if I 'ave?' Rollo demanded aggressively, as if he had taken Joey's words as a criticism. 'The bloke who paid me ain't goin' to complain, is 'e? An' it ain't no skin off my nose if this bugger's up an' died on us.'

But the wharfinger was not dead, and even as Rollo was speaking, he started to make small, painful movements.

'Ain't it time we was gone?' Chas asked.

'No 'urry,' Rollo said. He looked down at the man on the ground. ' 'E ain't goin' to be causin' us no trouble, now is 'e?'

'No, 'e ain't,' Chas agreed with a grin.

Rollo walked round the wharfinger, inspecting his handiwork, then swung his leg and kicked the man hard in the ribs.

'That should keep 'im in 'ospital for a couple o' days more,' he told his pals, 'an' for no extra charge, neither. Still, I supp'se we better get movin'. Give us that titfer, will yer, Chas?'

Chas passed him the wharfinger's top hat, and, after a second's thought, Rollo crammed it down on Joey's head.

Just the feel of the unfortunate wharfinger's hat was enough to send a shudder running through Joey's whole body. He reached up, with a trembling hand, to pull it off.

'Leave it where it is,' Rollo ordered him.

'But I don't want it,' Joey protested.

'Maybe yer don't, young shaver,' Rollo said. 'Maybe yer don't. But it's what *I* want that goes, an' I want yer to 'ave it.'

Rollo decided that the gang would spend some of their ill-gotten gains in a pub called The Waterman's Rest, down by Elephant Stairs. It was a run-down boozer, full of the lowest sort of casual labourers and drunken costermongers. It certainly wasn't the kind of place where the customers wore silk top hats, and Joey's earned him some strange looks. Twice, he tried to take it off, but each time Rollo clamped his hand on his wrist to prevent him.

'Keep it on,' the gang leader said threateningly.

'But everybody's starin' at me,' Joey protested.

'So bleedin' what? Keep it on. It suits yer.'

Chas and Blackie were in high spirits, since not only had they been paid the ten shillings for their work, but they'd found another eight in the wharfinger's pocket.

'Eighteen bob for 'alf an hour's work,' Chas gloated. 'Not bad, is it, Joe?'

'No, it ain't,' Joey said, trying to keep his voice steady – and wishing he was a hundred miles away from this pub and these hooligans.

'Did yer see 'ow we did it?' Rollo asked.

'Yes, I saw it,' Joey said.

Not only had he seen it, but he would never forget it – Chas lifting off the hat, Rollo bringing down the cosh, the sound of the crack on the wharfinger's skull, the way the man had just collapsed as if he no longer had bones in his legs.

'Well, the next time we do somefink like that, you can 'elp us,' Rollo said. 'Think 'e can 'andle the cosh, Blackie?'

'I think so,' Blackie replied. 'Like yer said, 'e's got a lot o' spirit in him.'

Rollo clamped his hand down on Joey's knee. 'See 'ow much we like yer, Joe?' he said. 'See what a big chance we're givin' yer?'

'Yes,' Joey mumbled. 'Thanks, Rollo.'

And all the time, he felt himself drowning in panic and kept thinking, 'What am I goin' to do *now*? What *am* I goin' to do now?'

He couldn't just tell Rollo he didn't want to be part of the gang any more, because he'd just seen them commit a violent crime, and they'd only let him see it *because* he was one of them. Yet to *stay* one of them, he was going to have to do something similar himself. And he couldn't – he simply couldn't.

There was only one way out, he decided as he sat there, clenching his hands to stop them trembling. He was going to have to tell Tom all about it. He was going to have to ask his big brother to get him out of this mess.

CHAPTER ELEVEN

The small lecture room in National Telephone Company's training school had three rows of chairs in it, but by the time Annie arrived the first two had already been filled, and she was forced to take a seat at the back.

Once she was seated, she looked around her. There was a dais at the front of the room, with a teacher's desk resting on it and a blackboard hanging behind it.

Just like my old school in Lant Street, she said to herself.

And she would have giggled at the thought, had it not been for the fact that while match girls might sometimes do such a thing, young ladies who were training to be telephone operators never did.

She turned her attention to the other trainees. There were six chairs in each row, she counted, but only three girls – including herself – on the back one.

Annie hoped that none of the girls who'd attended the same interview board as her would be on this course, because they'd be bound to remember what she'd said about her mother and her maid, Peggy – and if they mentioned it, she was sure she'd die of embarrassment. Whatever had possessed her to tell those whopping lies?

'It was that chubby girl's fault,' she thought. 'If she hadn't started bragging about supervising her own packing, I'd never have said what I did.'

But she knew, really, that she couldn't put the *whole*

blame on the chubby girl because – when all was said and done – nobody had forced her to start fibbing.

'Well, in future I'll know better and I'll keep me gob shut,' she promised herself. Yet even as the idea flitted across her mind, she knew she was making a promise she'd never be able to keep.

Annie looked at the two girls sitting on the same row as she was, and was relieved to find that neither of them seemed familiar. Then, without making it too obvious, she began to examine the backs of the heads of the girls in front. No, she didn't think she recognised any of them either.

'Thank 'eavens for that!' she whispered softly to herself.

The door at the back of the room opened, and a severe-looking woman in a dark dress entered and walked up to the dais. There had been some soft mumbling up to that point, but now all the girls fell silent.

The woman surveyed the room, a grim expression on her face, and when her gaze swept the back row Annie felt an urge to stand up and confess to some wrong-doing – though she couldn't actually think of anything she might have done wrong in the short time she'd been in the training school.

'Good morning, young ladies,' the formidable woman said. 'I am Miss Dobbs.'

'Good morning, Miss Dobbs,' the young ladies chanted.

'You have all been selected to fill very responsible positions,' Miss Dobbs told them. 'In my youth, the telephone had not even been invented . . .'

'I can believe that,' Annie thought. 'In her youth, the 'orse an' cart probably hadn't been invented.'

'. . .but now it is an indispensable part of the life of London,' Miss Dobbs continued. 'From the wholesale merchant who begins his honest labours at four o'clock in the morning, to the gentleman of leisure who calls the last cab from his club well after midnight, everyone in this great city of ours depends on the telephone for their comfort and convenience.'

Annie tried to imagine her dad saying, 'I depend on the telephone for my comfort and convenience,' and almost had an attack of the giggles again.

'I will now call the register,' Miss Dobbs said, opening a book which had been lying on the desk. 'Miss James?'

'Here, ma'am.'

'Miss Cuthbertson?'

'Here, ma'am.'

'Miss Benson?' Miss Dobbs raised an eyebrow. 'Oh, I do beg your pardon . . . The Honourable . . .'

'It's just *Miss* Benson,' a girl on the front row said firmly. 'And I'm here, ma'am.'

'Oh crikey!' Annie gasped.

The back of the girl's head hadn't looked familiar, but Annie recognised her voice all right – she was the big-boned girl with the wide mouth who'd been sitting in the opposite corner at the interview.

'It would have to be her, wouldn't it?' Annie thought miserably. 'She could see through me right from the start – I could tell that, because while some of the other girls were takin' me seriously, she was almost laughin'.'

When Miss Dobbs had finished calling the register, she outlined what lay ahead. The first part of the young ladies' training would consist of operating dummy switchboards . . .

'. . . using the set of clear and precise instructions which the company will provide.'

Once they had mastered the clear and precise intructions, they would work in pairs . . .

'. . . one of you acting as the operator and the other as the subscriber.'

An' maybe my partner will be Miss Benson, Annie thought. Won't that be fun?

Finally, when Miss Dobbs considered they were proficient enough to deal with the public, they would progress to a real telephone exchange and would work side by side with an experienced operator for several more weeks.

'And only when *she* is happy that you have reached the required standard will you be trusted with a switchboard of your own,' Miss Dobbs said grandly.

She led them to the room where the dummy switchboards were installed. 'You will notice that there are a number of black over-gowns hanging on those pegs,' she said.

Just like the aprons at the match factory, Annie thought.

'You will each be given one of these gowns,' Miss Dobbs continued. 'Now, why is it, do you think, that the company should go to the expense of providing such garments for you?'

None of the fifteen young ladies present seemed willing to volunteer an answer.

'Why do *you* think it is, Miss . . .?' the instructress asked.

To her horror, Annie realised that *she* was the person Miss Dobbs was pointing to.

'Miss . . . Miss Clarke,' she stuttered.

Well, she'd got that part of Miss Dobbs' question right – she really was Miss Clarke. But what was the answer to the other part? Being a telephone operator wasn't dusty work like match packing, so what possible reason could there be for them wearing over-gowns?

'Well, Miss Clarke?' the instructress said, with a hint of impatience in her voice.

Annie looked around at the other girls, as if she hoped to find the answer written on their faces. How smart they all were in their new, expensive dresses and . . .

That was it!

'It's so we won't waste time lookin' – looking – at what all the others are wearing,' Annie said.

Miss Dobbs gave her a smile that promising pupils everywhere would have recognised.

'Quite correct, Miss Clarke,' she said. 'An operator's time is far too valuable to the company to be wasted on mere female vanity. And now, if you would care to take your seats, we can proceed with our first lesson at the switchboard.'

The lesson lasted until noon, and then Miss Dobbs announced that it was time for luncheon. The dining room she led the young ladies to was long and thin, with two tables running from one end of it to the other, and could have accommodated many more than the fifteen people who now entered it.

It wasn't as posh as the ABC restaurant that Harry had taken her to, Annie thought, but with its bright, cheerful paintwork and the pictures on the wall, it was a considerable improvement on the canteen at the match factory.

'There is no prearranged seating,' Miss Dobbs told them. 'You may, therefore, sit wherever you wish.'

What Annie Clarke wished was to sit as far as possible from the girl – what was her name again? Miss Benson – who'd heard her tell all those lies about her family. While most of the trainees chose to congregate near the door, Annie made her way to the far end of the room and squeezed herself into a corner. Let the others think she was standoffish – she didn't care as long as it kept the Benson girl away from her.

The Benson girl looked around the room, spotted Annie and made a beeline for her.

'The company will provide you with a free luncheon today,' Miss Dobbs told the trainees, 'but as from tomorrow, you will be expected to pay what I think you will find is a very modest price.'

The Benson girl sat down in the seat right next to Annie's.

Why's she doin' this? Annie wondered.

'You must decide between you each day what joint of meat you would like to eat the following day, and the kitchen will order it,' Miss Dobbs continued.

If only she'd chosen a seat next to some of the other trainees, she could have ignored Miss Benson, Annie realised. But that was impossible with the two of them trapped together in the corner.

'Or, if you prefer it that way, you may bring in your own chop and the cook will prepare it for you,' Miss Dobbs said. 'And now, young ladies, I will take my leave of you. Enjoy your meals, and perhaps use this opportunity to get to know your neighbours.'

'Why did she have to go and say that?' Annie thought. 'Why couldn't she have told us we had to eat in silence, like they used to do in school?'

Maybe they could get through the whole meal without

talking. After all, Miss Dobbs hadn't actually said they'd *got* to speak to each other, had she?

'My first name's Belinda,' Miss Benson said, holding out her hand. 'What's yours?'

There was no way out of it, Annie decided. 'Annie,' she said, shaking the other girl's hand.

'I'm so pleased to meet you again, Annie,' Belinda replied. 'I say, that was quite a stroke you pulled at the interview, wasn't it?'

'Quite a stroke? I'm not sure I know what you mean.'

Belinda laughed. 'All that cock-and-bull about having your own personal maid. Your father isn't really rich, is he?'

'No,' Annie admitted. 'My father's – my *dad's* – a stevedore at St. Katherine's Docks.'

'How splendid!' Belinda said. She laughed again, in a rich, throaty way.

'There's nothing to be *ashamed* of in being a docker,' Annie said, 'but I can't see what's so splendid about it, either.'

Belinda shook her head. 'No, I didn't mean that,' she said. 'I mean, how splendid of *you* to bamboozle all those stuck-up little bourgeoises at the interview.'

'Do you really think so?' Annie asked, taking it as a compliment although she was not at all sure what *bourgeoises* meant.

'Yes, I really do think so,' Belinda said, 'and after you'd left, I carried on your good work.'

'How d'you mean?'

'I told them your uncle was probably one of the directors of the company.'

Annie giggled. 'Yer never did!'

'Trust me, dear girl – a Benson never lies when there's more fun to be had in telling the truth. That's practically our family motto, you know.'

'Is it?' Annie asked, thinking that she had never met anyone quite like Belinda Benson before.

Belinda glanced up at the table where the rest of the girls were sitting. 'Listen,' she said, 'I'm looking for a chum, and most of this lot seem as stuffy as the ones we were interviewed with. So would you care to apply for the position yourself, by any chance?'

'Would I what?'

'Care to apply for the position. It's sort of like being lady's companion, except that you don't get paid for it.'

'If you put it like that, I don't see how I can turn down the chance,' Annie said with a smile.

When Colleen heard the knock at the front door, her eyes went straight to the gin bottle, and it was not until it was safely hidden that she made her way shakily up the passage to see who'd come calling on her.

She was surprised to find Lil Clarke standing there, because this was the time of day when Lil usually gave her front parlour a thorough – and totally unnecessary – cleaning. And she was even more surprised when Lil, instead of saying what she'd come about, squeezed past her and headed resolutely for the kitchen. Still, once Lil *was* in, there was little that Colleen could do but to totter tipsily after her.

By the time Colleen had reached her kitchen, Lil was already sitting down and looking around her.

'Where d'yer 'ide it?' Lil asked.

'I beg your pardon?'

'Where d'yer 'ide the gin? I'd say that since this ain't washin' day, yer've probably 'id it in yer copper.'

Colleen gasped. 'How did you know?' she asked.

'It's an obvious 'idin' place.'

'I didn't mean that.'

'I know yer didn't. Yer meant 'ow did I know about yer secret drinkin'? Well, there's no such thing as secret drinkin' with gin – I could smell it on yer breath the minute yer opened the door.'

'Would you . . . would you like a drop of it yourself?' Colleen asked nervously.

Lil shook her head. 'Gin ain't the answer for me,' she said. 'An' it ain't the answer for you neither.'

In all the months they had been neighbours, Lil had never spoken to her like this – and Colleen felt her hackles rising.

'Now listen to me, Lil . . .' she said.

'No, *you* listen to *me*,' Lil replied firmly. 'An' yer might as well sit down while yer doin' it, because if yer don't, I'm goin' to 'ave to stand up again, an' these old pegs o' mine can't take the weight of a long talk these days.'

'So we're goin' to have a long talk, are we?' Colleen said. There was defiance in her voice, but even as she spoke she was lowering herself carefully onto one of the kitchen chairs. 'An' just exactly what are we goin' to talk *about*?'

'I was startin' to get the picture without anybody 'avin' to tell me anyfink,' Lil said, 'but then yesterday your George came round to see me an' . . .'

'He had no right to do that!' Colleen exclaimed, feeling her anger bubbling up again.

' 'E only did it 'cos he worries about yer,' Lil said. 'An' 'cos 'e loves yer.'

Colleen had been holding all her feelings inside her for a long time, but now she felt them start to spill out.

'I know he loves me,' she sobbed. 'I love him an' all. An' I treat him so badly, what with drinkin' all the time, an' keepin' him out of his own bedroom . . .'

Lil reached across the table and gently stroked the crying woman's hair. 'If yer know it's wrong, then why do yer keep doin' it to 'im?' she asked.

'Because I'm so desperately unhappy,' Colleen said. 'Because I know he really wants to have children an' I can't give him any.'

'It's too early to say that for sure.'

'We've been married goin' on for two years. Isn't that long enough to be sure?'

'Let me tell yer me own story, will yer?' Lil asked.

'All right,' Colleen agreed.

'They say it's always more difficult gettin' pregnant the first time, but it wasn't for me. I didn't plan on 'avin' Annie at all. Why, Sam an' me wasn't even married at the time.'

Colleen looked up, astonished. Could it really be Lil – a woman who put respectability next to godliness – telling her this?

'You weren't married?' she asked, just to check that she hadn't misheard.

'No, well, Sam was in the army, you see,' Lil explained awkwardly. 'An' he knew 'e was goin' overseas, but 'e didn't know when. So I thought to meself, "Gal, yer love 'im an' 'e might never come back. Do yer want to let 'im go without knowin' what it would be like to be in 'is arms in bed?" '

'An' so you let him have what he wanted,' Colleen said.

'What we *both* wanted,' Lil corrected her. 'Just the once – but it was enough. Anyway, I 'ad our Annie while 'e was away, an' 'e'd not been back five minutes before I was carryin' our Eddie. We 'adn't planned that, neither.'

'It's so easy for you,' Colleen said bitterly.

' 'Ang on till I've finished me story,' Lil told her. 'After I 'ad Eddie, I knew Sam wanted another gal, so I said to meself, "Right, we'll 'ave her soon, so that she can grow up with 'er brother." Well, a year went by an' nuffink 'appened, so I went to the chemist's an' got some stuff that was supp'sed to give yer a kiddie if yer 'usband so much as looked at yer. Well, I took it till I was nearly livin' off the stuff, but that didn't make no difference neither. So in the end, I just gave up.'

'But what about your Peggy?'

'That's just it, gal. As soon as I'd give up 'ope – as soon as I stopped forcin' all them rabbit glands into meself – I got pregnant with our Peggy.'

'So what's your point?'

'Me point is that there's such a thing as tryin' too 'ard. An' it might be all that tryin' that's puttin' the kibosh on it for yer. George is a good, lovin' 'usband to you an' he can . . .' Lil hesitated. ' 'E can . . . what I mean is, when yer upstairs, the both of yer together . . . when 'e's . . . when yer . . .'

In spite of her deep misery, Colleen couldn't help being amused at her neighbour's discomfort. 'When he's . . . when I . . . what?' she asked.

'When 'e's finished doin' what men do, 'e's not the only one that's left feelin' 'appy, is 'e?'

198

'No,' Colleen admitted. 'He's not the only one that's left feelin' happy.'

'Then stop worryin' for the moment about what yer want an' start enjoyin' what yer've got,' Lil advised her. 'An' if after a couple of years yer still don't 'ave a bun in the oven, I'll take yer down to the chemist's meself an' see if them rabbit glands are any more use to you than they was to me.'

Colleen smiled sadly. 'You're a good neighbour, Lil,' she said.

'Bugger bein' a good neighbour,' Lil told her. 'It's not gratitude I'm after – I want to 'elp yer solve yer problems as I know yer'd 'elp me. So will yer do as I ask yer?'

'I'll try,' Colleen promised.

'Yes, well, in the end I supp'se that's all any of us can do,' Lil said philosophically.

It was getting towards the worst time of year for the river policemen – a time of year when a freezing wind could blow from the north-east for hours on end, and rain pelt down mercilessly on the duty boats for shift after shift. Even the toe bags – waterproof sacks with a warm inner lining which the oarsmen put their legs into and then pulled up to their waists – did little for the Wet Bobs when there was weather like that.

'Still, whatever the conditions, the river still 'as to be patrolled,' Harry Roberts thought as he pulled hard on his oar and watched the Tower of London glide past.

He found his mind turning to Annie Clarke, as it often seemed to these days. He'd been seeing her for over six months, and he was getting nowhere with her. Not that he could blame the girl herself. She wasn't a tease like some he'd known. She'd made it quite plain that she didn't want to get romantically involved with anybody – and she'd been as good as her word.

He should give her up, he told himself. But it wasn't that easy. For a start, she was the prettiest girl he'd seen in a long time – and the best company. So apart from the fact that she wouldn't let him kiss and cuddle her, she really was the ideal companion for the little outings they went on together.

Yet it was more complicated than just that. He felt protective towards her – didn't want to see her end up in the clutches of a hooligan like Tom Bates. And, if he was honest with himself, he had to admit that even if the other man had been of shining character, his pride would still not have allowed him to see Tom succeed where he had failed – at least, not without a fight.

The boat was drawing level with Customs House Stairs when Harry noticed the young girl standing at the top of the steps.

'Let's go in closer to the bank,' he said to Jack Davies.

'Spotted somefink I've missed again, 'ave yer, 'Arry?' Jack asked, shaking his head in admiration.

'Maybe I 'ave, an' maybe I 'aven't,' Harry replied. 'I can't be sure until I get a better look.'

He thought he recognised the girl, but what would *she* be doing on Customs House Stairs? And though he didn't know her mother that well, he was sure Lil Clarke would never have allowed her daughter to go out on a day like this without a proper overcoat.

Peggy's latest mark was the captain of a steamer anchored just off Galley Dock. He didn't seem to speak much English, but that could be an advantage if you knew how to handle it right.

'. . . an' me dad just can't work no more, yer see, so we 'ave to keep sellin' all our cloves if we want to put food on the table,' she explained slowly and clearly.

'I deed not realize zer was such terrible poverty in England,' the captain said sympathetically. 'Are zer not places – poor 'ouses I sink zey are called – where your familee could go?'

'They won't 'ave us,' Peggy said artfully. 'It's not like where you come from, yer see. Over 'ere, they don't give tuppence fer the poor an' starvin'.'

From behind, a hand clamped, gently but firmly, on her right shoulder.

The Law! It had to be the Law!

Peggy felt her knees turn to water. She wanted to turn round – but she didn't dare to.

The foreign captain was looking quizzically over her head at whoever was standing behind her.

'It's all right, sir,' said a man's voice. 'I'll handle things from here on.'

'But zis little girl was telling me she was starving,' the captain said. 'She 'as zeese pawn tickets and . . .'

'The pawn tickets are fakes, sir. And as for the little girl, her family might not 'ave that much, but she's never short of an 'ot meal before she goes to bed.'

'I see,' the captain said. He gave Peggy a reproachful look. 'You are not a nice little girl at all,' he told her, and then he walked quickly away.

Peggy glanced desperately at where Pedro had been lurking only a few seconds earlier, but there was no sign of him now. So he'd deserted her, she thought bitterly – left her to face the consequences alone!

She felt the hand on her shoulder begin to turn her around, and had no power to resist it. She looked up and stared into the face of the sandy-haired man who, in his turn, was staring gravely down at her.

' 'Ello, Mr Roberts,' she said, her lip beginning to quiver.

The Clarkes' kitchen had the air of a courtroom about it. Lil, sitting at one end of the table, was displaying all the ferocity of a prosecuting counsel, while Sam, at the other end, looked as if he had not yet made up his mind whether he was the judge or defence attorney. The accused – Peggy – stood against the wall, staring down at her boots and sniffing occasionally.

'Beggin' outside the Customs House,' Lil stormed. 'Worse than beggin'. "Usin' false pretences" was what Constable Roberts called it. That's the same as stealin', that is.'

'I'm sorry, Mum,' Peggy said.

'Sorry ain't good enough. What you deserve – an' what

yer goin' to get – is a bloody good thrashin'. Ain't that right, Sam?' Lil said, appealing to her husband for support.

Sam shook his head. 'I've never taken me belt to any of me other kids,' he told her, 'an' I ain't about to start now with Peggy.'

'Yer've never taken yer belt to the others 'cos yer've never 'ad to,' Lil argued. 'Look at Annie – learnin' to be a telephonist an' goin' out with a nice young man who'll probably end up as a Chief Inspector one day. Look at Eddie – an apprentice mechanical engineer. An' then look at this one – little better than a common criminal.' She rounded on Peggy. 'Yer do realise, don't yer, that if it 'ad been any other policeman but Constable Roberts who'd found yer, yer'd 'ave been in clink by now?'

'Yes, Mum,' Peggy said – and sniffed again.

Lil turned back to her husband. Sam's face was a perfect picture of anguish, and she knew whatever punishment was inflicted on Peggy, it would probably hurt him just as much as it hurt the child. Still, it had to be done.

'All right, so yer too soft to give 'er a thrashin',' she said, although she knew that, for all her talk, she herself would never have allowed Peggy to be beaten, 'but yer do agree she's got to be punished for what's she's done, don't yer?'

Sam nodded sadly. 'We've been poor at times, Peggy,' he told his daughter, 'but we've never stole to get what we wanted.'

'I know, Dad.'

'For the next six months, yer to come straight back from school every day – and once you *are* 'ome, yer'll *stay* 'ome. There'll be no goin' out on the weekend, neither.'

Sam glanced at his wife, who nodded briefly.

'An' yer not to see that Pedro again – little 'ooligan that 'e is,' Lil told her daughter.

'I don't *want* to see 'im again,' Peggy said. 'I thought 'e was me friend, but the minute there was any trouble, 'e run off an' left me. That ain't 'ow friends be'ave.'

'Well, at least yer've learned *somefink* from this sorry business,' Lil said.

Peggy looked up. Her eyes were red and her chin was

quivering slightly. 'I know I deserve me punishment, honest I do,' she said. 'An' I don't mind stayin' in the 'ouse for an 'ole year if yer want me to. But can I buy me goat now I've got the money?'

'No, you can *not* buy yer goat!' Lil exploded. 'That money ain't yours to spend, 'cos yer got it by lyin' an' cheatin'.' A sudden thought struck yer. ' 'Ow much 'ave yer got, anyway?'

'Twenty-three an' sixpence 'apenny.'

'Twenty-three an' sixpence 'apenny!' Lil repeated, thoroughly scandalised. 'That's nearly as much as yer dad earns for a week of 'ard, 'onest work. When I think of all the lies yer must 'ave told to collect twenty-three an' sixpence 'apenny, I could die of shame, I swear I could!'

'It's not like I could give it back, is it, Mum?' Peggy argued. 'I got a penny 'ere, an' a tanner there. I'd never be able to find all the people what gave it to me. So couldn't I buy me goat with it instead?'

'Yer might not be able to give it back, but yer can't keep it, either,' Sam said.

'So what *can* I do with it?'

'Yer'll 'ave to give it away to charity.'

'But Dad . . .' Peggy protested, the tears flowing down her cheeks now.

'An' that's the last word I'm prepared to 'ear on the subject,' Sam said firmly.

Peggy gave her boots another short inspection, then said, 'Dad . . .?'

'I've warned yer, Peggy,' Sam told her.

'I wasn't goin' to argue no more,' his daughter said. 'I just wondered what charity yer was goin' to give me money to.'

'I 'aven't really thought about it yet,' Sam admitted.

'Well . . . could I choose it?'

Sam looked questioningly at his wife.

'I can't see any 'arm in that,' Lil conceded.

'So I can choose?' Peggy asked.

'Yes, yer can choose,' Sam said.

Peggy wiped her eyes with the back of her hand. She was beginning to look much more cheerful.

'So 'oo are yer goin' to give the money to?' Lil asked, intrigued to discover what had brought about her daughter's sudden change of mood.

'The Battersea Dogs' Ome o' course!' Peggy said.

When Annie arrived home, bursting to talk about her first day at the telephone school – and especially about Belinda Benson – she found her mother still sitting at the kitchen table and staring down at the knot-holes in the wood.

'Whatever's the matter, Mum?' she asked.

'Yer sister's been arrested,' Lil said glumly.

'Arrested!' Annie exclaimed. 'What for? And where is she now?'

'She's upstairs in 'er bed,' Lil replied, as if it were a silly question. 'Where else would yer expect 'er to be at this time o' night?'

With a sigh, Annie sat down opposite her mother. Talk of her own day would clearly have to wait until she'd heard the full story of Peggy's.

'Start at the beginnin', Mum,' she said. 'An' if yer can, do try to stick to the point.'

Lil told her everything that Peggy had confessed, from the day on Hampstead Heath when she'd met Pedro right up to the moment of her "arrest". 'An' if it 'adn't been for Constable Roberts, yer sister would 'ave landed 'erself in really serious trouble,' she said as she reached the end of her tale.

'Yes, I suppose she would,' Annie admitted.

' 'E brought her all the way 'ome 'imself,' Lil pressed.

'That was kind of him,' Annie said cautiously.

'There's not many men would 'ave gone to so much trouble,' Lil pointed out.

'I expect it's because he knows the family,' Annie said.

Lil laughed for the first time since she'd learned about her younger daughter's criminal activities. 'Because 'e knows the family!' she said. 'Get off with yer, Annie Clarke! It's because 'e knows *you* 'e did it. Because 'e's ever so sweet on yer.'

'I never asked him to be sweet on me,' Annie said, wishing she could change the subject.

'Course yer never asked,' her mother agreed. 'Yer never do ask for things like that – yer just grateful when they 'appen.'

'I've only just started me training.'

'So what are yer saying? That yer can't afford to get serious with a bloke, because 'e'd want to get married and then yer'd 'ave to give up yer job?'

'Something like that.'

Lil beamed with pleasure. 'Well, that's just where yer've landed on yer feet, ain't it?' she told her daughter.

'How do you mean?'

'From what I've seen of 'Arry Roberts, I'm pretty sure 'e'd wait for yer for a few years if 'e 'ad to. An' when yer did decide to settle down, well, police constables can earn up to thirty-three an' six a week these days.'

'How do you happen to know that?' Annie asked.

'I . . . er . . . looked into it. Anyway, 'ow I found out is neither 'ere nor there. Thirty-three an' six is a very good wage for any man, an' from what I've 'eard about 'Arry, 'e'll be gettin' 'imself a promotion before long.'

'He *is* a very nice bloke,' Annie admitted, 'but . . .'

Lil's eyes narrowed with suspicion. 'But what?' she asked.

'I don't love him, Mum,' Annie said, beginning to feel like an animal caught in a trap. 'I'm sure I don't.'

' 'Ow can yer be sure of anyfink like that at your age?' Lil said. 'Love ain't all violins an' roses, yer know? Yer can't expect yer 'eart to pound an' yer 'ead ter swim all the time.'

'They do when I'm with T . . .' Annie said. She stopped – but was too late.

'When yer with *'oo*?' Lil demanded.

'Forget it, Mum,' Annie said.

'No, I ain't goin' to forget it,' her mother said angrily. 'Yer were goin' to say, "They do when I'm with Tom Bates." Wasn't yer?'

'Yes,' Annie confessed.

'I don't understand yer at all,' Lil said. 'Yer 'ave a chance of a fine young man like 'Arry Roberts, an' yer've got the nerve to tell me yer might be fallin' for an 'ooligan like Tom Bates.'

'Mum . . .' Annie pleaded.

But Lil was not to be silenced.

'Well, I'll tell yer this much for nuffink, Annie Clarke,' she continued. ' 'Arry will always be welcome in the 'ouse, but there's no place 'ere for Tom Bates.'

'And what about me?' Annie said, starting to get angry herself now.

' 'Ow d'yer mean?' asked Lil, who seemed to be coming off the boil just as her daughter was heating up.

'What if I got serious enough about Tom to think of getting married to him?'

'I'm tired,' Lil said evasively. 'It's been a very upsettin' day for me.'

'Answer me, Mum,' Annie insisted.

'If you disgrace the family by marryin' Tom Bates, then there wouldn't be no place for you in this 'ouse, either,' Lil said.

CHAPTER TWELVE

Joey Bates had just reached the end of Lant Street when the big double doors of the fire station flew open and a fire engine, its bell ringing furiously, was pulled into the road by two strong horses.

'Bloody marvellous!' Joey gasped, as the driver skilfully guided his horses through a tight half-circle turn so that they were facing the river. 'Bloody incredible!'

He gaped at the firemen on the back of the engine – big, confident blokes which shiny helmets and axes in their belts. One of them, he saw, was Fred Simpson, the bloke his sister Mary was always eyein' up.

The fire engine set off down Southwark Bridge Road at a gallop, its bell ringing even louder now. Joey watched it go and imagined what it would be like to be a fireman – to charge around the streets of London and to risk your life runnin' into burnin' buildings to rescue people trapped inside. Now that was where *real* excitement lay, he thought – not in breakin' windows or sneakin' up be'ind people and knockin' 'em senseless like the 'ooligans did.

As Joey reached Lant Place, he saw two young men lounging under the nearest lamppost. One of them was thin, with cunning eyes, the other huge and stupid-looking.

'Oh Gawd – it's Blackie an' Chas!' he said to himself.

If the hooligans had been further up the street, Joey

would have turned round and made a run for it – but as they were so close he could almost touch them, he had no choice but to carry on sauntering up the street.

'Watcha, Chas! 'Ow yer doin', Blackie?' he said in the chirpy style that the Newington Hooligans affected.

' 'Ow are *you* doin'?' Blackie responded. 'We ain't seen much of yer, lately. 'Ave yer been sick or somefink?'

'No, I've just been busy,' Joey said – because it was considered bad form among the Hooligans ever to admit to feeling ill.

'So yer fightin' fit, are yer?' Blackie asked slyly.

'Never felt better,' Joey said.

'That's good – 'cos Rollo's got a bit 'o work he wants yer do to tonight.'

Joey felt his stomach churn. 'Tonight!' he gasped. 'Why didn't yer tell me about it before now?'

'The job's only just come up,' Blackie said. 'Anyway, why *should* I 'ave told yer before?'

'To . . . to give me time to get ready for it,' Joey stuttered.

Blackie chuckled. 'Time to get ready? Why d'yer need time to get ready? All yer 'ave to do is sneak up be'ind a bloke an' crack 'im over the bonce with yer cosh. Ain't that right, Chas?'

He should have told his brother Tom about the mess he'd got himself into, Joey thought desperately. He should have told him long ago! And he had been meaning to do it – honest he had – yet somehow, whenever he had the chance, he could never bring himself to say the words.

And now it was too late!

'We'd better get goin',' Blackie said. 'We got to meet Rollo in Tooley Street in 'alf an hour.'

'The job's in Tooley Street?'

'That's right.'

'But that's where we – where *you* – did the last one,' Joey pointed out.

'So what?' Blackie asked.

So the whole thing felt wrong – very wrong. 'I've just got to go 'ome for a minute,' Joey said.

'Go 'ome? What for?'

'To see me mum.'

'Why? 'Ave yer got to get yer ole lady's say-so before yer can go out an' crack somebody over the 'ead?' Blackie asked with a sneer on his face.

Joey forced himself to laugh. 'No, it's nuffink like that. I've got . . . I've got a message to deliver. An important message from one of 'er customers.'

Blackie looked at him suspiciously. 'Is there any back way out of yer 'ouse?' he asked.

'No,' Joey said.

'All right,' Blackie said. 'Yer can go 'ome an' give yer old lady 'er message, but if yer not back in five minutes, we'll be comin' in after yer.'

Joey lifted the latch and stepped into the hallway.

'Is that you, Joey?' his mother called from her front parlour-workshop.

'Yes, it's me,' Joey said. 'Is our Tom 'ome yet?'

'Course 'e ain't,' May replied. 'There's a lot o' shippin' in the Pool today, an' 'e's makin' 'is money while 'e can.'

'So when are yer expectin' 'im?'

'I've no idea. 'E could be 'ere in 'alf an hour, or 'e might not turn up till midnight.'

Why had Tom chosen that night – of all nights – to be workin' late, Joey wondered. He tried to think about what he should do next, but it was hard to come up with a plan when your heart was beating nineteen to the dozen and you were breaking out into a cold sweat.

He couldn't stay in the house, that was certain, because if he did Blackie and Chas would come in after him – and then his mum would know all about it.

He couldn't climb over the back wall and persuade the neighbours on the other side to let him out of their front door, either – that would be leaving his mum to the Hooligan's mercy.

A note! He would leave a note for Tom! With trembling hands, he rummaged through the drawers of the kitchen dresser and found a piece of paper and a pencil.

209

Dere Tom, he wrote, *I am in big trouble with the Newington Ooligans. They want me to do a job for em on Tooley Street tonite an i avent got the guts to tell em no. Please help me.*

Joey

He looked at the note, wishing he could say more, but knowing there wasn't time.

'An' what do I do with the bloody thing now I've wrote it?' he asked himself.

He couldn't give it to his mum, that was dead cert. He'd have to leave it somewhere in the house and hope that Tom found it. He ran quickly upstairs to the room he shared with his brother and laid the note on Tom's pillow.

'See it, Tom!' he prayed. 'Please see it.'

He had rushed up the stairs to leave the note, but he came down them again at a snail's pace, taking each reluctant step as if his legs were made of lead.

At the front door he stopped and looked longingly at the parlour where his mum was still working. He would have given anything to be able to go in there and give her a hug, like he'd done when he was younger – but how could he do that now without her guessing that something was wrong?

'I'm goin' out, mum,' he said.

'What about yer supper?' his mother asked. 'I've got yer some nice neck of lamb.'

'Keep it warm for me,' Joey said. 'I won't be long.'

And then, before his mother had a chance to say anything else, he flung the door open and rushed out into the street.

The cart stopped in front of Number Thirty-six, and George climbed down.

'Usual time in the mornin', Mr Taylor?' the carman asked as he was about to pull off again.

'Usual time,' George agreed.

What a bloody life it really was, he thought to himself, as he took his latch key from his pocket. Out all day graftin' in the wood yard, and then home again to an empty house. Still, sometimes he was glad to find the house empty, because when Colleen *was* there, and had one of her black moods on her . . .

He was just lifting his key to the lock when the door opened and, to his surprise, he saw a smiling Colleen standing there.

'Aren't you supposed to be down at The Goldsmiths' by this time?' he said.

'I asked the gaffer if I could take the day off, an' he said yes,' Colleen replied.

Asked the gaffer if she could take the day off? George thought, as he followed his wife down the passage. Was that what had really happened – or had it been more the case that, seeing the state she'd turned up for work in, the landlord had decided it would be best to send her home?

'I haven't touched a drop all day, if that's what you're thinkin',' Colleen said, reading his mind.

'I didn't . . . I wasn't . . .' George said, doing his best to cover his confusion.

'I can't blame you for jumpin' to that conclusion,' Colleen told him. 'There've been days lately when I've hardly been able to stand.'

This was a change – for Colleen to admit that she was drinking heavily. Normally, when *he* brought the subject up, she'd fly into a rage and accuse him of persecuting her just because she took the occasional nip.

George pushed the parlour door open, and instead of the sticks and rolled-up newspaper which usually greeted him in the hearth, there was a blazing fire.

'Let me take your crutch off you and help you into your chair,' Colleen said.

'Thanks,' George answered, because although he didn't really need the help, it made him feel good that Colleen was offering it.

She took the crutch and he steadied himself on her shoulder. How long had it been since they'd got so close to each other, he wondered. It felt like months.

Colleen sat down in the chair opposite his, and smiled uncertainly at him. 'How were things in the wood yard today?' she asked.

'Same as they always are,' George replied. 'Would you mind tellin' me what this is all about, Collie?'

'What's what all about?' Colleen replied.

George shrugged. 'You takin' the day off work an' waitin' at the door for me. The fire blazin' away an' . . .'

'An' the fact that I've not been drinkin'?' Colleen asked.

'That an' all,' George admitted.

'Do you remember what it was like when we first got married, George?' Colleen asked. 'You'd be in your chair an' I'd come to you an' sit at your feet . . .' She stood up, walked across the room and then knelt on the floor, resting her head against his good leg. 'It's nice this, isn't it?' she said.

'Yes, it is,' George agreed, but at the same time he couldn't help wondering how long it would last – how long it would be before Colleen went into one of her depressions and started searching for the gin bottle.

Colleen tilted her head and looked up at him. 'What would you like me to make for your supper?' she asked.

'I don't mind,' George said, stroking her hair and wishing things could always be as they were now.

'But if I gave you the choice – if you could have anythin' in the world you wanted – what would it be?' Colleen persisted.

George thought about it for some time. 'Leg of pork,' he said finally.

'On its own?' Colleen asked playfully.

'No,' George said. 'I'd like it with apple sauce, roast potatoes, carrots an' swedes.'

'It'll be fifteen minutes,' Colleen said, getting to her feet. 'Can you wait that long?'

'Fifteen minutes! But you can't whip up a feast like that in fifteen minutes.'

'I can if the pork's already in the oven – an' it is,' Colleen told him from the doorway, 'an' if the vegetables are already half-cooked – which they are.'

'What's goin' on?' George asked.

'I just wanted to give me husband a decent meal for a change,' Colleen told him. 'An' afterwards . . .'

'An' afterwards, what?' George said.

'An' afterwards, I thought we might have an early night for once,' Colleen replied.

★

Tooley Street was shrouded in fog again, as it so often was during the winter months.

'A perfec' night for pullin' a job, ain't it?' Rollo said to the others, as they all stood in a circle halfway down the alley.

'Perfec',' Blackie agreed.

'Just the number,' Chas chimed in.

'What about you, Joe?' Rollo asked, looking right into Joey's eyes. 'Don't you think it's a perfec' night for it?'

'Yes,' Joey said weakly.

How much time had passed, he wondered, since he'd first spotted Blackie and Chas loitering at the corner of Lant Place? An hour? An hour and a half? However long or short the time, it felt to him like an eternity.

'We'll be doin' things a bit diff'rent tonight, young shaver,' Rollo told him.

'Diff'rent?' Joey said, his feeling of doom mounting with every second that passed. ' 'Ow do yer mean – diff'rent?'

'Last time there was three of us – Blackie blockin' the wharfinger's way, Chas takin' 'is tifter off an' me givin' 'im the wallopin'. Yer remember that, don't yer?'

'Yes, I remember,' Joey said.

'Well, tonight there's going to be just you,' Rollo told him.

'But I can't do it all by meself,' Joey protested.

'Course you can. I'll grant yer, it's easier with three, but we don't want to make it easier, do we? 'Cos this is yer test – this is the night yer prove yerself to us.'

'No, it ain't,' said a voice from the other end of the alley. 'It's the night yer plan to shop 'im to the bobbies.'

The gang spun round in the direction of the voice and saw a black shape in the fog.

'Who the bleedin' 'ell are you?' Rollo demanded.

But Joey already knew who he was – and his heart leaped.

The black shape began to move closer towards them, and soon they could all recognise it.

'You tell me little brother 'e's got to do a job, but yer've already tipped the wink to the coppers, so they're swarmin' all over the place, an' the minute Joey tries anythin', they nab 'im,' Tom said. 'That *was* yer plan, wasn't it, Rollo?'

'Yes,' Rollo admitted, 'that was me plan.'

'An' all so yer could get yer revenge on me.'

'I bleedin' 'ate yer, Tom Bates, an' I'd rather see you 'urt than 'ave an 'undred pound in me pocket.'

'But yer plan ain't goin' to work, is it?' Tom asked. 'Not now I'm 'ere.'

'No,' Rollo agreed, 'but this is much better, ain't it? Yer've got no Borough Gang be'ind yer now, an' no crowd on 'Ampstead 'Eath to come an' help yer. There's just us an' you – an' yer goin' to get the beatin' of yer life, Tom Bates.'

'Just you an' me,' Tom suggested. 'Man to man – like it's s'pposed to be?'

'Mam to man!' Rollo sneered. 'Yer must think I'm cracked or somefink.'

'You can use yer cosh an' I'll fight with me bare 'ands,' Tom told him.

'It's very kind of yer to make the offer,' Rollo said, 'but yer see, I don't need to make no deals with you, 'cos I've got yer just where I want yer.'

Rollo put his hand in his pocket and pulled out his cosh. At almost the same moment, Chas produced an iron bar from up his sleeve and Blackie began to unbuckle his belt.

'Leave 'im alone,' Joey screamed. 'If yer want to 'urt anybody, 'urt me.'

'Get lost, yer little pipsqueak!' Rollo said contemptuously.

In a blind rage, Joey flung himself at Rollo, wanting to maim him, kill him – do anything, at whatever cost to himself, as long as it would protect his older brother.

It was a heroic effort – but a wasted one. Rollo lashed out with his big fist and Joey experienced first an agonising pain in his mouth and then another in his back as he was slammed against the wall. He tried with all his remaining strength to stay upright – to launch himself at Rollo for a second time – but his legs buckled beneath him and he fell to the ground.

By the time Joey managed to raise his head again, Rollo

and his pals were no longer near him, but were advancing slowly up the alley towards Tom. And Tom was just standing there – waiting for them.

Chas and Blackie went in first, big Chas wielding his iron bar above his head, and Blackie slashing the air with his belt. Tom punched Chas on the jaw with his right hand, while with his left he grabbed the belt and jerked Blackie forward onto his waiting raised knee.

Joey saw both the hooligans go down. But they wouldn't stay down, he knew that – and besides, Rollo was moving to take their place. Joey raised himself painfully to his feet and began to hobble towards his brother.

Rollo caught Tom a hard blow on the right arm with his cosh, but Tom's left fist buried itself in Rollo's stomach, and the hooligan sank to his knees. Tom spun round to face Chas and Blackie – who were already starting to get up – and saw his brother.

'Run for it, Joey!' he shouted.

'I can't just . . . leave yer 'ere,' Joey gasped, still fighting painfully for breath.

'It won't do no good to 'ave both of us gettin' beat up,' Tom said, lashing out with his foot and knocking Chas to the ground again.

'But . . . but I'm yer brother,' Joey protested.

'Think of our mum,' Tom said, grabbing Blackie and swinging him against the wall. 'She don't want to 'ave two sons in trouble. Spare 'er that, at least.'

Rollo was starting to get his wind back, and Chas was standing midway between Joey and Tom, waiting to attack whichever of them came closest to him first.

'Let me stay with yer,' Joey pleaded. 'Let me stay with yer an' fight by yer side.'

'Bugger off!' Tom ordered him. 'Bugger off now, or I'll never forgive yer.'

Joey turned round and headed for the end of the alley. Walking was painful at first, but then it got easier, and by the time he drew level with Battle Bridge Stairs, he was running.

And he needed to run, he thought. He needed to get away as fast as he could.

What was it Tom had said?

Think of our mum. She don't want to 'ave two sons in trouble.

Well, she'd have one son in trouble, there was no doubt about that – because before he was even fifty yards clear of the fight, Joey heard police whistles cutting their way through the fog and the sound of pounding feet heading for the alley.

' 'Ere yer are,' Lil said, sliding a cup of bedtime cocoa across the kitchen table to her elder daughter.

'Thanks, Mum,' Annie said.

They were both doing their best to sound friendly, but relations between them had been distinctly frosty since Lil had issued her ultimatum about Tom.

Annie was just about to take a sip of her cocoa when there was the sound of loud banging on the front door.

'Gawd! Whoever could that be at this time 'o night?' Lil asked worriedly.

'It's a bit early for Santa Claus,' Annie said. 'An' anyway, doesn't he usually come down the chimney?'

The banging started up again, even louder and more insistent this time.

'I'll thank you not to make jokes about it,' Lil told her daughter. 'It ain't funny! I don't like it, an' I wish yer dad wasn't workin' a ghost down at the docks tonight.'

'Well, seeing as he is, I'll go and answer it – before whoever's out there knocks the door down,' Annie said.

'Take the poker with yer, then,' Lil advised her.

'Don't talk daft, Mum,' Annie said. 'This is Lant Place, not Pentonville. Besides, if somebody was out to hurt us, do you think they'd wake up half the street first?'

'Yer prob'ly right,' Lil admitted. 'But I still don't like it. Respectable people don't go round knockin' on other respectable people's doors when most respectable people are gettin' ready for bed.'

Annie made her way up the hall – conscious that her mother was hovering behind her with the poker in her hand – and opened the front door to find Joey Bates standing there.

The boy was obviously in a state. He looked scared and pale, and his lips had started to swell up – but most disturbing of all was the pleading look in his eyes.

'Is it me you want to see?' she asked.

'Yes,' Joey gasped, as if she were the answer to a prayer.

Annie turned round to her mother. 'You can go back to the kitchen and finish your cocoa, Mum,' she said.

'Who is it?' Lil asked.

'It's nobody for you to worry about.'

Lil stood on tiptoe so she could look past Annie and out into the street. 'It's one o' the Bates kids,' she said. 'It's the brother of that 'ooligan Tom.'

'I know who he is, Mum,' Annie replied, turning round and ushering her mother back down the passage.

'An' 'e's been fightin',' Lil said. 'Yer've only got ter look at his face to see that.'

'I know that as well, Mum.'

'Well, I don't want him standin' on my front doorstep. Not at this time o' night! Not with a face like that!'

'I'll get rid of him, then,' Annie said. 'Only it'd be much easier to do if you weren't standing there. So why don't you go back to the kitchen and leave it all up to me?'

'All right,' Lil agreed reluctantly. 'But I told yer it couldn't be nobody respectable.'

Annie waited until Lil had closed the kitchen door behind her, then went back to the front step and said, 'What's brought you round here at this time of the night, Joey?'

'They've arrested our Tom', Joey said. 'They've got 'im down at the police station right now.'

A wave of giddiness swept over Annie, but she fought it back because she knew that now was the worst possible time for her to lose her head.

'What's he done?' she asked.

'Nuffink.'

'He must have done *something*. The police don't go around arresting people without a reason.'

' '*E* ain't done nuffink,' Joey insisted. 'I was the one what was in trouble. All 'e did was try an' get me out of it.'

'I think you'd better tell me the full story,' Annie said.

And Joey did – from the moment he'd first seen Rollo and his gang at Hampstead Heath right up until the second Tom had made him run away.

'If you weren't there till the end, how can you be so sure he's in gaol?' Annie asked, nursing a faint hope that Tom might have found some way to escape.

'I went back after it was all over,' Joey explained. 'There was still a few coppers around, an' I asked one of 'em what 'ad 'appened. 'E said some 'ooligans 'ad been fightin', but there wasn't anyfink to worry about, 'cos they was all be'ind bars.'

So it must be true, Annie thought – her Tom really was in the hands of the police!

'Who else have you told about this?' she asked.

'Not a soul,' Joey said. 'I daren't tell me mum – it'd break 'er 'eart. An' I couldn't think of nobody else but you to turn to. Will yer 'elp him, Annie?'

'Of course I will,' Annie said.

The only problem was that although she was willing to do whatever she could to help him, she couldn't think of *anything* she might do which would be of any earthly use.

The fog had lifted a little overnight – just enough for the blue light to have lost its fuzzy edge and for the man standing underneath it to be clearly identifiable as a policeman.

'Can I be of any 'elp to yer, Miss?' he asked as Annie approached him.

'I've come to see Constable Roberts,' Annie said.

The policeman consulted his watch. 'At a quarter to six in the mornin'!' he said.

'He's on the early shift,' Annie explained. 'He should be tying up his boat in about fifteen minutes.'

The policeman looked at her suspiciously. 'Members o' the public don't normally know so much about policemen's movements,' he said. ' 'Oo exactly are you?'

'My name's Annie Clarke.'

A smile spread across the constable's face immediately.

'Annie Clarke!' he said. 'That would explain it. Yes, I've 'eard all about you.'

'You have?' Annie asked in amazement.

' 'Arry can't stop talkin' about yer,' the policeman said. 'An' now I've met yer for meself, I can understand why.'

'Could I please see him?' Annie asked.

'Course yer can, Miss Clarke. An' since it's you, I'll even take yer down to the landin' stage, so yer can meet 'im as soon as 'e comes in.'

The landing stage jutted out onto the river behind the police station. It smelled of new rope and tar, and when Annie stepped onto it the boards beneath her feet groaned in protest.

'I'll 'ave to get back to me post,' the constable said. 'You'll be all right 'ere on yer own, won't yer?'

'I'll be fine,' Annie assured him.

In fact, she preferred to be alone, because she had some thinking to do.

The constable left, and Annie just stood there, looking out into the darkness. Across the river, in Rotherhithe, the lights of the public houses twinkled like stars, and on the water itself, the dark shapes of long barges slid silently by.

'I've got to get my thoughts in order before Harry gets here,' Annie told herself.

She'd come to see him for much the same reason as young Joey Bates had come to see her – because she couldn't think of anyone else to turn to. But now she was here, she had no idea what she was going to do or say.

There was the sound of oars softly sculling through the water, and out in the darkness she saw the lamp on the front of the police duty boat. The boat got closer, and she could make out Harry, pulling on the oars with his powerful arms.

He was a fine-looking man, she thought – a good, steady man, too. She could understand why her mother would be delighted if she fell in love with him. But love isn't something you can plan, she said to herself, something you can turn on an' off like a tap.

Whatever young women might wish would happen, they sometimes fell for the most inconvenient men;

wastrels and scoundrels, philanderers and rogues – and penniless watermen who would probably soon be ending up in prison.

Harry lifted his hand from the oar and waved cheerfully to show that'd he'd seen her. Annie waved back, though in her present mood waving was the last thing she felt like doing.

The boat glided up to the jetty and Harry and his partner stepped ashore. Harry tied the boat up to its mooring and double-checked the knot. Then the two men walked up the steps where Annie was waiting.

'Jack, this is my ga . . . my friend Annie,' Harry said.

'Please to meet yer, Annie,' Jack said – and sounded as if he meant it.

' 'Adn't yer better go an' report in at the front desk, Jack?' Harry said.

'Report in at the front desk?' Jack replied, with his eyes still on Annie.

'That's right,' Harry said. 'We wouldn't want the desk sergeant comin' lookin' for us, now would we?'

Jack reluctantly turned away from Annie and looked at his partner quizzically. 'Why should the Sarge come lo . . .?' he asked – and then the penny dropped, and he grinned. 'Oh . . . I see what yer mean, 'Arry. I'd better go an' find the Serge before 'e comes searchin' for us. Will you two be all right on yer own?'

'We'll be just fine,' Harry assured him, grinning back.

'Well, I'll be seein' yer around, Annie,' Jack said, and made his way towards the back door of the police station.

Harry took Annie's hands in his own. 'This is about the nicest welcome I've 'ever 'ad off a shift,' he said. 'But what's it all in aid of?'

There was no easy way to approach the subject, Annie thought, so she'd probably best come straight to the point.

'Tom's in trouble.'

Harry's face clouded over, and Annie felt his hands tighten around hers.

'What's 'e done?'

'He's been arrested for brawling with some hooligans in Tooley Street.'

Harry nodded, as if that was just the sort of thing he might have expected. 'Well, if that's what the charge is – an' with 'is 'istory of trouble makin' – young Mr Bates is lookin' at six months inside. Maybe even more.'

'But it wasn't his fault,' Annie protested.

'It never is,' Harry said cynically.

'It really wasn't,' Annie persisted. 'Tom's brother Joey got himself involved with the Newington Hooligans, and all Tom was trying to do was rescue him before he got into serious trouble.'

Harry let go of her hands. 'Yer know, Annie,' he said sadly, 'when I saw yer standin' on the jetty – at six o'clock in the mornin' – I thought yer must have come down 'ere because . . .'

'Because what?' Annie asked.

'It don't matter now,' Harry said. 'So what *is* the reason yer've come 'ere?'

'I want you to go to the magistrates' court and speak up for Tom,' Annie told him.

'Yer want me to *what*?'

'To go to court and speak up for Tom. Tell the magistrates that he's changed his ways, and he's really not to blame for what happened in Tooley Street last night.'

' 'E could call you as a character witness if he wanted to,' Harry said.

'I know he could,' Annie agreed, 'but my word wouldn't count for much, would it?'

'Yer a very respectable young woman with a good job in the telephone company . . .' Harry began.

'But I'm not a policeman,' Annie said. 'And you are! If you were behind Tom, it would carry real weight. So will you do it, please? For me?'

Harry walked to the edge of the jetty. For perhaps two or three minutes he stood completely still, gazing at the dark water which was lapping gently against the pier. Then, finally, he turned round and walked back to Annie.

'I'll be honest with yer,' he said. 'The way that I feel about yer meself . . .'

'That's got nothing to do with Tom!' Annie interrupted. 'Nothing at all.'

'Let me finish,' Harry said, with quiet authority. 'The way that I feel about yer meself has got nothin' to do with the way I feel about you an' Tom Bates.'

'Hasn't it?'

'No, it 'asn't. I still wouldn't like yer knockin' about with 'im if I was yer dad or yer uncle.'

Or my mother, Annie thought, remembering the way Lil had turned on her when she'd started to explain how she felt about the young waterman.

' 'E's not good for yer,' Harry continued, 'an' as far as I'm concerned, 'im goin' to prison for a spell could be the best thing that could 'appen to you – 'cos it'd give yer time to see what a mistake yer've been makin'.'

'And you'd let an innocent man go to prison just for that?' Annie said angrily.

'Tom Bates isn't innocent,' Harry told her. 'Oh, 'e might not be guilty *this* time, but there's plenty of things 'e's done in the past that he ain't been punished for yet.'

Whatever Harry might say, Tom didn't deserve to go to prison, Annie thought to herself. It had been years since he'd been involved in any trouble, and ever since he'd left the Borough Hooligans he'd been nothing but a hard-working man who'd given most of the money he'd earned to his mother.

His mother! How would poor May Bates feel when she learned that on top of all the struggles she'd already been through, her eldest son was going to gaol? It would break her heart, Joey had said, and Annie could believe that it would.

And what about Tom himself? He was tough enough to stand six months or a year in prison, but when he came out he would have a criminal record, and he'd never get a decent job again. Yes, six months or a year in prison, and his life would be ruined.

'Please speak up for him in court, Harry,' Annie begged.

'No,' Harry said, folding his arms across his chest. 'Me mind's made up.'

222

Annie searched desperately for some argument she could put to him that would make him change that stubborn mind of his – and when she found one, she hated herself for it.

'Suppose Tom didn't need to go to prison for me to see the mistake I've been making by going around with him,' she said. 'Would you help him then?'

'How d'yer mean?'

'Suppose I promised never to see Tom again.'

'An' where would that leave you an' me?' Harry asked.

'It would leave us exactly where we are,' Annie told him.

'For 'ow long?' Harry wondered.

'I don't know for how long,' Annie confessed. 'Until . . . until you get fed up with me, I suppose.'

'Seems to me there's an awful lot of "supposin' " goin' on,' Harry said.

'I know,' Annie admitted.

Harry stroked his chin thoughtfully.

'I can't make no promises meself,' he said, 'but I'll look into what 'appened, an' if what yer say is true, then I'll do what I can for Tom Bates.'

'Thank you, Harry,' Annie said.

And then she turned away so he wouldn't see the tears in her eyes.

CHAPTER THIRTEEN

A long line of people had already gathered in front of the Tower Bridge Police Court by the time the clock struck ten.

And what a line it was! Annie thought. Shabbily-dressed men and women, some of them with their heads swathed in bandages, were jostling and cursing each other.

'I'm afore you.'

'No yer ain't. I been waitin' 'ere since 'alf past seven.'

Children who had been queuing with their mothers for hours, now found themselves being thrust aside.

'But I want to stay with yer, Mum!'

'I can't take yer into the court, darlin'. Yer'll just 'ave to wait 'ere while I tell the beak what a bleeder that man 'oo calls 'imself yer father really is.'

Annie herself was stuck in the middle of this mad, confused huddle, next to an Oriental gentleman in baggy trousers who seemed completely oblivious to his surroundings and was peacefully reading a book of squiggly writing.

'Half of London seems to be here,' she said to herself. 'Half of *disreputable* London, anyway!'

On the last stroke of the clock, the big double doors of the court were opened.

'Now then, lets 'ave some order,' said the stern-eyed policeman on duty.

The crowd quietened down immediately and filed meekly into the courtroom under the policeman's intimidating gaze. Annie grabbed an aisle seat and looked around her. At the front of the court was a raised desk behind which the magistrate would sit. To the left of it was the dock, and though it was empty now, Annie could picture Tom standing in it – and shuddered at the thought.

She turned around. Three policeman stood at the back of the room, talking to one another in the hushed tones that are always used in court – but Harry, who was Tom's only real hope of freedom, was not one of them.

'There's still plenty of time for him to turn up,' she told herself. 'There's still plenty of time!'

A uniformed usher stood up in front of the magistrate's bench.

'Silence!' he called, in a voice which boomed throughout the courtroom.

The magistrate entered and took his place at the bench. He was an old man with a bushy white beard and hard, calculating eyes.

'He doesn't look as if he'll have much sympathy for other people's mistakes,' Annie thought, with a sinking feeling in her stomach. She looked around again – and there was still no sign of Harry.

Perhaps because Tom's case was so important to her, Annie had expected it to come up almost immediately. But that was not the way the Police Court worked. Before the more serious offences could be dealt with, there were a host of more minor matters for the magistrate to consider.

Annie listened with growing impatience to the long line of supplicants. A woman with a black eye swore out a complaint against her brutal husband. She was followed by a weedy little chap who said he wanted to swear out the same thing against his 'old lady'.

'You are the master of your own house,' the magistrate told him. 'Go home and be a man.'

'That's easy enuff for you to say, Yer Worship,' the victim complained as he was being ushered out by the policeman on duty. 'You ain't seen the size of 'er!'

Next came a long-haired inventor with a model of a wire-less telephone which the Patents' Office had refused to register.

'But does it work?' the magistrate asked.

'It will,' the inventor said. 'Eventually.'

'But it doesn't work *yet*, does it?' the magistrate persisted.

'No,' the inventor admitted.

'Then you can't possibly expect the Patents Office to register it, can you?' the magistrate asked.

The inventor did not see the point and mumbled something about 'a conspiracy against me' as he was being led away.

Annie looked around the court once more. There was still no sign of Harry. Now, her impatience with the trivial cases which had to be settled before Tom's disappeared and she began to feel grateful for them – because the longer they took, the more time it gave Harry to get to the court. If he was coming at all.

Following the inventor was a young man who complained that his 'gal' had broken off their engagement but refused to return his ring, and then a grocer who wanted a warrant issued against a man who had written him a bad cheque. A widow dressed in little more than rags told the court that if she had a mangle she could make an honest living as a washerwoman, and the magistrate decreed that a grant should be made to her out of the Poor Box.

In a strange way, seeing these cases cheered Annie up a little. The magistrate might be a hard man, but he tempered it with mercy. And he was no fool – so surely he'd be able to see that Tom wasn't guilty of anything but trying to do his best to keep his brother out of trouble.

When the last of the appeals had finally been dealt with, the door to the gaolers' room was opened and the first of the prisoners – a man charged with begging – was marched into the courtroom.

'I ain't no beggar,' he claimed from the dock. 'I 'ad this 'ere box 'o matches to sell.'

'Only *one* box of matches,' the magistrate mused.

'That's right, guv.'

'And what would you have sold once that had gone?'

The beggar gave the magistrate the sort of pitying look which those who know the ways of the world reserve for those who don't. 'Use yer loaf, guv,' he said. 'Who's goin' to take a poor man's last box of matches off of 'im?'

Annie bit her nails in frantic frustration. Suppose the beggar hadn't been arrested, she thought. Suppose a few of the supplicants had decided to put off coming to court until some other day. If that had happened, Tom's case would have been over by now – and Harry would have missed it.

What was it that he'd said to her on the jetty of Wapping Police Station?

If what yer say is true, then I'll do what I can for Tom Bates.

And it *was* true – so why hadn't he kept his word and turned up to speak for Tom?

'You promised,' she said aloud.

'I did what?' whispered the fat woman who was sitting right next to her.

'Sorry,' Annie whispered back. 'I was just thinking aloud.'

'You want to watch yerself, gal,' the woman told her. 'They'll lock yer in a padded cell if yer keep doin' that.'

And they'd lock Tom up, too, without Harry to help him.

The beggar was sentenced to a twenty-shilling fine or two weeks in gaol – as were the four young men who came next and were charged with gambling at pitch-and-toss on a public street.

'An' if they got a fortnight for what they've done, what's he going to give Tom?' Annie thought worriedly.

But it seemed that the magistrate was not always so severe. The next person to appear before him – a girl who had attempted to commit suicide – wasn't given a prison sentence as the law allowed, but instead was handed over to the care of a dockside missionary who promised to see that she was given honest work.

The moment that Annie had been both waiting for and dreading finally arrived. The door to the gaoler's room opened once more, and Tom and the three Newington Hooligans were marched into the court and herded towards the dock.

And still Harry had not appeared!

The clerk read out the charge and a police sergeant was called to give evidence.

'I was informed by a hanonymous source that there was goin' to be a robbery on Tooley Street last night at around nine o'clock,' he said. 'Accordin'ly, in order to prevent such an occurrence, I stationed me men at various points along Tooley Street at approximately a quarter to nine.'

'And did you actually see any robbery about to take place?' the magistrate interrupted.

'No, sir.'

'Then what *did* you see?'

'We encountered the four men in the dock, Yer Worship. They was down an alley just off Tooley Street, in the act of committin' a breach of the peace.'

'What kind of breach of the peace?'

'They was knockin' the blue blazes out of each other, sir.'

Even distressed as she was, Annie couldn't help noticing that whereas the Newington boys really did look like they'd had the blue blazes knocked out of them, Tom had only a few minor scratches. For a moment, she couldn't help feeling proud of him – and then she realised it would have been better if he'd been the one who'd been battered and bruised, because as it was, he didn't look like the victim at all.

She studied the faces of the four men in the dock. Rollo, Chas and Blackie all wore expressions which mixed innocence with shame – as if to say, 'We didn't *think* we was doin' anyfink wrong, Yer Worship, but if we was, we're very sorry.'

Tom, on the other hand, was staring straight ahead of him, without a hint of emotion on his face, as if *he* didn't give a damn about what the magistrate thought.

'You have no proof that these young men were the ones who were actually planning the robbery you'd been tipped off about, have you?' the magistrate asked the sergeant.

'No, sir,' the policeman admitted. 'Although we did find offensive weapons lyin' near them in the alley.'

Tom was still staring at the back wall. Annie coughed loudly, and when he turned in her direction, she willed him, with her eyes, to try and look as contrite as the other three defendants.

It didn't work, as she'd known that – Tom being Tom – it wouldn't. When he turned away again, his face was as blank as ever.

'What sort of offensive weapons did you find, sergeant?' the magistrate asked.

The policeman consulted his notebook.

'A hiron bar, a belt with a 'eavy buckle, and a sandbag cosh, Your Worship.'

'That's only three weapons,' the magistrate said, glancing at the four men in the dock.

'That is correct, sir.'

The magistrate looked questioningly at the prisoners, and Annie wished once again that Tom would somehow try to alter the expression on his face.

'Do any of the four defendants have a previous criminal record?' the magistrate asked.

'Not as such, sir,' the sergeant admitted. 'Which is to say that none of 'em 'ave ever been charged with anyfink. But all of 'em are known to the police, an' all of 'em belong to – or *'ave* belonged to – 'ooligan gangs.'

Annie saw the lines on the magistrate's face harden.

'I have no use for hooligans,' he said. 'They are the scourge of London. Why, I myself have had the front windows of my house completely shattered by a such a group of young thugs.' He regarded the prisoners with intense dislike. 'Have any of you anything to say before I pass sentence?' he asked.

'It was 'is fault,' Rollo said, looking as innocent as a newborn babe and pointing at Tom. ' 'E set on us.'

The magistrate's expression changed from one of loathing to one of shrewd curiosity.

'He set on you?' he said. 'But there are three of you and only one of him. Is he a madman?'

'Well, I don't think 'e's exactly right in the 'ead, if that's what yer mean, Yer Worship,' Rollo said. 'Certainly seems to 'ave a vicious streak to me.'

'Tell me exactly what he did,' the magistrate said.

'He crept up on us, see. An' then he started attackin' us with them weapons of 'is.'

The magistrate raised his eyebrows. 'You're saying that all the weapons – the belt and the bar and the cosh – were his?' he asked incredulously.

'That's right,' Rollo agreed.

'And how did he manage to use them all at once?'

'Beg pardon, sir?'

'He has only two hands, hasn't he?'

Rollo grinned. 'Oh, I see what yer mean,' he said. 'The fact is, 'e threw the iron bar at one of me pals, an' then started settin' about us with the cosh and belt.'

'And what have you got to say for yourself?' the magistrate asked Tom.

'Nuffink, sir,' Tom said.

Nothing! Annie thought. Nothing! Why didn't he just tell the magistrate the truth – simply explain what had happened?

And then she understood. He couldn't tell his story without dragging his brother Joey into it – and that was the one thing he was not prepared to do.

The door at the back of the court opened. Harry Roberts entered the room and immediately began an urgent, whispered conversation with one of the policemen on duty.

'There are certain discrepancies in your testimonies,' the magistrate told the accused, 'but I am satisfied that all four of you are guilty of a serious breach of the peace and so I am going to . . .'

Harry stepped forward. 'Your Worship?' he said.

'Yes, what is it?'

'Do I 'ave yer permission to address the court?'

'Is it relevant to this case?'

'Yes, sir.'

'Then you have my permission.'

'My name is Constable Harold . . .' Harry began.

'I know who you are, Constable Roberts,' the magistrate interrupted. 'You have appeared in my court a number of times before, and have always been, I may say, a credit to your uniform.'

'Thank you sir,' Harry said. 'I'd like, if I could, to make an appeal on be'alf of one of the prisoners in the dock.'

'Is that the young man you mean?' asked the magistrate shrewdly, pointing at Tom.

'That's correct, sir.'

Tom's indifferent gaze melted away to be replaced by astonishment as he looked at Harry – and then by accusation as he turned round to Annie.

'Proceed, Constable Roberts,' the magistrate told the policeman.

Harry hesitated, as if, even at this point he was thinking of changing his mind.

'Say something, Harry!' Annie prayed silently. 'Please say something – anything – that will save my Tom.'

'Tom Bates ain't always been no angel, sir,' Harry told the magistrate, 'but over the last few years 'e's been workin' 'ard an' supportin' the rest of 'is family.'

'And you know that for a fact, do you?'

'Yes, sir. I've been checkin' with the people 'oo live up 'is street an' the watermen at Battle Bridge Stairs 'oo 'e works with. That's why I nearly didn't get 'ere on time to speak up for 'im.'

'I see,' the magistrate said. 'Carry on, constable.'

'I'm not sayin' 'e ain't guilty as charged,' Harry continued, 'but I do believe that 'e didn't go lookin' for trouble last night. In fact, though I can't prove it, it's my opinion that 'e went down to Tooley Street to *prevent* trouble.'

'There *were* only three weapons recovered,' the magistrate said thoughtfully.

'An' given 'is good behaviour recently an' the fact that 'is mother depends on 'im, I'd ask that the court shows 'im mercy this time,' Harry concluded.

The magistrate frowned. 'I am not sure you quite understand the implications of making such a plea,' he said. 'Do you realise that you are virtually staking your whole reputation on the belief that the defendant, Bates, will keep well within the law from now on?'

'Yes, sir, I do realise that,' Harry said.

The magistrate's frown deepened.

'Let me spell it out further,' he said. 'Should Bates commit some more serious crime in the future, there will be those who will blame at least part of it on any leniency I show him today – leniency which would be based on your recommendation. In other words, they would blame *you*. Do you understand *that*?'

'Yes, sir.'

'Should such a situation occur, it would certainly damage a very promising career,' the magistrate warned him. 'It might even cost you your job. Now, Constable Roberts, do you *still* wish the court to show this young man mercy?'

Harry looked directly at Annie and then turned back to face the bench. 'Yes sir, I do,' he said.

The magistrate sighed, then nodded his head.

'Very well,' he said. 'On your recommendation, I will give the defendant Bates a twelve-month suspended sentence. Baliff, see that his property is returned to him.'

'Thank you, sir,' said Tom, stepping down from the dock.

'On the other hand,' continued the magistrate, 'I am determined that the rest of the defendants – the ones I am convinced were really carrying the weapons – should not get off so lightly. You will each serve a six-month sentence.'

'I'll get yer for this, Tom Bates,' Rollo hissed as the bailiff began to lead Tom away. 'I'll find a way to get yer for it if it's the last thing I ever do!'

Annie went straight from the court room to the Central Telephone Exchange on St. Paul's Church Yard, but she had already missed lunch, and it was not until tea time that she got a chance to discuss her problems with Belinda Benson.

'Now let me get this straight,' Belinda said when Annie had told her the whole story. 'Your dashing policeman promised to save your handsome boatman, but only when you promised in return to give the boatman the proverbial elbow.'

'That's right,' Annie agreed.

'Sounds a bit like blackmail to me,' Belinda pronounced. 'Smart, though. And I can't say I blame him for seizing the opportunity when it was presented to him.'

'It isn't like that,' Annie protested. 'Harry honestly does think that I'd be better off without Tom. And even after I'd made my promise, he still wouldn't have spoken up if he'd thought that Tom really was guilty.'

'Still, it does leave you in a bit of a mess, doesn't it, old girl,' Belinda said.

'I suppose it does,' Annie admitted.

'Of course, there's nothing to stop you from breaking the promise, is there?' Belinda reflected.

'That isn't the way I was brought up,' Annie said.

Belinda chuckled. 'And how *were* you brought up, my little Cockney sparrer?' she asked. 'Poor but honest?'

'That's right,' Annie replied earnestly. 'When you're poor, you've got to have a reason for believing you're worth something – a reason that doesn't have anyfink – anything – to do with money or possessions. So you find a set of decent rules for yourself and you stick to them through thick and thin.'

'My God, you're not just a Cockney sparrer – you're a philosopher as well!' Belinda exclaimed.

'It's not funny, Belinda,' Annie said.

The intensity of her words had an instant sobering effect on her friend.

'Sorry, old girl,' Belinda said. 'Forget myself sometimes. Bad habit – must try to break myself of it.'

'Besides,' Annie said, 'I owe Harry something. He didn't just give up a bit of his free time to get Tom off, you know. By speaking up like he did, he was gambling with his own future.'

'Gambling with his own future? How was it a gamble? I thought you said that your handsome waterman had completely given up a life of lawlessness.'

'He has. But has *it* given him up? He didn't want trouble last night, but he still ended up in the dock. And who's to say for sure that it won't happen again? So you see, Harry really *was* taking a risk.'

'His choice,' Belinda told her.

'I'm not sure it was – not entirely, anyway. The magistrate kept trying to talk him out of it, and there was one moment – when Harry looked across at me – when I knew that all I had to do was nod, and he'd take the magistrate's advice. But I didn't nod. So in a way, I feel responsible for Harry. Can you understand that?'

'I'm not sure,' Belinda admitted. 'But there's one thing I do know. The more I hear about the messes that love can get you into, the more I give serious consideration to becoming a bloody nun.'

It was dark when Annie and Belinda left the telephone exchange, but at least there was no freezing fog for once.

'Why don't we go to the ABC for a bite to eat,' Belinda suggested. 'My treat.'

It had been the ABC that Harry had taken her to the day of her first interview – back when life was much less complicated.

'I don't really feel like eating,' Annie said.

'Stuff and nonsense!' Belinda replied, sweeping aside the objection in her customary manner. 'Do you good to get some food inside you. Besides that, I . . . I wanted to do something to make up for being so bloody insensitive earlier.'

'It's very kind of you to offer, Belinda,' Anine said, 'but I just couldn't . . .'

'Chap watching us,' her friend interrupted. 'On the other side of the street. Rather good-looking, actually.

Annie looked across the street. Several people were walking purposefully in both directions, and a wagon loaded down with winter hay was slowly trundling up the street – but there was no sign of a man watching them.

'Well, I can't see him,' she said.

'Hidden behind the wagon at the moment,' Belinda replied. 'Patience, dear girl – all will be revealed.'

The wagon moved on, and Annie saw that there was indeed a man watching them.

'Oh crikey!' she said. 'It's Tom.'

The young waterman stepped into the street and walked towards them.

'Looks a bit annoyed if you ask me,' Belinda said. 'What do you want me to do – push off, or stay and give you moral support?'

'I think it might be better if you went,' Annie told her.

'Right you are,' Belinda replied. 'I never was one to stay around when I wasn't wanted. You will tell me all about it in the morning, won't you?'

And without waiting for an answer, she sauntered off down the street.

Annie turned to face Tom. Belinda had been right – he looked annoyed, if not downright angry.

'Hello, Tom,' she said as he drew level with her.

'What did you give 'im?' Tom demanded.

'Sorry, I don't . . .'

'What did you give Constable Harry-bloody-Roberts to get 'im to speak up for me?'

'I . . . I didn't give him anything,' Annie stuttered. 'You heard what he said in court. He'd been to talk to your neighbours and the other watermen, 'an he'd decided for himself that you weren't to blame for the fight.'

' 'Arry Roberts wouldn't 'ave lifted 'is little finger to 'elp me without you gettin' 'im to do it,' Tom said. 'Why, left to 'imself, 'e'd 'ave been more than delighted to get me out of the way. So I'll ask yer again, Annie – what was it that yer give 'im? Did yer let him 'ave 'is way with yer?'

Annie was overcome with a fury as blinding as the one which had struck in Battle Bridge Lane the night that Tom had dared to suggest that, having become a telephone operator, she would soon forget her old friends. And like then, she now acted without thinking, raising her hand and slapping Tom as hard as she could.

'That's the second time yer've done that to me,' Tom said, the rest of his face almost as red with anger as his cheek was from the slap.

'It's the second time you've *deserved* it!' Annie retorted. 'Sometimes I really hate you, Tom Bates!'

Her words were like cold water to his blazing temper, and he bowed his head for a second.

'Yer right,' he said. 'I *did* deserve it. I shouldn't 'ave said what I did, Annie an' I'm very sorry.'

But his apology was not enough for Annie at that moment – nowhere near enough.

'It's not just an insult to me,' Annie screamed. 'It's an insult to a fine policeman who puts his duty above everything and would never – *never* – have done what he thought was wrong in return for – as you say – *having* me!'

'I'll take yer word for what yer say about 'Arry Roberts,' Tom said, 'an' I'm sorry if I've been unfair to 'im as well as you. It's just that I care about yer so much, an' the thought of you an' 'im . . . I could picture it all in me mind, yer see, an' . . .'

'Well, nothing happened, so there was nothing to picture,' Annie told him.

'I know,' Tom said. 'Can yer forgive me?'

Annie felt her anger slip away as Tom's had.

'Well, of course I can forgive yer,' she said.

'Do yer know what was goin' through me 'ead all the time I was in that dock?' Tom asked. 'All the time I knew for certain that I was goin' to go to prison?'

'How could I know?'

'I was thinkin', "If they lock me up, the worst thing about it will be that I won't be able to see Annie".'

'Please, Tom . . .' Annie begged.

'An' then when 'Arry Roberts started speakin' up for me an' I thought – well, yer know what I thought . . . Honest, Annie, I don't know 'ow I stopped meself from goin' mad then an' there.'

'Forget it,' Annie said. 'It's all over now.'

Tom smiled. 'Yer a wonderful gal, Annie,' he said. 'I'd been plannin' this to 'appen at a different time in a different place, but after what we've both been through today . . .'

'Planning what to happen in a different time and a

different place?' Annie asked, alarmed that she might already know the answer.

And suddenly Tom was down on one knee in front of her – right there in the street.

'I love yer, Annie, an' I know yer love me,' he said. 'Will yer marry me?'

A passing couple saw him kneeling there and smiled at one another, and a workman on the other side of the road shouted, 'That's the spirit, son!'

'Get up, Tom. Please!' Annie urged.

Tom was smiling even more broadly – and confidently – now.

'I'll stay where I am until yer give me a yes or no,' he said playfully.

'Don't keep 'im waitin' too long, gal,' called the workman. ''E'll get arfritis if 'e's down there much longer.'

She wanted to say yes – God, she wanted to say yes – but she'd made a promise and she had to stick to it.

'I can't marry you, Tom,' she said.

'Can't marry me?' Tom said, poleaxed. 'What d'yer mean – *can't*? Are yer sayin' yer don't love me?'

'Yes . . . no . . . I don't know . . .' Annie confessed as she grew more confused by the second.

Tom stood up, put his hands on her shoulders and looked down into her eyes.

'If yer don't love me like I love you, then I can understand yer turnin' me down,' he said. 'But yer 'ave to tell me straight that that's the reason.'

Annie gazed into his eyes and knew that whatever else she said to him, she couldn't tell a lie.

'I . . . I don't want to talk about it,' she said.

'Be fair with me, Annie,' Tom told her.

'You're just going to have to accept the fact that I can't marry you and that I can't . . . can't see you again.'

'Yer keep sayin' *can't*. What's to stop yer?'

'I don't have to explain,' Annie said defensively.

The light of understanding suddenly came to Tom's face.

' 'Arry Roberts made yer promise that, didn't 'e?' he

demanded. 'I knew there 'ad to be some price for 'is speakin' up for me – an' that was it!'

'It . . . it wasn't quite as simple as that,' Annie said uncertainly.

'Don't yer know I'd 'ave gone to jail for ten years – for twenty years – rather than 'ave somethin' like this 'appen?' Tom said.

'I only did what I thought was best,' Annie said.

'An' yer won't break yer word once yer've given it, will yer?' Tom said.

'Would you have an ounce of respect left for me if I did?' Annie asked him.

Tom didn't answer. Instead, he grasped his hair in his hands and pulled it as hard as he could. Annie reached forward to touch him, but he brushed her arm aside.

'Yer've ruined me, Annie Clarke,' he said. 'Yer've ruined the both of us.'

He walked rapidly away down the street. Annie watched him go through eyes blurred with tears, and then he turned a corner and was lost to her.

CHAPTER FOURTEEN

It was two days after Tom Bates' appearance in front of the Tower Bridge magistrate – and over a month after the start of Peggy's period of punishment – when Lil Clarke raised the subject of an excursion for her younger daughter. Not that it was that simple, of course – for as Sam often said, 'My old lady'll never go anywhere direct while there's a chance of wanderin' off round the 'ouses.'

Sam and Lil were alone together in the front parlour when Lil started her 'wanderin'. He was quietly reading the evening newspaper, she was doing the ironing – and thinking.

' 'Ow are things down at the docks these days?' Lil asked, out of the blue.

'Not too bad,' Sam said, laying down his newspaper in the confident belief that Lil was about to give him a lot more fun than he could ever have got from *The Advertiser*.

'What I mean is, are yer likely to be workin' Saturday?'

Sam shook his head. 'Not very likely at all. We should 'ave unloaded all the wheat off of *The Pride of Quebec* by then, and there's nothin' else due in until Monday morning.'

The flat-iron Lil had been using was almost cold and so she swapped it with a second one, which had been heating up on the hob over the fire.

'That money our Peggy scrounged is still in the jug on

the mantelpiece,' she said. 'It ain't doin' nobody no good just sittin' there, is it?'

'Well, why don't yer post it to the Battersea Dogs' 'Ome like yer said yer were goin' to?' her husband asked.

'I don't believe in keepin' charity at arm's length,' Lil said. 'If yer givin' money away, then yer should make the effort to see just what it is yer givin' it to.'

'Yer mean, Peggy should go to the Dogs' 'Ome an' 'and it in personal?'

'Well, it is 'er money – in a sort of way.'

'An' goin' to the Dogs' 'Ome would give 'er a day out – in a sort of way – wouldn't it?' Sam said with a twinkle in his eye.

'I s'pose it would,' Lil agreed, as if the idea had just occurred to her.

'An' you're always accusin' *me* of bein' too soft with the gal,' Sam said.

'So yer are,' Lil countered.

'Then what about you?'

'I'm not bein' soft on 'er, if that's what yer suggestin'. I'm just bein' . . .'

'Bein' what?'

'I'm just thinkin' of 'er welfare. It'd be educational for the gal to see the Dogs' 'Ome.'

'Educational, yes,' Sam said thoughtfully. 'So when are yer thinkin' of takin' 'er?'

'That's what I was wonderin' about meself,' Lil said. 'I've got so much on me plate, what with Christmas comin' up an' everyfink, that I can't see me 'avin time until the New Year. But really, we should 'ave given 'em the money long before then.'

The puzzle was falling into place. Sam smiled to himself, then forced his features into an expression of shocked horror.

'Yer surely not goin' to send the gal all that way on her own, are yer?' he asked.

'Well, no,' Lil admitted. 'There's at least two changes o' tram between 'ere an' the Dogs' 'Ome. She's a bit too young – an' a bit too dreamy if I'm bein' honest – to 'andle all that by 'erself.'

'So what the dickens *are* we goin' to do?' Sam asked, scratching his head thoughtfully.

'It is a problem,' Lil agreed.

'I don't think we could ask our Annie to do it,' Sam said. 'She still seems a bit upset about that Bates lad.'

'That Bates lad, indeed!' Lil snorted. 'She's well shot of 'im, if yer ask me.'

'An' our Eddie's spendin' every free minute he's got down at the garage,' Sam pointed out.

'Yes, that's turned out really well,' Lil said. 'I must admit, I 'ad me doubts at first, but I've never seen 'im as keen on anyfink as 'e is on messin' about with them motor cars.'

'So who *is* going to take our Peggy?' Sam wondered aloud. Then he slapped his forehead with the palm of his hand. 'O' course! It's obvious when yer think about it.'

'What is?'

'Since I'm not workin' Saturday, I could take her meself.'

'Well, that would be kind of yer,' Lil said.

She turned away, so that Sam would not see the smile on her face. It was remarkable, she thought, that after all the years they'd been married, it was still so easy to twist her husband around her little finger.

The lady who dealt with them at the Battersea Dogs' Home was called Mrs Briggs. She wore a brown apron over her silk dress and couldn't have been more charming.

'You can rest assured this will be put to very good use,' she said as she carefully counted out Peggy's one pound three shillings and sixpence ha'penny.

'Do a lot of people give yer money?' Peggy asked.

'Well, yes, they do,' Mrs Briggs replied.

'As much as I 'ave?'

'Some of them give much more.'

'Oh!' Peggy said, disappointed.

'Of course, the ones who give more are people like businessmen and bankers,' Mrs Briggs added hurriedly, 'and they can easily afford it. But I don't think I can remember such a big contribution by a young lady like yourself before. Wherever did you get it all from?'

'Part of it come from the broken milk jug dodge . . .' Peggy began, and would have said more if her father hadn't hugged her to him and gagged her mouth with his arm.

'She's been savin' 'er money up for ages,' he said. 'She's very fond of animals.'

'Then before you go, we must give you a short tour of the place,' Mrs Briggs said.

'That'd be real nice,' Peggy agreed.

Mrs Briggs took them to the kennels – though cages was probably a more accurate word – which ran the length of the courtyard wall. There were about ten animals in each, and though some of them came from clearly recognised breeds, there were others which looked as if they'd been put together from spare parts.

'Ain't they all luverly,' Peggy said fondly.

'Yes, they are,' Mrs Briggs agreed.

'An' 'ow many dogs do yer get brought in to yer in a year?' Peggy asked.

'About twenty-two thousand,' Mrs Briggs said.

Twenty-two thousand! Peggy counted the number of dogs in the cage in front of her and tried to work out how much space it would take to house twenty-two thousand.

'An' d'yer manage to find good 'omes for all of 'em?' she asked their guide.

Mrs Briggs looked a trifle uneasy, as if she'd had this question put to her by little girls before, but had never yet been able to come up with an answer which been both satisfactory and truthful.

'We do manage to find good homes for most of them,' she said cautiously.

'An' what 'appens to the rest?'

'Well, they . . . they . . .' Mrs Briggs said, floundering a little. 'Look at that lovely little puppy over there.'

But Peggy was not about to put off. 'I s'pect yer put the sick ones to sleep, don't yer?' she said, practically.

'Well, yes,' Mrs Briggs said, not at all sure whether she was glad to be off the hook or not.

'An' the ones that nobody wants, the old an' ugly ones, I s'pect yer put them to sleep as well, don't yer?'

'Sometimes,' Mrs Briggs admitted.

'Does it 'urt?' Peggy asked.

'Oh no!' Mrs Briggs assured her. 'In Sir Benjamin Richardson's new lethal chamber, they don't feel a thing.'

'That's all right then,' Peggy said.

'All right?' Sam said, surprised to hear the words coming from the mouth of his younger daughter.

'They can't keep 'em all 'ere,' Peggy explained, 'they 'aven't got the room. An' if they turned 'em loose, they'd only starve to death or get knocked over by a tram.'

'Quite correct, young lady,' Mrs Briggs said with some relief. 'And quite sensible, too.'

'I'm goin' to work with animals when I'm grown up, yer know,' Peggy told her.

'Are you?' Mrs Briggs asked.

'Yes,' Peggy said. 'An' if yer goin' to work with animals, yer 'ave to love 'em – but yer can't afford to be soft about 'em.'

Sam looked down at his daughter in total amazement. She might be a bit of a dreamer, he thought to himself, but she was certainly not a fool.

When they were waiting at the stop for the next tram back to Southwark, Peggy took her father's hand and said, 'Thanks, Dad. I 'ad a really good time.'

'An' would yer like a dog of yer own when yer a bit older?' Sam asked.

'Yes,' Peggy said seriously. 'It'd be very useful.'

'Useful? Useful for what?'

'For keepin' me goat in order.'

Sam shook his head. 'Yer never goin' to let us 'ear the last about goats, are yer?' he asked.

'No,' Peggy agreed, 'not until I've got one.'

Then she smiled at him – a sweet, loving smile – and it was as much as Sam could do to stop himself rushing off and finding her a goat right then and there.

When Colleen Taylor went to answer the bell in the Bottle and Jug Department of The Goldsmiths' Arms, she found

Mary Bates standing there and gazing up at the mounted mirror which reflected an image of the saloon bar.

'What can I do for you, Mary?' the barmaid asked.

Mary, her eyes firmly fixed on the mirror, did not seem to hear. And now Colleen noticed two other things about her. She wasn't carrying a jug, and she was wearing her Sunday best.

Colleen looked at the mirror herself, and saw the back of a head covered in curly blond hair – which she knew belonged to Fred Simpson, the fresh-faced fireman.

'If only I was bit older,' Mary sighed.

'If only you were a bit older – then what?' Colleen asked.

The words seemed to snap Mary back to reality. She tore her eyes away from the mirror and looked, finally, at Colleen.

'Oh, I . . . er . . . nuffink,' she mumbled.

It wasn't fair to laugh at young love, and Colleen did her best to hide her smile. 'Can I get you anythin', Mary?' she said, sure enough to bet money on it that the girl had no idea at all that she'd been asked the same question before.

'I . . . er . . . come in for some ale,' Mary replied.

'Where's your jug?'

Mary looked down at her hand as if she was surprised to find no jug there. 'I . . . er . . . must 'ave lost it,' she said. 'I'll be losin' me own 'ead next.'

You've already lost *that*, Colleen thought, but aloud she said, 'You'd better go back home an' get another one, then, hadn't you?'

'That's right,' Mary agreed, 'I'd better go back 'ome an' get another one.' She backed towards the door, her eyes glued to the mirror again. 'I'll . . . er . . . see yer tomorrow, Colleen,' she said as she bumped into the door handle.

As Colleen went back to the saloon bar, she allowed the smile she'd been hiding to come to her face, and when Fred Simpson ordered his next drink she said, 'You've got an admirer, Fred.'

'An admirer! Me?' Fred said, as if it was the most inconceivable thing in the world. 'Who is she?'

'Oh, I couldn't tell you that,' Colleen replied. 'Barmaids are a bit like priests, yer know – we get to hear an awful lot, but we're supposed to say nowt.'

Fred grinned. It really wasn't surprising that Mary Bates was mooning over him, Colleen thought. It was true that he still had the face of a kid, but it was a handsome face for all that. And he had the body of a strong man, with thick arms and broad shoulders. She remembered the day the hooligans had burst into the pub. That Rollo character hadn't wanted to take Fred on, had he? Even though he'd been armed with an iron bar.

'I'll tell yer what I'll do – I'll bribe yer,' Fred said. 'I'll buy yer a drink, an' then, when it's gone to yer 'ead, yer can just sort o' 'int at who me admirer is.'

Colleen laughed. 'It's not a bad idea,' she admitted, 'but it won't work. I don't drink any more, you see.'

It was no lie. Ever since she'd had her talk with Lil Clarke, she hadn't touched a drop.

'Go on! Just 'ave the one,' Fred urged her. 'After all, it is very nearly Christmas.'

'Aye, time flies by, doesn't it,' Colleen replied. 'An' no thank you, I won't have a drink, Fred.'

The young fireman shrugged. 'Well, yer can't say I ain't asked,' he said. 'Will yer be goin' 'ome for the 'olidays?'

'No,' Colleen replied. 'We can't manage it this year.'

She hoped that her face wasn't giving her away, because what she'd just said this time was *far* from the truth. Mr Wilkins had assured her that he could spare her if she wanted to go and see her family for a few days, and George had said that he could see no problems with him taking a few days off.

But perhaps she was speaking the truth after all, because what she really meant was that *she* couldn't manage it – couldn't manage seeing all her small nephews and nieces, as long as she had no children of her own.

Don't worry about it, she thought, reminding herself of Lil's advice. Don't worry about it and it'll happen.

But it hadn't happened, had it?

★

Tom Bates knew that he was somewhere in Rotherhithe, but he couldn't have put a name to the street he was tramping down now. He'd been walking for hours – walking aimlessly in an attempt to take his mind off Annie.

'An' it ain't workin',' he told himself.

He thought back to the last time they'd spoken, outside the telephone exchange. He'd meant every word of what he'd said to her there. He *did* love her. And she *had* ruined him!

He was approaching the end of the street, and from the pub on the corner came the sound of a piano and people singing. He was tempted to go inside, but he knew that if he did, he would only drink himself legless – and he hadn't sunk that low yet.

'D'yer fancy 'avin a nice time, darlin?' asked a woman's voice from the shadows.

Tom came to a stop under one of the gas-lamps.

'I can't see yer proper,' he said. 'Come out 'ere where I can get a better look at yer.'

The woman stepped forward. She was wearing an elaborate feathered hat and a shabby frock which clung tightly to her hips and bosom. In her dress and her bearing, she was no different from any of the other few dozen prostitutes who worked the waterfront around Rotherhithe, but she had a nice voice – and that was why he had stopped.

'Only cost yer a shillin',' the woman said.

She was keeping her distance, hovering a few feet away from the gas-lamp like a moth which senses it is in danger.

'I still can't see yer proper,' Tom told her. 'Come a bit closer to me, will yer.'

She took a step or two towards him. She was younger than most of the women who worked the docklands, and under her caked-on make-up, he could tell, she was a very pretty girl indeed.

'Well, d'yer want to or not?' she asked, a hint of impatience in her voice now.

What could be the harm? Tom asked himself. If he did take her somewhere and lose himself in her arms for half an hour or so, who would he be hurting?

'What's yer name?' he asked.

'Rosie.'

'Roise what? Rosie Lea?'

The girl laughed. 'That's right,' she agreed. 'Rosie Lea.'

Tom reached into his pocket and took out his money. In the light of the streetlamp, he counted it out. Two shillings.

'Yer could 'ave me all night for that,' the girl said.

Tom handed the money over to her.

'I'll tell yer what, Rosie Lea,' he said, 'why don't yer go an' get yerself a good supper, then go back to yer room an' wait for me to come an' join yer?'

'Yer a very trustin' bloke, ain't yer?' the girl said. ' 'Ow d'yer know that I won't give yer the wrong address an' just make off with yer money?'

'Yer've got an honest face,' Tom told her.

The girl studied him for several seconds.

'S'ppose I did like yer told me, 'ad me supper 'an then went back to me room to wait for yer,' she said finally. 'I'd be wastin' me time – 'cos yer won't be comin', will yer?'

'No,' Tom agreed. 'I won't be comin'. It's been nice meetin' yer, Rosie Lea.'

And without another word, he set off once more on his relentless march to nowhere.

It was half past midnight. The final customer had been persuaded to leave The Goldsmiths' Arms, the shutters were up, and Colleen had just finished the last of the washing up.

'I'll be off, then, Mr Wilkins,' she said, reaching up to the rack for her coat.

'Just a minute,' the landlord replied. 'Before yer go, I think we'd better 'ave a little talk.'

'A little talk?' Collen repeated. 'Is somethin' wrong with the way I'm doin' me job?'

'Yer might say that,' Mr Wilkins told her. 'To be honest, I'm startin' to get worried about yer, Colleen.'

'Worried?'

'Echo in 'ere, is there?' the landlord asked. 'Look, I appreciate 'avin' good people workin' for me as much as the next man does, but sometimes I think you do *too* much. Yer always 'ere before yer shift starts, and whenever we're short-'anded it's you what steps in to fill the breach.'

'I like to keep busy.'

'I'm sure yer do, but yer wearin' yerself out. Why don't yer take a few days off, like I suggested?'

'I'm quite all right,' Colleen said firmly. 'Honestly I am, Mr Wilkins. I don't need a holiday. I wouldn't know what to do with meself if I was on holiday.'

But on her way back up Lant Place – when she noticed that the gas lamps looked unusually fuzzy and that she was starting to breathe irregularly – Collen began to think that Mr Wilkins had been right about her doing too much.

The further she went, the more difficult it became to go on. Her head was pounding now, and though the air which enveloped her was almost freezing, she felt herself breaking into a heavy sweat.

It's just a cold, she thought. But she had had colds before – influenza, too – and they hadn't felt like this.

After what seemed like hours, she finally reached her own front door. It took quite a while to find her latch key in her pocket, and even once she had it in her hand, it didn't seem to want to fit into the lock.

'What's the matter with you?' she snapped irritably at the offending key.

She tried to insert it two or three times, but it just kept skidding away from the hole, and in the end it must have been the sound of metal scratching against metal that brought George to the front door, just in time to catch his wife as she fainted into his arms.

Colleen was slowly coming to, but she decided to keep her eyes closed for the moment. The last thing she remembered, she'd been trying to open that bloody awkward front door of hers, but now, from what she could feel with the flats of her hands, she was obviously lying in bed.

She opened one eye cautiously, and focused it on the wallpaper. She recognised the pattern immediately, which she supposed must mean that she was in her *own* bed.

Well, that was a relief anyway she told herself, but who was this strange man she'd just noticed hovering over her?

'And how are we feeling now, Mrs Taylor?' the strange man asked her.

'I don't know about you, but I feel awful,' Colleen replied. 'It's almost like I've been sick or somethin'.'

But that hadn't been what she'd meant to say. She wanted to ask him a question – if only she could remember what it was.

'You *have* been sick,' the man said. 'All over your hallway. Is it the first time it's happened to you, or have you being doing it a lot, recently?'

It was hard to think when your head was full of cotton wool, but Colleen did her best – because the very last thing she wanted was this man running to Mr Wilkins and telling tales about her overdoin' it at The Goldsmiths'.

'I said, have you been being sick quite a lot recently?' the man repeated.

'I might have been,' Colleen said cautiously. 'Two or three times, anyway.'

'Have you had any aches and pains? Especially in the area of the lower back?'

Colleen was starting to get annoyed. 'You try standin' on your feet for twelve hours a day, an' see if you don't get a few aches now an' again,' she said.

The man chuckled, though Colleen had no idea what she'd said that was so funny.

'Have you talked these symptoms of yours over with your mother?' he asked.

'Me mother lives in Cheshire,' Colleen said, thinking to herself that he must be really stupid if he didn't even know that.

'Well, have you discussed them with anyone else? An older neighbour, perhaps?'

'Why should I have?' Colleen demanded. 'It's none of their business, is it?'

'What about your menstrual cycle?'

'Me what?'

'Your monthly discomfort. Is it normally very regular?'

'No,' Colleen said. 'When I'm worried, it goes all haywire.'

'And are you worried now?'

The question which had been lurking at the back of Colleen's mind had finally wriggled its way to the front, and now she determined to put it without delay.

'Just who are you?' she asked. 'What are you doin' here? An' what's my monthly discomfort got to do with you, anyway?'

The man chuckled again. Really, it was very annoying.

'Oh, I'm sorry,' he said. 'I never introduced myself, did I? My name's Dr Rankin. Your husband called me just after you collapsed, and now that I've examined you, I'm inclined to think that . . .'

'That I've been overworkin' in the pub,' Colleen snapped, thinking as she spoke that these irrational bouts of temper weren't like her. 'Well, I haven't!'

'No, I wasn't going to say that,' the doctor told her. 'I was *going* to say that while we can't be sure yet, you're showing all the classic symptoms of someone's who's expecting a baby.'

A clock – somewhere on the other side of the river – struck two, and Annie turned restlessly in her bed. She'd been lying there for over three hours, she thought to herself.

Three hours! And she was still no closer to sleep than she'd been when she'd first laid her head on the pillow. Yet how could she hope to sleep when there was a yearning inside her – a yearning for Tom – which was almost eating her away?

She remembered that evening on Battle Bridge Lane, when the fog had been snaking its way up from the river and she and Tom had been walking along arm in arm. He'd said she'd soon forget her old friends, and she'd slapped him. And then . . . ah, and then.

She could almost feel his powerful body pressing against her as it had that night. She could taste him in her mouth, and her thighs tingled as if, even now, his hands were caressing them.

How she wished that after they'd been interrupted – after they'd heard the voices coming out of the fog – they'd gone somewhere else and finished what they'd started! Just to have known what it was like to make love to him once would have made all that followed bearable. But she'd thought she had all the time in the world.

And now it was too late.

In the bed at the other end of the room, Peggy stirred and uttered the single word, 'Goat!' A sad smile came to Annie's face. It must be wonderful to be a child, she thought, to have simple desires which were not complicated by jealousy or duty or promises you couldn't bring yourself to break however much you wanted to.

She drifted off into sleep, and in that sleep she was back in the fog, with Tom by her side. But this time it was different – this time, when they heard the voices, the wall they were leaning against just melted away, and suddenly they were standing in a room draped in swirling silk and satin.

'I'm goin' to undress you now,' said the Tom of her dream.

'Yes! Please!' Annie begged.

At his gentle touch, her clothes seemed to fall away from her, and soon she was completely naked.

Tom stepped back to look at her – and gasped with amazement.

'Yer perfect,' he said.

'Course I'm not,' Annie told him awkwardly. 'No woman is.'

'Well, yer look perfect to me.'

'Then that's all that matters.'

Tom picked her up in his powerful arms and suddenly she saw the bed – a huge bed, floating serenely across the room like a great white swan.

Tom laid her on the bed, and now, though she had not noticed it happen, he was naked, too. She looked at his powerful shoulder muscles, at his broad chest . . . at the thing between his legs which showed the urgency of his need for her.

'You're perfect,' she said.

'Course I'm not,' Tom replied with an easy grin. 'No man is.'

'Well, you look perfect to me.'

'Then that's all that matters.'

He kissed her breasts, he kissed her belly, he kissed the hidden, secret area which even she herself had hardly ever been able to touch without a feeling of guilt.

And then he was astride her, entering her and sending shocks of pleasure through her body which she would never have imagined possible.

She locked her ankles behind his back – she didn't know why, it just seemed right – and the sensations became so intense that she thought she would pass out . . .

She was awake again, lying in her lonely bed. She ran her hands over her cotton nightdress, pretending that it was Tom who was stroking her firm breasts. She let her right hand make its way between her legs, and with one finger began to rub herself gently.

And as she did these things to herself, she wept softly. Her heart would always be Tom's, she thought, no matter what happened to her in the future. But her body – sooner or later – would betray him.

More tears trickled from her eyes. She cried herself to sleep and dreamed of Tom again, but this time, he was not lying beside her and almost driving her out of her mind with his love-making – this time he was dead.

PART FOUR: A DEATH ON THE RIVER

Spring 1902

CHAPTER FIFTEEN

Spring came early that year. The sun, forcing its way through the grey winter clouds, bore down on the snow which lay heavy on the streets of Southwark, then sat back and smiled as the last of the melting enemy retreated down the gutters of Lant Place and disappeared, with a last gurgle of protest, down the drains.

With the white mantle of winter cast off, the new season began to move apace. Buds sprouted on the trees in All Hallows churchyard and daisies pushed their way up on the waste ground near St. Evelina's Hospital. Birds who had survived the winter basked in unaccustomed warmth, while those which had travelled from foreign lands swooped around the roof tops in search of suitable sites for their summer homes. Nor were the swallows and swifts the only creatures to return to London – the spring also brought with it Nettie Walnut, the old tramp who had been calling on Lil Clarke for nearly twenty years.

'An' she really don't look a day older than the first time I set eyes on 'er,' Lil thought, looking at Nettie, who was sitting at the opposite side of the kitchen table.

But though she didn't look any older, it was hard to imagine Nettie ever having been young, either. Her nose was hooked, her eyes small and deep set, her mouth a long gash edged with the thin lips. All in all, she had a face that looked as though it had been carved out of wood, and a skin which shone as if the craftsman who'd created her had devoted days to polishing it up to perfection.

'We 'spected yer to be comin' round some time in November, like usual,' Lil said as she offered Nettie a cup of tea and a slice of bread and marge.

'Meant to come then,' the old tramp answered briskly. 'Only I was busy – too many things on.'

Lil wondered what a vagabond, who carried everything she owned around in one small bundle, could possibly have been busy *with* – but thought it kinder not to ask.

'Well, it's nice to see yer, whenever yer can find time to come,' she said.

'Yes, I likes to cheer people up,' Nettie replied. 'It's me main purpose in life, as yer might say. So tell me what's been 'appenin' round 'ere while I's been away.'

'We got new neighbours since yer last called,' Lil said. 'A young couple. Luverly people. 'E's got a wooden leg an' she's goin' to 'ave a baby in August.'

' 'S nice 'avin' babies,' Nettie said, taking a clay pipe out of one of the pockets of her ragged dress and lighting it with a match she struck on the heel of her oversized boots.

' 'Ave you ever 'ad any children, then?' Lil asked.

'No,' Netti replied, puffing away happily at her pipe. 'But me mam did.'

'Yes, I thought she prob'ly would 'ave 'ad,' Lil said, wondering what it would be like to see the world through Nettie's eyes. 'So where will yer go tonight? Down to St. Saviour's Work'ouse?'

'That's right,' Nettie said. 'I allus go there. Well, they'd be disappointed if they found out I'd been in London an' not stayed with them.'

'Would they, Nettie?' Lil asked, doing her best to hide her smile behind her teacup.

'Course they would,' Nettie said. 'The Walnut's 'ave been stayin' at St. Saviour's for two 'undred years.'

This time, even with the help of the tea cup, Lil couldn't keep her amusement in.

'It's true,' Nettie protested. 'One of the fellers what works there showed me the old work'ouse records.

Course, I couldn't read 'em meself, but 'e said that Ebenezer Walnut – 'e must 'ave been me great-great-great-grandad – first stayed at St. Saviour's in seventeen-oh-six, an' there's been what 'e called "an unbroken line" of us visitin' it ever since.'

'So your family 'ave been tramps for two 'undred years!' Lil said, amazed.

'Much longer than that,' Nettie told her. 'We was tramps when Good Queen Bess was on the throne. I gots me whole family 'istory up 'ere,' she tapped her head, 'an' one day, I might get somebody to write it all down.'

It suddenly occurred to Lil that though she had lived two streets down from the workhouse ever since the day she got married, it was as unknown to her as if it had been a thousand miles away.

'What's St. Saviour's like, Nettie?' she asked, with new-found curiosity.

'Like any other work'ouse, more or less,' the old tramp replied in a tone which suggested that she considered it a particularly stupid question.

'An' what's any other work'ouse like?' Lil asked patiently.

'Like St. Saviour's,' Nettie said.

It was unusual for Lil to be on the *puzzled* end of a conversation, and she was not quite sure she liked the feeling.

'What 'appens when yer go there, Nettie?' she asked.

'You mean, from the start?' Nettie asked.

'Yes, that's what I mean,' Lil agreed, glad to be getting somewhere at last.

'Well, first we queues up,' Nettie said, ' 'cos they've only got so many places, an' if you doesn't get there early, there's no room for you. Then, around six o'clock, the porter opens the door and lets us in. Once we's inside, we gets split up – the men go one way an' the women and kids the other. The men gets searched to see if they's got more than fourpence on 'em – 'cos if they 'as they're not allowed in. The porter tries to take their pipes an' tobaccer off 'em an' all, but the men usually 'as 'em hidden.

'Where?' Lil asked.

Nettie grinned. 'You'd be shocked if I told you some of the places as they hides their pipes, love,' she said. 'Anyway, once we's inside, they insists we all 'as a hot bath, which I don't mind, once in a way. Then we 'as supper – a pint of gruel an' six ounces of bread. Then we goes to bed – 'cos they got real beds in there, you see.'

'Go on,' Lil said.

'How does you mean?'

'What 'appens next?'

'Well, we goes to sleep, o' course.'

'I mean, in the morning.'

'In the mornin' we wakes up an' 'as breakfast,' Nettie said.

'What do they give yer for breakfast?' Lil asked.

Nettie looked at her oddly. 'Bread an' gruel, o' course,' she said. 'An' after that, we gets put to work, don't we?'

'What sort of work?'

Nettie shook her head.

'Doesn't you know anythin'?' she asked. 'The women's set to cleanin' an' washin, and the men picks oakum – an' oakum, in case you doesn't even know what that is, is what you gets when you undoes rope. They uses it to make boats watertight.'

'I see,' Lil said.

'We 'as dinner – bread 'an cheese – then we does some more work till it's time for supper . . .'

'Bread and gruel,' Lil supplied.

'What else would it be?' Nettie wondered. 'Then, in the mornin', after breakfast, they shows us to the street, an' we can't go back for at least two night.'

'But I thought people lived in the workhouse all the time,' Lil said, horrified at the prospect of them being shown the street after such a short time.

'They're not casuals like me,' Nettie told her. 'They's the reg'lar inmates you's thinkin' of. A fine time of it, they 'as.' She licked her lips. 'They gets real meat for supper, four an' an 'alf ounces each. An' porridge for breakfast. They gets more interestin' jobs, an' all – some of the men even gets to make furniture and cobble boots.'

'Wouldn't you like to be one o' the reg'lar inmates yerself, Nettie?' Lil asked.

The old tramp shook her head. 'They'd 'ave me, o' course,' she said. 'They thinks the world of me down there. But I enjoys me freedom too much to be anythin' but a casual.' She glanced up at the clock on the kitchen wall. 'What's the time, missus?' she asked.

'Nearly four o'clock,' Lil said.

'Then I's'd better be on me way if I doesn't want to spend the night under a bridge,' Nettie replied. 'I's lookin' forward to a good old natter with the other casuals.'

'What do yer natter about?' Lil asked, intrigued.

'Why, you lot what live in 'ouses,' Nettie said. 'Us tramps see a lot of things. I bets that by tomorrow, I knows more of what goes on round 'ere than you does.'

Lil laughed. 'I'm sure yer will, Nettie,' she said, never dreaming as she spoke just how valuable Nettie and her tramp friends were going to be in the difficult days which lay ahead.

On Sunday, Annie and Harry took the train to Epping Forest. It was a perfect day for walking and, picnic baskets in their hands, they set off to explore the woods. Annie loved it all – the springy earth under her feet, the air which was filled with the smells of wild flowers, damp moss and new leaves, the chirping of the birds and scurrying of small animals.

'I could live here, Harry,' she said.

'Get on with yer,' Harry replied good-naturedly. 'Yer might like it well enuff for a day, but yer a city gal, born an' bred. Put yer out 'ere, an' it wouldn't be long before yer started missin' the pavements an' the gas-lamps.'

'Maybe you're right,' Annie said. 'But you have to admit, it is lovely out in the woods.'

'Anywhere's lovely when I'm with you,' Harry said.

And Annie, not knowing what she could say in return, said nothing at all.

They had been walking for over two hours before Annie confessed that she was getting a little tired.

'Yer see what I mean,' said Harry triumphantly. 'Yer missin' the trams already.'

They found a convenient clearing which they both agreed was the perfect spot to stop, and sat down to eat the dinner that Lil had packed for them. It was a sumptuous feast of potted beef sandwiches, chicken legs and hard-boiled eggs.

'She's done us proud,' Harry said with relish.

Done *you* proud, you mean, Annie thought, because it was a fact that Lil had a soft spot for Harry, and had made more effort for him than she would have done even for her own family.

They finished their food and then lay on their backs and looked at the bright blue sky which floated just above the treetops. It seemed to Annie, happy and relaxed as she was, that something wasn't quite right. And then she realised what it was – no tram cars rattling noisily by, no costermongers shouting out their wares, no clip-clopping of horses hooves. Apart from the birdsong and rustling of the leaves in the breeze, the wood was silent, and she and Harry might have been the only two people left in the world.

When Harry rolled over and put his strong arms around her, she did not resist. Nor did she try to stop him when he kissed her on her mouth with more passion than he had ever dared show before. It was only when she felt his eager hands caressing her bosom that she decided he had gone far enough.

'No, Harry!' she said.

But the hands did not stop exploring, and she could feel his hot breath on her neck.

'I said no!' she repeated, starting to panic now.

His hands continued to fondle, his body pressing urgently against hers. She pushed at his shoulders with all her might, though she knew that if he was really deter-mined, there was nothing she could do – nothing at all.

The hands released their hold, the body ceased to press, and Harry rolled away from her.

For at least a minute, she just lay there, gasping for breath and listening to her heart pound against her ribs. And then she turned to look at Harry. He was sitting a couple of feet away from her, the expression on his face a strange and disturbing mixture of humiliation and remorse.

'I'm sorry,' he said.

'It . . . it doesn't matter,' she gasped, still having trouble with her breathing. 'You . . . you just got a bit carried away, that's all.'

'It *does* matter,' Harry insisted. 'I should 'ave been able to control meself better than that. I should 'ave done things properly, right from the start, shouldn't I?'

'Properly? I don't know what you mean.'

Harry raised himself until he was on one knee, just like Tom had been outside the telephone exchange.

'Will yer marry me, Annie?' he asked.

She should have expected this, she supposed, but she hadn't – and now she had no idea how to deal with it.

'Are you really serious?' she asked.

'I've never been more serious in me life.'

'But you must know that I don't love you.'

'Yer might learn to, if yer give yerself the chance.'

'But what if I tried and I still couldn't?'

Harry shrugged his shoulders. 'I'm prepared to risk it if you are. An' whatever 'appened, I'd been a good 'usband an' a lovin' father.'

'I know you would,' Annie said regretfully. 'But I'm sorry, Harry . . . it just isn't enough.'

Harry bowed his head. 'I see,' he said.

Annie stretched across and put her hand on his arm. 'You've been nothing but good and decent to me since the first time we met, Harry,' she told him. 'And if, after this, you want to stop seeing me, I'll quite understand.'

Harry shook his still-bowed head.

'No,' he said. 'I don't want to stop seein' yer. I shouldn't 'ave tried to push yer today, either into marriage or . . . the other thing. I'll wait till yer ready – even if it takes an 'undred years.'

It was Wednesday afternoon, almost the middle of the

working week. Tom Bates stood half-way up Battle Bridge Stairs, watching the barges float by as slowly and lethargically as did his days, and reflecting on the fact that if he hadn't had his mum and his sisters depending on him, he'd probably have joined the army.

Or the circus. Or the tinkers, he thought to himself. Maybe I'd even 'ave gone to Australia.

Anything to take him away from Lant Place, where every lamppost – every crack in the pavement – reminded him of Annie Clarke.

'Well, if it ain't Tom Bates,' said a sneering voice behind him. ' 'Ow are yer gettin' on, me old pal?'

Tom spun round, only to see Rollo standing and glowering at him from the top of the steps.

'I didn't want no trouble the last time, Rollo,' he said evenly. 'And I don't want none now.'

'Just come out of the Scrubs, I 'ave,' Rollo said, slowly walking down the steps towards Tom. 'Six months, I did. Blackie an' Chas was there with me. But I didn't see you, did I?'

'You was standing next to me in the dock,' Tom said. 'You know what 'appened as well as I do.'

Rollo stopped, two steps higher up than Tom.

'Oh, I know what 'appened,' he said. 'You got that bobby to speak up for yer.'

'I never asked 'im to do it,' Tom replied.

'Well, maybe yer did and maybe yer didn't,' Rollo said. 'But yer got off, anyway. D'yer 'ave any idea what life's like inside the Scrubs, Tom?'

' 'Ow could I?' Tom asked.

'I was kept in a cell all on me own,' Rollo told him. 'Oh, it wasn't solitary confinement – I could 'ave stood that, not speakin' to anybody. No, what I 'ad was a bleedin' sight worse. People comin' round every day. The governor an' the chief screws, the chaplain an' prison visitors – all droppin' into me cell an' askin' if everyfink was all right. An' you can bet yer last tanner I 'ad to say yes or there'd 'ave been trouble. They even sent me a schoolteacher once, to ask if I'd like to learn to read proper. Well, I gave 'im pretty short shrift – an' got the birch for it!'

'I never wanted yer to go to prison,' Tom said.

'Didn't yer, now?' Rollo said. 'Well, the fac' is, I ended up there. An' I could 'ave stood it all if I'd just known that you was there inside with me.'

Rollo took another step down the Stairs.

'Watch 'im, Tom,' warned Dick Sharp, one of the other watermen, who'd been listening to the exchange from further up the Stairs.

Rollo rounded on him. 'Keep out o' this,' he said threateningly. 'This is between 'im an' me. Ain't that right, Tom?'

'Yes,' Tom agreed. 'It's between you an' me.'

'You sure yer don't want any 'elp, Tom?' asked Bill Rose, another waterman, who was standing at the bottom of the Stairs.

'Yes, I'm sure,' Tom replied, never taking his eyes off Rollo for a second.

'D'yer want to know what I was thinkin' all the time I was in prison, Tom?' Rollo asked.

'If yer want to tell me.'

'Well, it's this. I was thinkin' I'd be a lot 'appier in me own mind if I could be sure that sometime you'd 'ave to do a bit of sufferin' of yer own.'

His hand went into his pocket, and when it came out again, it was holding something.

'Look out! 'E's got a gun!' called Bill Rose.

Rollo raised his cheap pistol and aimed it at Tom's head. The young waterman flung himself up the steps, hitting Rollo square in the chest with all his body weight.

The two men went down. Rollo tried to twist his pistol round and fire, but Tom already had his left hand clamped tightly around his enemy's wrist. For a moment, they teetered on the edge of the step, and then, still locked together in combat, they began to roll down towards the river.

As they bounced from step to step, first one on top and then the other, it was impossible to say which of them would triumph. They hit the moorings on the landing stage with a crash, and both men grunted as the wind was knocked out of them.

Tom rolled away from his opponent and climbed shakily to his feet. He had the pistol in his hand.

'Yer never did learn to fight fair, did yer, Rollo?' he gasped.

Rollo looked up at him. 'Only a bleedin' idiot like you fights fair,' he said through clenched teeth.

'Set the Law on the bugger, Tom!' Dick Sharp shouted.

' 'E wants locking up again, an' that's the bleedin' truth!' said Bill Rose.

Tom hesitated, but only for a second, then glanced down at his old enemy. 'Get yerself out of 'ere, Rollo,' he said. 'Get yerself out of 'ere while yer still can.'

'Give me me gun back,' Rollo said.

'No gun,' Tom told him. 'That stays with me.'

Rollo climbed painfully to his feet and hobbled up the Stairs. At the top, he turned round and shook his fist at Tom.

'I'll be back for me revenge,' he shouted. 'An' if yer beat me the next time, I'll be back again. The only way yer goin' to be finished with me, Tom Bates, is when one of us kills the other.'

'So will you be seeing that dashing policeman of yours over the weekend?' Belinda asked Annie during the Friday lunch break.

'I do wish you wouldn't keep calling him *my* dashing policeman,' Annie said.

'But you will admit to the "dashing" bit of it?' Belinda said mischievously.

'Not dashing, exactly,' Annie told her, 'but there's no doubt he cuts a fine figure.'

'And you've been going around with him for . . . how long is it, now? Nearly a year?'

'Something like that.'

'A year, and you still haven't succumbed to his amorous advances, have you?' Belinda mused.

'Yer what?' Annie asked, forgetting for the moment that she was a telephone operator who'd paid out her hard-earned wages to learn to talk nicely.

'Don't understand me, heh?' Belinda said. 'Now, let me see, how would you say it on the other side of the river? I've got it!' She twirled an imaginary moustache under her nose. 'You still haven't given him his supper.'

'You really are an awful person, Belinda!' Annie said, feeling herself start to blush.

'You haven't, have you?' Belinda persisted. 'I'd be able to tell if you had.'

'No, I haven't,' Annie admitted.

But the previous Sunday, in Epping Forest, she'd come as close to it as she ever had. Because even when she'd pushed Harry away, there'd been a part of her which had wanted to give in, a part of her which had cried out for his caresses, for the feel of his body pressing down on hers.

She would probably do it soon, she thought. She couldn't bring herself to marry him, but at least she could succumb to his amorous advances – give him his supper! And why not? Now that she had lost Tom, there was no one she wanted to save herself for.

Sam and Peggy were standing in the queue outside the Zoological Gardens in Regent's Park.

'Now remember,' Sam told his daughter, 'I'm takin' yer to the zoo on one condition.'

'Yes, Dad,' Peggy said.

'An' what is that condition?'

'I forget.'

'In that case,' Sam said, 'we'd better turn round an' go 'ome right this minute.'

'I'm think I'm beginnin' to remember,' Peggy said quickly.

'I thought yer might,' Sam replied. 'So what is it?'

Peggy pursed her lips as if she was going to have to force the words out. 'I can go an' see the goats,' she said.

'But . . .?' her father prompted her.

'But I'm not to give yer any grief about gettin' one meself,' Peggy finished reluctantly.

'Correct,' Sam agreed.

'Strewth! It's enough to turn me back to a life o' crime,' Peggy whispered under her breath.

The gardens were in a festive mood that sunny Saturday. The spring flowers had only recently reached their full glory and everywhere was ablaze with colour. The people, too, seemed to have dressed for the occasion. The young women all wore their brightest frocks, and the young men accompanying them had new straw boaters perched rakishly on their heads. And everyone – from the youngest toddling child to gravest old gentleman – was carrying a brown paper bag stuffed full of buns and nuts.

'I read in the newspaper that it costs around four thousand nicker a year to feed all these animals,' Sam told his daughter. 'An' it'd cost a blessed sight more than that if it wasn't for all the grub the visitors bring 'em.'

'I wonder just 'ow much it would cost me to feed a go . . .?' Peggy began.

'What was that?' Sam asked sharply.

'Nuffink, Dad,' Peggy replied.

They strolled towards a corner of the gardens where a military band was playing.

'I think we'll stop 'ere for a bit,' Sam said.

'Do we 'ave to?' asked Peggy, who was more than anxious to be elsewhere.

'Yes, we do,' her father replied. 'I like a nice bit o' music now an' again.'

He got more of it than he bargained for. The bandstand was close to the wolf pit, and as soon the instrumentalists struck up a new tune, the wolves were joining in the music with untrained howls of their own invention.

Peggy stuck her fingers in her ears. 'Crikey, Dad, that's even worse than you singin' in the bath,' she said.

'Yer a cheeky young devil, ain't yer?' Sam said fondly. 'Come on, let's get it over with.'

'Get what over with?' Peggy asked innocently.

'The goats,' her father told her. 'The blinkin' goats.'

★

There were several of the creatures bounding over the rocky ground in the middle of the goat pit.

'*Capra hircus*,' Peggy said.

'Yer what?' her father asked.

'That's its proper name – *capra hircus*. I looked it up in the library.'

'An' what else did yer find out about 'em?'

Peggy closed her eyes. 'Ruminant, quadruped,' she recited. 'Forming with sheep the "caprine" section of the Bovid . . . Bovidae family.'

Sam laughed. 'An' what exactly does that lot mean?' he asked.

'It means they make very good pets,' Peggy told him.

'Is that right?' Sam said. 'Well, I'll tell yer somefink. Yer mother'd never stand for 'avin' one of them in the back yard. The smell alone'd put 'er off.

Peggy closed her eyes again. 'The male goat (commonly called the "billy") is characterised by a strong offensive smell, especially during the rutting season,' she quoted. 'This fact 'as given rise to the erroneous impression among many people that all goats have an unpleasant odour.'

'Could I 'ave that again, please?' Sam asked. 'An' in English this time, if yer don't mind.'

'People are stupid when they say goats stink.'

'Then what was that about a "strong offensive odour"?'

'Well, the billy goat does pong a *little* bit,' Peggy admitted. 'But only when 'e's feelin' romantic.'

'Thank you for explainin' that to me,' Sam said. 'Shall we go an' see some of the other animals, now?'

'I s'ppose so,' Peggy replied, forcing herself to tear her eyes away from the goats.

They made their way towards the hippopotamus enclosure.

'Are yer 'appy, Peggy?' Sam asked as they walked along hand in hand.

' 'Appy?' Peggy replied. 'Who wouldn't be 'appy when they were in the zoo?'

Sam smiled fondly at his daughter. It was easy to make sure your kids were happy when they were young, he thought, but when they got older it could be more of a problem. Eddie was all right – as long as he had his engines to play with, the rest of the world could go hang itself as far as he was concerned. But Sam worried about Annie. *She* hadn't been happy – not really happy – since that time young Tom Bates had been arrested.

Lil had told him not to worry. 'Our Annie's better off without Tom Bates,' she said. 'An' that 'Arry is ever such a nice lad.'

A nice lad he might be, but Annie didn't sparkle when she was with him – which she should have done if he'd been the one for her. And Sam didn't share his wife's opinion of Tom Bates, either. What he'd done down on Tooley Street – sticking up for his brother like that – had shown real character. And when all was said and done, character was what a man looked for in a son-in-law.

A crowd had gathered outside the hippo enclosure, and was peering curiously through the railings.

'I wonder what's goin' on 'ere,' Sam said.

'Maybe one o' the 'ippos 'as gone off its chump an' bitten its keeper's 'ead off,' Peggy suggested helpfully.

But the keeper's head was still very much on his shoulders, and he was standing next to the huge animal, tempting it – with a bun – to keep its mouth open while another man gazed in at its teeth.

'What do they want to go tormentin' the poor dumb creature for?' asked a large woman with hennaed hair and a sulky expression. 'It's a scandal, that's what it is.'

'They ain't tormentin' it,' said a man who looked as if he thought he knew everything. 'The bloke what's lookin' into its mouth is a dentist. I 'eard 'im say so.'

The sulky woman seemed somewhat mollified. 'Oh well,' she said, 'if they're measurin' him for false teeth, then I suppose it's all right.'

Sam and Peggy exchanged glances and then hurried away, not breaking out into hysterics until they were a good distance from the woman with the hennaed hair.

'An' 'ippo with false choppers!' Sam said between bouts of laughter. 'Can yer imagine it?'

'I wonder where 'e keeps 'em when 'e's asleep,' Peggy giggled.

'In a big glass o' water by the side of 'is bed, o' course!' Sam told her.

They laughed until their sides were splitting. Some of the other visitors looked at them a little strangely, but they didn't care. They were a father and daughter, out together and having a good time – which was just how it should be.

'Come on,' said Sam, when they'd finally calmed down. 'Let's go an' see if they're measurin' the giraffe for spectacles.'

And that, of course, started them both off again.

They found no spectacled giraffes, but Peggy did ride on the elephant twice, and when they got home they were both tired and happy.

It had been a perfect day, Sam thought as he sat in his favourite chair reading the paper – though looking back on it later, he would forget its perfection and see it simply as the last spot of calm before the storm came crashing down on all their heads.

Dawn was just breaking as the police duty boat drew level with Billingsgate Fish Market, and the gaslamps that had been burning throughout the night were already starting to lose their brilliance in the gentle pink glow of the early morning sun.

Harry Roberts looked across the water at the two steamers, fitted with ice tanks, which had arrived from the north-east coast sometime during the night and were now moored next to the market. 'The bridges should be comin' down any minute now,' he told his partner.

No sooner had he spoken than the metal bridges were lowered from the quay onto the steamers' decks. And no sooner were the bridges in place than a line of market porters started to dash down them like a swarm of hungry ants.

'Just look at 'em,' Harry,' said. 'Every time I feel like grousin' about me job – yer know, when it gets too cold or the wind starts cuttin' through me like a knife – I think o' them blokes, and suddenly it don't seem so bad after all.'

Traffic was operating both ways on the bridges now, with some porters going down empty-handed and others climbing back up with boxes of fish on their heads.

'What's wrong with bein' a porter?' Jack Davies inquired. 'Seems like steady work to me. I mean, people always gotta eat, ain't they? An' fish is the poor man's beefsteak.'

'Oh, the work's steady enough,' Harry agreed. 'But Gawd, it must be bleedin' borin'. Think about it. 'Ow would you feel about gettin' up for work if yer knew yer'd be doin' exactly the same thing today that yer did yesterday? At least in the Bobs there's always somethin' new 'appenin'.'

'That's true enough,' Jack agreed.

'Take this shift we're just finishin',' Harry continued. 'It's been a quiet one, 'asn't it?'

'Dead quiet.'

'An' if we was to get paid for what we'd done, we wouldn't be drawing much in wages this week. But even now, when we're 'eadin' back to Wappin', there's still a chance that somefink new an' interestin' might come up.' Harry took one of his habitual glances up the river and then pointed. 'Look at that, for instance.'

Jack's eyes followed Harry's finger and settled on a shape bobbing up and down in the water.

'It doesn't look like nuffink more than a bit of ole sackin' to me,' he said.

'An' maybe that's all it is,' Harry agreed. 'But it won't do us any 'arm to go an' 'ave a look, will it?'

Jack grinned. 'Yer a proper devil for findin' work for yerself, ain't yer? 'Arry?' he said.

'I always was,' Harry told him, grinning back.

They rowed at a leisurely pace at first, preserving their energy, like all good oarsmen, for when it might be needed. But as they got closer – as they began to see that the object was not a piece of old sacking at all – they redoubled their efforts.

'Not that there's any real 'urry,' Harry said as he pulled

hard on his oars. 'Whoever 'e is, the poor bloke's long past needin' our 'elp by now.'

The corpse was floating face down, but even so it was possible to guess that he was a big, well-muscled man.

'D'yer think it's a suicide?' Jack asked as they drew closer to the body.

'Could be,' Harry replied. 'Or it could be an accident. These bloody watermen just won't learn to swim, yer know. I've even offered to give some of 'em classes, but they'll 'ave none of it.'

When they were alongside the dead man, they stopped rowing and Harry reached for the boathook. With expert ease, he caught it in the victim's collar and pulled him gently toward the boat.

'I'll get 'old of *im*, an' you get 'old of *me*,' he told his partner.

Harry reached into the water and groped about until he had located the dead man's armpits. Then, placing his hands under them, he heaved the body aboard.

'What d'yer make of 'im?' he asked.

Jack examined the dead man. 'From the way 'e's dressed, I'd say 'e was an East-ender,' he pronounced. 'Round about twenty-one or twenty-two.' He touched the corpse's cheek with the back of his hand. 'An' from the feel of 'is skin, I'd guess 'e 'asn't been in the water long.'

Harry nodded his approval.

'I think yer right,' he said. 'I wouldn't put it at more than a few hours meself. Check through 'is clothes an' see if 'e's got any identification on 'im.'

Jack put his hand in first one of the corpse's jacket pockets, and then in the other.

'Nuffink. Not a sausage,' he said.

'See if 'e's got an inside pocket. People sometimes keep their valuables in there.'

Davies unbuttoned the jacket, peeled back the left lapel – and froze!

'Somefink the matter?' Harry asked.

But words seemed to have failed Jack Davies for the moment, and he merely pointed at the dead man's shirt.

Harry saw immediately what had knocked his partner off balance. Just at the level of the corpse's heart, there was a small, neat hole, edged in rusty brown.

'Is it . . . is it . . .?' Jack stammered.

'A gunshot wound?' Harry asked. 'Oh yes, I don't think there's any doubt about that.'

The colour which had drained from Jack's face when he made the discovery was slowly starting to return.

'Sorry I lost me 'ead,' he said. 'I ain't never seen anybody who's been shot before. Did he do it to 'imself, d'yer think?'

Harry shook his head. 'From what I've seen of suicides, they usually shoot themselves through the mouth or temple,' he said.

'Then it's murder!' Jack gasped.

'Looks that way,' Harry said calmly. He shifted his gaze from the wound to the victim's face. 'There's somefink familiar about this bloke, yer know.'

'Yer mean, yer think yer might 'ave nicked him sometime?'

'No, I'm sure I've never nicked 'im meself, but 'e was definitely in some sort o' trouble the last time I ran into 'im.'

'Maybe yer remember seein' 'im in some court or other?' Jack suggested.

'That's it!' Harry agreed. 'The last time I saw 'im, he was standin' in the dock at Tower Bridge Police Court, charged with causin' a breach of the peace in Tooley Street.'

'So who is 'e, then?'

' 'E is – or rather 'e was – a Newington 'Ooligan by the name of Rollo Jenkins.'

CHAPTER SIXTEEN

Since Rollo Jenkins was discovered floating slightly closer to the south bank of the river than he was to the north, it was decreed that the inquest on him should be held in the Southwark Coroner's Court. So it was that the day after fishing the man out of the Thames, Harry Roberts found himself pushing the mortal remains of Rollo in a police ambulance – really no more than a covered pram on wheels – into the mortuary at the back of the court.

There were three other bodies there, each of them lying in its own long metal box.

' 'Ave yer got much on today, Mr Philips?' Harry asked the big genial man who served as the coroner's officer.

'Not a great deal,' Philips replied cheerfully. He pointed to two of the boxes. 'They're a couple of suicides. One hung himself in the outside lavvy. The other threw himself under the express train from Brighton – and you can imagine the mess he's in.'

'Yes, I can,' Harry said.

Philips pointed to the third box. 'That's an old tramp we picked up near the workhouse. Drank himself to death, by the look of his nose. And then there's yours,' he continued, patting the ambulance Harry had just brought in. 'Four altogether. Shouldn't be more than a morning's work. The coroner won't like it much, but I expect the jury will be pleased.'

Harry nodded. Jurymen were paid two bob a day whether there was one inquest to sit through or twenty-five. The coroner, on the other hand, received thirty shillings per inquest, and would probably have been much happier if he'd had quite a few more corpses to pontificate over.

'I've scheduled your case to be the first one,' Mr Philips said. 'After all, you don't want to be stuck in this place longer than you have to be, do you?'

'That was very kind of yer, Mr Philips,' Harry said.

The coroner's officer tapped his big nose with one finger. 'You've always played fair with me, Harry, so there's no point in making life difficult for you. Besides, yours is the simplest case of the lot.'

'The simplest!' Harry exclaimed. 'Since when 'as a murder been simpler than a suicide?'

'Perhaps I shouldn't have said *simplest*,' the coroner's officer amended. 'What I really meant was, it'll be quickest of them all to deal with.'

'Why's that?'

'Well, as you know, we usually summon a couple of the dead man's relatives to give us a picture of what he was like in life, his mental state just before his death, and so on.'

'Yes?'

'In this case I couldn't find anyone who even admitted *knowing* Rollo Jenkins, – let alone being related to him. So the only people called to give evidence will be you and the doctor.'

The jurors were sworn in and taken to the mortuary to view the bodies. They emerged again – some of them looking slightly green – and took their places in the jury box. Then Mr Philips called the first case, and Harry stepped up to give his evidence.

He and his partner had noticed the body in the river just after dawn, he told the court in the clear, precise manner he had perfected over the years. They had fished it out, and he had realised that the dead man was Rollo Jenkins.

'What can you tell the jury about the man Jenkins?' the coroner asked.

'That he was the leader of a gang known as the Newington 'Ooligans an' that he caused far more trouble than we could ever prove against 'im, sir.'

'He had a criminal record, did he not?'

'Yes, sir. I meself was present in the Tower Bridge Police Court when 'e was sentenced to six months in Wormwood Scrubs for disturbin' the peace.'

'And did he have any enemies that you know of?'

' 'Ooligans always 'ave enemies, sir. Especially when they're gang leaders, like 'e was.'

'Could you perhaps give us a few examples?'

Harry shrugged. 'Members of rival gangs,' he suggested. 'Members of 'is own gang 'oo fancy takin' over the leadership from 'im. Shopkeepers 'oo've got tired of payin' out to the gang in order not to 'ave their winders smashed. People 'oo've been robbed by 'em an' know full well who's done it, but don't 'ave any evidence to take to the police. Tradesmen 'oo . . .'

'Thank you, Constable. You've given us a very full list,' the coroner interrupted him.

'I've 'ardly started, sir,' Harry said.

'Nevertheless, I think we've heard enough to establish that any number of people might have wished the deceased ill,' the coroner said. 'You may step down now, constable.'

Harry went back to his seat and turned his attention to a stocky man who was sitting at the back of the room with a bowler hat on his lap. The man seemed to take considerable interest in the proceedings, and at one point had even taken out a notebook and written something down. He could be a reporter, Harry thought, but he knew all the court reporters – at least by sight – and this bloke was a complete stranger to him.

The coroner called the only other witness, a doctor who testified that the cause of death was a bullet in the heart.

'You're quite sure of that, doctor?' the coroner asked.

'Absolutely,' the doctor replied. 'There was very little water in his lungs.'

'And what does that lead you to infer?'

'That he didn't drown. That he was already dead when he first entered the river.'

'Thank you, doctor.'

After the coroner's guiding remarks, it took the jury little more than a minute to reach its verdict.

'We find the deceased, known as Rollo Jenkins, was murdered by a person or persons unknown,' the foreman announced.

'I agree with your verdict,' the coroner said. 'And now, if we might proceed to the next inquest, Mr Philips . . .'

The stocky man with the bowler hat was standing on the pavement outside the court, and the moment he saw Harry leaving he took a couple of quick steps to the right, deliberately blocking the constable's way.

'Can I help yer?' Harry asked.

'My name's Walton,' the man told him. 'I'm an inspector in the Detective Branch.'

'Pleased to meet yer, sir,' Harry said.

'Are yer indeed?' the inspector replied drily. 'I was listenin' to yer evidence in there. Yer gave me a couple of good leads on motive – rival gangs, angry shopkeepers an' so on.'

'Gave *you* a couple o' good leads?'

'That's right. Now it's officially a murder, it's a job for the Detective Branch.'

'I see,' Harry said.

'I'm not sure yer do entirely, Constable Roberts,' the inspector told him. 'I've been doin' a bit of checkin' up on you. An' d'yer know what I found out?'

'No, sir.'

'That yer a good copper, but yer take it all far too personal. As far as you're concerned, it's *your* river yer patrol, an' the blokes up to no good on it are *your* villains, Ain't that right?'

'I find lookin' at it that way 'elps me to do me job better,' Harry said, thinking that if this bloke wasn't his superior officer, he'd be tempted to give him a real pasting.

' "Dogged", that's what they call yer,' Walton

continued. 'Well don't go gettin' "dogged" on this case. I've worked 'ard to get where I am, an' I'm not about to 'ave some bright young bobby stickin' 'is nose in where it's not welcome. 'Ave I made meself clear?'

'Oh yes, sir,' Harry said. 'I think yer've made yerself *very* clear.'

'I'll be off about me business, then,' Walton said. 'An' remember what I told yer. It ain't your case no more – so the best thing you can do is forget all about it.'

Harry stood in the court doorway and watched Walton stride purposefully away. So they'd taken his case off him, had they? he thought angrily. And now it was a job for the detective branch, was it? Well, he was the one who'd fished the body out of the water – and he was the one who was going to find out who'd put it in there.

'Suppose that you were going to – oh, what were those words you used? – suppose you were going to succumb to your man's amorous advances,' Annie said. 'How exactly would you go about it?'

Belinda, who was energetically chewing her way through a pork chop, almost choked.

'How would I do what?' she asked, when she'd finally be able to soothe the piece of meat down her throat with a drink of water.

'Go about it?' Annie repeated.

Belinda smiled mischievously. 'I'd probably start by uncrossing my legs,' she said.

'Oh, do be serious!' Annie said exasperatedly.

'All right,' Belinda agreed. 'I'd invite him up to the house for the weekend, I suppose. Then I'd suggest we play a game of tennis – because tennis dresses are quite skimpy, you know, and it'd give him a proper look at the goods . . .' She stopped, realising exactly what she was saying. 'That wouldn't work for you, would it? You don't have a tennis court, do you?'

'Not unless me dad's built one in the back yard while I've been at work,' Annie admitted.

'I don't suppose you have Hunt Balls south of the river,

either, do you?' Belinda asked, with just a trace of her mischief creeping back into her voice.

'Not that I've noticed,' Annie said.

'Then it is a problem,' Belinda told her. 'I mean, people get so upset if you're wicked in public, don't they? No chance you could take him to your house, I suppose?'

'You must be joking,' Annie replied. 'There's always somebody in – if it's not mum and dad, it's Eddie or Peggy – an' even if they were all out by some miracle, they'd soon find out from the neighbours that I'd been "entertaining" a man on me own.'

'No chance he'd wear a disguise, is there?' Belinda asked. 'Pretend he'd come to read the gas meter or was a tally man?'

'I don't want to do it like that,' Annie said.

'You're probably right,' Belinda agreed. 'That would be only one step up from being unceremoniously deflowered in some back alley after the pubs have closed.'

'So what *am* I going to do?' Annie asked.

'You could take him to Epping Forest again, only this time when he starts with all the hot breath and panting, you let him know the feeling's mutual.'

'And how do I do that?' Annie asked, though she was sure that if it had been Tom she'd been taking to Epping Forest, she would have needed no instruction.

'Oh, there's dozen of ways to go about it,' Belinda said. 'You could nibble his ear. Or tickle the back of his neck, ever so gently, with your finger. Then again, you could simply grab his . . .'

'Grab his what?'

'No, that's not a good idea since it's your first time. You'd probably be better just sticking to ear nibbling.' Belinda leant back in her chair and smiled the smile of a teacher who is pleased to see a promising pupil coming along well. 'So you're finally going to give your dashing policeman his supper, are you?' she asked.

'Yes, I might as well,' Annie replied.

'Might as well!' Belinda repeated. 'You're not exactly burning up with the flames of passion, are you?'

'It's the one thing he wants from me that I can give him,' Annie said. 'And I must admit, I'm curious about it myself. Anway, why are you making such a big fuss? It's just part of life, isn't it?'

'That's certainly one way of looking at it,' Belinda agreed, eyeing her strangely.

It felt odd to be doing a round of the pubs in Newington in his ordinary clothes, but Harry reminded himself that this was an unofficial investigation he was conducting and his uniform would have been completely out of place.

How many boozers had he visited already, he wondered. Ten? Twelve? The number was unimportant, because he would keep searching until he found what he was looking for – no matter how long that took.

It was at a run-down pub called The Green Man that he finally struck lucky and spotted the two hooligans – one with shifty eyes and the other with a vacant expression – whom he hadn't seen since their last appearance before the Tower Bridge magistrate.

They were standing at the counter, drinking pints of porter with whisky chasers. They seemed to have got themselves a new tailor since the last time he'd met them, Harry thought, because although the jackets they were wearing were extremely gaudy, they looked quite expensive too.

Harry walked to the bar and took up a position to the right of Blackie. 'Hello, lads,' he said. 'D'yer remember me?'

The two hooligans turned their heads towards him.

'Yes, we remember yer,' Blackie said. 'Yer a bleedin' copper, ain't yer?'

'Has another bleedin' copper called Inspector Walton been round to see yer?' Harry asked.

Blackie grinned. ' 'E's been round all right – but 'e ain't seen us.'

'I expected yer to turn up at Rollo's inquest,' Harry said, 'what with 'im bein' a pal o' yours an' all that.'

The hooligan shrugged. 'We was out o' town. Anyway,

what would 'ave been the point o' turnin' up in court? 'E's dead, ain't 'e? There's nuffink *we* can do for 'im now.'

'Yer could 'elp us to find the bloke who did 'im in,' Harry pointed out.

Blackie took a thoughtful sip of his pint.

'I'm surprised yer even lookin' for 'is killer,' he said. 'After all, Rollo was only an 'ooligan, wasn't 'e? An' who gives a bugger what 'appens to 'ooligans?'

'I give a bugger,' Harry replied. 'It was my patch 'e was found on – that makes 'im my responsibility. An' I'm goin' to keep lookin' for 'is murderer until I find 'im.'

The two hooligans exchanged meaningful glances.

'Let's go somewhere a bit quieter, where we can 'ave a serious talk,' Blackie said.

Somewhere quieter turned out to be the saloon bar of The Burning Bush, another pub just a few doors down from The Green Man. There were two courting couples in the bar when they arrived, but at a gesture from Blackie, they quickly got up and left.

The hooligans led Harry to a table in the corner, and all three of them sat down.

'Are yer really serious about not givin' up till yer've found out 'oo killed Rollo?' Blackie said.

'That's what I said, ain't it?' Harry replied.

'It'll cost yer a drink,' Blackie said, and while Harry went up the bar to get them, the two hooligans had an urgent, whispered conversation.

Harry returned with three pints and placed two of them in front of Chas and Blackie.

'A whisky to 'elp it down would 'ave been nice,' Chas complained.

'Bugger the whisky,' Harry said. He turned to Blackie. 'Tell me what yer know.'

'The last time we saw Rollo was a few hours before he was fished out o' the river,' Blackie said. 'We were in a pub in Rother'ithe. Rollo left just before it closed.'

'Can anybody confirm that Rollo was there?'

'Con-what?'

'Can anybody else back up yer story about Rollo bein' in this pub with yer?'

'They could,' Blackie said, 'but they ain't about to.'

'Why not?'

'Well, this partic'lar pub don't exactly keep to reg'lar licensing times, yer see – an 'oo'd be fool enough to admit they'd been drinkin' after hours?'

That was true enough, Harry thought to himself. Why should any of the rough costermongers and dockers who patronised that sort of place risk getting a pound fine to catch the killer of a toe-rag like Rollo Jenkins?

'So what time was it when Rollo left the boozer?' Harry asked.

'About a quarter past one.'

'And why didn't you go with 'im?'

' 'E didn't want us to, did 'e? See, 'e said 'e'd arranged to meet somebody down by the river. Said 'e 'ad some unfinished business to deal with.'

'An' I don't s'ppose 'e bothered to tell yer what the name of this person 'e was meetin' was, did 'e?' Harry asked.

'Well, that's where yer wrong, Mr Bleedin'-smart-alec-copper,' Blackie said. ' 'E did tell us.'

'An' who was it?' Harry demanded.

'Tom Bates,' Blackie replied.

The two men stood on the river bank looking out over the water. At their backs was the borough of Rotherhithe and the pub – not more than a couple of minutes from this spot – where Chas and Blackie said they'd seen Rollo Jenkins for the last time.

'D'yer mind if I ask yer what we're doin' 'ere?' Jack Davies asked. 'I mean, we are off duty, yer know.'

'Course we are,' Harry Roberts replied. 'That's 'ow we 'appen to 'ave the time to try out a little experiment.'

'An experiment! Ain't that grand! I s'ppose that's why yer've brought them with yer,' Jack said, pointing to several spars of wood which had been tied together with rope.

'That's right,' Harry agreed.

'Any particular reason yer've brought *just* that amount?'

' 'Ow 'eavy would yer say Rollo Jenkins was?'

' 'Bout twelve an' an 'alf stone.'

'An' that's just about 'ow 'eavy that wood is.'

'When are yer goin' to tell me what this experiment o' yours is all in aid of?' Jack asked.

'I'm not,' Harry replied. 'I'm doin' somefink the Detective Branch don't exactly approve of, an' I don't want me partner gettin' involved with it.'

'Then why am I 'ere at all?' Jack wondered.

'Because I need a second man at the oars,' Harry told him.

'Well, it's nice to know I'm useful for somefink,' Jack said, sounding a little aggrieved.

Harry consulted his watch. 'It's about time,' he said.

'Time for what?' Jack asked. 'Oh, I'm sorry, yer don't want me gettin' involved.'

'Give me an 'and to get this wood into the river, will yer, Jack?' Harry said.

'Oh, I can do that without gettin' involved, can I?'

Harry grinned. 'Yes, yer can do that without gettin' involved,' he said.

The two men picked up the spars, waded out in the water until it came up to their knees, and then lowered their burden down onto the surface.

'I name this wood The Good Ship Waste o' Time,' Jack said. 'An' may Gawd 'elp all who sail in 'er.'

For a second or two, the spars simply bobbed up and down, then they did a half turn, were picked up by the current and started to move off down river.

'An' now what do we do?' Jack asked.

'An' now we get in the boat an' follow them,' Harry told him.

'Course we do,' Jack replied. 'Bit stupid of me even to ask, wasn't it?'

When the floating timber and the boat both drew level with Billingsgate, Harry told his partner to stop rowing and took out his pocket watch.

'Yer wood's gettin' away,' Jack said.

'Don't matter now,' Harry answered. 'It's served its purpose.'

'An' just what was its purpose, exact'ly?' Jack said.

'I told yer . . .' Harry began.

'Yer told me yer didn't want me gettin' involved,' Jack interrupted him. 'Well, I'm yer partner, an' everyfink I know about the river, I've learned from you. If there's any glory to be got out o' this, I want me share . . .'

'There might not be . . .'

'. . . an' if any trouble comes from it, then I want me 'alf of that as well.'

Harry gave his partner a searching glance. 'All right,' he said finally. 'I talked to a couple of Rollo's pals who told me 'e left a pub in Rother'ithe at about a quarter past one on Sunday night.'

'Go on,' Jack said.

'Give 'im ten minutes to walk down to the river an' another five for an argument, an' 'e would 'ave gone into the water about 'alf past. Now the wood represents Rollo . . .'

'I'd managed to work that bit out for meself,' Jack said.

'An' we put it into the water at about the same point on the tide, as near as I could estimate it. So it should 'ave taken just about as long to get from Rother'ithe to Billingsgate as Rollo's body did on Sunday night.'

'An' did it?'

'Not to the minute – but close enough.'

'Which tells yer what?'

'Which tells me that Blackie and Chas were probably tellin' the truth about that pub Rollo was in, and what time 'e left it.'

'So what are yer goin' to do now?' Jack asked.

'Now I'm goin' to make a few inquiries about the bloke Rollo's pals say 'e went out to meet,' Harry said.

Even from the corner of Tooley Street, you could hear the sound of singing coming from The Duke of Clarence. It was known to be a lively pub on most nights of the week,

Harry thought, but when it was holding a "friendly lead", as it was that evening, the number of customers – and the din – was more than doubled.

He stopped for a moment and studied the black-boarded card which was his invitation.

'THE DUKE OF CLARENCE', BATTLE BRIDGE LANE
A SELECT HARMONIC MEETING
will take place at the above house
for the benefit of the widow and children of the late
Ted Collins
Who died after a short illness leaving a wife and
seven children. The late T.C. being a good supporter
of these meetings, it is the wish of the undersigned
that his and our friends will support
the widow in her hour of need.

Harry scanned through the names of 'the undersigned' . . . Bill Cowley, Bob Fricker, Joe-the-butcher, Bandy Chambers, Deafy, Tiger Willis . . . There were a few minor villains amongst them, but on the whole they were decent, hard-working people.

'He read on . . Ginger Brown . . . he was a waterman from Battle Bridge Stairs, and so were Bill Rose and Dick Sharp. Yes, they would do for a start.

'Nice to see yer, Constable Roberts,' said the doorman when he handed in his card.

'I never miss a friendly lead if I can possibly 'elp it, Sid,' Harry replied.

It was true. He considered it both a duty and an honour to attend to these meetings, and to play his part in seeing that the dead man got a decent send-off. But he hadn't gone there to pay his respects to the memory of the late Ted Collins that night – he was much more interested in learning exactly what had gone on between Rollo Jenkins and Tom Bates.

Harry stepped through the door and into the pub. There

were watermen at every table, and at the far end of the room a large, red-faced man was just beginning a monologue.

'It's a curious thing to reflect sometimes
On the various incidents passin' around.
To think of the number of 'orrible crimes
Whose authors 'ave never as yet been found.
A murderer's 'and may be clasped in ours,
In the grasp o' friendship, warm an' true.
Should we love it the less or cease to caress,
If we only knew?'

Harry looked around him and spotted Dick Sharp and Bill Rose. He made his way to their table. 'Mind if I join yer?' he whispered.

'Course not, Constable Roberts,' Dick Sharp said.

'Yer should 'ave come earlier,' Bill Rose told him. 'Yer've missed 'alf the fun.'

He might have missed some of the fun, Harry thought, but if he'd come earlier he wouldn't have found the watermen as much at their ease as they were now – and he wanted them relaxed for when he started his questioning. He signalled to the waiter.

'Three pints o' best, please.'

'Very kind of yer,' Bill Rose said.

'Think nuffink of it,' Harry replied, hoping he would get value for his money.

The red-faced man was reaching the end of his monologue.

'Let us succour the frail ones, bearin' in mind
That though in this world we meet not our due
For a kind act done, a crown may be won
In the world to come – If only we knew!'

The audience applauded enthusiastically.

'Beautiful,' Bill Rose said.

'Brings tears to yer eyes,' Dick Sharp agreed.

The performer, made even more red-faced by the

acclaim, bowed and returned to his seat. His place at the front of the room was taken by the chairman of the friendly lead.

'We're goin' to take a little break now,' he said.

'What the bleedin' 'ell for?' someone called out good-naturedly.

'To give yer all time to lubricate yer throats before the singin' starts,' the chairman responded.

'Fair enough,' the heckler agreed.

Harry turned to the watermen at his table. 'I 'ate to bother yer when yer 'avin a night out,' he said, 'but I was wonderin' – d'yer think yer could 'elp me with this little problem I've got at the moment?'

'If we can,' Bill Rose said.

Harry took a photograph out of his pocket and handed it across to him.

' 'Ave yer ever seen this man?' he asked.

The waterman peered at the picture. ' 'E don't look well, does 'e?'

Since the photograph had been taken in the morgue, that was hardly surprising, but Harry thought it best not to mention that fact to the watermen.

' 'Ave yer seen 'im?' he repeated.

' 'E does look familiar,' Dick Sharp admitted. 'Yes, I 'ave seem 'im – an' I'll tell yer where. He come down to the Stairs last week, lookin' for trouble.'

'What sort o' trouble?'

' 'E 'ad some kind o' grudge against one o' the watermen. They 'ad a real barney on the steps.'

'Who 'ad?'

'The bloke in the photo an' Tom Bates.'

'That's right,' Bill Rose agreed. 'I recognise 'im meself now. A really nasty piece o' work 'e was. Said the trouble between 'im an' Tom'd never be over till one of 'em 'ad done for the other.'

'I thought there'd be murder then an' there,' Dick Sharp chipped in. ' 'E 'ad a gun, yer see.'

'An' did 'e actually fire it?' Harry asked.

' 'E would 'ave done if 'e'd 'ad the chance,' Bill Rose

chuckled. 'But Tom didn't *give* 'im a chance, did 'e? 'E was up them steps an' 'ad the gun off the other bloke before yer could blink.'

'What 'appened to the gun,' Harry said.

'Well, Tom certainly didn't give it back to that Rollo bloke, did 'e?' Bill asked.

'No, 'e didn't,' Dick agreed.

'So 'e must 'ave kept it, mustn't e?' Bill concluded. A sudden look of concern came into his eyes. 'Tom won't get into any bother for that, will 'e?' he asked. 'I mean, 'e didn't start it.'

'No,' Harry promised. ' 'E won't get into any bovver for *that*.'

It was the following morning, in the locker room of Wapping Police Station, that Harry gave Jack Davies a brief summary of what he'd found out.

'So yer see, Tom Bates 'ad the motive, 'e 'ad the means an' 'e 'ad the opportunity,' he said when he'd reached the end. ' 'E was the one who killed Rollo Jenkins, all right.'

'Very clever,' Jack said gloomily. 'An' now yer know who the murderer is, what are yer goin' to do about it?'

'Take it to the Super.'

'Take it to the Super!' Jack repeated. ' 'Ave yer gone completely off yer 'ead?'

'I don't see I 'ave a lot of choice,' Harry replied.

'Listen, if it was anybody else yer'd got the goods on, I'd be *pushin'* yer into the Super's office,' Jack told him. 'But it ain't anybody else – it's Tom Bates, for Gawd's sake! Yer spoke up for 'im in court . . .'

'I know I did . . .'

'. . . an' the magistrate said that if 'e did somethin' more serious, it'd be a blot in yer copybook. And there's nuffink more serious than murder. Yer'll be ruined.'

'Yer not tellin' me anyfink I 'aven't thought out for meself already,' Harry said sombrely.

'It just ain't worth ruinin' yerself over somebody like Rollo,' Jack argued. ' 'E was a guttersnipe – the lowest o' the low. Tom Bates prob'ly did everybody a favour by killin' him, 'cos if 'e'd lived, 'e'd 'ave ended up killin' somebody 'imself.'

'We don't know that for sure,' Harry had argued. 'An' anyway, it ain't our choice to make. We've got to foller the law through, 'cos if *we* don't, 'ow can we expect anybody else to?'

'Yer not goin' to change yer mind whatever I say, are yer?' Jack asked.

'No, I'm not,' Harry admitted.

'Then yer'd better get it over with, 'adn't yer?'

The Superintendent toyed thoughtfully with an india-rubber band which lay on the desk in front of him.

'This case rightly belonged to the Detective Division,' he said. 'I'm surprised you weren't told that, Constable Roberts.'

'I was, sir. But it seemed as if once I got me teeth into it, I couldn't let go.'

The Superintendent frowned. 'Irregular. Highly irregular. Having said that, however, you do seem to have uncovered a great deal more in your investigation than Inspector Walton did in his.'

'I just got lucky, sir.'

'If there's one thing I can't stand in my men, it's false modesty,' the Superintendent said irritably. 'What you did was a fine piece of police work – and you know it!'

'Thank you, sir.'

'A fine piece of police work,' the Superintendent repeated, 'and the fact that it will probably lead to the termination of your very promising career is nothing short of tragic.'

'Yes, sir,' Harry agreed. 'Ain't that the truth?'

How long had it been since they'd arrested him on Battle Bridge Stairs, Tom wondered. Two hours? Three? He had no way of telling in this small windowless, clockless room. However long it had been, the handcuffs they'd slapped on him were starting to chafe his wrists now, but he was buggered if he was going to ask the man sitting opposite him – Detective Inspector Walton – if he could take them off. Tom didn't want any favours from the police.

'So yer knew Rollo Jenkins well did yer, Bates?' Walton said.

'We've been over all this before,' Tom said wearily.

'Then let's go over it again,' Walton snarled. 'When yer were the leader of the Borough 'Ooligans, yer 'ad a serious fight with Rollo, didn't yer?'

'That was years ago.'

'But yer punch-up on Tooley Street wasn't years ago, was it? An' that fight yer 'ad with 'im on Battle Bridge Steps only 'appened last week.'

'If yer speak to any of the other watermen, they'll tell yer that I didn't start it,' Tom said.

'No,' Walton agreed, 'but by the time it was over, yer 'ad Rollo's gun in yer pocket, didn't yer? Where's the gun now, Tom?'

'I threw it in the river.'

'An' why should yer 'ave gone an' done that?'

' 'Cos I 'ad no use for it.'

'Didn't yer, indeed?' Walton asked. 'Not even to shoot Rollo Jenkins with?'

'No,' Tom said firmly.

'Where were yer on Sunday night, then?' Walton demanded. 'An' don't say yer were at 'ome, 'cos we've already checked with yer mother, an' she said yer didn't get in till after three. So just what exac'ly were yer doin?'

'Walkin',' Tom said.

'Walkin',' Walton sneered. 'Walkin' until three o'clock in the mornin'! Now why should yer want to do that?'

Because walking helped take his mind off Annie Clarke. Because if he kept walking long enough, he would sometimes fall asleep through sheer exhaustion and – if he was lucky – he could spend a night without the vision of Annie coming to haunt him.

'I'm waitin' for yer answer,' Walton said.

'I was walkin' 'cos I felt like it,' Tom told him.

'Yer a lyin' little toerag!' Walton said, finally losing his temper. 'Yer went up to Rother'ithe where yer met Rollo

Jenkins and shot 'im with 'is own gun. An' then yer dumped 'is body in the river an' went 'ome. Now isn't that what really 'appened?'

'I didn't do it,' Tom said.

Walton sighed heavily. 'I've 'ad enough of this,' he said. 'Thomas James Bates, I am formally chargin' you with the murder of Rollo Jenkins. Yer not obliged to say anythin' but anythin' yer do say may be taken down an' used in evidence against yer.'

'I'm not guilty,' Tom said.

Walton smiled. 'So you say,' he told his prisoner. 'But guilty or not, if I know my juries, yer'll swing for it.'

CHAPTER SEVENTEEN

As Annie walked into the saloon bar of The Goldsmiths' Arms, she couldn't help wishing the butterflies in her stomach would go away.

'It's plain stupid, being nervous like this,' she told herself. 'You've made yer decision, an' now you should stick to it.'

She took a seat at a table in the corner of the bar and looked up at the clock. It was just nine-thirty, which meant that Harry should be arriving any minute.

She practised variations of her planned speech in her mind.

'Why don't we go to Epping Forest on Sunday, Harry?'

'I'm getting sick of being stuck in the Smoke. What about a trip to the country?'

'Have you ever picked your own mushrooms, Harry? I'm told they're delicious.'

Oh yes, it sounded very easy in theory, didn't it? But what if Harry didn't want to go? What if the memory of what had happened the last time made him turn her down? Then what should she do?

If Belinda had been in her place, she'd probably have nudged Harry in the ribs and said, 'Don't be a bloody fool, old chap, I'm taking you out to the woods to give you your supper!' But somehow, Annie couldn't see herself acting like that.

'Do you want anythin' to drink, Annie?' called a voice from behind the bar.

Annie looked up. 'No thanks, Colleen,' she answered. 'I think I'll wait till Harry gets here.'

She watched Colleen as the barmaid reached up – with difficulty – for some glasses on the top shelf. There was no wonder she found it a struggle – though she was only five months pregnant, she was already the size of a house.

The saloon door swung open and Fred Simpson walked in. The young fireman's baby face was as white as baking powder, and seemed to have aged at least twenty years since the last time Annie had seen him. 'Crikey, what's happened to Fred?' she wondered.

She thought of calling him over to ask him what was wrong, but Fred, looking neither left nor right, headed straight for the bar counter.

'Give us a double whisky, Colleen!' he said. 'Quick!'

'Whisky?' replied the barmaid, who had automatically reached for a pint pot the moment she'd seen him come in. 'But you never drink spirits. Are you sure you wouldn't rather have a pint?'

Fred shook his head. 'It's whisky I need after the shock I've 'ad.'

'Bad news, was it?' Colleen asked sympathetically, as she poured the drink.

'Couldn't be much worse,' Fred told her. 'I've just 'eard that a pal o' mine 'as been arrested – for murder.'

'Murder!' Colleen slid the glass across the counter to him, and when the fireman started to fumble in his pockets for change, she said, 'Forget it. Have this one on me.'

'Thanks,' Fred said, taking a generous gulp. 'It shook me up, I can tell yer. 'I mean, I was only 'avin' a drink with 'im the other day – in this very pub.'

' 'E's not one of *my* regulars, is he?' Colleen asked.

The fireman nodded. ' 'E only lives just up the road – in Lant Place.'

'In Lant Place!' Annie thought. She found it hard to believe that anybody from up her street was capable of *murder*.

'What's his name?' Colleen asked.

'Didn't I say?' the fireman replied.

'As a matter of fact, you didn't.'

'It's Tom Bates I'm talkin' about.'

'Tom!' Annie gasped. 'It can't be Tom!'

Fred swung round to face her.

'I'm . . . I'm sorry, Annie,' he stuttered. 'I didn't see yer there. If I 'ad, I'd've broke the news more gradual, knowin' 'ow you and Tom . . . knowin' what 'e . . . anyway, I'm really sorry.'

'It can't be Tom!' Annie insisted.

'It's right enough, what I'm tellin' yer, gal.'

'And who's he supposed to have killed?'

'A bloke called Rollo or somefink. They say 'e shot 'im clean through the 'eart.'

A nightmare vision swam before Annie's eyes . . . Rollo and Tom squaring up to each other, both their faces twisted into masks of ugly hatred . . . Rollo taunting Tom until he could stand no more . . . Tom raising the pistol, pointing it at Rollo's heart, hesitating for a second, and then pulling the trigger . . . Rollo falling to the ground, with his blood spurting everywhere . . . crimson . . . everywhere . . .

No! She couldn't believe it! If Tom *had* killed Rollo, it would have been with his bare hands, not a pistol.

The door opened and Harry walked in. Annie felt a great surge of relief flow through her. 'Harry'll know what to do,' she thought. 'Harry'll find some way to prove that Tom's innocent.'

Harry kissed her lightly on the cheek. 'What can I get yer to drink?' he asked.

'Tom's been arrested,' Annie blurted out. 'For murder!'

'I know,' Harry said.

'You knew!' Annie exploded. 'You knew and you didn't find some way to get a message to me?'

Harry sighed and sat down. 'What would 'ave been the point?' he asked.

'You just sat back and let me hear it as common gossip in the pub!' Annie said angrily.

'I'm sorry. I should have thought,' Harry admitted.

'Well, let's forget that now,' Annie said, calming down a little. 'The important thing is to come up with a plan that will get Tom out of this awful mess.'

Harry shook his head. 'There's nuffink you, or anybody else, can do for 'im.'

'What do you mean by that?'

'The evidence against 'im is watertight.'

'How would you know that?' Annie asked suspiciously.

'Because I'm the one who collected most of it,' Harry replied, looking straight into her eyes.

'You . . . you collected most of it?'

'That's what I said.'

'You did it to spite me!' Annie screamed.

'I don't deserve that,' Harry told her.

'To spite me! Because you know that I love Tom and I could never love you!'

Harry grabbed her wrist and squeezed it – tightly.

'Listen to me,' he said. 'I worked 'ard at gettin' 'im arrested – yes – because I think 'e's guilty. But if I thought 'e was *innocent*, I'd work just as 'ard at gettin' 'im off. Yer know that, don't yer?'

'Yes, I know it,' Annie said, bowing her head. 'I'm sorry, Harry, I had no right to say those things to you.'

Harry released his grip on her wrist. 'An' *I'm* sorry if I 'urt you,' he said, 'but bein' a good copper's the only thing that matters to me – apart from you. Now, shall we 'ave a drink.'

'No,' Annie said, lifting her head again. 'No, Harry, we won't. I can understand why you did what you did – but I never want to see you again.'

And she stood up and fled from the pub.

When Annie arrived home, her parents were already sitting down and eating their supper.

'I suppose yer've 'eard all about Tom Bates gettin' 'imself arrested,' Lil said.

'Yes, I've heard,' Annie replied.

'Well, all I can say is "good riddance to bad rubbish".'

'Shut up, Lil, for Gawd's sake!' her husband warned her.

'I will not shut up!' Lil said. 'I told yer right from the start that he was a thoroughly bad lot, an' now look what 'e's done – gone and killed somebody.'

'It's not true!' Annie said passionately. 'Tom wouldn't . . . Tom couldn't . . . kill *anybody*.'

'The coppers wouldn't 'ave arrested 'im if 'e hadn't done it, would they?' Lil countered.

Sam slammed his fist down on the table. 'I'm *orderin'* you to shut up, Lil!' he said. 'Right now!'

Lil turned to her husband in astonishment. 'Sam Clarke!' she said. 'In all the years we've been married, yer've never ordered me to do anyfink!'

'Well, maybe that's because I've never wanted anyfink badly enough before,' Sam replied.

'An' why should yer want . . .? What's so important about Tom Bates that . . .?' Lil asked, before finally drying up.

'What's so important about Tom Bates is that yer daughter's in love with 'im,' Sam said.

Lil laughed. 'In love with 'im! Go on with yer! Oh, I admit she might 'ave 'ad a bit of a crush on 'im at one time, but that's as far . . .'

'Ask 'er!' Sam said.

Lil turned to face her daughter again and hardly recognised the face she saw. She remembered telling the neighbours the day Annie was born that the girl would take a ray of sunshine with her wherever she went. But there was nothing to remind her of the sun in Annie's face now. It was as pale as death and as full of grieving as any widow's.

'Go on – bloody well ask 'er!' Sam insisted.

'Are yer . . . are yer in love with Tom Bates?' Lil asked.

'Yes, Mum,' Annie said in a voice so quiet that her mother could hardly hear it. And then she burst into tears.

Lil jumped up from her chair and threw her arms around her daughter. 'There, there, my little darlin',' she cooed softly. 'Everyfink's goin' to be all right.'

'He didn't do it, Mum,' Annie sobbed.

'Of course 'e didn't do it,' Lil agreed, stroking her daughter's hair. ' 'Ow could anybody you're in love with 'ave possibly done an 'orrible thing like killin' somebody?'

As he approached the docks, Sam's mind was more on the previous evening than what was going on around him, so it was it not until Bert the Chaplain called to him that he even noticed the other man.

'Oh, 'ello, Bert,' he said absently. ' 'Ow are yer gettin' on?'

'Doing fine,' Bert told him.

Sam took a closer look at his old regimental padre. Bert's cheeks were a mass of veins and his eyes as red as blood. If he was doing fine now, Sam would have hated to see him when he wasn't.

'Well, it's good to see yer up an' around again, anyway,' Sam said.

Bert licked his dry lips. 'I really need a drink, Sam,' he said.

Of course he did. When didn't he? 'Just a minute,' Sam said. He reached into his pocket, but when he brought his hand out again, there was no money in it.

Bert, who already had his own palm held out in expectation, looked down at the empty hand in horror.

'Please, Sam . . .' he begged.

'Don't worry, I'll buy yer a drink,' Sam told him, 'but this time I'll come with yer.'

'Come with me?' said Bert, raising his eyebrows in surprise.

'Yes,' Sam replied. 'The way things are goin', I think I could use a drink meself.'

The pub Bert took them to was The Cock and Lion on Alderman Stairs. It was a run-down, filthy place, yet Bert looked around it as if it were home.

Sam went up to the bar and ordered a pint for himself and a large whisky for his companion.

'Give me the cheap stuff,' Bert called out to the landlord, and then to Sam he said, 'It's not to save you money. I've got used to the taste.'

They sat down at a rickety table near the door. Bert took a slug of his whisky and immediately seemed more alive.

'There's something troubling you', he said in a voice that took Sam back to the old church parades. 'I noticed it the moment I saw you. Why don't you tell me what it is that's weighing you down?'

'I should think yer've got enough of yer own troubles without wantin' to know anyfink about mine,' said Sam, beginning to wish he's gone straight to the docks.

'I used to be a good listener,' Bert persisted. 'Quite a lot of the men used to come to me with their worries, you know.'

'That was a long time ago,' Sam said gruffly.

'Once you have the knack for listening, I don't think it's something you ever lose,' Bert replied with growing confidence. 'So go on, Sam – unburden yourself to me.'

Well, why the hell not? Sam thought. After all, what harm could it do? 'It's me eldest daughter,' he said.

'What about her?'

'The bloke she's in love with 'as got 'imself in trouble with the coppers, an' it's breakin' 'er 'eart.'

'How serious is this trouble he's got himself into?'

'Just about as bad as it could be. 'E's been arrested for killin' somebody.'

Another sudden change came over Bert. The moment he'd taken a sip of whisky, his face had relaxed, but now the tightness and desperation were back again.

'Was this a very recent murder?' he asked cautiously.

'Last Sunday.'

'And what's the name of the young man your daughter is in love with?'

'Tom Bates.'

There was definite panic in Bert's eyes now. He looked swiftly around the bar to see if anyone was listening to them, then leant across so that his mouth was almost touching Sam's ear.

'I'm not a very brave man, Sam,' he whispered. 'I wouldn't be in the state I'm in now if I was.'

'I'm not follerin' yer.'

'Not brave at all,' Bert repeated, 'but I do owe you something for all the kindness you've shown me.'

'Yer still not makin' sense.'

'I don't mix with decent, honest people, like you do, Sam. The ones I know are the sinners – the lawless. I live with them, I see their abominations daily, and sometimes, to my eternal shame, I even do some of their dirty work for them.'

Was he raving? Sam wondered. Had the drink finally rotted his brain to such an extent that all he could talk now was nonsense.

'Listen, Padre, there's no point in yer gettin' all worked up,' he said soothingly. 'I'm sorry now I ever told yer about me daughter.'

'Let me finish what I was telling you,' Bert pleaded. 'Please let me finish before my courage fails me.'

There was something in his tone which said that he would not be denied. 'All right,' Sam agreed, 'but make it quick.'

'The chap who got himself murdered – his name was Rollo Jenkins, wasn't it?'

'Yes, it was. Did yer know 'im?'

'No, but I knew *of* him. And I know that he was involved in something big on the river.'

'Somefink big?'

'Something criminal. I'm not sure what, exactly, but there was a lot of money involved. And he started getting greedy, you see, so his associates – and I don't know their names, either – decided he'd have to be disposed of.'

'An' are yer sayin' that they went an' 'ired Tom Bates to dispose of 'im?'

'No, of course not. He was killed by one of his own gang – one of the Newington Hooligans.'

'Who else knows about this?' Sam asked.

'In the sort of criminal circles I move in, almost everybody's heard about it,' Bert told him.

'Then if we could just get one or two of the people who know the truth to come forward . . .' Sam said.

'They wouldn't!' Bert assured him. 'Not one of them would lift a finger to save this Tom Bates. Why should they? He's not one of their own.'

'Tell me some more about this big job on the river,' Sam said.

Bert shook his head. 'I've told you all I dare,' he said, 'and that's probably more than enough to get me killed.' He knocked back what was left of his whisky in a single gulp. 'If you see me around the docks again, don't speak to me,' he continued. 'Look straight through me as if you don't know me from Adam.'

He got unsteadily to his feet. For a second, Sam toyed with the idea of forcing him back into his chair. But it would have been pointless. He couldn't have been bribed into saying any more. He couldn't have been threatened into it, either – because you couldn't frighten a man who was already nearly dead with fear.

'Good luck to yer, Bert,' Sam said softly.

The Padre didn't answer. Instead, he took one last, panicked look around him and then staggered towards the door.

If Annie had given the matter any thought, she would have realised that the Wapping Police Court was very similar to the one at Tower Bridge. Here, too, she would have noticed, there was an iron dock, a uniformed usher and a row of unsmiling policemen. Here, too, a stern magistrate sat at his bench, listening to a series of complaints and ruling on a rag-bag collection of cases involving drunk and disorderly behaviour, begging and street brawling. But she didn't think about it – hardly, in fact, noticed her surroundings at all.

There was only room in her mind for one thought – she would soon be seeing Tom. She remembered the last time she'd watched him standing in the dock, and how worried she'd been that he might be found guilty. How trivial her old worries seemed now that he was facing not a few months in prison, but death by hanging!

The door to the gaolers' room swung open and Annie looked up expectantly, only to have her hopes dashed by the sight of a grey-haired man with a hangdog expression being shepherded towards the dock by two policemen.

The man was accused of counterfeiting, and stood in silence, guilt written all over his face, while the sergeant in charge of the case began to outline his evidence.

It was at some point in the middle of the policeman's testimony that the magistrate began to frown, and by the time he had finished, the look had turned into a definite scowl.

'Have I got this clear?' he asked. 'You found all the tools a coiner might use – the melting pot, the electric battery, the plaster of Paris et cetera – not in the accused's place of residence, but in another house entirely. Is that correct?'

'Yes, sir,' the policeman admitted, 'but we have sufficient reason to believe that they were his tools.'

'Well, you have not given *me* sufficient reason to believe,' the magistrate said. He turned to the man in the dock. 'I have no doubt of your guilt,' he told him, 'but based on the evidence presented to me I cannot, in all conscience, commit you to prison pending trial by jury. Case dismissed! You are free to go.'

The coiner could not believe his luck. 'Thanks, Yer Worship,' he said.

'Let the same thing happen to Tom!' Annie prayed. 'Please let the same thing happen to Tom!'

The door to the gaolers' room opened again, and this time it was Tom who was brought in.

'How pale he looks!' Annie thought miserably. Yet he wasn't cowed as the previous defendant had been – he kept his head held high and looked straight ahead of him with clear, unafraid eyes.

Inspector Walton made his case. The police knew that there had been bad blood between the accused and the dead man for some time. They could prove that the accused had had a gun in his possession. They could produce witnesses who would swear that on the night of his death, the victim had said he was going to meet the accused, and Bates could provide no satisfactory alibi for the time of the murder.

All the time Walton was speaking, Annie studied the magistrate's face, hoping to see the same signs of doubt as had appeared on it in the previous case. But there were none.

When the inspector had finished, the magistrate turned his attention to Tom. 'Does the accused have anything to say?' he asked.

'I didn't kill Rollo,' Tom replied in a steady voice. 'I didn't 'ave no arrangement to meet with 'im. I didn't even see the bloke on the day 'e died.'

'The evidence would suggest otherwise,' the magistrate told him. 'You are to be remanded in custody until such time as you will appear in the Central Criminal Court to answer the charges which have been laid against you.'

Annie heard a muted sob from the other side of the room, and turning, she saw May Bates.

'Oh, you poor woman!' she thought.

May was not alone. Her daughter Mary sat on one side of her, and Fred Simpson on the other. They were both doing their best to comfort her – but what comfort could they offer?

The two policemen indicated that Tom should step down from the dock, and when he had done so, they stood one each side of him and marched him back towards the gaolers' room.

Tom walked as steadily as if he were going about his normal business instead of being taken off to jail, but just before he reached the door he lifted his arm and ran a finger quickly round the inside of his collar.

'See that?' whispered the man sitting next to Annie. ' 'E can feel the rope around 'is neck already.'

May Bates was waiting for Annie when she emerged from the magistrate's court.

'It was very good of yer to come, gal,' she said. 'I think it 'elped my Tom, knowin' yer were there.'

'I didn't even realise he'd seen me,' Annie admitted. 'I was watching the magistrate, hoping he'd . . .'

' 'Opin' 'e'd what?'

Hoping he'd show some doubt – hoping he'd throw the case out! But he hadn't, had he?

'It doesn't matter now,' Annie said. 'You're sure Tom saw me?'

'Saw yer? 'E couldn't take 'is eyes off yer all the time that copper was talkin'. I don't think 'e even remembered 'e was in court till the Beak asked 'im if 'e'd got anyfink to say for 'imself.'

'And what he *did* say was that he'd never seen Rollo,' Annie remembered. 'Do you know where he was that night?'

'Walkin',' May told her.

'Walking? At one o'clock in the morning?'

' 'E's been doin' that a lot ever since . . .'

'Ever since what?'

May bit her lower lip and looked as if she would cheerfully have bitten her tongue as well. 'Ever since yer broke up with 'im,' she admitted.

The full horror of what she'd just been told hit Annie with the weight of a sledgehammer.

'You're saying that if I'd still been seeing him, he wouldn't have been out on his own and the police would have no case against him,' she said.

'Yer mustn't blame yerself,' May told her.

'Mustn't blame myself!' Annie repeated. 'Who else do you think I've got to blame?'

It was Colleen's night off from the pub, and she and George were sitting quietly and contentedly in their cosy parlour.

'D'you fancy a cup of tea, luv?' she asked. Then she smiled. 'I beg yer pardon,' she said, in a fair imitation of Lil. 'Would my ole man like me to get 'im a cup o' rosie?'

George laughed appreciatively. 'I wouldn't mind a cuppa, now you come to mention it,' he said. 'But I'll be the one who makes it. You spend enough time on your feet in that pub.'

But she wouldn't be able to work in The Goldsmiths' for much longer, he thought as he filled the kettle. Though she was only five months into her pregnancy, the bulge in her stomach was already huge, and he sometimes caught himself wondering whether it was a baby elephant she was carrying.

There was a knock on the front door. 'I'll get it,' George called out.

'But you're makin' the tea,' Colleen replied.

'I'll do that an' all,' George told her. 'You just sit back. You're resting for two.'

He opened the front door to find a grim faced Sam Clarke standing there. 'Is there anythin' the matter, Sam?' George asked, and then he thought, of course there's somethin' the matter. Didn't Collie tell you how Annie rushed out of the pub after she heard about Tom Bates being arrested?

'I need yer 'elp,' Sam said. 'I need yer brains.'

Despite the serious expression on Sam's face, George couldn't help laughing. 'My brains!' he said. 'What's wrong with your own?'

'They're corporal's brains,' Sam told him. 'They're all right for most things, but no good when there's a really big problem. An' the problem I've got now is so big yer could block the road with it. *That's* why I need you, George. I need a sergeant's brains.'

'All right,' George agreed. 'D'you want to come inside an' talk it over?'

'No,' Sam said. 'I'd rather do all the talkin' next door, if it's all the same to you.'

'Fine,' George said. 'I'll just make Colleen a cup o' rosie an' then I'll be with you.'

Annie, Sam and George sat at three sides of the Clarkes' kitchen table, while Lil, who hated being still even for a moment, was ironing next to the fire.

'The problem is that there's a fair number o' people who know Tom didn't do it, but none of 'em'll speak up for 'im,' Sam said after he'd told George about his talk with Bert. 'So just 'ow do we go about provin' his innocence?'

'I don't know,' George admitted. 'Me sergeant's brains seem to be lettin' me down.'

'If only we could persuade someone to step forward,' Annie said desperately. 'Perhaps we could offer them a reward or something.'

Sam looked expectantly at George, but the ex-sergeant shook his head. 'There's three things wrong with that,' he said. 'First of all, you probably couldn't raise enough readies to make it worth their while. Secondly, if you *had* got the money, they'd probably be too frightened to testify – your old padre as good as told you that. An' thirdly, even if we did get over them two problems, a bought witness is worse than useless.'

The room lapsed into gloomy silence, the only sound the swish-swish-swish of Lil's flat iron.

'We have to do *something*!' Annie said, after a minute had passed. 'We can't just sit back while they go ahead and hang my Tom.'

'It's like bangin' yer head against a brick wall,' George confessed. 'No, it's worse than that – it's like comin' up against one of them fortresses we had to storm in the Sudan an' India. D'yer remember 'em, Sam?'

' 'Ow could I ever forget? Yer'd look up at 'em and yer'd wonder 'ow we were ever goin' to manage to get inside.'

'But was allus *did* get in,' George mused. 'We some'ow managed to find a weak spot in the defences an' make a breach in it. That's what we need to find here. A weak spot.'

'I don't see what good all this army talk's doin',' Lil said from her ironing board. And then she relented and added, 'Sorry, George. I know yer tryin' yer best.'

'Would you mind goin' over that inspector's evidence again?' George asked Annie.

'If it'll help,' she replied. 'He said that there'd been bad blood between Tom and Rollo for a long time.' George nodded. 'And that he could produce half a dozen witnesses who'd seen Tom take Rollo's gun off him on Battle Bridge Stairs. Is this doing any good?'

'Not yet,' George admitted, 'but go on.'

'He also said he'd got witnesses – Blackie and Chas – who'd swear that when Rollo set out that night, he said he was going to meet Tom because he . . .'

George banged his big fist down onto the table.

'That's it!' he said. 'That's the weak spot. I know where we can make the breach.'

'Yer do?' Sam asked. 'What was it our Annie just said that's made yer so . . .?'

'Blackie and Chas said Rollo had arranged to meet Tom, but accordin' to Tom, he hadn't, so . . .'

'Tom may 'ave been lyin' about that,' Sam pointed out.

'He wasn't!' Annie said fiercely.

'I'm not sayin' he killed Rollo,' Sam told his daughter, 'but 'e might 'ave *seen* 'im, an' then later decided it was wisest to keep quiet about it.'

'I heard him deny it in court,' Annie said, 'and I *know* he was telling the truth.'

'Anyway, there wasn't time for Rollo to go and meet both Tom *and* his killer,' George said.

'You're right,' Sam agreed.

'So Blackie an' Chas are the ones who were lyin'. Now why would they want to do that?'

'Because they wanted to shift suspicion from themselves!' Annie said excitedly.

'Or from someone else,' George said cautiously. 'Let's look at what we know about Rollo's killer. One: according to Sam's padre friend, he's a member of the Newington Hooligans . . .'

'There's dozens o' them,' Sam reminded him.

'. . . an' two: he's also in the gang who are pulling this "big job" on the river. Now there can't be dozens of hooligans involved in that, can there?'

'I s'ppose not,' Sam conceded.

'And that's where we find our breach,' George continued. 'Say there are only four Hooligans in this river gang – then we know that one of them is the murderer. Even better, say there's only Chas an' Blackie – it must be one of them.'

'I don't see 'ow that'll help get Tom off,' Sam said.

'One step at a time,' George told him. 'Once we know all that, we can go to the police with our information. They'll interrogate all the suspects, and you can bet your last shillin' that one of the ones who *wasn't* responsible for Rollo's death will inform on the killer in order to save his own skin.'

'It might work,' Sam admitted. 'At least, it's the best thing we've come up with so far. But exac'ly 'ow are yer goin' to find out which 'ooligans are mixed up with this job on the river?'

'By followin' Chas an' Blackie, findin' out where they go an' who they spend their time with.'

'Followin' 'em!' Sam said. 'Use yer loaf! 'Ow can *we* follow 'em? We ain't got the training for that kind o' work. A one-legged man an' a docker followin' a couple o' hardened criminals – they'd 'ave us spotted in the first five minutes.'

'I suppose you're right,' George agreed gloomily. 'But if we can't follow them, then how the devil are we goin' to . . .'

'What yer really need is five or six people,' Lil said. 'People yer get so used to seeing around the streets that yer 'ardly notice 'em any more.'

'You mean like postmen or road sweepers?' George asked.

'Or tramps,' Lil said with a smile. ' 'Ave I told yer about my friend Nettie Walnut?'

Tooley Street looked just as it always did on weekday mornings. Trams were rattling up and down the road. A bill sticker was pasting an advertisement for the latest show at The New Savoy onto a convenient wall. A beer-boy was weaving his way in and out of the stream of foot traffic and using the pole from which his cans of beer hung as encouragement to other pedestrians to clear a passage for him. And, of course, there were tramps – but then there were always tramps.

Blackie and Chas sauntered past the top of Morgan's Lane. It was at this very corner, only a few months earlier, that they had ambushed the wharfinger and stolen his hat. But they did not think of that now. Their days of cracking heads at ten shillings a go were behind them. They had finally landed themselves in 'the big time'.

If the two hooligans had bothered to look around instead of gazing insolently straight ahead, they might have noticed the grey-haired tramp in a coat so long that it flapped around his ankles. This particular tramp was heading in the

306

same direction as they were – and not only in the same direction, but also at the same speed. When they stopped to look in a shop window, he stopped in front of one further down the street. When they set off again, so did he. It was as if, a disinterested observer might have thought, the tramp was following them.

Blackie and Chas could have turned down Tanner Street, in which case they would have encountered another tramp – an oldish man with a wall-eye. But they didn't. Instead, they continued along Tooley Street until it became Dockhead Road. There they passed a third tramp, a woman sadly afflicted with warts. The woman hardly looked up as they went by, but the second they'd gone she shot a questioning glance in the direction of the tramp with the long, flapping overcoat.

The man pointed his finger at the backs of the two hooligans and nodded, just once. Then he turned around and headed back the way he'd come, while the woman set off after Chas and Blackie.

Tom walked at a steady pace, making sure – as per prison regulations – that the distance between himself and the man in front of him neither lengthened nor shortened. He was not allowed to turn and look, but he knew that the prisoner behind him would be doing exactly the same thing, and the one behind him, and the one behind – so that though there were several dozen men walking round and round the exercise yard, each was as isolated as if he'd been alone.

Tom looked at the man just ahead of him. He was wearing an expensive frock coat and a silk top hat, while the prisoner *he* was following was dressed in little more than rags. It helped to have money in prison, just as it did everywhere else, he thought. A man with money could rent nice furniture for his cell and have his meals sent in from restaurants outside the gaol. A man with money could afford a solicitor to advise him on his case.

But would having a lawyer really have made a difference? he wondered. The evidence that Harry Roberts had collected would have convinced *him* if he'd been on a jury, and was certainly enough to hang him twice over.

He wasn't afraid of death, but if it had to come, he wished it could be in some other way – saving a child from a blazing building, or fighting for his country. 'There's somefink degradin' an' 'umilatin' about endin' yer life at the end of a rope,' he thought to himself.

Yet however he looked at it, it seemed as if only a miracle could save him from that.

CHAPTER EIGHTEEN

Nettie Walnut was not at all happy with the way things were going. In the week that she and her fellow tramps had been following Blackie and Chas, they'd managed to lose the hooligans *five* times. Of course, she told herself, it was very easy to lose people when there were a lot of other folk about and you had to be careful you weren't spotted yourself. Still that was no consolation to Annie Clarke, was it? She thought Annie was a lovely lass, and it broke Nettie's heart to see the disappointment on the poor girl's face every time the tramps had to report another failure.

'Well, I isn't goin' to lose 'em today,' Nettie promised, keeping her eyes firmly on the two young men who were walking along twenty yards in front of her.

Blackie and Chas came to a sudden halt in front of a pawnbroker's. The hooligans hesitated for a second, as if they were unsure about something, then stepped into the shop. They were not inside long. Barely half a minute after they had entered they were chased out again by a small man with an angry red face.

They made a strange sight out there on the pavement, the red-faced man shouting furiously, and the two thugs – who could have made mincemeat of him if they'd wanted to – cowering under the hail of his words. Nettie took a chance and moved a little closer to them.

' 'Ow many times 'ave I told yer not to come 'ere?' she heard the red-faced man demand.

'We was gettin' worried, not 'avin' 'eard from yer, Mr Stone,' Blackie said lamely.

'The reason yer 'aven't 'eard from me is 'cos until the boat docks, I've nuffink to bleedin' tell yer,' Stone told him. 'What are yer worried about? That I'll cut yer out of the job?'

'Well, we were startin' to think . . .' Blackie began.

'Listen,' Stone said, calming down a little, 'if that's what's on yer mind an' yer want to keep in touch, then why don't yer just . . .'

He glanced up the street and saw Nettie standing there, lighting her pipe. He gave her a suspicious look, and when he talked to the two hooligans again, it was in a whisper.

There were four of them sitting round the Clarkes' kitchen table – Annie, Sam, George and Nettie Walnut.

'You're sure that's what they said to each other?' George asked Nettie.

'I couldn't swear them was their exact words,' Nettie admitted, 'but they's pretty close.'

'So what do we know for a fact,' George said, looking down at his notes. 'We know that the two of them went to see this pawnbroker on Adam Street . . .'

'Which is close to the pub where Rollo was supp'sed to 'ave 'ad 'is last drink,' Sam pointed out.

'. . . close to the pub where Rollo was supposed to have had his last drink,' George agreed. 'We know that he was furious they'd turned up, and that he shouted something at them about the job they were pulling and told them not to worry about being cut out of it. Is that right, Nettie?'

' 'S right,' Nettie said.

'But you didn't hear what he said about how they were to keep in touch. It's a pity, that.'

Yes, Annie thought in quiet desperation, it *was* a pity. There were a lot of things which were a pity.

Tom was staring at the ceiling of his cell and thinking about death when he heard the key turn in the lock. The door swung open, and two wardens were standing there.

'On yer feet, six-o-three. There's a bloke 'ere to see yer,' one of them said.

'A bloke? What bloke?' Tom asked.

'No questions, six-o-three,' the second warden said sharply. 'Prisoners ain't allowed to ask questions. Prisoners just do what they're told.'

The two guards marched him across the yard and stopped in front of a door which was almost directly opposite his cell. 'In yer go,' the first warden told him.

Wondering what exactly was happening, Tom turned the handle and stepped through the door. The wardens did not follow.

The room was sparsely furnished, with just a table and two chairs. On one of the chairs sat a man in a frock coat. He was around thirty, Tom guessed. He had a sharp nose, and small, ambitious eyes. He smiled by way of greeting, but it was not a warm smile.

'Sit down, Mr Bates,' he said, indicating the free chair.

It seemed so long since he had been anything but six-o-three that for a moment Tom didn't react. Then he pulled out the chair and sat down as he'd been instructed.

The man reached into his pocket and pulled out a packet. 'Cigarette?' he asked, offering it across the table.

Tom took one, and the man lit it for him. Tom inhaled deeply, and felt the nicotine, which he'd grown unaccustomed to in prison, go straight to his head.

'My name is Hardcastle,' the man said. 'I'm a barrister, and I've come here to tell you that I wish to defend you.'

'I can't afford a lawyer,' Tom said.

Hardcastle laughed. 'Of course you can't,' he replied. 'I'd be taking you on as a *pro bono publico* case.'

'As a what?'

'I am prepared to waive my usual fee.'

Tom looked at Hardcastle suspiciously. 'What's in it for you?' he asked.

'The satisfaction of seeing justice served.'

'I don't believe yer,' Tom said flatly. 'An' unless yer straight with me, yer can leave right now.'

The lawyer sighed. 'All right, Mr Bates,' he said. 'Your case has aroused considerable public interest, and naturally when it comes to trial some of that interest will be focused on the barrister who defends you. It will make my name, even though, on this occasion, I am bound to lo . . .'

He broke off and coughed.

'What were yer about to say?' Tom asked.

'I was going to say that whatever the outcome of the case my reputation will be enhanced,' Hardcastle said.

'No yer weren't,' Tom told him. 'Yer were goin' to say that it'd be good for you even though yer bound to lose.'

'Perhaps I was,' the barrister admitted, 'but I was wrong to do so. You can never tell with a jury which way they'll jump.'

'Do *you* think I did it?' Tom demanded.

'That is neither here nor there,' Hardcastle said.

Tom stood up. 'Thanks for the cigarette, Mr Hardcastle,' he said, 'but I think I'd rather take me chances on me own.'

'You're a fool, Bates,' the lawyer hissed.

'Yer might be right about that,' Tom agreed. 'But there's not much I can do about it now, is there?'

The tramp with the long, flapping overcoat was not surprised when Blackie and Chas went into the telephone kiosk in Ludgate Circus. Indeed, he would have been surprised if they hadn't, since that was what they'd done – at precisely twelve noon – every day since their visit to the pawnbroker's in Rotherhithe.

Usually the tramps were told to keep a good distance from the hooligans, but today the instructions had been changed, and as Blackie picked up the phone, the man in the flapping overcoat edged closer to the kiosk.

'Yes, Mr Stone,' he heard Blackie say. 'Right, Mr Stone . . . Same time tomorrer?'

The tramp in the flapping overcoat had heard all he needed to, and hurried away.

★

'If the phone call today was to Stone, then we can assume that all others have been as well,' George said to the group huddled round the Clarkes' kitchen table.

'Specially since they always make 'em at the same time,' Sam agreed.

Annie had been sitting there quietly, her hands clenched together, but now, suddenly something seemed to snap.

'This ain't doin' any good!' she screamed. 'It ain't doin' any good at all!'

The poor girl was exhausted, George thought, looking at her drawn features and bloodshot eyes. He wished he could tell her that everything was going to be all right, but he knew that it would be cruel to raise her hopes too high.

'We have got *somewhere*,' he said carefully. 'We know that Chas and Blackie are definitely workin' with Stone, on this "big job" of his.'

'An' that Stone's prob'ly the bloke who decided Rollo 'ad to die, even if it was Blackie or Chas who actually pulled the trigger,' Sam added.

'But we ain't got enough to go to the police with, 'ave we?' Annie demanded.

'No,' George admitted. 'We haven't.'

'Then it's bloody useless, all this follerin' people an' all this takin' notes, ain't it? Because my Tom's still in gaol, and they're goin' to 'ang him – I know they are.'

'George an' yer dad are doin' the best they can, Annie,' Lil said quietly from the other side of her ironing board. 'We're *all* doin' the best we can.'

'Well, it ain't good enough!' Annie shouted – and then she put her hands to her face and started to sob.

Sam made a move to reach out for his daughter, but Lil shook her head. 'Let 'er cry it out,' she said. 'She'll feel better when she's cried it out.'

For several minutes they all sat there, not speaking, hardly breathing – just watching Annie break her heart. Then the sobbing stopped, and Annie took a deep breath.

'I'm sorry, Dad. I'm sorry, Mr Taylor,' she said in a calm but shaky voice. 'I didn't mean it when I said that what you'd found out was useless. But I think we've taken things as far as we can on our own. What we need now is professional help.'

'Professional 'elp?' Sam said. 'And just where do yer intend to get professional 'elp from?'

A look of resignation came to Annie's strained face. 'Where d'yer think?' she asked.

He saw her waiting on the corner the moment he stepped through the front door of Wapping Police Station, but though his heart leaped, he still had some pride left, and instead of walking over to her, he waited for her to come to him.

'Hello, Harry,' she said.

' 'Ello, Annie,' he replied stiffly. 'An' to what do I owe the honour of this visit?'

'I need your help,' Annie said.

'If it's about Tom Bates again, yer wastin' yer time,' Harry said. 'I couldn't do anyfink for 'im now, even if I wanted to.'

'I think you could,' Annie said firmly. 'With what we've been able to find out . . .'

'Who's we?' Harry interrupted.

'Me and my dad and Mr Taylor.'

'You and yer dad an' Mr Taylor,' Harry scoffed. 'What a team! An' I s'ppose yer all trained detectives, are yer?'

'Of course we're not trained detectives!' Annie said. 'That's why we need you on our side – because with what we've been able to find out, you should be able to track down the people who really killed Rollo Jenkins.'

'Tom Bates killed Rollo,' Harry told her. 'That's the plain an' simple truth, an' that's the verdict the jury will bring in when 'e comes to trial.'

'Won't you at least spare a couple of minutes to listen to what we've got to say?' Annie pleaded.

'Why should I?' Harry asked. 'Yer broke my 'eart, yer know, Annie Clarke.'

'I never meant to,' Annie protested.

'Maybe yer didn't,' Harry replied. 'But that don't make it any easier to bear.'

Annie searched around for something she could say to persuade him to change his mind – and suddenly, she found it.

'The last time I asked you to help Tom, you made me promise to do something,' she said. 'Do you remember?'

'O' course I remember.'

'You made me promise not to see Tom again. And I kept my word, didn't I?'

'Yes,' Harry agreed, 'you did.'

'And I'll keep my word over the promise I'm about to make now,' Annie said.

'What promise?' Harry asked.

'If you'll do everything you can to get Tom off the murder charge, then I promise I'll marry you,' Annie said.

Harry sat at the Clarkes' kitchen table reading through George's careful notes, while Annie, George and Sam looked on, waiting impatiently for him to finish, but not daring to speak in case it broke the flow of his concentration. Even Lil, though she was still standing by her board, had stopped ironing so as not to disturb him.

Finally, Harry laid the notes aside and turned to George.

'Yer've done a good job for somebody who ain't 'ad no trainin' in proper police work, Mr Taylor.'

'Thank you,' George replied.

'An' I'd say that yer definitely on to somefink,' Harry continued. 'This Wally Stone is a well-known fence, an' the fact that 'e told Chas an' Blackie to stay away from 'is shop was as good as admittin' that they're workin' for 'im.' He turned his attention to Annie. 'But all it proves it that they're up to some dirty business. It don't signify that Tom Bates didn't kill Rollo Jenkins.'

'But it will,' Annie said. 'I know it will. It *has* to.'

'We'll see,' Harry said dubiously. 'Now, if we are goin' to carry on with this investigation of yours, then it's time we got it on a proper footin'.'

'Couldn't yer just do what George suggested?' Lil asked. 'Yer know, pull Chas an' Blackie in, an' get one of 'em to admit that the other did the shootin'?'

'We ain't got no *grounds* for pullin' 'em in,' Harry said. 'No grounds at all.'

'Then how do we go about *getting* grounds?' Annie asked.

'As far as I can see, our best chance is to catch 'em in the act of pullin' this big job. Then, once we've got 'em down in the cells charged with that, we can start askin' questions about Rollo's murder.'

'That makes sense,' George said.

'Now yer say yer've got these tramps of yours followin' 'em wherever they go,' Harry continued.

'That's right,' Sam agreed.

'Only it ain't a perfect system, 'cos every once in a while they lose sight of 'em, don't they?'

'Yes,' George admitted. 'They must have lost them six or seven times altogether.'

'An' what 'appens if they lose 'em the day they pull the big job?' Harry asked.

'Then we've got nothing,' George said gloomily.

For a moment Harry's face was as grim as George's, and then it lit up as if he had just had a brilliant idea.

'Call 'em off completely,' he said.

'Yer what?' Sam said. 'If we did that, we'd 'ave no chance of catchin' Chas an' Blackie in the act.'

'Yes, we would,' Harry told him. 'Because they won't make their move till they've 'ad orders from Wally Stone. An' 'ow are they goin' to get them orders?'

George's mouth fell open.

'By . . . by telephone,' he gasped.

'Correct,' Harry said. 'That's why yer tramps are no good to us any more.' He turned to Annie. 'What we really need is somebody inside the telephone company.'

'He's here!' Belinda Benson hissed.

Annie looked up from her switchboard and gazed across the long room to the supervisor's desk near the door. Belinda was right. Harry had arrived and was conducting an earnest conversation with Miss Barnett, the supervisor.

'I wonder what he's saying,' she thought. 'I hope to God he can persuade the old battle-axe to help us.'

It would not have surprised Miss Barnett to hear herself described as an old battle-axe – one had to be quite severe when dealing with flighty young ladies – but in her own mind she knew it was far from the truth. Away from the responsibilities of work, she was quite different. In the privacy of her own home she became a person who loved needlework and cats, and – though she would never have admitted it to even her closest friends – positively *adored* romantic novels.

It would be true to say, however, that neither her secret life nor the one she put on public display had prepared her for the suggestion this handsome young policeman had just made her.

'I've never heard such a thing in my life!' she said. 'It's quite out of the question to do what you ask without direct authorisation from my superiors.'

'Yes, but that's the problem, yer see,' Harry told her. 'We 'ave reason to believe that one of yer superiors is in on it.'

If he'd grabbed her by the waist and kissed her passionately, he couldn't have shocked her more.

'One . . . one of my superiors?' she stammered. 'In on it? But . . . but *which* one?'

Harry smiled winningly. 'If we knew that, Miss Barnett, I would never 'ave 'ad to come botherin' you, now would I?' he said. 'But it could be *any* one of 'em, yer see.'

Miss Barnett twisted her hands together uncertainly.

'If only you had a warrant from the magistrates or a letter from your own superiors,' she said.

'Too much of a risk,' Harry told her. 'That might leak out – an' the last thing we want is somefink that'll warn the guilty parties and scare 'em off.'

'My first loyalty it always to the Telephone Company . . .' Miss Barnett said.

'An' so it should be,' Harry agreed. 'That's why it's all the more disgraceful that somebody the company 'as trusted with 'igh office 'as been abusin' that trust.'

Miss Barnett hesitated. On the one hand, she was not the sort of person to do anything without written authorisation. On the other hand, this policeman, for all that he was quite young, did seem to carry with him a certain amount of authority of his own. And he had a very nice smile – not that that had anything to do with it.

'It might help if you were to explain it to me all over again,' she said.

'Of course,' Harry replied. 'We know that somebody is stealin' a lot of money from this company, an' that 'e has to be an 'igh up to be able to do it. We also know 'oo 'is accomplice on the outside is. Now what we 'ave to do is to find some way to get the accomplice to give us the official's name.'

'But . . .' Miss Barnett objected.

'I shouldn't really be tellin' yer all this, yer know,' Harry said, smiling again. 'But some'ow yer seem to 'ave a way of wormin' it out of me.'

Miss Barnett, who'd never thought of herself of having a way of worming anything out of anybody, positively glowed with pleasure. 'Go on,' she said.

'The best way to get the name of the man we're after is to listen in to the accomplice's calls,' Harry said.

'And it would only involve eavesdropping on just one line, would it?' asked Miss Barnett, weakening.

'Just the one line,' Harry agreed.

Miss Barnett wished he'd stop smiling. Policemen *shouldn't* smile so much. She looked around her, searching for some objection to his plan with which to support her weakening resolve.

'You couldn't put a policeman in here,' she said, with some relief. 'He'd be noticed right away.'

'We don't need to put a policeman in,' Harry replied. 'We've been plannin' this investigation for months, an' we've taken the precaution of makin' sure one of our people was already 'ere.'

Miss Barnett was almost as shocked as she'd been when she learned that someone high up in the company was being light-fingered.

'Do you mean to say that one of my young ladies is a . . . a . . .' she gasped.

'A police agent?' Harry supplied. 'Exactly. So all yer've got to do is instruct yer other operators to pass all calls from this partic'lar number over to 'er, and she'll do the rest.'

Miss Barnett looked around the room at the operators and realised, with some envy, that one of them was involved in something really exciting. But which of them?

'Who is she?' she asked Harry.

The policeman winked at her. 'I believe you know 'er as Annie Clarke,' he said.

Annie could bear the suspense no longer. Turning away from her switchboard, she risked a quick glance at the desk. She need not have been so cautious. Harry was just shaking hands with Miss Barnett, and the supervisor had eyes for no one but him. And he was smiling back at her – which must mean that she'd agreed to do what he'd asked!

Annie breathed a sigh of relief.

'So that's your dashing policeman, is it?' Belinda whispered from the switchboard next to hers. 'It's a pity you had to promise to marry him. I would rather have fancied a crack at him myself.'

'Yer takin' yer bleedin' time gettin' me me number, ain't yer?' Blackie said into the telephone mouthpiece.

This was not the first occasion on which there'd been a delay. Every time he'd rung Wally Stone in the last two or three days, it had taken the operator at least a couple of minutes to put him through.

'Connecting you now,' a female voice told him.

Blackie heard a ringing sound and then a harsh voice said, 'Stone 'ere.'

'It's me, Mr Stone. Blackie.'

'We're on for tonight,' Stone said.

Blackie felt his heart give a little jump. A few more hours and he'd be richer than he'd ever imagined possible.

'Yer better give me the details, Mr Stone,' he said.

'The steamer yer want is the *Simon Bolivar*,' Stone told

319

him. 'It'll anchor in the middle of the river, off Jerusalem Wharf. Yer not to go anywhere near it till well after midnight.'

' 'Ow'll we get out to it? By skiff?'

'By skiff! Of course yer don't go by skiff. Yer couldn't fit all the bloody cargo in a skiff, could yer?'

'Then 'ow?'

'There'll be a barge called the *Christina* moored at Pickle Herrin' Stairs. Yer'll take that.'

'I don't know 'ow to sail no barge,' Blackie protested.

'I 'ired yer as muscle, not brains,' Stone said cuttingly, 'so it don't exac'ly come as a surprise to me to 'ear yer say that.'

'Well then, Mr Stone . . .'

'There'll be a bloke name o' Mike waitin' for yer on the *Christina*. 'E'll do all the clever stuff. 'Ave yer got that?'

'Yes, Mr Stone.'

'Then get this as well,' Stone said. 'It don't matter if yer get stopped an' searched by the Wet Bobs before yer pick up the cargo, but we can't risk it once yer loaded. So what yer do is, you sail maybe an 'undred yards away from the steamer an' yer drop anchor for the night. Then in the mornin', when there's a lot o' traffic movin' on the river, yer can slip away as easy as yer please. Understand?'

'Yes, Mr Stone.'

'Then you tell me what yer've got to do.'

'Drop anchor about an 'undred yards from the steamer an' slip away in the mornin'.'

'Right,' Stone said. 'Just make sure yer do it like that, an' this time tomorror we'll all be laughin'.'

It was more than she'd had any right to hope for, Annie thought, when she heard the click which meant that Stone had hung up. She knew the place, the time and who would be involved. Yet she was far from sure she had enough to save Tom.

What was it Harry had said?

Our best chance is to catch 'em in the act of pullin' this big job. Then, once we've got 'em down in the cells charged with that, we can start askin' 'em questions about Rollo's murder.

It had sounded like a good plan when Harry had outlined it, but now she was beginning to have her doubts. Harry, she knew, would keep his word if he could – but would he be in any position to? It wouldn't be Harry who was interrogating the hooligans, but one of his superiors. And why should that man, handed one of the most important cases to turn up on the river for years, give a fig about the fate of a penniless waterman?

'I can't leave it up to Harry,' Annie told herself. 'I *daren't* leave it up to Harry.'

Which meant she would have to fall back on her second plan. And though even the thought of it made her feel giddy with fear, she knew she really had no choice if she were to keep the hangman's rope from Tom's neck.

'Is anything the matter?' Miss Barnett asked.

'I'm not feeling very well,' Annie told her. 'Would it be all right if I took the rest of the day off?'

'Of course, Miss Clarke,' said the supervisor, winking at her conspiratorially.

There were barges on the Thames which were scarcely more than lighters with sails, but the *Christina* was not one of them. She was a proper, sea-going craft, and when Mike – a thin, nervous man – showed Blackie and Chas the space below deck where they could store the cargo and sit out the night, the two hooligans agreed that it would do them very well.

A good stiff breeze had blown up earlier that night, and the barge – sailing without lights – had no difficulty at all in covering the distance from Pickled Herring Stairs to the steamship *Simon Bolivar*.

Blackie signalled, once, with his shuttered lantern, and there was a responding flash from the deck of the steamer.

'Right, get yerselves ready,' Blackie whispered hoarsely to the other two men.

There was a sound of cranking machinery up above them, and, slowly but surely, a net was lowered from the *Simon Bolivar* onto the deck of the *Christina*.

It was now that the dangerous part of the job really

began. Earlier, if they had been intercepted by the river police as they were sailing towards the ship, they could probably have talked their way out of the situation. Afterwards, once they were moored with the cargo safely in the hold, there was no reason in the world why they should raise any suspicion. But now, as members of the *Simon Bolivar*'s crew lowered the heavy metal bars, they were at their most vulnerable – and they knew it.

They worked as quickly as they could. Blackie, standing on deck, passed the bars to Chas, who was by the hatch. Chas in his turn handed them over to Mike, who stashed them below. Then the net was hauled back up, and the whole process began again.

There were times during those nerve-wrecking few minutes when Blackie wished that there had not been quite so much gold to stash, but he told himself he was being a berk. Less gold would have meant a quicker getaway, but it would also have resulted in a smaller cut for him. And Blackie – who had killed Rollo Jenkins in return for the promise of a bigger share – would not willingly have given up one shilling's worth that he didn't have to.

At last the loading was completed and the *Christina* slid away from the *Simon Bolivar*, sailed a little way up the river, and dropped anchor, just as Wally Stone had instructed.

'It's as good as over,' Blackie thought, as he lounged in the hold, one hand resting against the stack of gold, the other holding a bottle of whisky. 'As good as over. Just a few more hours an' we'll be in the clear.'

From the top of Pickled Herring Stairs, Annie Clarke and Joey Bates peered out over the darkness of the river.

'I think they've settled down for the night,' Joey said.

'Are you sure?' Annie asked anxiously.

'Course I ain't sure,' Joey replied. 'But if they ain't dropped anchor yet, they'll 'ave to do it soon. Didn't that Stone bloke tell 'em not to sail far?'

'That's right, he did,' Annie agreed.

'Then we might as well get started,' Joey said, setting off down the steps to where the skiff was moored.

Annie grabbed his arm. 'You don't have to do this, Joey,' she said.

'Like 'ell I don't!' Joey replied.

'It could be dangerous,' Annie pointed out.

'You don't need to tell *me* that,' Joey answered, 'I *know* Chas an' Blackie, remember?'

'And aren't you scared?'

'Out of me wits!'

'Well, then?'

'Look, Annie,' Joey said, 'our Tom is in prison because of me . . .'

'That's not the only . . .' Annie began.

'Because of me,' Joey repeated firmly. 'An' I'll do anyfink I can to get 'im out again.'

Annie nodded, accepting the fact that he had the right to make his own choices. 'Then let's get it over with,' she said.

The two of them walked down the stairs and stepped into the small skiff.

Blackie was sitting on a packing case next to the pile of gold bars, a half-empty bottle of cheap whisky in his hand.

'Go easy on that,' Mike said nervously.

'Eashy on it?' Blackie slurred. 'Why should I go eashy on it? All we gotta do is sit 'ere an' wait.'

'What if somefink went wrong?' Mike said.

'Nuffink *can* go wrong,' Blackie said. 'Can it, Chas?'

'Not a thing in the 'ole wide world,' Chas replied, taking the bottle from Blackie and pouring a slug of the rough spirit down his own throat.

'I still don't . . .' Mike began to say – and then he stopped suddenly and a look of fear came to his face.

'Wha's the matter?' Blackie asked.

'I thought I 'eard somebody up on deck,' Mike told him.

' 's just the timbers creakin,' Blackie said. 'Get lotsa . . . lotsa timbers creakin' on a boat.'

Overhead, there were a series of heavy thuds which could only have been footfalls. 'Bleedin' 'ell!' said Blackie, climbing shakily to his feet and reaching for his iron bar.

'I told yer,' Mike said hysterically. 'I said yer should 'ave stayed off the booze.'

'Drunk or sober, I can still 'andle whoever's up there,' Blackie growled.

The hatch slid open and a pair of feet appeared at the top of the ladder. Then the feet moved down a rung, and the hem of a dress became visible.

'It's . . . it's a bloody woman!' Chas said.

As Annie made her way down the ladder, she was counting silently to herself, 'Eleven hundred, twelve hundred, thirteen hundred, fourteen hundred.'

She had reached seventeen hundred by the time she got to the bottom step and turned to face the hooligans, who were standing one each side of the gold.

'Well, well, what do we 'ave 'ere, then?' Blackie asked, grinning horribly.

'I'm Annie Clarke,' Annie said.

'Are yer now?' Blackie said. He looked up the ladder at the second person who was descending into the hold. 'An' I see yer've brought young Joe Bates with yer.'

'That's right,' Annie agreed. 'It's as much Joey's business as it is mine.'

'What is?' Blackie asked.

Annie walked over towards Blackie and pointed at the bars of gold bullion.

'We want some of this,' she said.

'Yer what?' Blackie asked, amazed.

'We want some of this,' Annie repeated. 'Not a lot. Just enough so that we can hire a good lawyer for Tom.'

Blackie squinted at her in the dim light of the oil lamp.

'I know yer,' he said. 'Yer were in court that day me an' Chas got sent down for six months.'

'That's right,' Annie agreed.

'An' now yer want us to give yer some gold, so yer can get Tom Bates off *again*?' Blackie asked.

'You owe it to him,' Annie said.

'I don't owe Tom Bates nuffink,' Blackie told her.

Annie had continued her silent counting even while she'd

been talking, and now she reached three thousand five hundred. That was enough. That *had* to be enough.

'It's *your* fault Tom's in gaol,' she screamed, stamping her foot loudly on the floor. 'Your fault and nobody else's. You know he didn't kill Rollo Jenkins' . . . Stamp! . . . 'Nobody knows *better* than you!' . . . Stamp! . . . 'If you don't give me the gold, I'll go straight to the police and tell them all about it.'

Blackie grinned again. 'Will yer now?' he asked. 'But ain't yer forgettin' just one tiny little thing?'

'What thing?'

'Yer got on this barge by yerself – but yer only get off it again if I let yer.'

He signalled to Chas, who moved over to the ladder and blocked their escape.

'You can't keep us here for ever,' Annie said defiantly. 'You'll have to let us go in the end.'

'I don't 'ave to do nuffink of the kind, gal,' Blackie said. 'Oh, yer'll leave 'ere, all right – but when yer do, it'll only be as food for the fishes.'

'Yer can't do that, Blackie . . .' Mike croaked from the corner where he'd been crouching since Annie and Joey had appeared. 'Yer just can't.'

'You keep out of this, yer toe-rag,' Blackie warned him. 'Comin' 'ere like she 'as – seein' the gold – she ain't given us no choice but to get rid of 'er.'

'You wouldn't . . . you wouldn't really kill me, would you?' Annie gasped.

'For what I'm gettin' paid, I'd kill me own gran'muvver,' Blackie told her.

'Like you killed Rollo?' Annie asked.

'Yes,' Blackie agreed. 'Like I killed Rollo. Gettin' greedy, wasn't 'e? Wanted more than 'is share. Mr Stone didn't like that. Mr Stone promised me twice as much if I got rid o' Rollo.'

'And did you have any part of this?' Annie asked, turning to Chas who was still standing casually at the bottom of the ladder, though now he had a wicked-looking knife in his hand.

'Yes, I 'ad a part in it,' Chas said.

'I don't believe you,' Annie said. 'You haven't got the guts to shoot anybody.'

Chas flushed angrily. 'Blackie shot 'im, but only 'cos 'e was the one who had the gun,' he said. 'If it'd been my pistol, I'd've pulled the trigger, don't yer go 'avin' any doubts about that. An' I 'elped to drag 'is body down ter the river, didn't I, Blackie?'

'Yer did,' Blackie agreed.

'So you're each as guilty as the other,' Annie said.

Blackie had been holding his iron bar since he first heard noises up on deck, but now he raised it above his head.

'It's a real shame I've got to do away with a pretty girl like you,' he told Annie.

She backed away from him, but in the small space below the deck of the barge, there was nowhere to run.

'Joey!' she called, and turning towards him she saw that he was retreating, too – retreating from Chas, who had his wicked knife pointing straight at the young man's throat.

Annie felt her hand touch the side of the boat. She could retreat no further. If she moved now it would have to be to the left or the right, and whichever she chose, it wouldn't make much difference.

'Don't struggle, gal,' Blackie said, in an almost kindly manner. 'Yer'll find it'll all be a lot easier for yer if yer don't fight back.'

The overhead hatch was flung open, and suddenly a large man in a blue uniform was sliding down the ladder. Chas whirled round – but not quickly enough. The sandy-haired policeman grabbed his knife arm and twisted it behind his back.

' 'Elp me, Blackie!' Chas cried out in pain and shock.

He hadn't needed to say that. Blackie had already abandoned Annie and was advancing on the policeman.

'Be careful, Harry!' screamed Annie.

But by now two more coppers had slid down the ladder, and before Blackie got anywhere near Harry, they had the hooligan firmly in their grips.

Harry clicked handcuffs onto Chas, and his two

companions swiftly manacled Blackie. Mike, still quivering in the corner, was plainly going to put up no resistance.

'Take 'em to the duty boat,' Harry said to the other policemen. Then he turned to Annie. 'I didn't like yer doin' it,' he told her. 'But I 'ave to admit that yer 'andled it wonderfully.' He chuckled. 'Mind you, with all that footstampin' yer did, I thought yer were goin' to sink the barge before they'd have time to say anyfink.'

'I had to make sure they didn't hear you climbing aboard,' Annie said. An anxious expression came to her face. 'Did you hear it all?' she asked.

'Oh yes, we 'eard it,' Harry assured her. 'Blackie did the shootin' 'cos it was 'is gun, but Chas 'elped 'im to dump the body into the river.'

'And that will be enough to get Tom off, won't it?' Annie said.

'More than enough,' Harry agreed. He put his hand softly on her shoulder. 'An' now yer don't need me 'elp any more, will yer still keep yer promise?' he asked.

'Yes,' Annie said. 'I'll still keep my promise.'

'An' I'll promise *you* somefink,' Harry told her. 'Yer *will* learn to love me in time.'

But she knew she never would, and she turned away so he couldn't see the tears in her eyes.

PART FIVE:

LUVERLY DAY FOR A WEDDIN'

Summer 1902

CHAPTER NINETEEN

Dick Todd, the local milkman and the most bad-tempered man in Southwark, was driving his cart along Lant Place when Lil Clarke came out to her front door. Dick reined in his horse – and smiled.

'Mornin' Mrs Clarke!' he called out so cheerfully that Lil nearly dropped her milk jug. 'Luverly day for a weddin'.'

'It is,' Lil answered, recovering slightly.

'An' where's your Annie?'

'She's upstairs – gettin' ready,' Lil answered. 'Where else would she be?'

'Well, wish 'er all the luck in the world from me an' my old woman,' Dick said.

'Why don't yer do it yerself?' Lil asked. 'Yer comin' to the weddin', ain't yer?'

'O' course I am,' Dick replied. '*Everybody's* comin' to the weddin'. I just thought she might need a bit o' encouragement before'and. Yer know 'ow it is with these young gals. Sometimes they get cold feet at the last minute.'

'Not our Annie,' Lil said proudly. 'Once she's made 'er mind up about goin' ahead an' doin' somefink, there's nuffink that'll make 'er turn back.'

'I remember the day she was born,' Dick said. 'The fog was so thick that even me 'orse lost 'is way.'

'Yes, it was a proper peasouper,' Lil agreed. 'It was

nuffink short of a mirale that Mrs Gort – the midwife, yer know – ever managed to get through it.'

Dick sighed. 'Don't seem that long ago, does it?' he asked.

'Seems like yesterday,' Lil replied.

'Well, I can't 'ang about 'ere all day, natterin' to you,' Dick said, his face settling back into its customary scowl. 'Milk don't deliver itself, an' I can't expect the idle buggers who call themselves me customers to come to me, can I?'

He jerked on the reins and his horse set off at a trot. Lil glanced up at the bedroom and wondered how Annie was getting on.

Annie was being attended by two of her bridesmaids – Maisie Stowe, her old pal from the match factory, and Belinda Benson, her best friend from the telephone exchange. Of her third bridesmaid, her sister Peggy, there was no sign.

'She'll turn up, don't you worry,' Belinda said briskly. 'From what you said, she might be a bit woolly-headed but she'd have to have a ton of sheep's hair up there to make her miss her own sister's wedding.'

'Then there's the question of horses and carriage,' Annie fretted. 'Harry wanted to fix that himself, but our Eddie was so insistent that in the end I gave way and said he could do it. Now, every time I ask him about it, he goes all vague and says not to worry, he's got the matter in hand. But I can see myself walking to church – honestly I can.'

'Yer won't 'ave to walk,' Maisie told her. 'If the worst comes to the worst, me dad 'as promised that 'e'll take yer to the church in 'is cart.'

'Thanks, Maisie,' Annie said, although she might have been more reassured if she hadn't known that Maisie's dad was a rag and bone merchant.

As her bridesmaids fussed with her hair, Annie thought back over the previous couple of days.

Miss Barnett, her supervisor, had taken the news of her resignation much better than she'd expected.

'I'm surprised you've stayed on so long after the

telephone exchange had served its purpose,' she said. 'I realise, of course, that you can't tell me what your next mission will be . . .'

'I'm leaving to get married,' Annie told her.

'. . . but I have no doubt I shall be reading of your further exploits in the newspapers,' Miss Barnett continued. 'I've already started a scrapbook with clippings on the way you smashed that gold-smuggling ring.'

'I really am getting married,' Annie protested.

'Of course you are,' Miss Barnett agreed. 'Good luck to you, *Miss Clarke*,' she concluded, winking heavily.

Mr Archer, the interview board member with the kind eyes, had come to see her on her last day, too.

'I feel a bit guilty about resigning after all the trouble you went to to help me get the job in the first place,' Annie confessed to him.

And Mr Archer had smiled and said, 'Don't worry your head over it, Miss Clarke. I never expected that a lovely young lady like you would stay with us forever.'

The girls she worked with had presented her with a pretty enamel brooch, the kitchen staff had cooked her a special lunch of roast lamb and three veg, and then, almost before she knew it, she was out on the street – a telephonist no more.

Yes, that part of her life was behind her now, and in a few hours she'd be married – if, that was, her sister turned up in time and her brother managed to get horses and a carriage from somewhere.

Next door, at Number Thirty-six, George was polishing his boots and Colleen was making yet another adjustment to the dress she was to wear at the wedding.

'It fitted me two days ago,' she complained, 'and now, if I don't let it out again, I'll never get into the thing.'

George laughed. 'The joys of mother'ood,' he said.

Colleen laughed too. 'Oh, I don't mind, really,' she said. 'It's just that I'll be happier about feedin' and washin' the little mite – little mite! – than I am about carryin' it around inside me.'

'Well, you've not got much longer to wait,' George said. 'Almost exactly a month, isn't it?'

'That's right – just another month an' then . . .' Her face was suddenly creased with pain. 'Ouch!' she said.

'What's the matter?' George asked, alarmed.

'A bit of a cramp,' Colleen told him. 'I get it when I've been sittin' down for too long.'

She pressed down on her chair and pushed herself heavily to her feet.

'Are you sure you're all right,' George asked anxiously. 'Wouldn't you be better off in bed?'

'What – and miss Annie's wedding?' Colleen asked. 'I wouldn't do that for the world.'

Though Maisie and Belinda were still fussing around with her dress and veil, it was perfectly plain to Annie that there really wasn't much more to do – except worry!

And she had plenty to worry about. She was due at the church in a little over an hour and there was still no sign of her third bridesmaid or the transport which was going to take her there. Well, she could do without Peggy – though she'd rather not. But as regards the other matter . . .

'What exactly is your dad's cart like, Maisie?' she asked her bridesmaid anxiously.

'A grand little thing,' Maisie assured her. 'An' ever since I sent 'im word, 'e's been cleanin' it up to make it as spick an' span as yer could wish.'

'Still . . .' Annie said dubiously.

'An' yer mustn't worry about the smell, yer know, 'cos once yer've been in the cart for a couple o' minutes, yer 'ardly even notice it any more.'

There was a gentle tap on the bedroom door. Annie hoped that it was Eddie, with news of her carriage – but it was only her mother, who'd been using any excuse to pop in and out all morning.

This time, however, Lil had come on a real errand.

' 'Arry's downstairs,' she said. ' 'E'd like to see yer if yer've got a second.'

'Well, she hasn't,' Belinda said bossily. 'It's taking us all our time to get her ready as it is.'

'If it's only a second he wants, I think I can spare him that,' said Annie, who was just about fed up of being treated as if she were nothing more than a prize-winning exhibit at Crufts'.

'Yer can't go downstairs!' Maisie said, desperate to keep her there so she could fuss over her some more. 'It'd be bad luck if he saw yer now.'

A nice try, Annie thought, but she wasn't going to let her friend get away with it. 'Bad luck!' she said. 'I've heard it's bad luck if the groom sees the bride before the wedding . . .'

'Yes it is. It really is.'

'. . . but nobody's ever told me it's bad luck for the best man to see her.'

As she made her way down the narrow stairs – 'Watch yer dress!' Maisie called after her – Annie couldn't help thinking back to the day after her adventure on the *Christina*.

She remembered Harry appearing at the front door with a sad smile on his face, and remembered, too, wondering why the smile should be sad when he'd got everything he wanted.

'I've brought yer a present,' he'd said.

And she'd thought, 'He's brought the ring!' – the engagement ring which she knew she'd have to accept, because she'd given her word that she would.

But Harry hadn't reached into his pocket and pulled out any ring. Instead, he'd simply stood aside, so that she could see who was standing on the pavement behind him.

Tom! Tom, looking pale after his ordeal in prison – yet still her own, dear Tom. She'd wanted to throw her arms around his neck, but she remembered her promise – her two promises – to Harry, and so she stood frozen on the doorstep, looking questioningly at the policeman.

'I was only foolin' meself when I said yer'd learn to love me,' Harry had told her. 'Yer'd never really 'ave been mine, would yer – not in your 'eart?'

'I . . . I . . .' Annie had stuttered, not knowing what to think or what to do.

'I reckon I owe Tom somefink for all the sufferin' 'e's gone through,' Harry continued. 'So I've brought 'im to yer.'

'Does that mean . . .? Can I . . .?'

Harry had smiled, and there was genuine warmth in his smile this time – and happiness for her. 'Go on!' he'd said. 'Do what yer wanted to do the second yer saw Tom standin' there.'

And Annie had flung her arms around Tom and held him as if she never meant to let go of him again.

Harry was waiting in the overcrowded front parlour. He looked very smart in his new uniform with the three stripes on the sleeve, and Annie told him so.

'An' you look a picture,' he said. 'Tom's a lucky man, but he don't need me to tell 'im that.'

'What's brought you here, Harry?' Annie asked, suddenly starting to get worried. 'Has anything gone wrong?'

Harry laughed. 'No, yer can rest easy on that score,' he assured her. 'Everyfink's runnin' as smooth as clockwork.'

Except for a few small matters like missing bridesmaids and carriages, Annie thought.

'So if there aren't any problems, why have you come?' she asked Harry.

The policeman reached into his pocket and took out a large buff envelope. 'I'll give yer me own present at the reception,' he said, 'but this is from the bank in Peru.'

Annie opened the envelope and counted out ten crisp five-pound notes.

'Fifty quid!' she said.

'It ain't that much,' Harry told her, 'not when you think of 'ow much yer saved 'em by gettin' the gold back for 'em, but it'll give yer a bit of a start in yer new 'ome.'

'It's more than I expected,' Annie admitted. 'And what about you, Harry? How much did they give you?'

Harry shrugged. 'Nuffink,' he said. 'A policeman don't expect a reward for doin' 'is duty.' He took out his pocket watch and examined it. 'I'd better be gettin' back,' he continued. 'I've a lot to organise before this weddin' can take place.'

'Will anyone be coming with you, Harry?' Annie asked, hoping that someone was, because it might make the whole thing easier for him to bear.

'A guest, yer mean?' Harry said. 'Oh yes, I'll certainly be bringin' a guest.'

'A girl?' Annie asked.

'A gal,' Harry agreed.

He said it almost as it he were playing a joke on her, and Annie, despite her worries, found herself becoming intrigued.

'Do I know this girl?' she asked.

'Yes, yer might say yer know 'er.'

'Is she from Lant Place?'

'No, she ain't.'

Annie stamped her foot in mock-exasperation. 'Well, stop teasing, Harry, and tell me who she is,' she said.

Harry grinned. 'Yer just goin' to 'ave to wait an' see, Annie Clarke,' he said. 'Yer just goin' to 'ave to wait an' see.'

It was three-quarters of an hour before they were due to leave for the church that Peggy finally wandered into the house.

'An' where 'ave you been all this time, you young madam?' Lil demanded.

'Down the market,' Peggy said.

'Down the market! On the day yer sister's gettin' married!' her mother responded, outraged.

'That's why I went,' Peggy said sweetly. 'I was buyin' 'er a wedding present.'

It was then that Lil noticed the paper bag in Peggy's hands, and felt her heart soften.

'Well, it was kind of yer,' she admitted, 'though I'm sure our Annie didn't expect no present apart from the one the 'ole family was givin' her.'

'But this is special,' Peggy insisted. 'It's a way of sayin' thank you for 'er bein' such a good sister all these years.'

337

Lil stroked her daughter's hair. 'Yer can be a good kid sister sometimes, Peggy,' she said. 'So what 'ave yer bought 'er?'

Peggy held up the bag for her mother to see. 'Guess,' she said.

Lil would have said it was fruit, except the bag didn't look full enough. On the other hand, it wasn't the kind of container they gave you when you'd bought an ornament or brooch.

'I ain't got no idea what it is,' she told her younger daughter, a little irritably.

And then the bag chirped.

'Can yer guess now?' Peggy asked.

'Yer've never gone an' got 'er a blinkin' bird, 'ave yer?'

'It ain't just any bird,' Peggy said, offended. 'It's a Java sparrer, this is.'

'An' yer brought it 'ome in a paper bag! Why couldn't yer 'ave bought a cage for it?'

'I couldn't afford both them things,' Peggy exclaimed. 'An' I thought our Annie would prefer 'avin' a bird without a cage to 'avin' a cage without a bird.'

'But where are we goin' to keep it until we 'ave got a cage?' Lil asked, suddenly aware of how quickly time was passing.

Peggy looked around her. 'In the lavvy,' she suggested.

'That'd be a fine idea wouldn't it?' Lil said. 'An' what if somebody needs to go?'

Maisie appeared from upstairs.

'Annie won't let us do no more to 'er,' she said. 'Can I make meself useful down 'ere?'

And right then and there – out of the blue – Lil Clarke had an inspiration.

'Run up to Tom's mum's 'ouse,' she said. 'If yer quick, yer'll catch 'er before she leaves for the church. Find out if she's still makin' 'at boxes, an' if she is, ask 'er if we can borrow one. No, yer'd better make that 'ave one, 'cos it'll be no good to 'er once we've punched a load of 'oles in it.'

'Punch a load of 'oles in it!' Maisie said. 'Why ever should yer want to do that?'

'To let the air in,' Lil said.

'But why should yer want to let air into an 'at box?' Maisie wondered.

'Because if we don't the sparrer won't be able to breathe proper, will he?' Lil said.

'No, o' course he won't,' Maisie agreed, though she was no wiser now than when she'd asked the question.

Lil turned to Peggy. 'An' now, young madam, we'll see what we can do about gettin' you ready in time for this weddin' of yer sister's,' she said.

Annie, her three bridesmaids, and her mother, sat in the front parlour, all trying not to mention the fact that the coach had not arrived, but still jumping involuntarily whenever there was the sound of horses' hooves outside.

Finally, Lil said, 'Well, I 'ate to leave yer, Annie, but them of us who 'as to walk to the church 'ad better get goin' now.'

'Of course,' Annie said bravely.

'I'll stay with you, dear girl,' Belinda said.

'But if you do that, however will you get to the church in time to be my bridesmaid?' Annie asked.

'Oh, you'll have two bridesmaids even without me – more than enough,' Belinda said airily. 'And to tell you the truth, I'm much more interested in the festivities which follow than I am in weddings themselves.'

'Well, I would feel much better if you did stay with me,' Annie admitted.

'Then consider the matter settled.'

Lil, Peggy and Maisie got up and headed for the door.

'Just a minute, Maisie,' Annie said. 'On your way to the church, could you call in at your house and ask . . .' she gulped, '. . . and ask your dad to bring his cart round.'

'Course I could,' Maisie said cheerfully. 'It's been waitin' in readiness.'

'Waiting in readiness!' Annie thought when the cart arrived at the front door. 'Waiting in readiness for what?'

For shifting a load of old brass bedsteads? For

transporting a heap of smelly bones down to the glue factory?

And as if the cart itself was not bad enough, there was also Mr Stowe. He may possibly have done something to improve the appearance of his vehicle – though God knew, it didn't show – but he had done nothing at all about his own apparel. Annie looked him up and down, right from his unshaven chin and greasy neck-cloth to his cracked boots. Anyone further from her ideal coachman would be hard to imagine. And she couldn't help thinking that once she was up on the cart, riding behind him, people were more likely to think that she was something he'd got for the price of a child's windmill and a couple of balloons than a bride on her way to church.

'I can't do it,' she told Belinda. 'I simply can't arrive in a smelly old rag and bone cart.'

'It's not ideal,' her friend admitted. 'But it'd be better to arrive in that than not to arrive at all.'

'We'll give Eddie another ten minutes to turn up with the carriage,' Annie said.

'Even if he came in *five* minutes, you'd still be too late to arrive on time – or even fashionably late,' Belinda told her.

'We'll give Eddie another ten minutes,' Annie said firmly.

Sam Clarke stood at the doorway of the church, shifting his weight from one foot to the other. His new collar had felt fine when he'd put it on that morning, but now it was biting into his neck and almost cutting off his circulation.

He checked his watch again. 'Where the 'ell 'ave yer got to, Annie?' he said, almost under his breath.

If it had been Peggy who was getting married, he could have understood her being late. It only took the sight of some mangy stray cat or injured bird to distract his younger daughter from whatever it was she was supposed to be doing. But Annie just wasn't like that at all.

The vicar appeared at Sam's side. 'Still no sign of her?' he asked.

' 'Fraid not,' Sam admitted.

'I do have other marriage ceremonies to perform this afternoon,' the vicar told him.

'I know,' Sam said worriedly.

'We can wait for a few more minutes, but once the next party starts to arrive . . .'

A carriage appeared at the top of the street.

' 'Ere she is,' Sam gasped with relief.

But the carriage, containing quite another bride, went straight past the church.

'Another few minutes – no more,' the vicar said sternly, turning round and re-entering the church.

Sam gazed down the street. A dog cart was approaching, and so was a greengrocer's wagon, but of the carriage there was absolutely no sign.

'Come on, Annie, gal,' he said softly to himself. 'Don't go lettin' us all down now.'

Inside the church, Colleen Taylor shifted uncomfortably in her pew. She was having those pains again, but that probably came from sitting in the same position for so long.

In an attempt to take her mind off her discomfort, she looked around her. On her side of the church – the bride's side – she could see so many people who had been strangers to her only a little over a year ago, and now were almost old friends.

There was Mr Todd, the bad-tempered milkman, his head bent close to his wife's ear. 'As if he was complainin' about being kept waitin',' Colleen thought – then realised that he probably was.

Next to the Todds sat Mr Wilkins, the landlord of The Goldsmiths' Arms, and beyond him was Miss Crosby, Annie's old teacher from the Lant Street Board School. Nettie Walnut, looking very smart in the 'new' second-hand clothes Lil had insisted on buying her, was sitting close to the aisle.

'You're going to invite Nettie to your daughter's wedding, are you?' Colleen had asked when Lil had shown her the list of invitations. 'I mean, she is a tramp, you know.'

'Well, she did 'elp to get Tom out o' jail,' Lil had replied defensively. 'An' she's a very *respectable* sort o' tramp.'

Lil herself was on the front row, as befitted the bride's mother, and Colleen noticed that she was twitching nervously. She'd stopped briefly at the Taylor's pew on the way in and whispered something to Colleen about trouble with the carriage so maybe that was what was upsetting her.

Colleen switched her gaze to the other side of the aisle. What a sea of new hats there were! Hats with feathers sticking out of them, hats with bows around their edges – and hats with both!

May Bates, Tom's mother, had chosen a titfer with a large, lacquered ostrich feather, and Colleen thought it went very well with the smart lilac dress she was wearing. In fact, all the Bates family were well-turned out, despite their poverty. Puny little Joey – who had been responsible for half the trouble, but had turned out to be something of a hero in the end – had on a grey striped suit, and his two sisters, Doris and Mary, both looked splendid in their blue frocks.

Mary was turnin' into a real beauty, Colleen suddenly realised, and from the way Fred Simpson was gawpin' at the girl from his pew two rows back, she wasn't the only one who'd noticed it. Colleen remembered the way Mary had stared at Fred through the mirror in the Jug and Bottle Department of The Goldsmiths' Arms, and smiled to herself.

She let her eyes wander over to the front of the church. There were Harry and Tom, side by side as if they'd been mates all their lives, when the truth was that only months earlier they'd been at each other's throats. Whether they were old enemies or new lovers, there was something about weddings which just seemed to bring people together, Colleen thought.

She felt another twitch. The doctor had talked about something called 'contractions' that she would start to get when the baby was due, but since that wasn't for another month yet, it couldn't be them now. No, she was simply getting a stich from sitting in the same position for so long.

★

'It's the rag-and-bone cart or no wedding, I'm afraid,' Belinda said practically.

'What a choice!' Annie thought to herself.

This was her special day – the day she'd get married to her Tom – and there would never be another like it. She imagined herself looking back on it years later, and remembering arriving at the church in a rickety old cart, smelling of whatever it was that scruffy Mr Stowe had last carried.

'Oh, I could kill Eddie – I really could!' Annie thought as she looked hopelessly up and down the street.

All he'd had to do was go down to the stable on Union Street, where he used to work, and tell Mr Horrocks that he wanted a carriage for Saturday. A simple task! But he couldn't have done it, otherwise it would have been there by now. What a fool she'd been to think for a moment that Eddie . . .

Her train of thought was interrupted by a cacophony of noise coming from the end of Lant Place.

'What the . . .?' Belinda said.

'Cor blimey!' Mr Stowe added.

Annie looked down the street and saw what was causing the disturbance. A group of children were running towards her, shouting and whistling excitedly – but it was what they running *alongside* which really captured her attention! A magnificent motor car, the like of which had never graced the streets of Southwark before, was slowly and majestically purring its way in their direction.

The car stopped right in front of them. The driver was wearing a peaked leather cap and goggles. He took off the cap and a crop of wild hair sprung free. He lifted the goggles, and Annie saw that it wasn't a man at all – it was her little brother, Eddie. Yet somehow, sitting behind the wheel of the wonderful automobile, he didn't really look like her little brother any more, and Annie realised that without her even noticing it, he had begun to grow up.

Eddie grinned. 'Sorry I'm late,' he said, 'but I had a bit of engine trouble, Still, not to worry, now she's running as smooth as anyfink an' I'll 'ave yer at the church in two shakes of a lamb's tail.'

'This is what I call travelling in style,' Belinda said, stretching out her hand and stroking the upholstery.

'Yes, it even beats my cart,' Mr Stowe admitted.

'Get in then,' Eddie said.

'But . . . but can you drive?' Annie asked.

' 'Ow d'yer think I got the car down the street? Magic? I've been takin' lessons so I'd be able to give yer the sort o' ride to yer weddin' that yer deserve.'

And Annie realised both how foolish her question about his driving had been, and how nice her brother Eddie could be when he really tried.

'Come along, Annie,' Belinda said, taking her hand and leading her towards the automobile. 'After all, you don't want to keep your Tom waiting any longer than you have already.'

Almost in a dream, Annie stepped forward. Not two minutes earlier, she'd had visions of getting to the church in a smelly old rag-and-bone cart, and now she would arrive there in a far grander fashion than anyone had ever done before. What memories she would have when she looked back on it in years to come!

'You know, there's times I'm almost glad you're my brother,' she said to Eddie, leaning over and kissing him on the cheek.

Eddie blushed. 'There are times when I'm *almost* glad as well,' he replied.

CHAPTER TWENTY

Tom and Annie had considered all sorts of places where they might hold the wedding breakfast, and finally settled on the big, upstairs room of The Goldsmiths' Arms.

'An' a very good choice it was,' Tom whispered to his new wife as they sat in the back of the magnificent automobile on the way to the reception.

'Why do you say that?' Annie asked, detecting a teasing tone in her new husband's voice.

'Well, look at it this way,' Tom replied. 'After I've passed out through 'avin' too much to drink, it won't be far for yer to carry me 'ome, will it?'

'You'll do no such thing as pass out from too much drink, Tom Bates,' Annie replied with mock severity. 'My friend Belinda's told me all about what's in store for me tonight, and I've no intention of missing out on that just because you've had a skinful.'

Tom smiled that infectious smile of his.

'Yer seem to 'ave very 'igh expectations of me,' he said. 'I 'ope I can live up to 'em.'

Annie remembered the night on Battle Bridge Lane, and just the thought of it was enough to make her knees turn to water. 'You'll live up to them,' she said confidently.

The automobile pulled up smoothly in front of The Goldsmiths' Arms.

' 'Ere yer are, sir an' madam,' Eddie said. 'The finest hostelry in the 'ole of Southwark.'

Tom stepped out of the car, then held out his hand to assist his wife down. 'Thank you, my good man,' he said to Eddie. 'I'd give yer a tip, but I know yer'd only go an' spend it on somefink foolish.'

'You just wait till yer get the bill for all me drivin' lessons,' Eddie said.

'The bill for all your what?' Annie asked.

'Me drivin' lessons,' Eddie repeated. 'Well, I mean, since I only took 'em so I could drive yer to the church, it's only fair that you should be the one who pays for 'em.'

'Eddie Clarke, is there even a shred of truth in what you've just said?' Annie demanded. 'Because if there is . . .'

Eddie grinned. 'Yer can relax,' he said. 'The lessons are free – one o' the perks of me job. An' now, if yer'll excuse me, I'll return this borrowed car to the garage.'

'Yer mean it ain't really yours?' Tom asked, as if the discovery amazed him.

'Chance'd be a fine thing,' Eddie said, putting the automobile into gear and pulling away.

As they watched him disappear down Lant Street, Tom put his arm around Annie's waist. 'Are yer 'appy, Mrs Bates?' he asked.

'You know I am,' Annie told him.

With his free hand, Tom opened the door of The Goldsmiths' Arms. 'Well, it ain't exactly our own threshold,' he said, 'but I could carry yer upstairs if yer'd like.'

'Not a chance,' Annie replied. 'I want you saving your strength for tonight, if you remember.'

From her vantage point on the top table, Annie looked around her. Sharing this table with her and her husband were May, Joey, Doris and Mary Bates; Lil, Sam, and Eddie Clarke, the three bridesmaids and the best man. Another table, at right angles to the top one, contained the friends of the groom, while a third, also at right angles, accomodated the friends of the bride.

'It's a waste of time really, having a groom's side an' a bride's side,' Annie remarked to Tom. 'I mean, since most of the guests are from down our street, they could have sat at either table.

'Yes, it's a pity, that,' Tom replied.

'A pity? Why?'

'Well, if there's one thing I like at a weddin', it's a good punch-up, an' these lot are so friendly with one another I can't really see one startin'.'

Annie elbowed him in ribs.

'Ouch!' Tom said. 'That 'urt!'

'You're going to have to get used to it if you keep trying to be clever with me,' Annie replied.

'Now she tells me,' Tom said to Harry, who had been watching the whole exchange with an amused expression on his face.

'The joys of married life, eh?' Harry replied.

Who was Harry's mysterious guest? Annie wondered. And why hadn't he brought her to sit at the top table with him? She looked around the room. Could the mystery woman be Winnie Sanderson? No, she had a squint and hairy legs. Bettie Rogers, perhaps? No again, because she was head over heels with a young bloke in the army.

Then who *could* it be?

'Course I's been to more weddin's than I cares to remember,' Nettie Walnut told Colleen Taylor.

'Have you?' said Colleen, twisting in her seat to see if she could get more comfortable.

'Hundreds of 'em,' Nettie said. 'Some of 'em for tramps, 'eld by the side of the road, and some of 'em in big 'ouses with roofs an' real glass in the windows.'

Colleen winced as another of the inexplicable pains hit her.

'It's true!' Nettie said, taking Colleen's screwed-up expression as a sign of disbelief.

'I'm sure it is,' Colleen said.

'Why, I remember Lord Bancroft's weddin',' Nettie continued. 'What a show that was.'

'You were a guest at a lord's wedding?' Colleen asked, and this time her look *was* one of incredulity.

'Well, not so much a guest,' Nettie admitted. 'More what you might call an entertainer.'

It was almost as hard to accept the idea of Nettie as an entertainer as it would have been to swallow the notion that she might have had an invitation.

'Nettie the Gypsy,' the tramp told her. 'You puts an 'andkerchief around your 'ead and says, "Cross my palm with silver". Then you looks at *their* palms – all serious-like. "I see a great future for you" – as if they's goin' to 'ave anythin' else with all the money's they's got. "You's goin' to 'ave a very long life" – well, if they doesn't, they's not goin' to come an' ask for their silver coin back, now is they? "You's goin' to meet a tall, dark, 'andsome stranger" – an' it's more than likely they will. Oh, they just laps it up, I can tell you – superstitious idjuts that they is!'

Colleen put her hands down flat on the table and pushed herself to her feet. 'You'll have to excuse me for a few minutes,' she said.

She didn't want to seem rude to Nettie, but she was sure she'd burst if she didn't go to the lavatory soon.

The Goldsmiths' Arms had laid on a fine spread. There was mouth-watering glazed ham, roast beef which was so tender that you could have cut it with your fork. There was chicken, although, being the treat that it was, that didn't stay on the plates long. And there were oysters, jellied eels, whelks and cockles, without which any Cockney feast would have been considered a pretty poor show.

Wine was available too, but most of the women stuck to tea, while nearly all the men preferred their pints.

The people of Lant Place ate and ate until they were thoroughly stuffed, then sat back contentedly and waited for the speeches.

Sam, always one to oblige, rose to his feet. 'Ladies and gentlemen . . .' he began.

'Are yer nervous, Sam?' someone called out good-naturedly.

'Not yet,' Sam replied. 'I'm savin' me nerves for when I get the bill for this lot.' He waited for the laughter to die down, then continued. 'I've been thinkin' a lot about what advice I should give to the 'appy couple, an' 'ere's what I've come up with. Bein' married is a bit like bein' a docker.'

'Like bein' a what?' Lil said in a scandalised tone.

'Like bein' a docker,' Sam repeated. 'Yer see, there's 'ard times at the docks, an' there's 'ard times in marriage . . .'

'Yer supposed to be thankin' people for comin', not talkin' about bein' a docker,' Lil whispered.

'There's been times when I've been so sure there'd be no work for me that it's been 'ard to drag meself down to St. Katherine's Dock,' Sam continued. 'But d'yer know why I did it?'

'No! And they don't want to,' Lil hissed. 'For Gawd's sake, why don't yer make a proper speech, Sam?'

'I did it because there's always a chance that a steamer from Argentina'll arrive ahead o' time, or one of them tall sailin' ships from Australia'll 'ave caught a good wind an'll dock days before it was expected.'

'Please shut up, Sam! Yer embarrasin' the life out o' me,' Lil groaned.

'So what I'm sayin' to Tom an' Annie is that there'll be rough times ahead, but if they can manage to stick 'em out together, then one day their ship'll come in.'

'Oh, is that what yer meant?' Lil demanded. 'Well, why didn't yer just say so in the first place?'

'Take me as a fer instance,' Sam said. 'Me an' my old dutch ain't always 'ad it easy. Money ain't always been around an' there's been weeks at a time when we've done no more than scrape by. Then there's the kids. Yer kids can cause yer a lot of aggravation. Ain't that right, Peggy?'

'I don't know, Dad,' Peggy said innocently.

'Do I 'ave to start talkin' about broken milk jug dodges?' Sam whispered to her.

'Yer kids can cause yer a lot of aggravation,' Peggy admitted loudly.

'But with a good woman by yer side, yer can get through

anyfink. I know that's what I got – an' so 'as Tom,' Sam concluded.

He sat down to thunderous applause and shouts of 'Good ole Sam!'

' 'Ow did I do?' he asked Lil.

'All right,' his wife admitted, surreptitiously wiping away a tear from the corner of her eye, 'but I still think yer'd 'ave been better off just thankin' them for comin'.'

Harry was well into his speech by the time Colleen returned from the lavatory.

'. . . an' I know that the only reason Tom's chose me as 'is best man is so 'e can be sure yer won't get raided by the police . . .'

'Smart thinkin', Tom!'

'Who said all watermen were stupid?'

'. . . but I'm still very honoured ter to be standin' 'ere in front of yer today . . .'

Speeches were the last thing on Colleen's mind at that moment. The banter went completely over her head, and instead she concentrated all her efforts on trying to make it back to the empty chair next to her husband.

'What's the matter, luv?' George asked when he saw how ashen her face had become.

'Me water's broke,' Colleen told him.

'Your water?' George asked, mystified. 'What water?' Then, suddenly, his face turned as white as his wife's. 'You can't mean . . . you're not sayin' . . .?'

'I am!'

'But it's not due . . . it shouldn't be comin' . . .'

'Men!' Nettie Walnut said. 'They's hopeless, isn't they? Babies is like tramps, they doesn't go by no clocks. When you's delivered as many babies in ditches as I 'as, you knows that.'

'What are we going to do?' George asked, in a complete panic for perhaps the first time in his life.

Nettie leaned across the table towards Mr Wilkins – who was so thoroughly enjoying Harry's speech that he hadn't noticed anything amiss – and poked him sharply on the ribs.

'You's the gaffer of this boozer, isn't you?' she asked.

'Yes,' replied the startled landlord.

'An' 'as you got any beds in it?'

'O' course I 'ave. Upstairs – in me livin' quarters.'

'Then you better get this girl on one of 'em. Unless you wants her havin' her baby right where she's sittin'.'

It caused something of a sensation when George and Mr Wilkins helped Colleen to the door, but after a while everyone calmed down again, and Harry was allowed to finish his speech.

And then it was Tom's turn. He thanked everyone for coming – 'No talk o' dockers from 'im, yer notice,' Lil pointed out to her husband – and said that he and his wife would be leaving the next morning for a short holiday in Southend.

'An' what will yer doin' tonight?' some wit called out.

'I thought we might turn in early,' Tom said, and from the corner of his eye he saw that Annie was starting to blush.

'I'll bet yer'll be 'avin' a *really* early night!' the wit said. 'An' I can't say as I blame yer.'

The speeches were finally over, and since the band had not yet arrived, the guests were left to entertain themselves for a while.

Tom, for his part, handed the bridesmaids the presents he had bought them. There was a brooch for Maisie – and a book for Belinda.

'*The Karma Sutra*,' Belinda said appreciatively, reading the title on the spine.

'I don't know what it's about,' Tom confessed. 'Annie was the one who chose it.'

'And have you read it yourself, Annie?' Belinda asked.

'No,' replied Annie, blushing again. 'But I might want to borrow it off you some time.'

There was only one bridesmaid who had not received any present, and when Tom left them to go and look out of the window, she just about gave up hope of getting one – and did her best not to cry.

'Don't worry, I 'aven't forgotten yer, Peggy,' Tom said, turning round again.

'Aven't yer?' Peggy said, sniffing slightly.

'Course not. Very bad move, offendin' yer new sister-in-law right from the start.'

He grinned, but made no move to produce the promised present.

For an eternity – perhaps as much as ten or fifteen seconds – Peggy waited patiently, and then she said, 'Where is it?'

'Where's what?' Tom asked.

'Me present.'

'Oh, that. It's outside. Well, I mean, I couldn't bring it in 'ere, could I?'

'Why couldn't yer?'

' 'Cos it'd probably 'ave caused a riot if I 'ad done.'

'But what *is* it?' Peggy asked exasperatedly.

'Didn't I mention that?'

'No yer didn't.'

'Could've sworn I 'ad. Well, instead of me tellin' yer, why don't we both go an' look at it?'

All the way down the stairs, Peggy was turning over the possibilities in her mind. What kind of present could it be, that you could leave out on the street and would have caused a riot if you'd brought it into the pub?

And then she stepped out onto the pavement and realised that the reason Tom had gone over to the window earlier had been to see if her present had arrived. And there it was – tethered to the nearest lamppost!

'I was lucky to get one so young this late in the season,' Tom said as he watched Peggy cuddle the kid to her chest.

'Thank you, Tom,' Peggy said ecstatically. 'Yer the best brother-in-law a gal ever 'ad.'

'Just you make sure yer keep it under control,' Tom warned her. 'Otherwise, I know one mother who won't be thinkin' that I'm the best *son*-in-law a woman ever 'ad.'

The sound of the band beginning to play drifted up the stairs to the small landing where George stood, anxiously waiting for his wife to give birth.

'Don't panic,' he ordered himself. After all, what was there to panic about? Colleen was a strong, healthy girl, and he'd seen that she didn't overdo things during her pregnancy. Still, she was *very* big, and the baby was coming a *month* early.

George hesitated for a moment, then raised his big fist and tapped lightly on the door.

'What is it?' came the midwife's irritated voice from the other side.

'I was just wonderin' how things were goin' in there,' George said.

'They'd be goin' a lot smoother if yer'd just leave us alone to get on with it.'

'But I mean . . . is she . . . does she . . .'

'The contractions are comin' closer together. It shouldn't be long now.'

Joey Bates watched as his brother Tom whisked Annie gracefully around the centre of the room in the first dance.

He wished he could be big and strong like Tom. Rollo Jenkins had called him a runt, and he had to admit that though Rollo was just being nasty, there was a lot of truth in what he'd said.

'Stop feelin' sorry for yerself, Joey,' he told himself.

If he really wanted to change, he thought, then it was about time he started doin' something about it. There were gymnasiums all over the place – all he had to do was join one an' start workin' on his body. Maybe he'd make a boxer yet.

Annie and Tom reached the end of their dance, and all their guests cheered and whistled their appreciation. Then it was the guests' turn to have their bit of fun. Sam took his wife's hand and led her forward, Dick Todd grumpily agreed to dance with *his* wife – and Harry Roberts made a bee-line for Belinda Benson.

'Of course!' Annie thought.

How could she have been so stupid as not to see what was right under her nose? Harry had told her that she knew the girl he was bringing. Belinda had said she – what was her phrase – 'wouldn't mind a crack' at Harry. And the reason Harry hadn't brought his guest to the top table was because she was already there – as Annie's bridesmaid.

Annie watched as they danced with an easy familiarity which suggested this was by no means the first time they'd held each other. So just how long *has* it been going on? Annie wondered.

Tom, standing by her side, had noticed them, too.

'D'yer think we'll be goin' to another weddin' soon?' he asked.

Annie laughed. 'I shouldn't be at all surprised,' she told her husband.

Eddie Clarke was looking at the dancing, but his mind was somewhere else entirely. He was thinking of the talk he'd had with Mr Rockcliffe, his boss, just after he'd successfully completed his driving lessons.

'Yer instructor says yer a natural at drivin' automobiles, as well as at takin' 'em to pieces,' Rockcliffe had told him.

'Thanks,' Eddie had replied.

'An' I was wonderin' if yer'd like to take it further?'

' 'Ow d'yer mean?'

'The motor car race is still a bit of a novelty, but it ain't goin' to stay that way. In a few years' time, it'll be a proper sport like 'orse racin' an' football.'

'I 'ope yer right,' Eddie had agreed, 'but I don't see what that's got to do with . . .'

'They're goin' to need professional drivers – blokes who can get the very best out o' the machine. 'Ow would you fancy 'avin' a crack at it?'

How would he fancy having a crack at it? Racing round the track at unbelievable speeds? Risking his life battling against a bunch of maniacs who were determined to beat him whatever the cost? He'd love it!

The only trouble was, he couldn't see his mum bein' quite so enthusiastic.

Fred Simpson watched the dancing with growing gloom.

354

He wished he'd been born ugly, because ugly men could at least go out with ugly girls, whereas he, with that baby face of his, couldn't go out with any girls at all. It was ridiculous, he thought to himself, that such a face should be seated on top of a rock-hard body like his. It was ridiculous that such a face should belong to a fireman with two medals for valour above and beyond the call of duty. Yet he was stuck with it – stuck with the fact that no girl was ever likely to take him seriously.

He wished that he could go up to Mary Bates now and ask her if she would dance with him, but he was afraid of getting the same reaction he always had from other girls.

'Dance with you? I'd rather dance with me little brother.'

'Come back in about five years' time, Sonny, an' ask me again.'

'Does yer mother know yer out?'

He felt a tap on his shoulder and looked up to see Mary Bates standing there.

'Mum says yer were so nice to us while Tom was in gaol that I've got to ask yer to dance with me now,' she said.

'Yer don't 'ave to do that,' Fred told her. 'You go an' tell yer mum I've let yer off.'

A look of panic crossed Mary's face. 'Don't send me back,' she said. 'Mum'll be really mad if I don't get yer to dance with me.'

Fred grinned. 'Well, we wouldn't want that, would we?' he asked, standing up and taking her hand.

They glided around the floor together and the young fireman was happier than he remembered being for a long time. And then he realised that as soon as the dance was over and she had fulfilled her obligation, Mary would go back to her mother again – and he felt even worse than before.

'Fred,' Mary said.

'What?'

'Yer know I told yer that me mum made me come across an' ask yer for a dance?'

'Yes?'

'Well, she didn't. If the truth be told, I 'ad to talk 'er into it.'

'I'm glad yer succeeded,' Fred said, holding her ever so slightly tighter.

'Push down harder!' said Mrs Gort, the midwife.

'I'm doin' the best I can,' replied Colleen, who had never hated anyone in her whole life as much as she hated this woman who was deliberately torturing her.

'Harder!' the midwife repeated.

And Colleen did, if only to show her that you couldn't break an O'Leary by birth and a Taylor by marriage – however hard you tried.

'I can see the head!' Mrs Gort exclaimed. 'Keep at it! You're doin' well.'

Colleen pushed, Mrs Gort pulled, and a few minutes later the midwife was holding up a tiny baby in front of her.

'It's a girl!'

'She's beautiful,' Colleen told the midwife, who was the nicest, kindest woman she'd ever met.

Mrs Gort frowned. 'Don't stop pushin'!' she ordered Colleen.

'I . . . I don't understand,' Colleen gasped, feeling distinctly odd. 'Why should I keep pushin' when the baby's been . . .'

'Didn't you realise?' Mrs Gort asked. 'Yer 'avin' twins?'

'Thank you, it was an absolutely adorable wedding,' Belinda said.

'But you can't be going yet,' Annie said in surprise. 'The dancing's only just started.'

'I know,' Belinda agreed, 'and if it was up to me, I'd stay till the first cock crowed.'

'Then what's the prob . . .'

'It's Harry, you see. The poor chap is positively dying of hunger.'

'Dying of hunger? But it's not more than a couple of hours since the wedding breakfast.'

'I know, my dear girl, but he assures me that he's starving.'

'So are you going to a restaurant or something?' Annie asked.

Belinda's generous mouth broke out into a wide smile, and with her left eye she gave Annie a broad wink.

'No, not a restaurant,' she said. 'I thought I'd take him back to my place and give him his supper there.'

Colleen, exhausted but happy, lay in Mr Wilkin's big double bed with a baby on each side of her.

'One boy an' one girl,' she said. 'Are you pleased, luv?'

'Pleased!' George exclaimed, gazing lovingly first at his son, then at his daughter, then at his son again. 'Pleased doesn't even come near to how I feel. I've always been proud of you, Colleen, but never as much as I am today.'

There was a tap on the door, and when George shouted 'Come in!' Lil Clarke entered the room.

'Ain't they beautiful?' she cooed at the babies. 'An' ain't she a clever gal, 'avin' two at once, George?'

'George did have *somethin'* to do with it himself, you know,' Colleen pointed out.

'Somefink to do with it!' Lil snorted. 'Men'd do *that* whether it brought babies or not.'

'And wouldn't you?' Colleen asked mischievously, remembering how Lil had come to be pregnant with Annie.

Lil look flustered. 'I'm surprised at yer, bringin' some-fink like that up in mixed company,' she told Colleen. 'It would never 'ave 'appened in my day. I don't know what the world's comin' to since the Old Queen died, really I don't.'

'Was it me who brought it up?' Colleen asked, enjoying her neighbour's discomfort. 'I could have sworn it was you.'

'Yes, well, maybe it was,' Lil admitted. She swung round to face George. 'An' maybe us women *do* enjoy it sometimes, but that don't mean that you men 'ave any cause to go gettin' big 'eaded.'

'I wouldn't dream of it,' George assured her.

That unseemly topic disposed off, Lil turned her attention back to the babies. 'What are yer goin' to call 'em?' she asked.

'The little lad's goin' to be Ted, after George's dad,' Colleen said.

'An' we're goin' to call the lass Cathy, after Colleen's mam,' George added.

Lil nodded her head approvingly. 'Yer can't beat keepin' names in the family,' she told them. She walked towards the door. 'There's one or two other people downstairs who'd like to 'ave a look at yer babies, if it wouldn't be too tirin' for yer, Colleen.'

George and Colleen exchanged a quick, knowing glance.

'Let 'em all come if they want to,' Colleen said proudly.

The party had not slowed down in Lil's absence – if anything, it was more fast and furious than when she had left it. She looked around at all the happy faces – Mary Bates and Fred Simpson, who seemed unwilling to sit out a single dance; May Bates, so proud of the family she'd struggled to raise; Nettie Walnut, who was quietly slipping what remained of the food into her pockets; grumpy Dick Todd, who for once seemed to be . . .

And then she noticed that two very important faces seemed to be missing.

'Where's Tom an' our Annie?' she asked her husband.

'They've slipped off,' Sam said. 'Wanted a bit o' time on their own, I expect. An' who can blame 'em?'

Hand in hand, Tom and Annie stood on Southwark Bridge and watched the last of the sun's rays play on the water below them.

'I'm glad I come from Southwark,' Annie told her new husband.

Tom laughed. 'Whatever made yer say that?' he asked.

'I don't really know,' Annie confessed. 'Maybe it was seeing the people at the wedding – at *our* wedding.'

'What about 'em?'

'They all seemed so *special* to me, and I couldn't help thinking that if they'd come from somewhere else, they might have been different.'

'They *would* 'ave been different,' Tom said. 'Can yer

imagine Dick Todd as a duke, or my brother Joey as a Hottentot?'

Annie giggled. 'But you know what I mean,' she persisted.

'Yes,' he said, squeezing her hand. 'I know what yer mean.'

Annie looked up the river. It was still a busy, bustling place, even though only a few minutes of daylight remained. She watched a squat steamer making its way towards Tower Bridge, and the barges it was towing behind it reminded her of ducklings following their mother. She saw a pair of lighters, gliding slowly downstream. A police duty boat passed under the bridge, but Harry Roberts was not in it – he was elsewhere, getting his supper.

What interesting times they'd been since Tom had rescued her from the runaway beer barrel, she thought. She remembered how she'd battled to get her job with the telephone company, only to give it all up for love. She shuddered at the memory of Tom's arrest and the danger she'd gone through to get him released.

She thought of all her friends and neighbours – her mum, who usually started out judging anything by its 'respectability', yet in the end would always be ruled by her heart; her dad, who never missed a chance to see a funny side of things; her brother Eddie, who'd grown from a feckless youth into a young man with a purpose that was almost a mission; her sister Peggy, living in a furry dream world of her own; George and Colleen, who had had some rough times, but were at last proud parents . . .

'Yes, interesting times,' she murmured softly to herself. 'Very interesting times.'

'What was that?' Tom asked.

'Nothing. Just thinking.'

'Yer'll 'ave to give that up for a start,' Tom said, grinning. 'I can't abide wives who think.'

'Then you should probably have married somebody else,' Annie told him, punching him lightly in the ribs.

'Speakin' of thinkin',' Tom said, 'what did yer think of

359

yer dad's speech – all that about stickin' together, even when yer boat *don't* come in?'

'What did you think of it?' Annie asked.

'I thought it was wonderful.'

'And so did I.'

Darkness had finally fallen, and all there was now to remind them that there was still a river below were a few flickering lights, bobbing up and down at the prows of moored barges.

'Are yer ready to go 'ome now, Mrs Bates?' Tom asked.

'Yes,' Annie replied. 'I'm ready to go home now.'